"And in chute number four, we have Sam McPhee," said the announcer over the PA system.

The world stopped turning.

Applause erupted from the bleachers. Michelle stood at the rail and gripped the rungs hard. She knew she hadn't heard wrong. Oh, God. *Sam.*

Michelle looked at the chute at the end of the arena, and there he was. From a distance, he resembled any cowboy on a quarter horse. Yet she knew him. Knew the tilt of his head, the set of his shoulders, the fringe of sandy hair touching his collar. Sam appeared leaner, stronger, and quicker than ever. He retained that unique grace of movement she recalled so well. The years had hardly left a mark on him.

Michelle stared, spellbound, unable to move. He still had that slightly crooked grin that had once made her heart melt. . . .

The You I Never Knew

SUSAN WIGGS

WARNER BOOKS

A Time Warner Company

WARNER BOOKS EDITION

Cover design by Diane Luger
Hand lettering by David Gatti
Book design by H & H Roberts Design

Warner Books, Inc.
1271 Avenue of the Americas
New York, NY 10020

Visit our Web site at
www.twbookmark.com

 A Time Warner Company

Printed in the United States of America

First Printing: January 2001

10 9 8 7 6 5 4 3 2 1

To the women of my tribe:

my grandmother Marie
my mother Lou
my sister Lori
my daughter Elizabeth
who understand the necessary labors of loving

"Most of us become parents long before
we have stopped being children."

—MIGNON MCLAUGHLIN,
   The Second Neurotic's Notebook (1966)

Acknowledgments

Writing a book is a joyous act, but it's also a lonely one. The support, advice, and fellowship of professional advisors and friends anchor, motivate, and inform me, and for this I'm deeply grateful. In particular, to Robert Gottlieb and Marcy Posner of the William Morris Agency for pushing me off in a new direction, to Joyce, Christina, Betty, Barb, and Alice for reading the manuscript with open minds and blood-red pencils, to Kristin, Jill, and Debbie for moral support, to my gifted editor, Claire Zion, who held up the mirror that transformed this work, and to Sara Schwager for careful copyediting, to Sandra Brashen, M.D., Leslie Townsend, Peggy Moreland and Curtiss Ann Matlock for technical advice, and most particularly to Donna Roberts, who gave her father the gift of life and generously shared her story.

Saturday

Saturday

Chapter 1

After seventeen years, Michelle Turner was going back. Back to a past she didn't want to remember, to the father she barely knew, to the town where she grew up too fast, fell in love too hard, and wound up pregnant and alone.

During the long drive from Seattle to Montana, she rehearsed—under her breath so Cody wouldn't hear—what she would say when she got there.

"Hello, Daddy." Funny how she still thought of him as Daddy, even though he'd never been much more than a picture on the wall or sometimes a face on the TV screen late at night when his old movies played. "Sorry I didn't come sooner..." Sorry... sorry... sorry. All those regrets. So many of them.

Sorry wouldn't do. Gavin Slade—her father had kept

his professional name after retiring—knew damned well what had kept her away so long.

She flexed her hands on the steering wheel of the Range Rover and glanced over her shoulder at her son in the backseat. Cody was lost in the space between the headphones of his Discman. Maybe I'm the one who's lost, she thought. Here she was, thirty-five years old and the mother of a teenager, and the thought of facing her father made her feel like a kid again. Defensive. Powerless. Inadequate.

The Washington landscape roared by as she drove eastward, heading toward a place where she'd find no welcome. She and Cody had left their waterfront town house before dawn. The lights had still been shining in the steel skeleton of Seattle's Space Needle. By sunup, the Cascade Range had given way to rounded hills and scrubby flatland, then finally to high plateaus, a bare and colorless midwinter moonscape, a neutral zone.

She saw nothing out her window to interest the eye, nor to offend it.

Long ago, she used to be an artist, painting in savage color with emotions that spilled unrestrained over the canvas, dripping off the sides, because her feelings could not be confined to a finite space. But somewhere along the way she had reined in those mad and glorious impulses, as if a thief had come in the night and stolen the dreams inside her and she hadn't noticed they were gone until too late.

All that remained of the wild soul of her younger days was a cold, mechanical talent and a photographic eye. Airbrush and mousepad had replaced paint and canvas.

Her subjects had changed, too. She used to create art with passion and purity, whether it be a horse on her father's ranch or an abstract scramble of feelings. Inspiration used to govern her hand, and something far more powerful ignited her spirit. Once seen or imagined, the work rushed from her, generated by a force as strong as the need to breathe.

Now subjects came assigned to her by memo from the ad agency where she was up for full partner. She used a computer to design and animate dancing toilet brushes, talking dentures, or an army of weed-killer bags marching toward a forest of weeds.

Tugging her mind away from thoughts of work, she clicked on the wipers to bat away a few stray snow flurries. The day wore on. Spokane passed in a whisk of warehouses and industrial smokestacks. The interstate arrowed cleanly across the panhandle of Idaho. Between empty stretches of highway lay glaring commercial strip centers, tractor barns and silos, wood-frame houses huddled shoulder to shoulder against the elements. Deeper accumulations of snow formed crusty heaps on the side of the road. East of Coeur d'Alene, the landscape yielded to endless stretches of nothingness.

The monotony of the drive, and her purpose for racing across three states, caused an almost painful tectonic shift in her thoughts. Memories drifted toward dangerous places. Against her will, images from the past turned the barren snowscape to brilliant summer.

She saw herself as she was at eighteen. A little breathless at everything life had to offer. A little scared, but mostly happy and secure in her world. She finished high school with honors she didn't care about, a raw talent she didn't appreciate yet, and no sense of impending disaster. Her mother's cosmetic surgery was supposed to be routine. No one even considered the possibility that Sharon Turner would die from the complications.

In a shockingly short span of time, Michelle had found

herself alone and motherless—suddenly in need of the father she barely knew. She had expected him to hustle her off to college and breathe a sigh of relief when she was gone, but instead he'd surprised her. He had invited her to take a year off before college and spend the time with him in Montana. A year to grieve for her mother and to learn who her father was.

In that one brief season she experienced the events that were to shape her life: She learned what it was to be a motherless daughter. She fell in love. She became a painter. Not necessarily in that order. Everything sort of happened simultaneously. Even now, the years-old bittersweet ache rose as fresh as yesterday. It shouldn't still hurt, but it did, even though he was gone, long gone, from her life.

Except for the daily reminder he had left her.

She glanced into the rearview mirror again. Cody, who was sixteen and impossible, hadn't moved from his long-bodied position in the backseat. A tinny beat of heavy-metal music escaped from his headphones. He stared out at the endless swags of electrical lines strung along poles that bordered the highway. When a green-and-white sign welcomed them to Montana, his only reaction was to blink and shift position.

A billboard with a nauseating cartoon cowboy invited them to "Stop N Eat" in one mile.

"You hungry?" She raised her voice so he would hear.

He stuffed a wad of Fritos into his mouth. "Nope," he said around a mouthful of food. The roadside café, lit up by neon wagon wheels, disappeared in a smear of artificial light.

Just for a flash, she saw him as a toddler, cramming Cheerios into his cheeks like a baby squirrel. It seemed like only yesterday that he was her Cody-boy in Oshkosh overalls, with milk dribbling from his chin. That child was gone from her life now, she realized with a lurch of regret in her chest. He had slipped away when she wasn't looking. He'd vanished as swiftly and irretrievably as if he had wandered off at an airport, never to be found. In his place was this cynical, smart, exasperating stranger who seemed determined to push every button she had.

His sheer physical beauty then, as now, took her breath away. Only back then, she could tell him how adorable he was to her.

Now she could tell him nothing.

Cody had begged to stay in Seattle while she made this trip alone. He claimed he'd be fine, staying by himself at the town house. As if Michelle would consent to that.

Cody had even suggested that Brad could look after him.

Right. Brad couldn't handle Cody. Or wouldn't. And she was in no position to expect that level of support from Brad, their relationship notwithstanding. Her entire life was on hold until she dealt with her father.

A semi swung out and passed her, blasting its air horn. No speed limit in Montana, she recalled, and here she'd been dutifully doing sixty-five.

Life had trained her well for duty.

Defiantly, she pressed the accelerator. Sixty-five, seventy, seventy-five. She reveled in the speed, in the hum of the Rover's tires on cold bare pavement. Everything passed in a wavy smudge—streaks of cottonwood groves, shale rock ridges, coulees and brushy creeks, the blur of avalanche fence traversing the high meadows. The wind blew a dusting of snow along the highway. The snakelike motion and the subtle flickers of muted color were oddly exhilarating, and for a while she simply emptied her mind and drove.

The landscape lifted, a subtle change at first, but before long they would reach the high country of serrated crags, endless valleys, hanging alpine lakes. A chill of anticipation prickled her skin. Before long they would be at Blue Rock Ranch.

At Missoula, they turned northward, passing a giant statue of a Hereford bull at a combination tourist shop, café, and gas station.

"We're not in Kansas anymore," she murmured to Cody, but he didn't hear.

The Wild West kitsch was a sign that they had entered a different zone entirely, a land where the cowboy myth revolved around the solemn rites of rope and leather, where a sense of place and tall, endless skies surrounded and seduced her. Some said Montana was an empty land, but that wasn't quite right. It was just that the space was so vast it expanded the soul. She felt herself being drawn toward an encounter she had resisted for years. She tensed, unable to enjoy the beauty because this landscape held too many reminders of her past.

Highway 83 took them along the final leg of the journey. Against the brooding afternoon sky rose the peaks of the Swan and Mission Mountains. Shadows flickered in and out of coulees and valleys, creating a palette of sage and ocher and mysterious, restful earth tones that had no name.

"Cody, look!" She pointed out the side window. A huge herd of elk, winter migrants from the high country, grazed on the scrub-covered hills.

He stared at the milling herd, then yawned.

Well, what did she expect? "Gee whiz, Mommy" from a sixteen-year-old?

But oh, she wanted to share this with him, this sense of wonder inspired by the wild animals, the deep conifer forests and staggering snow-clad mountain peaks. A jewel-like chain of lakes bordered the highway. She wanted to tell him the lakes were formed as flood depressions in glacial moraines, filled when giant chunks of ice melted in each depression.

She wondered if that was what happened to people: When loss created a void that stayed empty too long, did the space fill up with ice?

They reached the turnoff for Crystal City, and the road began to climb in a series of sharp twists up into the mountains. Glacial violence made this harsh, craggy landscape as resistant to invasion as any man-made fortress. It took a special skill to breach it.

She hadn't driven in snow in ages, and the Range Rover fishtailed a little.

"Nice move, Mom," Cody observed from the backseat.

She gave silent thanks for the Rover's four-wheel drive. The tires gripped the sand-sprinkled snow. Forced to a Sunday-drive crawl, she saw everything with crystalline clarity. Open rangeland and broad meadows flowing past. A ring of mountains surrounding the valley like the walls of a mythical stronghold. Every tortuous inch of this road was familiar to her, so familiar that it made her eyes ache.

The valley slumbered in midwinter splendor, as if the entire landscape was holding its breath, waiting for the far-distant springtime.

She read the names on every rural mailbox they passed—Smith, Dodd, Gyenes, Bell, Jacobs. Most people who settled in the area seemed to stay forever. Each farm lay in perfect repose, a picture waiting to be painted: a white house with dark green shutters, a wisp of smoke twisting from the chimney, windowpanes glowing at the first touch of twilight.

There was a time when this sight had pierced her in a tender spot. She had painted this very scene long ago. Her brush had given life to the hillocks of untouched snow, to the luminous pink of the sunset, and to the fading sky behind alpine firs with their shoulders draped in white and icicles dripping from their branches. On a poorly prepared canvas with second-rate paints, she managed to convey a sense of soaring wonder at the world around her. It was a good painting. Better than good. But young. Impossibly, naively young as she had never been since the day she left this town in anguish and disgrace.

She wondered what had become of that painting. A part of her insisted that it was important to know. Creating that picture had been a defining act for her. It had opened a window into her future and sent her dreams off in a direction that would bring her joy and heartbreak for the rest of her life.

She peeked at Cody to see his reaction to their arrival. He stared out the window, his hands playing the air drums in his lap. His narrowed eyes were filled with nothing but indifference. She shouldn't be surprised. Indifference and contempt were the only emotions he exhibited these days.

A fading Rotary Club sign marked the city limits.

I'm back now, really and truly back. She knew it was just her imagination, but she heard a rush of wind as she felt herself going forward . . . into the past.

Across the Lions Club sign stretched a banner announcing the WINTER ROUNDUP—MARCH 2–3.

Great. That meant she wouldn't find her father at home. As the leading rodeo stock contractor in the state, he was bound to be at the arena. She punched his num-

ber into her cell phone—Lord, did *any*one but her father
keep the same number for twenty-five years?

"Blue Rock." A young voice, not her father's, answered. One of his personal assistants, she supposed.

"Is Gavin in? This is . . . his daughter, Michelle
Turner."

A pause. "I'm sorry, he's out for the evening. He was
expecting you tomorrow, ma'am."

"Is he at the arena?" she asked.

"Yes, ma'am."

She supposed she could go to his place, sit, and wait
for him, but she was too edgy to put the meeting off any
longer. The entire town would witness their reunion. Would
anyone remember her, and what had happened that year?
Would heads shake and tongues wag? Would they look at
her son and exchange knowing glances?

The next road sign posted a greeting from the Cal-
vary Lutheran Church: YOU'RE ENTERING GOD'S COUNTRY.

"I'll find him there, then." She hung up the phone.

Main Street stretched before her, cold and straight as
the barrel of a rifle. She passed the saddlery with its false
log façade, Ray's Quik Chek, the Northern Lights Feed
Store and Café, the Christian Science Reading Room,
LaNelle's Quilt and Fabric Shoppe, a bank, and a picket-
fronted bar that hadn't been there seventeen years ago.
Blue-and-white signs pointed out the turns to the county
hospital and the library.

On the other side of town was a flat-roofed restaurant hunched atop a knoll and surrounded by eighteen-
wheelers with their running lights on—the Truxtop Café.
She winced, recalling the last time she had set foot in that
place.

Crystal City was a part of Michelle Turner, no matter how hard she tried to forget that fact.

Every once in a while she used to fantasize about coming back, but in her mind it was always a triumphant return. Not like this. Not with her heart frozen, her world in disarray, and her purpose to save the life of the father she hadn't seen in seventeen years.

Chapter 2

Sam McPhee stared out the window at the ripples of snow on the hills behind his house. Though it was a familiar sight, he lingered there, watching as the last light of day rode the broken-backed mountains. The sight was a restful thing for a man to hold in his chest. In his youth, he'd carried the image with him no matter where he went, from Calgary to Cozumel, and when the time came to figure out where home was, he didn't need to look any farther than these hills.

He adjusted his hat and flexed his fingers into a pair of gloves. He straightened up and hitched back his hip, stomping his foot down into the boot, a characteristic gesture caught dozens of times by rodeo photographers.

Sam was a hard-bitten man, a loner who depended on no one, but sometimes the loneliness howled through him. Sometimes he wished he had someone to share these moments with, someone he could take by the hand, and say, "Look up at the hills tonight. Look at all those colors." After such a long time on his own, it shouldn't matter. But every once in a while, in the empty hover of time between evening and twilight, it did.

He flicked off most of the lights in the house, leaving one burning on the porch.

His boots crunching on the frozen drive, he went out to finish loading his trailer: saddle, tack, rope, blankets, Yellow Arrow liniment, an extra pair of gloves. These things were sacred to him and he handled them with the reverence and care of a priest performing the rites of consecration. They were the trappings of something so much a part of him that he couldn't even really think of it as a sport. Rodeo. His second love.

The sharp cold air needled his lungs as he crossed the yard to the bunkhouse, a squat log dwelling the former owners had remodeled into a guesthouse. Sam's partner in the horse ranch lived there now. He pounded on the door, then opened it. "Hey, Edward, you about ready?"

"Coming, coming. Hold your horses."

"My horses are already trailered, no thanks to you, pal."

"Yeah, well, I was busy," Edward called from the back bedroom.

"Did Diego get those stables done?" Sam closed the door behind him to keep in the heat from the woodstove.

"Diego took off. Got a job in a restaurant up at Big Mountain."

"Damn. That's the second stable hand we've lost this month."

"What you need is a slave," Edward called.

"Last time I checked, it was against the law to keep slaves."

"In this society," Edward said, "we call them kids."

"Yeah, well, I don't happen to have any handy." Sam didn't let himself dwell on it. "I guess I'll call Earl Meecham, see if one of his boys'll work after school each day."

Edward Bliss came out into the timber-ceilinged hall, a stack of folded blankets in his arms. Sam's partner was five-foot-two, half Salish Indian, and one hundred percent hell-raiser.

"What's with the blankets?" Sam asked.

"Ruby Lightning wove them. Asked me to put them out at the bake sale table tonight."

They climbed into the old Dodge truck, shivering against the chilled vinyl seats. The engine coughed in protest, then turned over with a flatulent blast of exhaust. Sam put it in gear and eased down the gravel drive. A thread of fiery orange sunset stitched across the peaks of the Mission Range. Foothills shadowed the lower pastures in shades of purple. The landscape looked bleak and cold, beautiful in a way few could admire.

He followed the dark rein of the road, glancing in the side mirrors to check the trailer. Rio and Zeus were probably dozing. The big quarter horses were used to the routine of loading up, driving, then waiting in the holding pen for a lightning ride that, in the old days, used to determine whether or not Sam got to eat that week.

"So what's Ruby up to lately?" he asked.

Edward took out a stick of Juicy Fruit, offering Sam the pack. "You ought to call her up and ask her."

Sam folded the gum in half twice and put it in his mouth. "Maybe I will. She doing all right?"

"You could ask her that, too."

An English teacher at the local high school, Ruby Lightning was also a single mom and an activist in the

Kootenai tribal government. She was scrubbed, earthy, and available, living in a frame house just a quarter mile down the road. They'd had some good times in the past, shared a few laughs, and could have shared more if he'd been so inclined.

Sam had simply stopped calling her. He wasn't proud of the way he drifted in and out of relationships. He'd tried marriage once and discovered it was a bad fit—like boots that were too tight. He didn't need a shrink to explain the parallels between his failed romances and his lousy childhood.

"How's that daughter of hers?" Sam wondered aloud.

"Molly's in the barrel-racing competition for sixteen-and-under."

"No kidding." It seemed only yesterday that he'd met little Molly Lightning, a dark-eyed waif, completely devoted to an old Welsh pony Ruby had bartered from Sam. Now Molly was nearly grown, slim and lithe as a bull-hide whip, probably leaving the halls of Crystal City High littered with broken hearts. Christ, where did the years go?

Like the best horses Sam had known, the girl had fire and heart. She also had, he recalled, a great mom.

Yeah, maybe he would give Ruby a call.

"How much does she want for those blankets?" he asked. Ruby was an expert weaver, using Montana-grown wool and traditional patterns and totems in her designs.

"Fifty bucks apiece," Edward said. "You want one?"

Sam grinned as he turned into the arena parking lot. "If I win the purse tonight, I'll buy them all."

"So you think you and old Rio'll win, eh, cowboy?" A gold tooth flashed in Edward's grin.

"Hey, we *always* win." It was a lie, and both he and Edward knew it. But there had been a time when Sam truly did rule the roping competitions. One winning ride used to net him $22,000, sometimes more. Most cowboys spent their winnings on silver-studded saddles and fancy rigs. Sam had used his for a different purpose altogether, a purpose that set him apart from other rodeo stars and made him something of an oddity in the circuit.

After he became a national champion, the trade sheets had a field day with him, focusing on the unorthodox choices he'd made. They'd documented his dazzling style, his natural grace in the sport. They'd published his hefty earnings. Plastered his face on calendars. For several seasons he'd been the golden boy of the circuit, the cowboy with a career plan.

What the reporters hadn't documented was the god-awful loneliness. The grinding tedium. The aches and bruises so deep they made him feel older than rock itself. It was a solitary life, traveling from show to show in a beat-up truck hauling a horse trailer, chasing down trashy, roped-out steers. But the prospect of another ride, another purse, had sustained him through the roughest times of his life.

"Nice rig," Edward said, as Sam drove past a white Ford 350 dually with a pristine white Cattleman trailer at least thirty-six feet long. Gleaming in the floodlights, the thing looked like a giant suppository.

On its side, in perfect custom commercial script, was a familiar logo in indigo paint: BLUE ROCK RANCH.

"Gavin Slade must've bought himself another new toy," Sam said. He used to resent everything Slade had and everything he was. But that was a long time ago.

Lately the whole town had been gossiping about Gavin in concerned undertones. Throwing his money away on expensive rigs wouldn't fix what was wrong. But it sure as hell wasn't Sam's place to tell Gavin that.

Edward spotted a cluster of women at the doorway

of the concession hall. "So hurry up and park already. I got people to see."

Despite his bantam-rooster stature, Edward Bliss was a ladies' man. He wrenched the rearview mirror toward himself, took off his Stetson, and checked his hair. He worked at flirting as seriously as he worked the ranch.

Sam yanked the mirror back and angled the truck toward his usual parking spot at the north end of the arena. "Damn," he said, cranking down the window and spitting out his gum.

"What is it?" asked Edward.

Sam glared at a late-model silver Range Rover with Washington plates. "Some idiot's parked in my spot."

Chapter 3

"This is totally bogus, Mom," Cody said through chattering teeth as they walked toward the main building of the arena. "I can't believe you're making me come to a Wild West show."

"It's not a Wild West show. It's a rodeo."

"I can't believe you're making me come anywhere near—shit!" Cody stopped walking and looked down.

"Horseshit, to be precise. Wipe your foot in the snow."

He got the worst of it off, grumbling the whole time. Somehow, it was impossible for Cody to be cool when he was scraping manure off his hundred-dollar Doc Martens.

"Can't we just go to his place and wait for him?" Cody demanded. "You said he had a guesthouse."

"Guesthouses—plural. My father never does anything part way." Blue Rock Ranch was the epitome of contemporary Western living: several thousand pristine acres complete with streams, ponds, and a compound of houses and barns that resembled a small, elegant village in a storybook setting. Some years back, *Architectural Digest* did a spread on the main house. And Michelle's father—never one to shun the public that validated his existence—made the most of it.

She had come across the article by accident. She'd been sitting at her drafting table at work one day, paging through magazines and looking at the ads to see what the competition was cooking up. Unsuspecting, she turned a page and found herself staring at a perfect shot of Blue Rock Ranch in high summer when avalanche lilies blanketed the hills and the grass was so green it hurt the eyes. The ensuing pages displayed room after perfect room. She recognized the window seat where she used to read and sketch, the rustic porch where she'd sat in the Stickley glider, spinning dreams she was absolutely certain would come true.

"So what say we go hang out in one of his 'plural' guesthouses?" Cody inspected the bottom of his shoe.

"No. We're here, and we're going to find my father."

"What's he doing out anyway? I thought he was sick."

"He's sick, all right, but not bedridden. His condition—"

"Jeez, it's cold." Cody stamped his feet on the straw-covered snow. "I guess if we're going in, let's go." He hunched his shoulders and headed for the main entrance. He never wanted to talk about her father's illness, never wanted to hear the details of what had to be done. He had a teenager's abiding horror of things medical and refused to consider his own mortality or that of anyone he knew.

Michelle bought tickets from a smiling girl with crooked teeth and loftily teased hair. "Right through there, ma'am." The girl gestured, displaying a lavishly fringed polyester sleeve.

"Don't say a word," Michelle warned Cody as they pushed through the turnstile. But the sarcastic look on his face said it all.

They found themselves amid a crowd of men in sheepskin-lined denim jackets and women in tight jeans with the creases ironed in blade-sharp. Michelle took a moment to inspect her son. Out of place would be putting it mildly. Torn black jeans with thick chains inexplicably draped from the pockets. A leather jacket studded with rivets along every seam. His hair was oddly colored—white sidewalls around his ears to show off a row of stainless-steel earrings, a long ponytail over the top and hanging down his back. The ends were still slightly green from when he'd dyed it for a Phish concert last summer.

Ah, but that face. Sullen, yes, but still so beautiful. *What happened to you, my precious boy?*

She resisted the urge to tell him to straighten his shoulders. Part of his determined coolness involved a studied slouch that gave his body the shape of a question mark.

Stand tall, like your father did.

Her stomach constricted nervously as they walked along the front of the bleachers in search of Gavin Slade. She'd see him soon. Good grief, what would they say to each other?

Their last face-to-face conversation had not been pleasant.

"I'm pregnant, Daddy."

Gavin had gone all stony-eyed. Then he'd said: "I'm not surprised. Your mother was careless, too."

"My *father* was careless," she'd shot back.

That same day, she'd left Blue Rock Ranch, vowing

never to return. But here she was, years later, her nerves strung taut with anticipation.

Heat blew into the arena through long tubes connected to generators. The smells of horse and leather and popcorn filled the air with poignant reminders of the past. Michelle couldn't help but notice the spot where she used to sit in the bleachers and watch the cowboys putting quarter horses through their paces. And there, in the middle of the arena, was the place where she'd lost her heart to a horse called Dooley.

She remembered the feel of the spirited animal beneath her as she learned the heart-tightening, dangerous joys of barrel racing. An experienced dressage rider, Michelle thought she knew how to handle a horse. But Dooley wasn't just any horse. He was a quarter horse bred for athletic ability, agility, and quickness, with Thoroughbred blood for extra speed and an explosive disposition. He took the turns around the barrels, expertly pivoting on one back leg. She still remembered the exhilaration of the flat-out run, the check at full speed, the turn 180 degrees around the barrel in a dizzying cloverleaf pattern. Across the years, she still could hear a voice calling encouragement, calling to the Michelle she used to be.

You're doing great for a city girl. Let him have his head. I think he likes you. . . .

Willing away the reminiscence, she watched a slim girl in black and turquoise ride into the ring on a piebald mare. Horse and rider flowed like water as they chased the cans. The girl, her shining black braid slapping as rhythmically as her quirt, wore a look of intense, exultant concentration on her face as she exited the course and the crowd applauded. The PA system blared an impressive time—17.5 seconds.

Ah, that smile, Michelle thought, studying the girl. Had she ever been that young? That happy?

Cody was watching the girl, too, and for once the expression on his face wasn't so snide. Even her urban animal of a son couldn't resist an event that featured beautifully dressed girls, powerful and good-looking horses, and fast action. Then he caught his mother studying him, and his rapt expression faded. "Well?" he asked. "You going to go find him or what?"

They passed the Chamber of Commerce table. She spotted a familiar face, and it gave her a start. Earl Meecham, owner of the Truxtop Café, was handing out flyers or coupons of some sort. He hadn't changed much— a little more paunch, maybe, a little more jowl. Shadowed by a ten-gallon Resistol hat, his grin reached from ear to ear.

Briefly, Meecham's eyes met Michelle's, but she could tell he didn't recognize her. She was a lot different from the girl with the long blond ponytail and the stars in her eyes.

Turning up the collar of her jacket, she moved toward the bleachers near the judges' booth. There, standing with one Lucchese boot propped on a hitch rail, a printed program clutched in his fist, was her father.

Instant panic set in. She had the urge to flee, to hide. *I can't do this.* Not here, not now. Yet at the heart of the panic lay something far more powerful. Love or hate or maybe a wrenching combination of the two. Resolve. *Duty.* She shoved the panic away.

Cody must have sensed her tension, because he stopped walking and followed the direction of her gaze. "That's him, isn't it?" His voice was bland, bored.

"Yes, that's him." The noise of the crowd and the

milling calves and horses fell away as she studied her father.

Gavin Slade. Thirty years ago he had been the hottest ticket in Hollywood, building a career on a body of tense, gritty Westerns and hard-edged police dramas. His rugged good looks had graced fan magazines and tabloids from *Life* to the *National Enquirer*. He was still good-looking, his face chiseled and lean, his air of command still evident, his magnetic charm still powerful.

At the height of his fame he had left Hollywood, migrating to Montana before it became fashionable to do so. He had discovered Crystal City during a location shoot and spent years building Blue Rock Ranch, becoming a rodeo stock contractor with an international reputation. Some of his bucking stock was better known than the champions who rode them. The people in the town lionized him. They considered him one of their own because he predated all the other California transplants. She'd never really known why he'd moved or what he hoped to find in Montana. Was he running away from the Hollywood rat race or was he running away from Michelle and her mother?

"He doesn't look sick," Cody observed, trying to appear casual but sounding relieved instead.

Gavin was a little too thin, perhaps, and maybe a yellowish cast haunted his complexion and the whites of his eyes, but Michelle allowed that the coloring might be from the arena lights. She took off her Gore-Tex gloves and stuck them in her pockets. Despite the midwinter cold, sweat dampened her palms. She wiped them on her jeans. "Let's go tell him we're here."

A short, bandy-legged cowboy carrying a stack of woven blankets jostled her as he passed, but she barely noticed. When she was a few feet away from her father, he glanced up. She didn't know this man well enough to read his expression. After all, she'd only spent half a year of her life with him. He'd always been a stranger to her. A stranger she called "Daddy."

"Michelle, honey." His trademark thousand-watt smile lit up his face, showing off his perfect teeth. "Come and give your old man a hug."

His arms went around her. She closed her eyes and inhaled. Clean laundry, breath mints, expensive aftershave. A strong embrace that enclosed her entirely. She told herself that it shouldn't feel this good. It shouldn't feel this right. He was a stranger. But when she drew back and looked up, tears swam across her eyes.

"Hi, Daddy."

"I didn't think you'd show up until tomorrow."

"We got an early start. The roads weren't bad, so we drove straight on through." She stepped back, blinking fast, refusing to shed the tears. "This is Cody."

Gavin's smile froze. She held her breath, hoping he'd look past the leather and chains, praying he'd see through the rebellious attitude. But Gavin had missed the wonder years with Cody, just as he had missed them with Michelle. He never knew the radiant joy of a toddler's face on Christmas morning, the triumphant exuberance of a nine-year-old who had just caught his first fish, the perfect tenderness of a boy holding a newly hatched duckling in his cupped hands, or his shy pride as he delivered breakfast in bed on Mother's Day.

Gavin saw only what stood before him now. His mouth took on the brittle edges of a false grin as he said, "Well, now. How do, youngster?" He stuck out his hand.

Cody took it briefly, then let go. "Okay."

Michelle found herself wishing she'd coached him for

this moment. Not that he would have listened, but shouldn't she have instructed him to be a little less sullen?

Awkwardness hung like a bad smell in the air. A dogie bawled in the pen outside. Michelle tried to will away her disappointment. What did she expect, that they'd fall into each other's arms just because one was her father, the other her son? That was something that might have happened in one of Gavin's old movies, not in real life.

She cleared her throat. "I knew we'd find you here."

"Wouldn't miss it, honey. Wouldn't miss it." He was the reason a town this size even had a rodeo. He needed a place to work his stock, and the arena had been built with civic funds—but with Gavin Slade in mind. He focused on the refreshment stand. "Can I get you two something to drink?"

"I think I'll go look around some." Cody jammed his hands into his pockets. His already sagging jeans lowered a notch. Michelle hoped her father didn't notice the *South Park* boxers that showed above the waistband.

"All right." She had promised herself she wouldn't try to force her father and son to get along. "Be back here in a half hour." As a reflex, she almost told him to stay out of trouble. She bit back the words. He generally took her warnings as invitations to step out of line. Watching him saunter away, she said, "I think he's a little tired and cranky from the long drive."

"How about you?" Gavin asked. "Can I get you something—coffee? A beer?"

"I'm fine."

He touched her shoulder. "Michelle. I feel stupid saying thank you for coming. How the hell can I thank you?"

She felt the color rise in her face. "Don't even try. I'm here. I'm going to help." She was filled with an impulse to milk this occasion, to bask in his gratitude. She was clearly the martyr here. She could use this to stitch together their tattered relationship.

But the impulse faded. That wasn't her purpose here.

"Help? Is that what you call it?"

"What would you call it, Daddy?"

"Hell, I don't know." He took off his hat and scratched his head. His hair was as thick and abundant as ever—but it had turned snow-white.

She hadn't pictured him white-haired. When she had reached him by phone, hearing his voice for the first time in seventeen years, she had envisioned the young, vital man he'd been during her eighteenth summer.

"I never meant for you to find out about my condition, Michelle," he said. The gravelly waver in his voice worried her. "And I sure as hell never meant for you to come riding to the rescue."

"This is one time you don't get to call all the shots, Dad." Out of the blue, a trust agreement had arrived in November. She'd been at work, fiddling on the computer with some coffee-bean graphics when a courier delivered a thick envelope bearing the logo of Blue Rock Ranch. She had nearly dropped the package in her surprise. Then she'd shuttered the blinds of her office, sat down at her desk, and opened the package. There was no cover letter, just little Post-it arrows indicating where to sign.

It had taken Michelle a few stunned moments to figure out what was going on. After nearly seventeen years of silence, her father was putting a staggering fortune in trust for her son.

She had broken a nail pecking in the phone number given on the trust agreement. The law firm in Missoula would tell her nothing, so she refused to sign the agreement.

That was when her father had called. He'd caught her

at home, loading the dishwasher and wondering why Brad hadn't phoned to tell her he'd miss dinner. The sound of her father's voice had banished her annoyance at Brad.

"Michelle, I've been sick."

She had closed her eyes and let out her breath. "What's the matter?"

"Damnedest thing. They call it end-stage renal failure."

"Kidney failure?"

"Yep. I had a spell of strep and ignored it, let it go on too long. There's a rare complication called glomerulonephritis—that's what developed. So far the tabloids haven't picked up on it, but the buzzards are circling."

The hated tabloids. They had made her childhood, as the daughter of a matinee idol, a nightmare. "So what's going to happen?"

Long hesitation. "I've started dialysis."

"Is there a cure?"

"Well, sort of."

"What's that supposed to mean, sort of?"

"My specialist in Missoula says I need a transplant."

"A kidney transplant." Comprehension burst over Michelle in a blaze so bright that she flinched. "From a living donor, right?"

"No. I'm on a waiting list for a cadaver."

Hearing the words, Michelle had the distinct sensation of stepping off a cliff. The knowledge of what she had to do came swiftly, pushing up through her like a geyser—unstoppable, filled with its own energy. She backed herself against the kitchen wall, sliding down it while the phone cord pulled to its limit. She knew she could stretch this strange moment out, make him talk to her, force him to ask, to beg, maybe. But instead, she shut her eyes and plunged right in.

"You don't have to wait for someone to die. I'll do it, Daddy," she practically whispered. "I'll give you a—"

Oh, Jesus. "—a kidney."

"Michelle?" Gavin Slade's movie-idol voice beckoned her back to the present. "If you're tired from the drive, we can leave right now."

"No, let's stay. I'm too wired to relax just yet." She had gone through nine weeks of multiple preliminary screening exams at Swedish Hospital in Seattle: blood tests, chest X rays, detailed urinalysis, sonograms and MRIs. Against enormous odds, five out of six antigens matched. Physiologically, she was a near perfect donor for Gavin. Because her father's health was otherwise excellent, he made the ideal recipient.

He sent her a look she couldn't read. "We've got a lot to talk about."

At least he acknowledged it. At least he acknowledged that he'd broken seventeen years of silence only because he needed one of her kidneys.

Michelle stared at the arena ring where the barrels were being removed. She was determined to keep her face neutral. *I will not be angry at him,* she told herself, as she had told herself ever since learning of his condition. Anger had no place in this matter.

"So you remember how to get up to Blue Rock?" he asked.

"I could do that in my sleep, Dad. I might even let Cody drive. He got his license last summer, and he's been bugging me all day."

Gavin nodded to a passing couple, but they didn't stop to chat. The barrel racing had ended, and it was time for team roping. People took rodeo seriously in Crystal City, and there wasn't a lot of socializing going on. That would come after, when winners and losers alike headed out to the Grizzly Bar, a local honky-tonk, for drinking and dancing.

"So your boyfriend decided not to come?" Gavin asked.

"He's snowed under at work." She tucked her chin into the collar of her jacket. "His name's Brad, and he's more than a boyfriend. We've been together three years."

"Getting married?"

Her cheeks filled with color yet again. *Marriage*. That would force her and Brad to define their relationship. "We're in no hurry."

"Well, I'd like to meet him. So he's a pharmacist?"

"He's part owner in a big pharmacy franchise. He's helped me a lot—understanding your illness and what's going on with this transplant. At one time he was thinking of becoming a doctor—a surgeon—but pharmacy suits him better."

At least, that was what he always said. Michelle realized, with a start, that she really didn't understand what lay in Brad's heart. Odd. She usually thought of the two of them as knowing each other so well.

An announcement crackled over the PA system, and Gavin perked up. "Michelle, I have to go over to the chutes. I've got some new saddle broncs I'm testing. You want to come?"

"No, thanks. I was just going to see what Cody's up to."

"You do that." Gavin started to walk away, then turned back. "Michelle?"

"Yeah?"

"It feels good to have you home."

"Ditto, Dad." She forced the words out. Everything felt strange, dreamlike, with the shadows of a nightmare hovering at the edges. It was just nerves, Michelle told herself. If all went well, she'd be back in Seattle in a few weeks. "See you up at the house later."

Michelle had no trouble spotting Cody in the bleachers at the far end of the arena. Having never been to a rodeo before, he probably didn't realize it wasn't the best place to view the action.

She opened her mouth to call out, then stopped herself. She saw exactly why Cody had parked himself there. The barrel racer—the one in black and turquoise—sat a few rows over, sipping a Dr Pepper and talking to the girl with the teased hair and fringed shirt. They appeared completely unaware of Cody, but then, he appeared completely unaware of them. And Michelle knew damned well he was burning up with awareness.

Good, she thought. Maybe he'd finally get over his obsession with Claudia Teller, his girlfriend since the start of the school year. Claudia was a beautiful pale predator who never met Michelle's eyes and who answered her admittedly chirpy questions with monosyllables. Claudia had introduced Cody to cigarettes and Zima, and probably to things Michelle hadn't found out about yet. There was no creature quite so intoxicating as a provocative teenage girl. And no creature quite so malleable as a teenage boy on hormone overload. A girl like Claudia could make Eagle Scouts steal from their grandmothers. She wore makeup with the brand name Urban Decay. She had bottle red hair and kohl-deepened eyes, and she was as seductive as Spanish fly on Cody's defenseless adolescent libido. The most popular girl in the school, she wielded her power over him with casual ruthlessness.

Since Cody had taken up with Claudia, Michelle felt herself losing her maternal hold on him. Her son was a stranger. When he lied to her, she didn't know what to do.

Maybe the sojourn in Montana was a test period, Michelle thought. Could she win her son back, or was he already lost to her?

The barrel racer didn't look quite so predatory. Perhaps he'd see her in school. Against his will, Cody was going to have to attend Crystal City High during their stay in Montana because his grades had been terrible lately. He despised the idea, but his grade-level advisor had laid down the law. Attend school in Montana or repeat the term.

Michelle wandered off, pausing at the baked goods table to admire a plush wool Salish blanket. Handwoven in rich earth tones, the design touched a chord in her. She thought of Joseph Rain, the master painter she had once studied with. His work had held echoes of these ancient motifs. On impulse, she went out to the car to get her checkbook. There was no cold quite so piercing as the cold of a Montana winter night. The new snow was powdery and light beneath her boots. The Swan River was almost frozen over. Only a miserly trickle down the middle remained, though in spring it would transform itself into a roaring gush of white water.

When she returned to the arena, Cody had moved down one bench closer to the girls. The calf roping had started, bawling dogies and lightning-quick horses kicking up dirt as the cowboys flew at them. The chase lasted no more than a few seconds, but there was a peculiar drama in the frantic flight of the calf, the moment the rope drew taut, the cowboy vaulting from his saddle to bind the feet, the flagger's arm streaking up to mark the moment.

". . . and in chute number four, we have Sam McPhee," said the announcer over the PA system.

The world stopped turning.

"Ladies and gentlemen, please put your hands together for Sam McPhee. . . ."

Time, breath, heartbeat, everything seemed to stop.

Applause erupted from the bleachers. She stood at the rail and gripped the rungs hard.

Sam McPhee. Sam is here.

Michelle prayed she'd heard wrong. But she knew she hadn't. Oh, God. *Sam.*

"Six-time national champion Sam McPhee retired from the circuit in 1992, but we're lucky to have his local talent here in Crystal City. . . ." The announcer droned on, enumerating accomplishments that didn't surprise Michelle one bit. The only thing Sam McPhee hadn't done right was stick around.

After a few moments, she remembered to breathe again. She looked at the chute at the end of the arena, and there he was. From a distance he resembled any cowboy about to rope a calf. Battered hat jammed on his head, the brim angled down, piggin string clamped between his teeth, coiled rope clenched in his fist.

Yet she knew him. Knew the tilt of his head, the set of his shoulders, the fringe of sandy hair touching his collar. She couldn't help herself. She moved along the rail to get a closer look.

Sam nodded briefly, almost imperceptibly, at the guy in charge of the chutes. The calf lunged out. Sam followed on a glossy-hided, athletic quarter horse. He roped and dispatched the calf with a speed that drew gasps of admiration from the crowd. Admiration for a six-time national champion.

Michelle stared, spellbound, unable to move, a fly caught in a pool of honey. Sam appeared leaner, stronger, and quicker than ever. He retained that unique grace of movement she recalled so well. More than brute strength, it was an aura of raw ability coupled with arrogant confidence. He waved to the crowd. Everyone knew he'd made the winning time. Everyone knew he was the champion.

Sam had it in spades—the star power and magnetism of a true pro. She got a good look at him as he led his horse, showman-style, along the rail. The years had hardly left a mark on him. He still filled a pair of jeans like a Levi's poster boy. He still had that slightly crooked grin that had once made her heart melt. Accepting the accolades, he still had that funny, enchanting "aw-shucks" manner about him.

And he was still caught up in the shallow thrills of the rodeo, she reminded herself with a superior sniff as a leggy brunette handed him a trophy, accompanying it with a kiss.

Was it the rodeo that had seduced him away from her? That had made him disappear overnight? She had never seen him again. Until now.

"That was kind of cool, wasn't it?" Cody came up behind her.

"What, the calf roping?" Good God, thought Michelle. Panic beat so hard in her chest it felt like a heart attack. Cody didn't know. She never thought she would have to tell him. *Good God.*

"Yeah, the calf roping, whatever." He watched the handlers, done up like clowns, shooing dogies into pens. "It was pretty cool."

Was it genetic? Michelle wondered. "I thought you were into wholesome pursuits like slam dancing and body piercing."

"How about driving, Mom? Can I drive from here to your father's place?"

Michelle nodded, thinking irrationally that if she gave in, she wouldn't have to deal with the other. "All right. You can drive."

For a few moments longer, he watched Sam with interest. And why not? The tall cowboy, with his easy smile and smooth way with the ladies, was sure to appeal to a boy's imagination.

Her heart chilled, aching in her chest. Sam was here. Sam and Cody were both here. And they didn't know about each other.

Chapter 4

It felt damned good to win. Winning always gave Sam a rush. Cheap thrills. They never lasted long, but they were easier to come by than the real thing.

"Nice ride." Edward Bliss fell in step with Sam while he walked Rio to cool out the big horse. "You done good, pardner." Beyond the paddock, some of the rigs were getting ready to leave, diesel engines idling.

"I guess I'll be buying all of Ruby's blankets." Sam led Rio in a wide circle. Steam rose from the quarter horse's body and plumed from his nostrils.

"You're too late. I just sold the last one. To a pretty blond lady I didn't recognize." Edward handed him a bottle of water.

"I assume you introduced yourself." Sam took a swig from the bottle.

"Nope. She was in a hurry. Had some whiny long-haired kid with her who kept saying it was his turn to drive."

"When you're a kid, it's *always* your turn to drive." Sam finished the water. Out in the parking lot, the sound of gunning engines roared. "So, you got a hot date?"

"Does a coyote have fleas?" Edward gestured at a plump, dark-haired woman in denims and a chinook jacket. She waved to him. "Pearl, from the bank. We're going up to Polson to have a few beers. Want to come?"

Sam grinned, thinking about the suggestion Loretta Sweeney had whispered in his ear when she'd given him the winner's trophy and check. "I've had a better offer."

Edward read his mind. "Loretta's a slut."

"That's what I like about her."

Edward took off. Sam bent to put on Rio's boots—he always put boots on the horses so they wouldn't damage their hooves in the trailer—when the whir of a spinning tire made the horse shy.

"Damn it." Sam dodged an iron-shod hoof.

A second later, he heard the unmistakable metal-on-metal crunch of two vehicles meeting. Rio grunted and flattened his ears. Looping the horse's lead around a rail, Sam went to see what the problem was.

"Shit," he said. "Shit, shit, shit."

The yuppie Range Rover from Washington had backed into his trailer. Its bumper was hooked into the rear, brake lights casting an eerie red glow over the dirty, churned-up snow. As Sam stalked across the parking lot, the yuppie gunned it again. With a wrenching sound of metal, the bumper unhooked. The Rover lurched forward.

Sam put two fingers to his lips and pierced the air with a loud whistle. "Hold on there!" he yelled, breaking into a run.

A few people stopped, shaking their heads when they

saw the damage. The driver's side door of the Rover opened and out jumped a slender teenage boy.

Great, thought Sam, eyeing the studded jacket and sleek ponytail. An underage driver to boot. He could see someone in the passenger seat of the Range Rover. The kid's date, maybe?

"Guess you had a little trouble backing up there," he said, keeping calm with an effort.

The kid tossed him an insolent glance. Light glinted off a small silver nose hoop. "Guess so. Sorry about your trailer. Insurance'll cover it."

The boy's nonchalance grated on Sam. Hell, he looked too young to have a license. A learner's permit—possibly.

When Sam thought of the time and expense repairs would take, he got more pissed. From the corner of his eye, he could see the boy's passenger rooting around in the glove compartment.

"Yeah, insurance'll cover it," Sam said, "but only after I fight with them for about six months. Tell you what— this looks like a few hundred dollars' worth of damage. You could come out to my place and work it off."

"Work it—"

"You know, work. Like with a shovel and a ton of horseshit." Sam dug in his pocket for a card with the ranch name and address on it. He held it out. "You show up to-morrow, and you can get started on the stables."

The kid didn't take the card. "Hey, I'm not from around here—"

"I never would have guessed," Sam snapped. "Look, you be there or—"

"He'll be there," said a soft voice behind Sam.

He froze, feeling a jab of premonition. *That voice.* He knew that voice. It was something the heart remembered long after the mind forgot.

He made himself turn slowly to face her. Awareness exploded over him, but there was only silence, and the smell of snow and exhaust, and a vague notion of folks walking to their cars in the parking lot. Each moment seemed endless, drawn out, excruciating. Denial reared in his chest, but he couldn't refute what his eyes were seeing.

"Michelle?"

"Hey, Sam." She had that same low, sweet voice and wide, fragile eyes, the same soft blond hair, cropped short now but curling in the same breezy way around a face he'd never forgotten.

The boy blew on his hands to warm them. "You guys know each other?"

"Reckon we do," said Sam, his gaze never leaving Michelle. Holy Christ, *Michelle Turner*. When he had first met her, she was the prettiest thing he'd ever seen in his life—long yellow ponytail, big blue eyes, a smile he liked better than air. Now she wasn't pretty anymore. She was beautiful, the way a goddess is beautiful, the way the moon is beautiful. Perfectly formed, luminous, chilly, and . . . distant. That was the word for it. Distant.

Where've you been, Michelle?

The unexpected quake of emotion pissed him off. He didn't need this, didn't want the memories she stirred up. Turning away from her, he tucked the card back in his pocket. "Look, kid, forget about the trailer."

The boy let out an explosive breath of relief. "Hey, thanks. That's pretty cool of you—"

"He'll be at your place tomorrow." Michelle's voice was flat, neutral. Sam had no idea what he was seeing in her eyes, her face. A stranger. Michelle had become a stranger. The person who had once been the sole keeper of every hope and dream he'd ever had was now a complete mystery to him.

"You don't have to—" he began.

"Yes, he does, and he will."

"*Mo-om,*" the kid said.

What an annoying little shit. Sam got prickly hearing some kid call Michelle "Mom." He felt even more weird thinking that somewhere in the world there was a guy the kid called "Dad." So where was he? Sam wondered. He knew he wouldn't ask.

"Now," she said, "where's your 'place'?"

He reluctantly held out the card. Their hands touched as she took it and stuck it in her pocket. A cold, impersonal brush of the fingers. A stranger's touch. What was he expecting? Fireworks? Electricity? Christ, violin music?

She wore a thick, artsy-looking ring that was more sculpture than jewelry. A wedding band? He couldn't tell. He wouldn't ask.

"I'll have Cody there in the morning," she said. "Is nine o'clock all right?"

"Yeah, okay. Nine o'clock."

"Mom," the kid said. "Do I really have to—"

"Get in the Rover, Cody," she said brusquely. "And *I'll* drive."

Chapter 5

Michelle shivered against the cold as she walked across the guest compound to the main house at Blue Rock Ranch. The moon was out, dazzling above the peaks of the Swan Range. She could see all the lunar craters as if through the lens of a telescope. Icy silver light poured invasively across the snow-covered meadows.

She experienced a gut reaction she hadn't felt in a very long time. It was a strange, impossible-to-forget combination of pain and ecstasy that always preceded inspiration. Artist's inspiration. Joseph Rain, who had been her teacher that long-ago summer, called it the touch of the damned, because it hurt, it burned, it was beautiful.

When was the last time she'd felt this desire, this ache? This sharp need to create an image, to speak in color and shape when there were no words?

She couldn't remember, because she had learned to squash the feeling as quickly as it came over her. She didn't have time. She was too busy at work, too busy with Cody and Brad.

But here? Would she be too busy here? The thought of actually having time on her hands frightened her, it really did. Back in Seattle she took a certain comfort in having so much to do that she never found time to think.

At the moment she couldn't do anything *but* think. Sam McPhee was here. He had a ranch called, according to the business card he'd given her, Lonepine. It was located up the old logging road between two hanging lakes. A guy who wasn't supposed to amount to anything had a place of his own. And first thing in the morning, she had to take his son to see him.

She hugged herself, staring up at the white winter moon, wondering if he'd guessed yet. Wondering if he would stay up late tonight, thinking about the past.

The garden gazebo rose like an ice sculpture in the middle of the front yard. She had been sitting on the steps of that gazebo, drawing, the first time she met Sam. She remembered the quiet of that afternoon, the scratch of her pencil on the Firebrand tablet she held in her lap. Joseph Rain had called Montana a "place of great breathing," his apt phrase for the expansiveness of the landscape.

"Nice picture," said a voice behind her.

She froze, charcoal pencil in hand, at the sound of that voice. It was nice, a baritone, but youthful, too.

"You think so?" she asked, getting up. And it was him, just as she had suspected—hoped, prayed—it would be. The boy from the training arena. She'd spotted him the day she arrived. Her first glimpse of him had been from a distance.

He'd been working in a round pen with a mare on a

lunge rope. She had been watching from the porch. He wore scuffed boots and blue jeans, a plaid shirt and battered cap with the Big Sky Feed Company logo on it. He was tall and rangy, like Gavin's favorite trail horse. She knew, to the very depths of her eighteen-year-old soul, that no one in the entire universe had ever looked so good in a pair of Levi's.

Up close, she noticed that he had sandy brown hair, a lean, suntanned face, and eyes the color of her birthstone.

"Yeah, I think so," he replied. "Haven't had much call to look at art, but that's a fine picture."

She stuck her pencil behind her ear, suddenly self-conscious in her cutoffs and cropped T-shirt. "I'm Michelle."

"I know. I've seen you around with your sketchbook."

He noticed. Hallelujah, he noticed.

Michelle had been drawing ever since she was old enough to hold a crayon. It was all she ever wanted to do, and she excelled at it, blazing like a comet through high school classes and special courses she took outside of school. Her inspiration and talent had served her well when she went to Montana to spend that precollege year with her father. Montana seemed so huge and limitless that she got into the habit of drawing constantly just to feel a measure of control over something so overwhelmingly vast and wild. She drew everything: the placid bovine face of a cow; a line of trees along the creek with the stars coming out behind them; the silhouette of a mare and her foal on the slope behind the paddock; a common loon nesting in a marsh.

"I never go anywhere without my sketchbook," she said.

"I'm Sam. Sam McPhee. I work for your dad." He

grinned, and her heart began to melt. If she looked down, she figured she'd see it in a puddle like hot fudge at her feet.

"I know." She grinned back, hoping her neck didn't go all splotchy the way it usually did when she blushed.

"So you're an artist?" he asked. Not with the hefty skepticism a lot of people exhibited when she told them her ambition, but with genuine interest.

"I want to be." She gestured at the sketch. "This is practice. I want to paint for real."

"You mean like on an easel with brushes and a palette and a beret and stuff?"

She laughed. "Exactly. Well, maybe not the beret."

"So do it."

"Do what?"

"Paint for real. Don't just say you're going to. You can't be an artist if you don't paint, right?"

"Guess not." She scuffed her foot against the gazebo steps. "You ever heard of Joseph Rain?"

"Sure," Sam said. "He eats at the café where my mom works. I heard he lives out on the Flathead reservation, but he's a recluse."

"Well, he's just about the most famous painter in the West," she explained. "I came here to study with him." Her father had arranged it all. Though the artist rarely accepted students, Gavin had sent him a box of her sketches and attached a very large check. Mr. Rain had kept the sketches, returned the check, and agreed to work with her—for a fee, not a bribe.

"Yeah? I'd heard he was an artist or something."

"He did a series of paintings for the National Trust." In her mind's eye she could picture them—deep burning emotional scenes that haunted her long after she had walked away from them. "I'm lucky he agreed to be my teacher."

"Is that the best offer you've had all summer?"

"So far." She dropped her sketchbook. Klutz, she thought.

Both she and Sam reached for it, their hands touching. He gave an easy laugh, keeping her hand in his.

The sound of Sam McPhee, laughing. The feel of his hand, touching her. These were the first things about him that she had loved. In the years that ensued, they were the things she remembered more vividly and more frequently than she wanted to.

She wished she had never come back. How would she bear the beauty of this place with its pure light, its slashing cold, and now Sam McPhee? Gritting her teeth, she let herself into the main house. When she stepped inside, she remembered her first visit here, how grand and solid everything had looked. Back then, she'd had her own room upstairs. Now she and Cody occupied a guesthouse. Gavin thought Cody would feel more comfortable in his own space.

"I'll be right out," Gavin called from somewhere upstairs. "Make yourself a drink."

She crossed the living room—a Ralph Lauren ad in 3-D—and stepped behind the wet bar. On a polished shelf, she found a heavy crystal highball glass and shook some ice from the undersized freezer. As she perused the bottles of exotic, expensive whiskey and liqueur, she tried to get her thoughts in some sort of order.

She tended to put things into compartments. Here, in this box—worries about Cody. She spent a lot of time sifting through them, never getting to the bottom, because every day he came up with a new challenge, from asking to get his eyebrow pierced to wanting permission to go to an overnight rock concert.

In another box—work. The agency liked her because she did good work and kept her clients happy. This spring, she would make partner and would earn more money than she ever dreamed of. The other partners lived in fear that she would leave them for a bigger, more lucrative firm, taking her clients with her. But why go elsewhere? To draw bigger, more lucrative ads for fertilizer and tampons?

Another box—Brad. After three years together, they hovered in the same spot where they had begun. They'd bought side-by-side units in a tony Seattle town-house complex, their outdoor decks divided by a wall of cedar planks. They were socially compatible. Sexually compatible. Financially compatible. Rough when it came to Cody, because he and Brad didn't get along.

Now she had a couple of other boxes under construction. Her father, whose life depended on her giving him one of her kidneys, took up a lot of space in her thoughts. For most of her life, he had ignored her, and only when his survival hung in the balance did he acknowledge her existence. A psychiatrist would have a field day with the two of them, she reflected wryly. Sharing their flesh, an organ, the mysterious life force—so damned symbolic. And—she kept telling herself not to think this but she couldn't help it—it was *icky*. There, thought Michelle. I'm a terrible person. Acting like Mother Teresa on the outside, while the coward inside trembled in horror at the ordeal to come.

And now Sam. Good God, Sam McPhee.

"I don't need a drink," she muttered under her breath, regarding the array of bottles. "I need a twelve-step program."

"Try the Booker's. Used to be my favorite."

She whirled around, startled. "Daddy. I didn't hear you come down."

He winked, looking spruce in a thick terry-cloth robe and leather slippers. "Light on my feet."

Obediently, she poured a splash of Booker's over some crushed ice. The first sip brought tears to her eyes. "That's lighter fluid, Dad."

"Good, huh?"

She coughed a little, feeling the rich amber liquid burn her throat. "You want something?"

He held up a tumbler. "My trusty cranberry juice. I've been on restriction for a long time."

A long time. When had he first fallen sick? How long had he suffered with no one to talk to about what was happening to him? Michelle didn't know him well enough to ask.

They sat together in the sunken living room. Rustic millionaire, she mentally classified it. Muted evergreen-and-burgundy plaid, peeled lodgepole pine, a massive field-stone fireplace. She stared intently at the flames lapping at a big log and sipped her single-barrel bourbon.

"So here I am," she said, hopelessly inane.

"Here you are. My angel of mercy."

She blinked fast, taken aback by the bitterness in his voice. "You're mad at me?"

"Hell no, honey, I'm mad at the world. Have been ever since the frigging diagnosis. I failed the medical standard for renewing my pilot's license."

"Daddy, I'm sorry." Everyone knew how much flying meant to him. A week seldom went by that he didn't take off, even for a little while, in his beloved airplane. He had brought her to Blue Rock for the first time in his vintage

P-51 Mustang, modified to accommodate two seats, and she used to love flying with him.

"Do you still have your plane?"

"Yep. I keep the Mustang out at the Meridian County Air Park. And a biplane for stunts." He held up his glass. "Can't even have a drink with my long-lost daughter. The kidney specialist has some diet Nazi monitoring me almost twenty-four hours a day."

"Does it help?"

"Yeah, kept me off dialysis longer than it should have. The biggest culprit is protein—damned hard to stay away from. Cheating isn't an option, either. If the kidneys have to work extra hard, it just hastens the breakdown. I guess that's why I'm resentful. And because I wish I was brave enough to just shoot myself rather than take a goddamned *organ* from my own child."

"Stop it." Michelle was starting to worry, trying not to show it. "We already agreed it's the right thing to do."

He fell silent, staring at the fire in the grate. His famous profile was illuminated by kindly soft light. He still had the charisma that made him a beloved icon in the world of film and a stranger to his family. After a while he let out a heavy sigh. "Anyway—" he clinked his glass against hers "—welcome home, long-lost daughter."

"I was never lost, Daddy."

"You stayed away a long time."

"You should have invited me back."

"Didn't think you'd want to come." He rubbed his cheeks, looking no less handsome than ever. Lord, the man was an android. Dorian Gray with bigger shoulders. He never seemed to age. Even sick and white-haired, he appeared tanned and fit, mature yet ageless.

"Dad, you should have asked me to come back. Before it was too late, got too awkward."

"What would you have said?"

She laughed humorlessly into the crystal highball glass. "I'd have told you to piss off."

"That's what I figured."

They finished their drinks, and somewhere in the house a case clock struck eleven. All the things they weren't saying to each other—about Cody, about the transplant, and now about the surprise cameo appearance of Sam McPhee—hung like cobwebs in the air between them. Why hadn't Gavin told her the father of her child was in Crystal City?

The prospect of an explosive, accusatory conversation held no appeal at this late hour. Without even speaking a word, they made a tacit agreement to avoid touchy subjects—for now.

Gavin looked tired. Frighteningly tired. And she could see, hidden in the folds of his robe . . . *something*.

"It's a sac of dialysis fluid," he said.

Her cheeks heated. "I didn't mean to stare."

"Not to worry. I don't have much dignity left since I got sick." He smiled, but there was a hardness in his face that gave away his fury and frustration. "The stuff in the sac flows through an abdominal shunt. Want to see?"

"Dad, please."

"Okay, I apologize. I stare at it too, sometimes, like it belongs to someone else. Can't believe my own body's turned traitor on me."

They sat for long moments, sipping their drinks and watching the fire, not speaking. The silence swelled. Only in the mountains in winter, Michelle reflected, did the quiet have this all-pervasive quality.

Suddenly she realized what she and Gavin were doing. Another battle of wills. Who would admit to being tired first? Who would make the first move?

No more games. She yawned elaborately, stretching her arms behind her head. "The Booker's did the trick."

"Guess I'll hit the hay, too." Gavin got to his feet. He was too good an actor to look relieved, but she figured he was. "You sleep in, now, Michelle. Since I didn't expect you until tomorrow, I didn't make any plans."

"Plans?"

He cleared his throat. "You know . . . appointments."

"Oh." The impending procedure was becoming more grimly real to her with each passing moment. "We can talk about that tomorrow."

"You got everything you need in the guesthouse?"

"It's fine." She stood, feeling awkward. "Thanks for stocking the fridge." She wondered if she should kiss him good night. Self-consciously, she lifted up on tiptoe, gave him a peck on the cheek, and let herself out the front door.

As she crossed the silent, starlit compound, she knew she wouldn't be sleeping in tomorrow. She had to take Cody to work at Sam's place. She had to figure out how to tell her son who Sam was without destroying him, without destroying them all.

Sunday

Sunday

t 8:45, Sam heard the growl of a motor and the grind of tires over snow. Out in the yard, Scout, the Border collie who ruled the ranch, launched into a barking frenzy.

Sam had taken Loretta Sweeney home early last night. He'd been up since six, and felt all jumpy in his gut; didn't even want his morning coffee. Damn it, he was a grown man. The last thing in the world he should be doing was getting nervous over seeing an old girlfriend.

Except that the words "old" and "girlfriend" didn't seem to apply to Michelle. Though their love affair had burned like a forest fire half a lifetime ago, she didn't seem old at all. Just . . . different. He remembered a girl with yellow hair and a quicksilver smile. Now she seemed far away and sort of fragile. But still so damned beautiful. And as for the girlfriend part—you didn't call your first grand passion a "girlfriend." The term was too inadequate to cover the delirium, the ecstasy, the sweaty palms and fevered dreams of that lost, intense season.

The sound of car doors slamming made him wince. Shit. He *was* nervous.

Going to the window, he expected to see Michelle's Range Rover. Instead, he spied Ruby and Molly Lightning getting out of their old Apache pickup. Scout's "who-the-hell-are-you" barking changed to "I'm-all-yours" whimpers of ecstatic greeting.

Sam gritted his teeth and tried to smile. Ordinarily he'd be glad to see Ruby and her daughter. But it wasn't an ordinary day. He was expecting Michelle, and he didn't look forward to entertaining her, the kid, and now these two.

He went out onto the porch. Sunlight glinted off the snow in the yard and driveway. A row of icicles dripped from the eaves. The Border collie nuzzled Molly's hand.

"Hey, ladies," he said. "You're out bright and early this morning."

Ruby propped an elbow on the battered hood of the pickup. She had a broad, pleasant face, one gold tooth, and an ease around people that made her a popular teacher at the high school. "Hey, Sam," she said.

"Hiya, Sam." Molly scratched the dog behind the ears. "Nice ride last night."

"You, too," he said.

Ruby opened the door of the truck and started rummaging around. "I heard you wanted to buy a blanket."

"Ma'am, I wanted to buy them all."

Molly rolled her eyes.

"I did," Sam said. "It gets mighty cold up here in the winter."

"Well, I brought you one." She held out a folded blanket.

At that moment, another car turned off the highway and started up the drive. The Range Rover. Scout launched into her watchdog routine.

Sam took the blanket from Ruby. The thick wool felt warm against his hands. Plenty warm. "Hey, thanks." He reached into his back pocket for his wallet.

Ruby reached around behind him and grabbed his wrist, holding it firmly. "Sam McPhee, don't you dare. It's a gift because you never let me pay you for delivering Glenda's babies."

He laughed. "Glenda's an Irish setter. She didn't need much help."

"Whatever. The blanket's to say thanks."

Michelle parked and got out of her car. And there stood Sam with Ruby's arm halfway around him, her hand pressed against his hip pocket.

He stepped back. "Morning, Michelle."

She inclined her head politely. Distantly. "Hello, Sam." The collie hung back, head tilted to one side, waiting to see how friendly this one would turn out to be.

"This here's Ruby Lightning and that's her daughter Molly over there."

"Pleased to meet you." Although Michelle smiled readily, the temperature seemed to drop a few degrees. "Look, if this is a bad time—"

"Not at all. You ladies want to come in for coffee?"

Ruby shook her head, winking at him. "I better get going. We've got church this morning."

Molly walked over from the paddock adjacent to the barn. A few of the horses, their coats thick with inch-long hair, stood at the fence waiting for their morning feed. "I could stay and help out with the horses," she called out.

Then Michelle's son got out of the Range Rover, looking as sulky and undernourished as a Calvin Klein ad. Interest sparked in his eyes when he spotted Molly, but he was quick to hide it with a squint that reminded Sam eerily of Gavin Slade. The kid would probably love having her around all day.

"Not today, Molly, but thanks for the offer," Sam said. He didn't want her to have to put up with the little hoodlum.

"My son's name is Cody," Michelle said, motioning him over.

It occurred to Sam that he didn't know the boy's last name, or if Michelle had a married name now. The kid shook his hair back. Stuck his thumb in the top of his belt. "Hiya."

"Hi," Molly said, transparent in her interest. She regarded the kid with the same fascination Red Riding Hood had for the Big Bad Wolf.

Ruby climbed into her truck. "See you around. Nice meeting you both."

Molly took her time getting in. "'Bye, Sam. 'Bye, Michelle and . . . Cody." The smile she sent him was way more than the kid deserved.

As the truck pulled away, a sense of amazement crept over Sam. Michelle had been dead to him. For seventeen years she had been gone, as permanently and irrevocably as if she had been buried six feet under. Now here she was, back again in all her beauty and all her strangeness, and he found himself vacillating between elation and rage. He found himself with a hard-on that made him glad his jacket was zipped.

"Cody's ready to get to work," Michelle said.

"Is that right?" Sam asked Cody.

The kid shrugged, slouching in the time-honored fashion of teens with attitude. "Guess so."

Sam flicked his gaze over him from head to toe. Shining light-colored hair cut too long in some places, too short in others. A leather jacket that would get him knifed in certain neighborhoods. Black jeans and designer combat boots.

The humane thing to do would be to give the kid one of the Filson coveralls from the stable lockers, but Sam wasn't feeling too humane about this guy.

"Let's go to the barn," he said, putting on his John Deere cap. "I'll introduce you to Edward and he can get you started."

"Started on what?"

Sam thought of the heap of manure Diego had left unshoveled. "Oh, I've got a real treat for you, Cody."

He turned to Michelle, flashing her a grin. She blinked at him as if his smile startled her. "Go on inside, Michelle. Make yourself comfortable. There's coffee in the kitchen."

She opened her mouth to say something, then seemed to think better of it and went toward the house. He stopped for a second and looked at her on his porch, and their gazes caught and held.

Though he made no move, a part of him stepped back, and he caught his breath. Michelle, here at his house. Looking as pure and brittle as the sun-shot icicles that lined the eaves above her, a dripping frame of cold and light. Sam felt as if he was in the middle of a dream. This wasn't real. *She* wasn't real.

Just then, the sun won its battle with the ice, and the row of icicles crackled and fell, coming away in slow motion and then falling all at once, stabbing into the snow-covered hedge in front of the porch. The sudden, glittering tumult seemed to startle her into action. She gave a brief, taut smile and disappeared into the house.

Sam started toward the horse barn, the collie leaping at his side. He didn't look back to see if the kid was following.

Situated inside the barn door was an office with papers, certificates, and permits plastered all over the wall, a cluttered kitchenette and coffee bar, and a refrigerator with a keg tap on the door. A pellet stove heated the room.

Edward Bliss sat with his feet up on a battered metal desk, a phone cradled between his shoulder and his ear, and a beatific smile on his face.

"Morning, Romeo," Sam said.

"I'll call you later, darlin'," Edward crooned into the receiver. He hesitated, listening, and his grin widened as he hung up. "You took the purse last night, boss, but I was the one who celebrated."

"So what else is new?"

"That biff on the back of your trailer. Did you see that? Looks like some idiot nailed you last night."

"As a matter of fact . . ." Sam stepped out of the doorway and motioned the kid into the office. "This is Cody. He's going to be helping out around the place. Cody, this is my partner, Edward Bliss."

Edward glanced up distractedly. Then he did a double take, looking from Sam to Cody and back again, his eyes wide. "Jesus H. Geronimo Christ—"

"Something wrong?" Sam knew Edward didn't care for punks, but he'd never known his partner to make such a snap judgment. So the kid had hit the trailer, so he'd made a mistake. It wasn't the end of the world.

Edward stood up, gathering the papers on the desk into a stack. "Nope, not at all. Cody's going to take Diego's place, then?"

"That's what I figure. For a while, at least." Sam hadn't even had time to ask Michelle how long she'd be visiting.

Scout lost interest in the entire situation and trotted out to the yard. Edward kept staring at the kid as if to drill a hole through him. Cody stared back, eyes narrowed.

"All right." Edward snapped his suspenders and reached for his battered plaid coat, flecked with hayseed and oat grains. "Let's get started."

Most of the stalls were empty, the horses turned out for the day since it promised to be sunny. The barn had the feel of a cathedral. Daylight streamed through high windows under the eaves, and the echo of footsteps sounded loud in the hush.

"So what do I do?" Cody asked, dubiously eyeing the area. Mild suspicion tinged his voice.

Edward opened the door to one of the stalls. "Simple. You move the manure out and the cedar shavings in."

The kid swallowed, staring at the floor of the stall. "Just this one?"

"Nope." Sam gestured down the length of the barn. "What've we got here, twenty jugs?" Sam told himself not to enjoy this, but he couldn't help it.

"Great," said Cody.

"Don't go into this one without Edward or me present." Sam showed him a roomy stall in the middle. "That's Sylvia. She's expecting, and she's getting kind of cranky."

Cody peered over the top of the half door. The roan mare flared her nostrils at him and laid her ears back in warning. Her sides fanned in and out like a set of bellows.

"Yeah?" Cody asked with the first spark of interest he'd exhibited since seeing Molly.

"The foal could come tonight," Sam said. "Sylvia's

showing signs of her labor. We'll be bathing her today and getting the birthing stall ready."

The mare glared white-eyed at the stranger. The boy glared back. Sam added, "Just relax, act a little friendly, and she'll warm up to you." He made a clucking sound in his throat. The mare's ears eased up, and she stuck her head out of the stall. Cody hung back a moment, then put out his hand. The mare sniffed his shoulder. He rubbed her nose and cheek, hesitantly at first and then with more force.

"Don't put any cedar shavings in Sylvia's stall," Sam said. "Sawdust and chips are bad for the foal. Straw only. Edward'll show you, and you can help hose her down, too. But remember—she's cranky."

"Just wait till we give her that phosphate enema," Edward said.

Cody winced. "I can wait."

Edward held out a pair of leather gloves and rubber pac boots. "Put these on and let's get started."

Cody looked askance at the boots, but took them and sat on a plastic milk crate to unlace his faux-biker shoes.

"I'll leave you guys to get after it." Sam started walking back toward the house, then turned.

"Glad you showed up," he called.

"Yeah, right." Cody tossed his hair out of his eyes and rammed his foot into one of the boots.

When Sam reached the doorway, he turned back one more time, intending to tell Cody to help himself to a drink from the barn fridge if he needed one. But the words froze in his throat.

The light from outside slanted down just so, and in the uneven yellow glow, Cody stood out sharply in profile. He straightened up and hitched back his hip, stomping his foot down into the boot, a motion so familiar to Sam it was like looking in a mirror.

He leaned back against the door of a stall, feeling as if he'd just been sucker-punched. He couldn't seem to grab a breath of air.

Slow down, McPhee, he told himself. Take it easy and think for a minute. Think think think. Think of the kid, and of Michelle's cold manner, her nervousness. Think of the look of amazement on Edward's face when he'd seen Sam and Cody standing side by side.

Think of the calendar, the years that had passed. Do the math.

Count the years.

Piece by piece, he put it together. The kid looked younger than sixteen, but Sam's first impression had been wrong. Cody *was* sixteen.

"Holy shit," Sam said under his breath. "Holy goddamned shit." An icy wind blew over him from outside, but he barely felt it. He stood motionless in the doorway of the barn and watched Cody wield the shovel. His slim form bent and straightened; the light from the cracks in the eaves streamed down over him, down over the shining sandy hair and the clean profile and the unsmiling mouth and the eyes that were not quite blue.

"Holy shit," Sam said again. Then he turned on his heel and strode away from the barn.

Chapter 7

S am McPhee's kitchen appeared lived-in but not fussed over. Stainless-steel appliances, tile countertops, a garden window with a few tired-looking potted herbs struggling along. A coffeemaker hissed beneath a set of wall hooks with an array of mismatched mugs bearing imprints of various feed brands and drug names. Drug names? Atarax. Was that a veterinary drug?

Brad would know, thought Michelle. Brad the pharmacy franchise owner. Her "boyfriend," Gavin called him.

Feeling like an intruder, she helped herself to coffee. She had a devilish urge to poke around the rest of the house, but she resisted and sat down at the table. A tabby cat leaped onto the seat of the chair next to her, peering solemnly through crystal eyes.

"Hi there." She offered a finger for the cat to sniff, then rubbed its fur. It turned its head nearly upside down beneath her scratching finger. "I bet you wonder what I'm doing here," she said, and sipped her coffee. "I'm wondering the same thing myself."

Outside, the wind kicked up whirlpools in the snow. The Border collie pounced on the snow dervishes, making a joyous game of it. In her wildest imaginings, Michelle had never dreamed she would find herself sitting in Sam McPhee's kitchen, drinking his coffee and petting his cat. He wasn't the sort she even thought of as *having* a kitchen, much less a cat.

It took all her self-control to stay seated, to keep from running outside, grabbing Cody, and driving away, not stopping until Seattle. She dreaded telling Cody the truth. She wasn't stupid; she knew her kid. Sam represented the sort of dad—the fantasy dad, the Disneyland dad—Cody had been secretly wishing for all his life. The swift ride, the cheap thrill.

What Cody was too young to realize was that the minute he gave himself to a guy like Sam, he was a goner. Sam would break the boy's heart the way he broke Michelle's so long ago.

But she was going to stay in Crystal City no matter what her instincts urged her to do. Because when it came to self-control, Michelle Turner was an expert.

On some level, she might even savor the visit, she told herself, watching the cat curl into a ball on the braided seat cover of the chair next to her. This morning she had awakened early to sunshine and new snow that had come silently in the night, covering every flaw of age and softening all the sharp edges of the world. The landscape looked as clean and stark as an unpainted canvas. The miles of white meadows and the mountains rearing against a tall cerulean sky had a calming effect on her; they always had. Here, she felt a sense of drama and richness she had been missing ever since her adolescence had given way to the brutal chaos of instant adulthood.

Though her mother had raised her in the hushed elegance of Bel Air, Sharon Turner had lived way beyond her means. Her unexpected death had left Michelle a legacy of unpaid taxes and debts. By the time all accounts had been settled, there was nothing left but grief.

Michelle could have prevailed on her father for help even after she'd left Crystal City. Writing checks was what Gavin Slade did best. But she had never asked. All the money in the world couldn't provide what she needed far more than monthly rent—love, support, stability. Money was the least of her problems, and it was the first one she solved.

On her own she built a life she could be proud of— a kid who, until recently, had been great; a waterfront town house filled with furniture from Roche-Bobois, a Lexus, a ski condo in Whistler.

Hers had been a life that hadn't slowed down since she'd fled Montana all those years ago. And now she was back, and she had no idea what to make of it, what to think, how to feel. Slowing down and giving herself time to think was dangerous. Seeing Sam again was even more dangerous. He had broken her heart once. She wanted to believe he had no power to do it again. But when she saw him at the arena last night, she knew a secret, fragile part of her still belonged to him.

All her instincts had rebelled against bringing Cody here this morning. But honor demanded it. Cody had trashed Sam's trailer, and he had to make amends.

Truth to tell, Michelle had been incredibly curious. She had always assumed Sam had never amounted to anything more than a rodeo bum, rambling from show to show until the inevitable injuries of his sport retired him. She used to picture him battered and stiff at age thirty, tending bar in some little Western town. He'd wear his champion's belt buckle, and behind the bar amid the array of beer nuts and whiskey bottles, there would be a few dusty trophies and photographs of him looking like a young Paul Newman.

There wasn't a single photo in sight in this kitchen, not even one taped to the refrigerator. Odd.

She finished her coffee and rinsed the mug, taking a long drink of icy tap water. The window over the sink framed the distant mountain peaks rearing against the sky. As she gazed out across the empty, perfect meadows, a wave of nostalgia had swept over her. She'd spent so little time in Montana, yet it seemed like the place where her soul had always dwelt. What a magnificent sight to greet Sam when he got up in the morning. How different it was from the soulless cocoon of her office at the agency in downtown Seattle.

Sam had managed to confound her expectations. He didn't seem to suffer any permanent injuries from the rodeo. He had a horse ranch with a comfortable house, sturdy outbuildings, covered and open-air arenas and pens. But in a way the place seemed as empty as her own town house.

Had he surrendered his dreams? Had it hurt? Had he simply awakened one morning to discover that the life he'd envisioned for himself didn't match the one he actually had? Did she dare to ask him?

"Of course not." Michelle stroked the cat. "It's none of my business."

As she watched out the window, a stocky dark-haired man on a tractor came out of the barn, towing a load of manure on a stone boat. The Border collie cavorted like a clown through the drifts of snow. Cody followed, wearing oversize boots and hefting a shovel over one shoulder. Amazing. He was actually working. It had been forever since Michelle had been able to make him do anything.

She took another drink, savoring the sweetness of mountain well water. Footsteps thudded on the back porch and a door slammed. She turned to see Sam standing in the kitchen doorway. Faded jeans, fleece-lined denim jacket, battered John Deere cap, gloves protruding from a hip pocket. The Marlboro man without the cigarette.

"I helped myself to coffee," she said uncertainly. "Want some?"

He ignored the question. He flexed his jaw, shifted his weight to one side. Though he barely moved, a subtle threat seemed to emanate from him. It was hard to explain, but Michelle sensed a dangerous turbulence in the air between them. Old intimacy mingled with fresh suspicion.

He took a step toward her. "So when were you planning on telling me I have a son?"

His blunt words pounded at Michelle, but she felt no shock. In the back of her mind she had known since last night that he would figure out the truth based on Cody's age. She folded her arms protectively across her middle. "God, if you said something to Cody—"

"What the hell do you take me for? Of course I didn't say anything. Thanks to you, I don't even know the kid." His gaze flicked over her, measuring her contemptuously from head to toe and back again. "So I guess that means you've never told him, either."

She returned his glare. "I didn't see the point. I didn't think he'd ever meet you."

He grabbed the back of his neck in a distracted gesture. "Jesus Christ. You had my kid, and you never told me."

"And this surprises you?" Too many years had passed for Michelle to feel bitter, but she did. The regrets, the resentment, the frustration, all came bubbling to the surface. "I was eighteen years old and pregnant. You'd run off to be a rodeo champ. Do you think I had the slightest idea how to track you down? And what makes you think I didn't try?"

"Did you?"

"Of course I did, Sam. I was in l—" She broke off, unwilling to continue down that path. "Are you telling me it should have been easy to find you? Did you and your mother leave a forwarding address? Did you stay anywhere long enough to have one?"

"Permanent addresses were never my mother's strong suit." His voice was low and hoarse. "We weren't all brought up in gated communities in Bel Air."

She flinched at the implication. She and Sam came from different worlds, though at eighteen they had sworn it didn't matter.

"I didn't have a whole lot of time to spend trying to figure out where you'd gone. I had a baby to raise. Beyond the twenty-four hours a day that took, I couldn't seem to squeeze in a missing-persons search."

"I deserved to know, damn it."

"Oh, right. So you could do what? Marry me?"

"So I could have a say in what you did with my kid. You never even gave me a chance."

"Tell me an eighteen-year-old cowboy wants a *chance* with a baby."

She was dangerously, humiliatingly close to tears. She refused to shed them. She had wept an ocean for Sam McPhee and he'd never come to find her. Crying now would only prove what Michelle had been trying to deny since seeing him last night. Seventeen years ago he had taken possession of her in ways she was too young to understand. She had never given herself so wholly to another person, nor taken so much from someone else. After Sam left, she had dreamed of meeting someone new, but she'd never found that depth, that completion, with any other person. So she learned to do without.

Michelle forced herself to get a grip, to stand up from the table so she didn't feel at a disadvantage. "This is stupid. We shouldn't argue about the past. We can't change what happened."

"Maybe not." Unhurried yet unrelenting, he walked toward her, stopping only inches from her. The smell of snow and wind clung to his clothes, underlying the unique scent of him. She thought she had forgotten it.

"Sam—"

"We've got a lot of talking to do." His low voice caught at her, mesmerized her. "Problem is, now that you're here, I want to do a hell of a lot more than talk."

"You're crazy." She didn't know this man anymore, but she could feel the anger and passion seething from him. She searched his face, wondering about the lines that fanned out from his eyes.

"Crazy? I've been called worse." He took another step toward her. "I couldn't sleep for thinking about you last night."

She inched back. "You came in here wanting to talk about Cody."

He stuck a thumb into his jeans pocket, his hip propped on the edge of the counter. "So talk. I'm listening."

This can't be happening, Michelle thought. "I don't know where to start."

"You had my child and you never told me." He spoke coldly, the words hard as stones. "How about starting there?"

"The day I found out I was pregnant, I went to see you. And you had left without a trace. I don't believe I owed you a thing."

The heat of his glare was a tangible thing; she could feel it blasting away at her. "I won't discuss this with you if you're hostile," she added.

"Excuse me if I'm a little disoriented by all this. It's not every day a woman I used to sleep with shows up with a kid she had sixteen years ago."

"I didn't know I'd find you here."

"Well, here I am, honey." He spread his arms mockingly. "I'm surprised your daddy didn't warn you."

She was surprised, too, but she wouldn't admit it to Sam. She wondered if he knew she and her father were strangers, and that only Gavin's illness had brought her back.

"We should be talking instead of arguing." She sat back down at the table, took a deep breath. "Maybe I was wrong. I should have searched high and low for you. But everyone said I'd get over you. Said I was better off without you, that I'd go off to college and meet someone who—" She broke off and shrugged.

"—wasn't a born drifter with a hopeless lush for a mother," Sam finished for her.

"I never said that."

"You didn't have to."

"I had to think about Cody, too. I spent my childhood ducking the paparazzi. I'm very protective of him in that way."

His eyes narrowed. "Oh, yeah, the tabloids would've had a field day with us. Gavin Slade's only daughter makes it with a ranch hand."

She flinched, knowing he wasn't far off the mark. As a child, she had shown up occasionally in the scandal sheets—a grainy photo taken through a long lens: *Gavin Slade's Love Child*, the caption always read.

A juicy story like an illicit Romeo and Juliet–style affair would have revived the attention she shunned. That was why she worked so hard to maintain her anonymity. Every once in a while a reporter in search of a scoop came sniffing around. One even snapped her photo when she was pregnant. The incident had scared her so much that she moved to Seattle, where no one knew her.

Sam sat down across from her. His hands were big, not as work-scarred as she would have thought. She caught herself staring at those hands, remembering how she used to rub Bag Balm on them to soothe the calluses.

"None of that old stuff can matter now, Michelle. What matters is that we have a son." He clenched his hand into a fist on the table. "A son. I can't believe it."

She was terrified to ask the next question, but she had to. "Sam, what are you going to do?"

"Do?"

"About . . . learning that Cody's your son." She tasted the burn of resentment in her throat. "Your biological son." Yes, that sounded better. More distant.

He studied her hands, and she wondered if he remembered the Bag Balm, too. On her right one, she wore a Cartier onyx ring. On the left forefinger, a large sapphire.

"Did you raise him alone, or are you in a relationship?"

She guessed that meant he wasn't thinking about the Bag Balm. *In a relationship*. It was such a modern thing to say. Like so many modern things, it had no meaning.

"Alone, more or less."

"Explain more or less."

"I've been with someone for the past three years. But

it's not—he's not—" Damn. How could she explain Brad? "He's not raising Cody."

"I see." Sam got up from the table and poured himself a cup of coffee. He seemed hesitant when he turned. "So did Cody ever ask about me?"

"Of course he asked."

"And you told him what? Obviously my name doesn't ring a bell with him."

"I was worried about the tabloids. So I left the father's name blank on his birth certificate."

"Christ—"

"Sam, I was young. Scared. I grew up with cameras shoved in my face every time I sneezed. I didn't want that for Cody, and I didn't want anyone to go snooping through records—"

"—and finding the name of a mongrel cowboy."

"Quit putting words in my mouth. I didn't know what to do."

"Didn't he want to know, just for him? Jesus, a name wouldn't have sent him off the deep end."

"A name's just . . . a name. And maybe I was afraid—" She stopped, wishing she could reel in the words.

"Of what? What were you afraid of?"

"That maybe he'd get mad at me one day and go off looking for you." The confession rushed out like air escaping a balloon. "Since school started this year, he's been . . . in rebellion."

Sam hesitated, took a sip of coffee. In his face she saw more than she wanted to see—interest, understanding. Compassion. "The kid's mad at the world, Michelle."

Ouch. He had seen that so quickly. "We've had rough times before. We've dealt with trouble. This year . . . is more difficult than most." Damn. She knew she should keep her thoughts to herself, but with Sam, it was hard.

Years ago he'd had that effect on her, and it hadn't changed. He still drew truths from deep inside her, made her say things better left unsaid.

"So what's going on?" he asked. "Is he having trouble in school?"

All right, thought Michelle. You asked for it. The good, the bad, and the ugly. "His last grade report was awful. Up until this year, he's been an A and B student. Now it's Cs and Ds. At first I thought it was a normal, predictable rebellion, but I don't see the end of it."

"Is he hanging out with his regular friends?"

"Not as much as he used to. He's got a girlfriend, and they're pretty exclusive."

"So what are you doing about his problems?"

"I'm working on it, Sam! Do you think this is easy? Do you think you could do better?"

"Is it my turn to take over? You had him the first sixteen years, I get the next sixteen?"

"I didn't bring him here because he's a troubled teen. I brought him here . . . to see my dad." She didn't feel like discussing Gavin's health with Sam. "My father's never met Cody." She got up from the table and went to the door. She was afraid. She was angry. And God help her, she felt an old, old yearning unfold in her heart, a burning ache she thought she had buried forever. "What time should I pick him up?"

Outside, Cody and the dark-haired man were loading bales of hay onto a flatbed truck. It was startling to see her son doing physical labor. It had been ages since he exerted himself doing anything more strenuous than lifting the telephone receiver.

"He'll be done around five, I guess," Sam said. "Edward can give him a lift over to your father's place."

"All right." Taking her jacket from a hook outside the kitchen door in the mudroom, she shrugged into it. "Sam?"

"Yeah?"

"You won't . . . say anything to him, will you?"

"Hell, no, I won't say anything. I don't even know the kid." He held open the door for her. He was as tall as she remembered, and broader in the shoulders and chest. His face was more deeply carved with character. His scent, God, why did she remember it so perfectly? Perversely, she had an urge to touch him, just once, but she resisted.

"'Bye, Sam."

"'Bye." He followed her out onto the porch and waited while she got into the Range Rover. "Hey, Michelle?"

She rolled down the window. "What?"

"That doesn't mean we're not telling him."

She leaned back against the headrest, closing her eyes. "Damn. I was hoping for a quick getaway."

"No such luck, Sugar. Tell him. I want him to know exactly who I am."

"But—" She opened her eyes. "All right. I'll tell him."

"When?"

"I'll . . . figure out the right time. Sam, I've got a lot on my mind. My father isn't well, and the next few days might be pretty difficult."

He stared at her for a long time. She couldn't read him. Didn't know him anymore. Yet that stare was as compelling now as it had been the first time she had met him. "All right. But I want him to know, Michelle. Soon."

Chapter 8

Cody felt like a cockroach in his grandfather's house—gross, unwelcome, and out of place. After shoveling horseshit at Lonepine all day, he wanted to shower for about nine hours and then crash facedown in his bed.

Instead, they were having dinner with Legendary Actor Gavin Slade. That was how Gavin was always referred to: Legendary Actor. Elder Statesman of Western Classics. In capital letters, like the guy was a walking headline or something. Lately, instead of showing him with his arm around some bimbo with big tits, the fanzines showed him alone on a horse, his cowboy hat pulled low over his brow. The headlines announced that he'd been in touch with aliens.

Cody liked the bimbo pictures better. It was pretty bizarre, thinking about his grandfather getting laid by women younger than his own mom, but it was even worse thinking about his grandfather dying of kidney failure. Mostly, he tried not to think of Gavin at all. It wasn't like Gavin thought about *him* all the time.

Cody had tried his best to weasel out of dinner, but he hadn't gained much sympathy from his mom. After crunching that cowpoke's trailer last night, he'd used up most of his goodwill points with her. Not that he had many to begin with. Since last summer she'd been driving him nuts, hovering over him, waiting to pounce the second she caught him doing something she disapproved of.

He'd tried a minor whine—*I'm too tired, I worked like a dog today*—but all he'd gained was the Look. That cold jackhammer of a stare still affected him sometimes, although he was getting pretty good at ignoring her lately.

When he was little, he used to be moved by the Look. He used to want to do just about anything to please her. Little by little over the years, he'd figured out that there was no way to please his perfectionist mother. No way to win a smile that wasn't sad at the edges, or to get praise from her that didn't demand things he didn't even know how to give.

So he quit trying, and he wasn't even sure she noticed. She was so lame, she and that loser Brad. All Brad cared about was making the almighty buck and showing off to the world that Cody's mom was his lady, like she was some sort of bowling trophy with boobs.

That was the only good thing about coming here. It gave him a break from Brad the loser.

"Hiya, Cody." Gavin Slade came into the living room. Unlike Cody, he looked exactly right in his surroundings. Jeans and a red corduroy shirt and cowboy boots. Big white hair that made his eyes look bluer than the heated swimming pool on the patio.

"Hi." Cody hadn't decided what to call his grand-father, and it would be too dorky to ask. Jamming his hands into his pockets, he pretended great interest in the objects arranged on a lighted glass shelf by the wet bar. After a couple of seconds, he didn't have to fake it anymore.

Holy shit. He was looking at an Oscar statue.

"That's pretty cool," he said, pointing to it.

"You think?" Gavin hooked a thumb into his back pocket like he was posing for a picture or something. Except he didn't even seem conscious of the pose—it was the natural way he held himself. "I guess so. I liked that movie. *The Face of Battle*. You ever see it?"

Only about a zillion times.

"I think maybe I caught part of it on TV once," he lied.

"It's about a misfit, a real loser. Nobody cared whether he lived or died. After a while, he quit caring, too. And in the end, that's why he was able to save his battalion. He quit looking for guarantees, and he made the sacri-fice."

Cody pictured the scene in his head. It was one of those film sequences the experts always showed when they were going over classic movies—the moment Gavin's char-acter stood alone on a tank-destroyer turret, the only vol-unteer of his battalion, shooting through a deadly hail of sniper fire at a 77mm tank gun. Like the image of Gary Cooper in *High Noon*, Gavin Slade's *Face of Battle* mo-ment had put him on the pages of the film history books. The memorable image showed a close-up of a face filled with nobility, anguish, and the wisdom of a man who knows he is about to die. It had become one of the most famous movie stills ever published.

"How come you stopped making movies?" Cody asked.

"It was always a job to me, to tell you the truth. A job I liked most of the time, and either loved or hated the rest." He had this intent way of speaking, leaning forward and lowering his voice so you had no choice but to listen. "The business is brutal, Cody. You live and die by the box office. Your looks and your image are everything. Sometimes you don't get a minute of privacy, and other times you can't buy attention for yourself. I got sick of the roller coaster. As soon as I could afford to retire, I got out of acting. I still coproduce things here and there, but it's pretty low-key. Haven't seen a film on the big screen in ages."

"Mom said the movie theater in town is closed down."

"That's a fact. They were going to tear the Lynwood down, so I bought it."

A spark of interest flashed in Cody. "Yeah?"

"I'd like to reopen, for old time's sake. One screen, maybe show some independent films."

"That'd be cool." Cody studied the other objects in the case—a baseball autographed by Joe DiMaggio, the stub of a ticket to a Beatles concert, a display of prize rodeo belt buckles, and photos of Gavin posing proudly by his vintage airplane. Pretty radical stuff, he decided.

His perusal drifted to a framed picture of his mom on a horse. "When was that taken?" he asked, to fill the silence.

"First summer after high school," Gavin said. "I invited her to spend a year up here before starting college. She studied painting with a local artist."

"She never finished college," Cody said, hearing contempt in his own voice. He didn't care. All his friends' parents had degrees and stuff. His mom had, well, her job. And him. And lame-ass suspicious Brad who lived in fear that Cody and his friends were going to help themselves to uppers or painkillers from his sample cases.

He looked at the picture, taken in a pasture with the mountains in the background. Slender and suntanned, long legs and bare feet, her head thrown back with laughter, she looked pretty amazing. For the past couple of years, his friends had been giving Cody a hard time about his mom. She was a lot younger than most moms. She looked like a shampoo ad or something. It was kind of cool sometimes, having a mom who was a babe, but mostly it was embarrassing as hell.

"I still have that horse," Gavin said.

"The one in the picture?"

"Yeah, that's Dooley. Your mom learned barrel racing on him."

"He must be pretty old."

"Twenty-something. Do you ride, Cody?"

"Not horses."

Gavin chuckled, showing perfect teeth. And his eyes— they had that crinkly, twinkly look Cody recognized from old movie posters. He didn't trust this guy. How did you know he was being sincere when he was an actor?

"I guess that'll change now that you're here," Gavin said. "Or maybe I'll take you flying once I pass my physical and get my license renewed. You interested?"

"We're only staying until you get through with your recovery period." Even that was too long for Cody. Worse, he had to enroll in the local high school here in Noplace, Montana. He had stormed for weeks in rebellion, but his mom was adamant. He got a minor reprieve this week— it was winter break in Noplace. But pretty soon he was going to have to be the new kid. A fate worse than death. "Mom says a few weeks or so. Then we're out of here."

Gavin's grin stayed fixed in place. But the movie-star

gleam in his eyes dimmed as if Cody's words were a light switch that suddenly turned it off. "Let's go see if supper's ready."

Cody felt kind of shitty as he followed his grandfather into a big dining room with fancy crystal and china laid out. What did the old man expect? Instant bonding, like on those long-distance phone commercials? He and Gavin Slade were complete strangers. After this transplant thing was over, they probably wouldn't ever see each other again.

Grandfathers made friends with grandsons when they were little and cute, not when they were sixteen, wearing a ponytail and combat boots. Not that Cody wanted to cozy up to the old man, anyway. It was gross, thinking about his illness. He had some kind of fluid bag attached to a tube going inside him, doing the work his kidneys were supposed to do. The very idea of it made Cody want to hurl.

His mom joined them in the dining room. She was smiling in a nervous way. Her gaze kept darting from her father to Cody. "Hi, guys," she said.

Gavin held a chair for her. It was corny but kind of nice seeing the old guy do that. Once, Cody had tried holding a chair out for Claudia. "What, like it's going to get away from me?" she'd asked, then cracked up. Cody had laughed, too.

Dinner was about the best thing that had happened since his mom loaded him into the car at the crack of dawn yesterday. Prepared by an Asian nutrition expert named Tadao, it consisted of pasta with fancy sauce, fresh bread, a bunch of grilled veggies, and a big salad of exotic fruit.

After shoveling away about nineteen pounds of food, Cody glanced up to see both his mother and his grandfather watching him. Neither of them had eaten much. Gavin was on some sort of low-protein diet. He couldn't eat things that made his kidneys work hard because they didn't function at all anymore.

"You must've worked up an appetite out at Lonepine today," Gavin commented.

"It's good," he said, and sucked down a whole glass of milk.

"Be sure you tell Tadao you enjoyed it," his mom said.

Shit. She was always doing that. No matter what it was—having a good meal, talking on the phone, whatever, she had to add her own little goody-goody twist on it. Her own little adjustment or correction. This morning he'd expected her to totally humiliate him in front of that girl, Molly. But for once his mom had shown mercy.

She'd seemed kind of flustered around Sam McPhee, like she couldn't quite decide what to make of him. Cody wasn't sure what to make of the guy either. He was okay, but Cody thought it was totally bogus of him to make him pay off the trailer damage with slave labor.

He helped himself to more milk from a cut-glass pitcher, feeling a slight sting from the blisters on his hand. *Blisters,* for chrissakes. He was pretty sure he'd never given himself blisters before. Especially not by shoveling horseshit.

He got the idea from that Bliss guy that Lonepine was some kind of hotshot horse breeding and training ranch. It was cool, working in a barn where a mare was about to give birth any minute. When it was time to go today, Cody had felt a twinge of disappointment. He wouldn't have minded seeing the horse being born. It would have given him a good story to tell Claudia.

Maybe the manure story was funny enough. But honestly, he hadn't felt much like laughing. There had been a moment, when he was alone in the barn, with the smells around him and the light falling between the rafters, that an odd feeling had settled over him. Maybe it was the quiet or the sense that he was totally alone; he didn't know. But it had felt kind of pleasant.

"It's nice to be together with the two of you," Gavin said suddenly, pressing his palms on the table as if he never planned to eat again.

"We let too much time go by," his mom said in a quiet voice.

"I know, Michelle," Gavin said. "I'm sorry. I can't tell you how many times I picked up the phone, but I never knew what I'd say—"

"Let's not do this, Daddy. Let's not drag up all the old regrets. We can't get back the years we lost. We can only go on from here."

Cody did his best not to roll his eyes. This was just what he'd been hoping to avoid—a big emotional scene where they go "I'm sorry I'm sorry" all over each other and then drag him into the middle of everything as The Grandson You Never Knew.

"Can I be excused?" he asked too loudly.

They both looked at him as if he had a booger hanging out of his nose.

"I told Claudia I'd call her."

"Girlfriend?" Gavin asked.

"Yeah." Cody felt about two feet taller just saying it. He loved walking through the halls at school, hearing everybody whisper: *He's going out with Claudia Teller. . . .*

"So can I be excused?" he asked.

His mom nodded. "Go ahead, honey."

"Thanks . . . for dinner," he said, then hurried out into the cold night. When he got to his own room, he collapsed on the bed, clicked on the TV, and realized that working outside in subfreezing temperatures all day had made him more tired than he'd ever been in his life. He was asleep before he even remembered he meant to call Claudia.

Monday

Chapter 9

Y ou're kidding, right?" Cody asked at the breakfast table.

"Don't talk with your mouth full." Cradling a coffee mug between both hands, Michelle regarded her son in the clear light of the mountain morning. His cheeks were stuffed with blueberry muffin. Chewing slowly, he washed it down with a big gulp of black coffee.

When did her son start drinking coffee—black, of all things?

He took a final swallow. "I said, you're kidding, right?"

She'd heard him the first time, but making him repeat himself for the sake of manners was ingrained in her. Funny how he'd never learned that lesson. The second time around, he was supposed to fix his tone of voice, ask his question politely and without food in his mouth. Yet in all his life, he'd never done it.

Maybe he kept thinking she'd get tired of correcting him. He'd worn her down on so many other matters. When he wanted something—ridiculously expensive shoes, a pierced ear, a snowboard—he became like water dripping on a rock: constant, incessant, wearing her away until she caved in.

"No," she said. "I'm not kidding. You're going back to Mr. McPhee's today."

"I'm not going." Cody jutted his chin defiantly and held up his hands, palms facing out. "I have blisters because I spent eight hours shoveling horseshit yesterday. Horseshit, Mom."

Michelle felt her lips twitch. Laughing now would enrage him, so she composed herself. "When Mr. Bliss dropped you off yesterday he said there was lots more work to be done and to be there at nine again."

"That sucks." He shoved back from the table, giving his long two-colored ponytail an insolent toss.

"What sucks is backing the car into a guy's trailer," she reminded him. *What sucks is that the guy's your father, and I have no idea how to explain it to you.*

"So go get ready." She put the mugs in the sink. "I need to phone Brad, and then we'll leave."

"Hey, I was going to call Claudia—"

"Later. When you get home tonight—"

Cody curled his lip. "I'll call her when I damn well please."

Her face felt hot, burning hot, yet the anger was directed at herself. When he spoke to her like this, she had no idea how to make him stop. It was frightening sometimes, knowing how completely out of her control he was.

"Let's not argue, Cody. Gavin and I have an appointment

in Missoula and we need to get going. In case you've forgotten, we're here for Gavin."

Cody tugged on his jacket, yanking out a pack of Camels, flashing them as he jerked open the door. "Yeah, I almost forgot. You're here to offer spare parts to your long-lost father."

The kid had great timing. He knew just when to pick a fight. She had to call Brad, drop off Cody, and accompany her father to Missoula. She didn't have time to deal with the rage and the hurt that had been ricocheting between her and her son since he turned sixteen.

The kid's mad at the world. Sam had seen that instantly.

She snatched up the phone and punched in Brad's number. He sounded groggy when he picked up.

"Oops," she said. "I forgot you're an hour earlier."

"Hey, babe." A sleepy smile softened his voice.

Michelle tried to relax, but she was too jumpy. "I wanted to call and say hi. I miss you."

"Miss you, too. Is everything okay out there? Do you need me to come out?"

What she needed, she realized suddenly, was for him to come without asking. To understand her well enough to know that of course she needed him. She was facing a terrifying ordeal; he was supposed to support her.

Dumb. If he showed up now, he'd be bored and fretful about missing work, and Michelle knew she'd feel guilty and that would make her cranky, and then she'd have a terrible attitude about the surgery. She shook her head, trying to veer away from that line of thinking. It was enough that he'd promised to fly in the day of the surgery.

"No, we're fine," she said. "Did anyone call?"

"Natalie." Distaste rumbled in his voice; he'd never

liked her best friend. An oft-unemployed cellist, Natalie Plum was the original free spirit. She drove a diehard planner like Brad crazy. "She's bringing her stuff over to your house today."

"Good. I was hoping she'd house-sit while I'm away. So how was your weekend?"

"Excellent. Dinner at Canlis with the Albrights. A round of golf at Port Ludlow. Babe, we should really look into getting a place up there. Mike was saying the lot values for the waterfront area have really shot up . . ."

She tuned out the monologue about real-estate investments. She did that a lot lately. He loved to collect things—resort property, sports equipment, luxury cars—displaying them to the world like hunting trophies. She admired his ambition, the way he was so driven to succeed in his career. In addition to the pharmacy, he had made a killing in the stock market, and money was an obsession with him. Sometimes she wished he'd slow down.

". . . he's a vascular surgeon at Swedish, got into the resort development on the ground floor . . ."

Michelle made the appropriate murmurs as her mind wandered further afield. She remembered the day she'd finally figured Brad out. He'd just put money down on a thirty-six-foot Hunter yacht, and she told him he was crazy. The vacation home, the ski lodge, the golf membership at Lakeside, the ski place at Whistler—he was wearing her out.

"Brad," she'd told him last summer while standing on the dock next to the gleaming new sailboat. "Wouldn't it be easier simply to *become* a doctor?"

His reaction had been unexpected and sharp. "No, goddammit. It wouldn't. What the hell sort of question is that?"

He so rarely spoke in anger that she didn't press. But

she knew she had touched a raw nerve. He used to want to be a doctor the same way she used to want to be an artist. Now he owned a chain of pharmacies and she was a commercial illustrator.

She listened patiently as he finished his recitation. She waited for him to ask how Cody was doing, but he paused in the middle of talking, yawned, and said it was time to get up and into the shower.

"Wish you were here," he said, the suggestion in his voice both sexy and familiar.

"Me too." Out the window she could see Cody puffing away on a cigarette. Dear God. Her kid was smoking, and she had no idea how to stop him. She wanted to tell Brad everything—that her father still had the power to make her cry. That Cody was doing his best to drive her crazy. That she had met Sam McPhee again.

That she couldn't think of anything but Sam—oh, shit. She'd have to tell Brad. How was she going to tell him?

"I'll call you later, Brad."

"Yeah. Take care, babe."

She gathered up her coat and purse, pausing to glance into the mirror over the hall tree. What, exactly, did one wear to meet a transplant team? They sounded so important, so intimidating. Would they think her red wool blazer was too boldly colored? Should she have gone with the black angora instead?

She shoved aside the ridiculous questions. She was nervous about the appointment. She was nervous about being with her father again. She was nervous about Sam. Clothes should be the least of her concerns.

She stepped into boots and went out to find Cody. He tossed his cigarette butt into the snowy yard.

Fixing a glare on him, she groped in her purse for

car keys. "You know, you really should take up bungee-jumping from live power lines. It's a lot less risky than smoking."

"Very funny." He got in the car.

She didn't want to launch into yet another big lecture about smoking, not this morning. She had to be focused on her father.

When she'd first found out about his illness and bullied Gavin into the transplant, she started some of the tests in Seattle. Once she'd qualified as a donor, she had donated some of her own blood for the surgery ahead of time, and it had been shipped from Seattle and stored. She had more blood and X rays taken, did a lung capacity test, and did the twenty-four-hour urine collection study, a delightful routine she hoped she didn't have to repeat.

She felt as if she had been holding her breath for twelve weeks, and she was about to let it all out soon.

At today's appointment, the team wanted to go over more details, schedule a renal angiogram, and make sure she was mentally prepared for this.

She was not doing so hot on that count.

"So," she said, flexing her hands on the steering wheel. "What did you think of Mr. McPhee?"

"He said to call him Sam. And the other guy said to call him Edward."

"So what do you think of Sam?" She tried to keep her voice light, casual.

"He's okay."

"Just okay?"

"You want me to think he's great for making me work in the freezing cold like a farmhand?"

"Ranch hand."

"Whatever."

"I think, given the circumstances, you're lucky to get off with a few days' work. So you like him?"

"Did I say that, Mom? And why do I have to like anyone around here? We're leaving as soon as you finish this thing with your—with Gavin."

"I'm not leaving him until the critical period is over." She shuddered inwardly, horrified by the possibility that the surgery wouldn't work, that her kidney would be rejected. "It wouldn't hurt to make a few friends."

Trying to push that worry aside, she watched the scenery. The morning sun on the majestic landscape brought out the harsh poetry of the high country. The sight of blanketed fields and soaring mountains filled her with a strange yet familiar yearning. The truth was, she needed the mountains, the air, the clarity of light found only in Montana in order to paint. And maybe she needed to be the person she had been all those years ago, too. A person who dared to love, dared to dream.

But she knew of no way to recapture that young, naive self. The disappointment ate at her, a quiet dull pain, the surrendering of hope. Sometimes she believed her gift was only slumbering or maybe frozen inside, waiting. When she was pregnant with Cody, she had enrolled in a small liberal arts college, and for one glorious semester she had painted. She had a rare talent, and she knew it. Her instructors knew it. The gallery owners who approached her knew it. But making a career as a painter would take years of work and study and time.

After Cody was born, reality intruded. She counted herself lucky to land an entry-level position at an ad agency. Late at night, after Cody was asleep, she'd fall into a dream world that was hers and hers alone. Those hours were precious; the work she did was dark, important, and expressive. She produced dozens of paintings, working from pain rather than joy, producing fast as she was wont to do. Perhaps a part of her understood that the creative burst would fade away.

Time crept on, eating secretly away at her soul. Inch by inch, her imagination and energy deteriorated until she simply stopped painting. She dropped her art classes and changed the direction of her dreams. It was easier to collapse on the sofa, take her precious baby boy in her lap, and read stories to him. Those paintings lay stacked against a wall in a spare closet. She rarely looked at them. Once Cody started school, she had more time to pursue her art, but she never did. The prospect terrified her. It was like standing in front of the door to a dark, forbidding room. She'd be nuts to go there.

At the firm she did good work, got promoted through the ranks, achieved some recognition in her field, and quit thinking about painting.

But sometimes she still wanted to. Oh, how she wanted to.

"I used to know Sam," she said carefully to Cody.

"I figured that out when he called you by name after I hit his trailer."

"He worked at my father's place. I met him when I came here after my mother died."

Before her death, Sharon Turner had advised Michelle to start college straight out of high school. Always chilly, self-absorbed, and distant, Michelle's mother had suggested a practical course of study in design or architecture. Her death had left Michelle adrift, vulnerable. Terrified. And then, like the cavalry riding to the rescue, Gavin had made his offer. "Don't go rushing off to college at a time like this, honey," he'd said, his charm and warm sympathy palpable. "You'll never again get a year of your life to do anything you want. I showed your work to a local teacher, and he agreed to meet you. Come to Montana."

And so she had gone, never asking herself what he expected from the relationship, what he hoped it would become. Perhaps she had wanted to believe he acted out of selfless compassion, opening his home to the grieving daughter who hardly knew him. If there was such a thing as the classic absentee Hollywood dad, Gavin was it. He had sent checks, phoned her, and showed up on significant occasions—her first ballet recital, her Bluebird fly-up, a dressage championship—and she'd been thrilled to stand back and let him be the center of attention. She remembered her first communion at All Saints in Beverly Hills, the girls in stiff white dresses and new gloves. She'd felt like a bride that day, and when her father, incandescent as the Holy Ghost and twice as handsome, came striding across the parking lot toward her, she'd squealed and wrenched her hand out of her mother's grip. Racing to greet him, she flung herself into his arms and he picked her up, swinging her round and round as she laughed with joy. She could hear camera shutters clicking and people whispering *Gavin Slade. It's Gavin Slade. He's even better-looking in person. . . .* The days with her father, few and far between, stood out vividly in her memory. When his visits ended she always experienced a gaping emptiness. The world was duller, flatter, when Gavin wasn't around.

She glanced over at Cody, waiting for him to say something else. Waiting for him to ask more about Sam.

But Cody said nothing, and neither did Michelle. It wasn't the right time to bring up all the events that started here so long ago. They'd need hours for that. You always need hours to recover after a bombshell drops into the middle of your life, thought Michelle. She pictured them buried by the rocks and relics heaved up by her confession. Each bit of rubble would have to be removed with care to avoid damaging the fragile, angry victim beneath it. Hours, yes. Maybe days. Maybe a whole lot longer.

When they arrived at Sam's place, Edward greeted them and set Cody to work loading avalanche fencing onto a stone boat on stout wooden runners. Sam was already gone, Edward explained, pointing at a snowmobile trail leading into the low, distant hills. A mountain lion had been lurking around, and Sam went to check it out.

Her eye wandered along the corrugated track while her knees turned to lime Jell-O. A reprieve, she thought weakly. For now, at least.

Chapter 10

Gavin insisted on driving to Missoula. Michelle couldn't discern his state of mind. He seemed quiet, preoccupied. A crimson rash marred the side of his neck. She wanted to ask him about it, but she didn't. Somehow it seemed too personal.

It was going to get worse before it got better, she knew. He'd told her this morning, a little sheepishly, that his last mistress had left him when she found out how sick he was. She'd recently sold her story to a sleazy magazine. Once it hit the stands, it was sure to bring the paparazzi flocking around like carrion birds.

Michelle felt a peculiar violence when she thought about the mistress. Her name was Carolyn and she was about Michelle's age. If I ever run into her, thought Michelle, I'll set her hair on fire. It was one thing to sponge off a guy when you're his mistress, but to sell the story after dumping him was disgusting.

The road to Missoula rolled out in front of the chrome-grilled truck, and the land was deep and stark, lit by a sun that shone brighter than anywhere else in the world.

"It's a boring drive to the city. You might want to get some shut-eye," her father said.

A little hitch of disappointment caught in her chest. Part of her wanted to talk with him, to get to know him. But another part kept its distance, circling warily around the whole bizarre situation. It would be noble indeed to insist she was going through this because of the selfless filial love she felt for him, but how much of that love was a sense of obligation?

And was there any way to tell the difference?

She used to know exactly what love felt like. She closed her eyes against the glaring snowscape and let the years roll away until she was back in the past again, the week before Thanksgiving, 1983. A fresh snowfall had blanketed the farm. Flush with excitement, she'd rushed into the guesthouse Gavin had set up as an art studio for her. There, on a sunny morning not much different from today, she had finished the best painting of her life. After laboring over theory and composition with Joseph, she had produced something of merit and value. She couldn't have known back then that she would never again equal that effort.

She had painted for hours, stopping when Sam came in from work, his cheeks chapped and his lips cool until he warmed them by kissing her. She was covered in paint and all awash with the wonder of creating a work that grew from every level of her heart. He'd peeled oranges for her and brewed steaming cups of tea while she worked. And when she took a break, he'd made love to her.

"It's unbelievable, Michelle," he'd said that chill November day, tackling her on the low sofa in front of the woodstove.

"I bet you'd say that if I was painting Elvis on velvet."

"Maybe." With the frank lust only teenage boys exhibit, he lifted her sweatshirt and unhooked her bra.

Michelle still remembered the way he kissed her neck, her breasts, her stomach. Trusting him, she relaxed and let it happen. Since the very first time they'd made love, he had created a world of sensation for her. Colors glowed brighter. Edges appeared sharper. When they struggled out of their clothes and came together, she saw a million glinting stars behind her squeezed-shut eyelids.

Later as they lay spent in each other's arms, she had listened to the beat of his heart, drifting, dreaming. She'd done a lot of pictures in the summer and autumn—landscapes and wildlife, abstracts with bold splashes of color and subtle shadows hiding in the hollows of space.

"I want to be an artist," she said.

"You already are."

"No, I mean I want my paintings to hang in exhibits where anyone who wants to can see them, even buy them."

"So go for it." His belief in her was unshakable and straightforward.

She had loved that about him, how he never doubted her. But what did he believe about himself? It used to worry her sometimes, how quiet he was about his own life, so she asked, "What about you? What do you want?"

He'd chuckled without a great deal of humor. "For my mother to quit fucking up."

Michelle hadn't known what to say. Tammi Lee Gilmer was holding down a waitressing job at the Truxtop, yet she knew Sam was concerned. If Tammi Lee's pattern held true, she'd go on a binge, miss work, lose her job, then collect unemployment until it ran out and she drifted to another town, dragging Sam along with her.

It was the only life he had ever known, and thinking about it made Michelle's heart ache.

"That's not what I meant, Sam. I meant you. What do you want for you?"

"For me?" He hesitated.

"Come on, you can tell me. What, do you think I'd laugh at you? I'm the one who wants to make a living as an artist."

"At least you know what you want."

"So do you. But you have to tell me." She figured he was headed for the rodeo circuit. Already, he'd placed in a lot of the local shows, riding her father's bucking stock, competing in team-roping and bulldogging. "Come on. Truth or dare."

He wiggled his eyebrows comically. "I'll take the dare."

"I want the truth."

Another hesitation. Finally, without looking at her, he said, "Would you believe medical school?"

Michelle had pulled back, studied him. The shaggy light hair, serious eyes, and a mouth that made her melt inside were all so blissfully familiar. But this was a stranger speaking. It was the first she'd heard of medical school. "Since when?"

"Since forever, I guess." He began getting dressed. The ranch hands were riding fence, and he was an hour behind because of their diversion. "I've never told anyone."

"I'm glad you spilled the beans. You should go for it, Sam."

He shook his head, flashing a self-deprecating smile. "I'm a high school dropout."

"You can get a G.E.D."

"I can't afford college."

"My dad could help with—"

"He wouldn't, and I wouldn't ask him."

"Then *I'll* ask him."

"In case you haven't noticed, I'm your dad's best roper. Why would he want to lose that? And why would I beg some rich guy's help? Believe me, I wouldn't be worth a bucket of spoiled oats if your dad ever found out how I've been spending my lunch hour."

"We're consenting adults."

"Right. You think that would make a difference to your old man?"

"He's been a hound dog for years. He's got no call to talk. I don't know why you insist on keeping this a secret. I *love* you, Sam."

He paused, touched her cheek. "Aw, honey. That's why we can't let him catch on. He'd try his damnedest to keep us apart."

"He can't keep us apart. It's a free country."

Sam had laughed at that. "Is that what they taught you in that fancy-ass girls' school in Cal-if-orny?" His smile was tinged with a weary tolerance that made him seem infinitely older and wiser than Michelle. "That's not the way the real world works. In the real world, the daughter of a rich movie star doesn't go out with a waitress's son. Believe me, your dad wants you to fall for some guy with a golf handicap, not a PRCA rating."

"That's dumb. Besides, I've fallen for you. And that's not going to change. Not ever." As they finished dressing, she had considered telling him that she was alarmingly late with her period. But she'd said nothing. If it was a false alarm, there was no need to worry him.

He took her hand. "Honey, I don't want it to change. That's why we're better off keeping this quiet."

His words made her feel hopelessly naive. There were differences between them, class differences she didn't want to see. Looking back, she realized that had been apparent to Sam right from the start. That was probably why he didn't think anything of simply disappearing one November night.

She had walked outside with him, into the dry cold and sunshine, bringing along the finished winter landscape.

"*Damn.*" He squinted in the direction of the training arena.

"What's wrong?"

"Jake Dollarhide. I think he saw us."

The foreman's son. She saw the gangly young man standing in the distance, and he was staring directly at them. "So what?" she'd said with breezy disregard. "Let Jake Dollarhide stare all he wants." She put the finished painting behind the seat of the truck.

"I can't take that, Michelle—"

"Yes you can. I'll paint a hundred more for you."

"Believe me, honey, this is enough."

She hadn't known back then that those would be his last words to her. That his last kiss would be a quick, furtive brush of his lips over hers. But after that moment, she had never seen him again.

"Ms. Turner, we're ready for you in Dr. Kehr's office."

Goose bumps rose on Michelle's arms as she entered a comfortable office with a generic but good-quality Robyn Bloss serigraph print on the wall behind the desk. Michelle studied it for a moment, remembering that she used to paint freely, in intense colors of her choosing, not in hues to match the burgundy wing chairs in doctors' offices where people waited for the bad news.

The Bloss print was supposed to be pacifying. To some it might have been. But to Michelle it was profoundly disturbing. Seeing that print was like looking into a mirror.

She seated herself in a leather armchair beside her father. A large window behind the desk afforded a view of the city, gray and bleak in midwinter, the river a colorless vein through the middle of town. Dr. Kehr, the nephrologist, sat opposite them, her ultraclean hands folded atop a stack of files and charts. She had a bland but pleasant smile, no discernible personality, and somehow meeting her for the first time made the whole situation starkly real.

They were going to cut out one of her kidneys and sew it into her father.

Sucking in a deep breath, Michelle shifted in her chair and waited for the rest of the team to arrive. They met Donna Roberts, the transplant coordinator, who was a registered nurse specializing in organ transplantation. Donna did a lot of touching and hand-holding, which Michelle didn't particularly need at that moment, but she figured she'd be grateful for later. Then there was Willard T. Temple, the psychologist and social worker. He could scuttle the whole thing if he didn't think her father and she were mentally prepared for it.

They would each have their own surgeons. They showed up in scrubs, alike as Tweedledee and Tweedledum but with firmer handshakes. Neither of them could stay long because, after all, they were surgeons and they spent all day cutting people, not talking to fading movie stars and their neurotic daughters.

To Michelle's surprise, one of the surgeons held the door open. "This way, Mr. Slade."

Gavin got up. Briefly, he rested his hand on her shoulder. "I'll be back shortly, okay?"

"You're not staying?" Panic pounded in her chest.

"I think they need to draw lines on me or something."

After the door closed, she scowled at Dr. Kehr. "He should be here."

Temple, who held a clipboard with a yellow legal pad, said, "Your father's been drilled on this procedure for months. We wanted a private meeting with you."

"Why?" *Oh my God. Are they going to tell me he won't make it?*

"Because if you have any uncertainty whatsoever about the transplant, we need to determine that. Living kidney donation is an emotional decision. It's natural to feel anxiety about the procedure, even though you want to help. You can speak freely to us. If you decide against the surgery, your father will be told you're not a good match. Our hope is to maintain the relationship between patient and donor, regardless of donation decision."

"I've made my decision," Michelle snapped, stung because she knew she and Gavin didn't have any relationship to maintain. "I already passed all the tests."

"We still have to do the renal angiogram," Dr. Kehr reminded her. "Chances are, you'll be a near-perfect donor. But there could be other issues that make you less than an ideal candidate."

"I'm here, aren't I?" she said fiercely.

"Sometimes there are emotional issues," Temple said in his low-key voice. "Your father indicated you've been estranged for many years. This decision—"

"Don't you get it?" Her voice rose. "There was never any decision to be made. You're welcome to explore my feelings all you want, but you're not going to get me to change my mind." She forced herself to glare straight into his eyes. "My father is dying. My kidney can save him. *That's* the issue, Dr. Temple."

He nodded briefly, and annoyingly made a note on his legal pad. "You should be aware that this procedure alone won't mend the estrangement between you and your father. Flesh and blood alone can't accomplish that."

"I just want him well again," Michelle said, painfully close to tears. "The rest . . . we'll deal with."

When Dr. Kehr started speaking, she was thorough, encouragingly so. She explained what everyone's role would be. She talked about recovery periods, follow-up care, side effects of the meds, and long-term prognosis. She took out badly drawn charts—medical illustration was not terribly lucrative—to show what would happen in the procedure.

That's what she called it. The Procedure.

"Unless the renal angiogram indicates otherwise, the surgeon will take the left kidney." The doctor pointed to the chart.

"I had no idea there was a difference." A heaviness weighted the atmosphere. Though he had left the room, her father's need pressed at Michelle, smothering her. Her hands in her lap ripped a Kleenex to shreds. Guiltily, she balled up the evidence and tucked it into her palm. Too late. Temple had seen. He made a note on his clipboard.

"Using the left kidney is standard," the doctor continued. "The connecting vessels are longer, so we've got more material to work with."

Michelle's hand, out of control now, stole back to press against her left side.

"You have a couple of options for entry." The chart was propped up again. "Later, we'll discuss whether it'll be the front or the back." Her finger traced incision lines on the chart. "Generally, we advise against the back entry, because although it's a more direct route, the recovery is quite painful due to the splitting of the rib cage."

Michelle wished she hadn't said anything about splitting her rib cage. It was hard to keep from looking terrified when the doctor talked like this.

"Also, an incision scar on the back might be troublesome," Donna added.

"What do you mean, troublesome?"

"In the fashion sense. If you like wearing dresses cut low in the back, the scar might show."

"That's not important."

"It doesn't seem like it now. But it's a consideration. A team in Seattle pioneered a harvesting technique that only requires a four-inch incision in the donor."

Harvesting. "That's good to know," Michelle said wryly.

"The long-term effects of having only one kidney are minimal. But there *are* long-term effects." Donna smiled pleasantly. She had honest eyes; Michelle liked her.

"You mean I should avoid cliff diving and logrolling?"

"That would be advisable, yes."

"Suppose I were to get pregnant." She had no idea where that came from; it just slipped out.

"You'd be at a higher than normal risk, but pregnancy isn't prohibited."

"Just asking." Quickly, to cover up her embarrassment, Michelle said, "Here's the big one. Will I be able to play the violin after the surgery?"

"Of course," the nurse assured her, though Michelle could tell from the smile in her eyes she knew this joke.

"Great," Michelle said. "I never could before."

"Just use good sense. Protect that one kidney."

By the time the meeting ended, Michelle was feeling both exhilarated and frightened. Her father came back as everyone was filing out. Dr. Kehr shook hands with her, and she held on to her longer than she should have. Her life and that of her father would quite literally be in this woman's hands.

"Any more questions?" Dr. Kehr asked.

Her father stood still and upright, looking heartbreakingly stoic. It was one of the things that distinguished him as an actor. He had a way of touching people's hearts without moving a muscle.

"Not at the moment," Michelle said. "You were really thorough. Dad?"

"No questions either. I've been doing my homework on this for months, so I guess I'm as prepared as I'll ever be." He sent the doctor a grin. Michelle could see her visibly falling for him. "Can we call you if any questions come up?"

"Of course." She held out a pale blue business card. "You have my home, office, pager, and cell phone. Call anytime." She walked them to the door. "Until next Saturday, then? If Michelle's final tests check out, Monday's our day."

Michelle held the stack of brochures and paperwork in front of her like a shield as they walked out of the hospital annex. "You want me to drive home?"

"No. I'm fine." Before long, they were heading back down the highway.

"The psychologist kept making notes on me," she remarked.

"Temple? He's got a bunch of notes on me, too."

"What do you suppose he was writing?"

Gavin stared straight ahead at the road. "I imagine he's wondering if we're up for this."

"That's stupid. You need a kidney, I'm a match, end of story."

He cleared his throat, seeming to draw words from a hiding place deep inside him. "You have every right to resent me, Michelle."

"I don't resent you."

"Sure you do. Christ, I don't blame you. I wish I'd been a father to you when you were growing up."

Before she could stop herself, she thought of her childhood, the older split-level home in Bel Air. Though there were plenty of single-parent families in Southern California, Michelle always focused on the unbroken ones. She couldn't help the sharp envy she felt watching her friends with their two doting parents. The terrible ache that would engulf her when she saw a girl playing Frisbee in the park with her father . . .

"Is it too late to be a father now?" she asked, the words surprising even her.

A long, awkward silence. His hand came across the seat, touched her shoulder. "I'm willing to try, Michelle. But remember, I'm new at this. I've got a lousy track record."

"What's that supposed to mean?"

He took his hand away. From the corner of her eye, she noticed a furtive flash of guilt in his expression. "You know, last time. You took off, and I didn't know what the hell to do. So I did nothing."

Michelle shut her eyes, but the memories rushed in. *"I'm pregnant, Daddy."*

"I'm not surprised. Your mother was careless, too."

"I figured that McPhee boy was up to no good," her father had said on that bitter November night.

She hadn't asked him how he knew it was Sam's. Jake

Dollarhide had probably ratted on them, just as Sam had predicted.

"I shouldn't have told you," she had said, scared and hurt by his reaction. "Sam will help me through this."

"Is that what he promised?"

"He will when I tell him."

Gavin had snorted with disbelief. "He's cowboy scum, and his mother is trash. Even if he says he'll stick by you, Tammi Lee will drag you both down. You'll be living in some trailer park trying to hold off the law from her. Don't look for any promises from him."

And—damn him—Gavin had been right. That evening when Michelle went to tell Sam about the baby, he was gone without a trace, the shotgun house he'd shared with his mother an empty shell.

"Michelle?" Her father's voice brought her back to the present. "You got mighty quiet there."

"I guess that's because there's so much to say."

Chapter 11

Sylvia was in labor. The mare had been restless all night, hadn't eaten. She was fully dilated, her sides bellowing in and out in the peculiar manner of laboring mares. She kept looking back at her own flanks as if they didn't belong to her. As Edward had taken such glee in showing Cody the day before, her udder was full, her nipples waxy, the milk veins distended. Now she was covered in sweat, a sure sign that her water would break soon.

Sam walked across the field where Edward Bliss and Cody were uncoiling snow fence, readying the slope for the avalanches the spring thaw would bring. He had to force himself to walk at an even pace, to keep his expression neutral when what he really wanted to do was rush headlong and gawk at his son. His *son*. His own flesh and blood.

How was it that Cody had been born and Sam hadn't realized it? Shouldn't he have felt some upheaval inside himself, some alteration in the most essential part of his being?

Babies were born all the time without their fathers knowing. Maybe Sam was no different from Calyx, the champion stud quarter horse that had sired Sylvia's foal. But he still couldn't understand how a baby boy with half his chromosomes had been born and he hadn't even felt a ripple in the pond water.

At the time of Cody's birth, he'd been running. After he and his mother had left Crystal City only hours ahead of the law, they hadn't made much of a home anywhere for a while. Hot checks, unpaid bills, and collection-agency notices had trailed behind them like kicked-up dust.

On that long-ago night, when everything had fallen apart, he hadn't even had time to button his shirt. In the months that followed, they stayed in motels with weekly rates, lay low in a couple of run-down trailer courts, even slept at a roadside park or two. Nothing lasted—not their jobs, not their money, not their luck.

Until the Lander rodeo. It had been pure dumb luck that the Valiant had broken down in Wyoming, right under the billboard for the annual summer event. Tammi Lee had scrounged up enough cash for a pint of Ripple, and Sam had walked into town, hoping to earn a few bucks helping out as a gate runner.

Instead, he'd encountered a guy lying on a stretcher, his face floury white and his severed thumb in a Dixie cup with a piece of ice. Sam had looked on with more interest than horror as the paramedics whisked the cowboy off to reattach his thumb.

It was a classic injury for a team roper. If he dallied the rope the wrong way, the tug of the fleeing steer could sever a thumb. The guy's roping partner had cast a worried eye at the pay window. He didn't want to disqualify himself, even though without a heeler, he couldn't compete. With nothing left to lose, Sam had stepped up. Everyone was so ball-squeezed by the accident that there hadn't been much discussion. They pinned a number on Sam and off he went.

By the end of the night he and the header had won the regional title and nine thousand dollars. Fired up by good fortune, he'd launched a new career by buying an old beat-up trailer and pickup. Then he'd gone looking for a horse. It took him four months to find Sherlock and several more good purses to acquire him, but the quarter horse was worth the trouble. He became Sam's business partner and best friend.

Sam went solo, specializing in calf roping. He didn't want to split his earnings with half of a team. Leaving his mother in a motel on the outskirts of Cheyenne, he took off in the pickup, entering rodeos from San Angelo to Calgary. At night he slept in the gooseneck of Sherlock's trailer and ate his meals out of fast-food bags. He often went home with a woman—there was no shortage of rodeo groupies, and they loved a winner—but he always felt hollow after those encounters. Always caught himself thinking too much of a soft-limbed girl with soulful eyes. He'd lie awake listening to the crickets and consider calling her, and once he actually picked up the phone.

"You got a lot of damned nerve, boy, calling here," Gavin Slade had roared at him.

Sam had braced his fist on the window of the phone booth, an ovenlike kiosk in Oklahoma City. "I want to talk to Michelle, Mr. Slade."

"Over my dead body. You stole from me, McPhee—"

"That's a damned lie." Over the months of rambling,

Sam had put the puzzle together. The day Jake Dollarhide had seen him and Michelle come out of the art studio, several hundred dollars had turned up missing from the foreman's cashbox. Sam had been set up, plain and simple. He wasn't certain Gavin was in on it directly, but it sure as hell was convenient timing—Sam being run off the day he'd been caught nailing the boss's daughter.

"Don't call here anymore," Gavin had warned him. He'd slammed down the phone.

Sam didn't try again. There was no point. His mom was in trouble, and he had to stay on the circuit. Michelle had to go to college. The impossibility of a rich girl–poor boy romance was finally real to him. Shame and hurt pride burned away the last of his innocence. Did Michelle believe he was a thief, or would she realize he'd been framed? Shoot, it really didn't matter.

By the end of that season, Sam had won enough purses to lease his mother a little clapboard house near Seguin, Texas. A year later, he'd passed his G.E.D. and saved up for college tuition. Between rodeoing and school and his wet-brained mother, he hadn't had time to come up for air, much less realize the only girl he'd ever loved had given birth to his son.

As he approached Cody, Sam told himself not to wonder about him as a baby, a toddler, a little boy. That child was gone now, and in his place was an angry teen. The hell of it was, Sam didn't know what to think. Did he really want to know this kid, learn his rage and his flaws, excavate his virtues from beneath the layers of resentment?

"Hey, guys," he said, scanning the fence. "How's it coming?"

"Okay." Cody stood back and gestured at the long line

of pickets curving under the brow of a hill where the avalanche danger was the worst. "I guess."

Sam held his breath. *Did she tell you, Cody? Did she tell you I'm your dad?*

Clearly not, judging by the kid's offhand manner. He held his shoulders hunched up, and his nose was bright red from the cold.

"See any sign of that cat?" Sam asked.

"You mean the mountain lion?"

"Yeah, Edward spotted a carcass last week."

"Snowshoe hare," Edward said. "How's Sylvia doing?"

"That's why I came to get you," Sam said. "It's time."

"What?" Cody snapped to attention, forgetting to sulk.

"Sylvia, the mare," Sam explained. "Her water's about to break, and the foal will come pretty fast after that."

"Yeah?" The kid's face brightened a hundred watts. He was a damned good-looking kid even with the ponytail and earrings. "Can we see her?"

As Sam returned to the snowmobiles, he concealed a smile. "You're not squeamish, are you, Cody?"

"Me? No, man. I got a stomach of iron."

The icy wind blasted their faces as they drove back to the barn, dismounting fast and running inside to attend the birth.

A low grunting sound issued from the birthing stall. A foaling kit, with OB sleeves, tape, the foaling record, a stopwatch, instruments, and drugs lay on a crate. Sam hurried in to find the mare bobbing her head up and down, pawing the straw and acting skittish.

"Everything okay?" Edward asked.

"Let's have a listen." Sam took a stethoscope from the foaling kit and pressed it to the mare's abdomen. The vigorous hiss and swish of her pulse reassured him. He could detect the faint racing pulse of the fetus as well.

But it was beating too fast and shallow for comfort. "Might be some fetal distress, possible dystocia."

"Should I call the vet?" Edward asked.

"Go ahead and put in a call, but I have a feeling the foal will arrive before the vet does. Let's see what kind of shape the amniotic sac's in when it emerges." He set his jaw against a curse. He loved this mare. He sure as hell didn't want to lose her.

"What's that mean?" Cody peered over the edge of the stall. "Dystocia. Sounds bad."

"It means a bad presentation and stress on the foal. Not great news. Edward," he called down the breezeway, "see if you can get the heat turned up higher in here. Don't want the baby to catch a chill." He indicated a bucket outside the birthing stall. "Cody, do me a favor and wrap her tail with that white tape. Then you can wash her perineum and teats, okay? If we don't get everything clean, we're risking infection."

"Wash her . . ." Cody gaped at him in disbelief.

"Teats. And perineum."

"What's a—"

"It's exactly what you think it is."

"Oh, man."

"You said you had a stomach of iron."

Cody grumbled, but he picked up the wrapping. Gingerly, he lifted the mare's tail, grimacing as Sam palpated the abdomen.

"Gross," Cody commented.

"A mare in labor urinates and defecates a lot," Sam said unapologetically.

"Great."

But the boy did a good enough job of wrapping the

tail; then he brought out the bucket of water and disinfectant. With all the diligence Sam could have hoped for, he scrubbed away at the teats.

"Hey," he said, "something's, um, dripping from her."

Sam examined the teats. "Colostrum."

"What does that mean?"

"It means you might want to hurry and get that perineum disinfected, because things are going to speed up pretty soon." Sam tried not to seem anxious. He and Edward had yanked foals many times before, usually with good results. But God. Sylvia. She was the best mare he'd ever had.

The kid took a deep breath and dipped a clean cloth. He lifted the wrapped tail and dabbed hesitantly at first. Then he blew out his breath in a show of determination, planted himself right behind her, and finished the job.

"You might want to stand a little to one side," Sam advised as Cody was rinsing. "Because if you're directly behind her when her water breaks—"

Too late. It broke before he could finish speaking.

She spewed like a fire hose, directly at Cody. The projectile of warm fluid, probably a couple of gallons of it, completely drenched the boy.

"Holy shit," he yelled, jumping back.

"Sorry." Sam bit the inside of his cheek to keep from laughing. "I tried to warn you."

"Thanks for nothing, man."

"You want to go find some dry clothes?"

Cody made for the door, then hesitated. "Will I miss anything?"

"The foal will come any minute now."

"I'll stay then." He ripped off his coat—the black leather thing Sam hated—and dropped it on the floor in the corner. And it was odd, but it seemed to Sam that the kid shed some of his cynicism along with the coat. He could look at Cody now and see a boy, eager and bright-eyed, his young face ablaze with interest.

"Holy shit," he said again. His eyes grew round.

The silvery-slick balloon of the amnion started to come through. "Lie down, baby," Sam said to Sylvia. "Lie down, there's a girl."

After a few minutes, she complied, lowering herself with a grunt of effort.

"Stay down, baby." Sam knelt by her head, holding it and murmuring in her ear. "Stay—"

With a defiant clearing of her throat, Sylvia lurched to her feet.

"That's bad, right?" Cody asked, his face paler than it had been a minute earlier. "She shouldn't be standing up, right?"

"It's better if she lies down," Sam admitted. "But it's pretty pointless to argue with a fifteen-hundred-pound horse. She—"

He broke off as the mare's sides began to fan violently in and out. "Here she comes," Edward said, returning from the office with a cordless phone in his hand.

Sam gave Sylvia's neck a pat. "Vet?"

"Up in Big Arm. He can't get here for an hour."

"Then we're on our own," Sam said. "Get down again, baby, there you are . . ." He coaxed gently, stroked her, massaged her. "Down, that's a girl." Eventually she obeyed. Sam hoped she'd stay put as he knelt to see how things were progressing. "Cody, give me a hand here."

The boy hesitated just for a beat. "Yeah, okay."

The foal was trying to present with its legs sticking up toward the croup, a dangerous situation. Sylvia rolled and twisted, driven by instinct to correct the position. When that didn't work, Sam nodded at Edward. "She needs some help turning it." He held the mare's head, murmuring mindless phrases, trying to soothe her. Edward and Cody stripped down to T-shirts to wrestle with the slippery emerging legs, Edward uttering low curses and Cody goggle-eyed with fascination and worry.

"I keep losing hold. Damn, that's narrow," Edward said, his hand caught inside. "Cody, are your hands smaller than mine?"

"I guess. You want me to try?"

Edward hesitated, then eased back when the contraction ended. He passed a tube of lubricant to Cody. "Here's what you do. We want the forelegs first, but turned this way, see?"

"Yeah." Cody smeared on the lubricant and took a deep breath. A few seconds later, his hand disappeared inside the mare. If the situation hadn't been so dire, Sam would have laughed at the expression on the kid's face. Edward coached him, instructing him to bring the legs down and around, working between contractions.

Sylvia grunted and pushed, expelling Cody's hand and then, pulse by pulse, the foal, hooves first. Cody didn't move out of the way in time but caught it against his knees, rearing back when the hindquarters slipped out.

"Easy there." Sam bent to examine the foal, suctioning out its mouth and nose. It gave a jerk of its bony body, then a strange cough, and began breathing on its own. Its pale muzzle took on the color of life. Its umbilical cord, still attached, pulsed in time with the mare's heartbeat. She stood with a lumbering effort, twisting to lick at her baby.

"Wow," said Cody, his eyes bugging out, his entire front covered with birth fluid, his mouth wide in a grin. "Wow."

Sam squirted iodine on the umbilical cord. He should have become a vet. Or a teacher.

Instead, he was a father who didn't know his son.

That, he decided, as he looked at Cody's sweat-streaked face, was about to change. Whether Michelle liked it or not.

The sac still hung from the mare, slapping against her hind legs. Sam saw the reflex coming, but before he could speak, she kicked out. In a flash of movement, the hoof caught Cody, right on the temple.

Chapter 12

As they approached Crystal City, Gavin kept his gaze fixed dead ahead, his jaw perfectly square, his hands relaxed on the steering wheel. Yet Michelle could tell—there was some subtle turbulence in his manner—that the hospital appointment had rattled him. Monday: 6:45 A.M. Perhaps knowing the precise day and time of the transplant was disconcerting.

It sure as hell was for Michelle.

"Are you all right?" she asked.

"I'm in end-stage renal failure," he said. "How all right can I be?"

"I'm sorry. I wish I knew what to say to you."

"You don't have to apologize for anything." He flexed his hands on the steering wheel. "I'm a lousy father, have been from the get-go. Being sick only makes me lousier."

"I don't know." She tried to keep her voice light. "A

true believer would say it's the universe's way of bringing us together."

"Are you a true believer, Michelle?"

She stared out the window. Long gray-white smudges of highway and snow. "I used to be."

He trained his eyes on the road. "When your mother told me she was pregnant, I panicked. I was just getting started in my career. I was in the most cutthroat business in the world, and I didn't think I'd make it on my own, much less with a family to care for. Kept seeing myself as a failure, pumping gas for a living, trying to make ends meet, chasing down bit parts and making everyone miserable. Didn't have a pot to piss in, Michelle. I had a rented room in Studio City and a risky role coming up."

His words sounded like lines recited from a script.

"That must have been *Shelter from the Storm*." The film had made him a star and a household name.

"As excuses go, it's pretty weak, but my career was everything at the time. I thought all a father did was send a monthly check, maybe show up for special occasions. The truth is, I never knew how to be a father, and I was too scared to try. Michelle, I'd give anything to change that, but I can't. It's one of the lessons people never seem to learn—that you can't change the past." He glanced sideways at her. "I just hope it's not too late to fix things."

"Why didn't you even try, Daddy? Didn't you know I needed you?" The anguished question burst from her.

"Michelle—"

The mobile phone chirped, startling them and shattering the tension in the truck. Michelle felt a twinge of annoyance. For once she and her father were actually beginning to talk, and now this. He clicked on the speaker phone. "Gavin here."

"It's Edward Bliss, from over at Lonepine."

"What can I do for you, Edward? You're on the speaker phone."

"Is Michelle with you?"

"I'm here." Like a sudden shadow, a chill swept over her. "Is everything all right?"

"Michelle, I'm at Meridian County Hospital. Your boy, he—"

"Jesus Christ." Gavin's foot pressed to the floor, and the truck shot forward, hurtling down the highway toward town.

"What happened?" Her chest pounded with dread.

"He's going to be okay," Edward said quickly. "He was kicked in the head by a horse."

"Oh my God—"

"It happens sometimes, it—" Static crackled, obliterating Edward's voice. As the peaks of the mountains plunged the road into gloom, the connection died.

"We'll be there in five minutes," Gavin said. "You got your seat belt on?"

Michelle nodded. She couldn't speak, could only hang on as they sped into town. The hardware store, the café, the municipal building and library passed in a blur. She died a thousand deaths, racing to get to her son. She imagined Cody, her beautiful boy, broken and bleeding in some emergency room, his head bashed in. *Please. Please. Please.* She could barely find the words to pray.

The truck screeched to a halt in front of the community hospital. Built of narrow reddish brick and small windows, it had an awning that stretched over the emergency entrance. She jumped out, dragging her purse along. The automatic doors hissed open. Lurching to the admittance desk, she was barely able to catch her breath.

"Cody Turner." The lump of dread in her chest started to hurt. "He's my son. He was kicked in the head—"

"—by Sam McPhee's mare," the attendant said. "Curtain area in the examination room, ma'am." She held up a clipboard. "Now, if we could just get some information—"

"Later." She raced down the hall. Earthtone linoleum, green-tiled walls, extra-wide doors with frosted glass windowpanes—were all hospitals alike? A nurse holding a tray of instruments was in the exam room. "You're the mother?"

The Mother. Spoken that way, it sounded so weighty, so dire. She straightened her shoulders, forced herself to get a grip. "I am."

The nurse, whose name tag read Alice O'Brien, nodded at an aqua-colored half curtain enclosing a wheeled cot. Blue jeans tucked into snowmobile boots showed at the bottom. She could hear a low, masculine voice murmuring something indistinct.

"The doctor's with him right now," Nurse O'Brien said.

Michelle parted the curtain. "Cody?"

"Hey, Mom." His voice was small. A flesh-colored patch covered part of his head. Rusty bloodstains streaked his hair. A bluish cast tinged his complexion. His clothes were wet, smeared with blood and a whitish slime. She wanted to touch him, hold him, scream with relief that he was conscious.

The other person in the cubicle was Sam McPhee. "Sam? Where's the doctor?"

Then she noticed what he was wearing. A green fiber gown and a pair of high-intensity lighted eyeglasses. Surgical gloves.

Michelle blinked fast, confused.

"Mom, Sam *is* the doctor," Cody muttered.

"He's what?" She stared at Sam. "You're what?"

"The doctor." Sam lifted a corner of his mouth. "Why do I feel as if I should apologize for that?"

"My God." She sank to a metal swivel stool beside the gurney. The information was coming at her too fast. "Okay, just tell me about Cody. He's a mess. Is he—"

"It's a head injury, Michelle. And he was lucky—it appears to be mild." Sam's voice was gentle. "The other stuff all over him is from the mare."

The nurse arrived with another tray and set it on a rolling table by Sam. The attending clerk came in, too. "Ma'am, you need to sign this."

"What is it?"

"A consent form."

She took the clipboard and lifted her gaze to Sam. He looked like a stranger in the gown and headgear, tall and slightly mystical, the high priest of some alien nation. "What am I consenting to?"

"Treatment. In this case that means you're authorizing me to debride and stitch this head wound."

"I don't want any stitches, man." Cody's lips were practically blue, stark against the shocked pallor of his face.

"We'll numb the area. Easier than going to the dentist," Sam said.

Michelle scribbled her name across the bottom of the sheet. On the next page, she swiftly answered a series of questions about Cody's health history, allergies, reactions to medication—all negative. The form under that was covered with small print. "What's this one?"

"An admit form," the clerk said.

"I want to keep him overnight," Sam explained. "His GCS scale was fifteen—that means all his neurological responses are fine. The CT scan showed a mild subarachnoid hemorrhage, so observation for a short period is probably the only treatment needed. We'll do a routine follow-up later, but I don't expect any complications."

Her hand trembled wildly as she signed. She heard her father come in. "Hey, Sam," he said.

"Gavin." Sam didn't look up from Cody.

Gavin seated himself in a molded-plastic chair inside the door. For a moment an eerie sense of unreality closed in on her. Here she sat, surrounded by her father, her son, and Cody's father in a situation straight out of a nightmare.

One thing at a time. She needed to force herself to concentrate on one thing at a time. "So tell me what happened."

"Cody was helping with a mare in labor," Sam said. "And doing a damned good job of it. Tweezers," he said to the nurse, and began to pick at the edges of the wound. "He helped Sylvia give birth to a gorgeous little filly. That's the good news. Hold this clamp, will you, Alice?"

"The bad news is," Sam continued, "Sylvia got a little antsy during the afterbirth and started kicking." He teased away the patch, revealing an alarming curved gash. The flesh gaped open, showing blood-drenched tissue. "Breathe through your nose, Michelle. This isn't pretty."

She rolled the stool closer to the bed. Cody's hand crept out from beneath the blue-paper sheeting and she grasped it, holding on hard. His fingers were icy cold.

"It's okay, Cody-boy," she whispered, calm now, although she knew that later she would fall to pieces. "Just hold real still."

He swallowed, his cheeks and his neck pale. For once he didn't sneer with disgust when she called him the old pet name.

Sam and the nurse cleansed the wound. Somehow she maintained a measured stoicism even though the large flap of skin and copious flow of blood terrified her. The wound was an upside-down crescent shape. She sat transfixed by Sam's hands, noting with a strange, horrified awe how deftly and delicately they worked, how sensitive they were.

His intense absorption in his work both reassured and frightened her. Like a rock tumbling in a stream, the revelation turned over and over in her mind. Sam had become a doctor. A *doctor*.

An ugly, sinking sensation spiraled downward through Michelle. She didn't want to feel this, didn't want to think this, but she realized she had convinced herself that Sam would never amount to anything more than a rodeo bum. That was how she had rationalized the past seventeen years. That was the excuse she gave herself for not moving heaven and earth to find him. She had convinced herself that he'd be a tumbleweed, a ne'er-do-well, hardly a fit father to Cody.

Yet now she saw that Sam had held on to his dream, pursuing it long after she'd abandoned her own.

Don't let me be this small, this petty, she thought. *Don't let me resent this.*

In the end, it was Cody who saved her from her own thoughts. The nurse turned on a pair of buzzing clippers. Cody squeezed her hand in sudden surprise and terror, and a powerful wave of love washed over her. Sam had become his dream, but she had become Cody's mother, and there could be no comparison.

"Mom," Cody said breathlessly.

She forced a smile. "I've been nagging you for months to get a decent haircut. I guess now's as good a time as any."

She couldn't be certain, but as Nurse O'Brien clipped away at the hair, Sam's mouth twitched, just a bit shy of a smile.

She shouldn't be surprised that he actually became a doctor. It made sense, after the way his mother raised him. He wanted a way to make people better.

The attending clerk brought Gavin a cup of water. Michelle had forgotten he was there. The glaring overhead light magnified the lines of fatigue around his eyes.

"Dad, you should go on home. It's been a long day."

"I'll stay."

"No, really. The last thing I need is for both of you to be laid up. I'd feel a lot better if you waited at home. I'll call."

"I'm staying," he said in his deep actor's voice.

He had known. He had known all along that the father of her son was a doctor, living here in Crystal City, and he had never bothered to tell her.

"Damn it." The coiled tension in her sprang up. "You make me nervous, sitting around and waiting. *Please,* Dad—"

"I'll give Michelle a ride home when we're done," Sam said, an edge of impatience in his voice. And he was right to be impatient. He had to concentrate, not mediate family squabbles.

Gavin hesitated; then he nodded and got to his feet. He came over to the table and gave Cody's shoulder a squeeze. "Take care now, you hear?"

Other than their first handshake, this was the only time she had seen him touch her son.

"Yeah," Cody said. "See you."

"We're going to numb the area now," Sam said. Nurse O'Brien finished clipping, then disinfected and draped the wound.

Because of the draping, she could no longer see his face. A calculated move, she surmised once she saw the needle Sam was using.

"This'll sting," he warned, being honest but not alarming. "You'll feel a pinch, and it'll probably make your eyes water."

Pretty smooth, thought Michelle. Giving the kid an excuse to cry if he needed to.

Cody squeezed again. She squeezed back. Sam injected Xylocaine in a few spots, then set aside the syringe.

"Okay, we have a few minutes to talk," he said. "Need to give the anesthetic time to work."

Michelle swallowed, the lump in her throat still painful. "So talk."

"It's a big laceration." Without touching Cody, he followed the curve of it with a finger. "Cody and that mare were really up close and personal. It could have been worse, but Edward removed the horse's shoes last night, because we knew the birth was imminent. So the damage is slightly less than it could have been."

She thought about the strange yet familiar smell on Cody's damp clothes. It was musky, faintly sweet, yet with an oceanic tang. The birth smell. Her son was drenched in it.

Sam pointed again. "See how this goes down to his temple?"

She nodded, thinking how delicate the tracery of tiny veins looked. How vulnerable. The terror pushed upward from her chest, but true to form she contained it.

"That means I'll be stitching in the region of his face, just here."

There was about an inch between his brow and hairline. The wound was stark there, the flesh amber in color from the disinfectant. "Now, I'm not a plastic surgeon," he said. "I usually refer cases like this to a specialist."

"But this is unusual?"

"Somewhat. I'm inclined to do this myself, here and

now. I can take a lot of tiny stitches—I had practice during a clinical rotation I did with a cleft palate specialist in the Yucatán."

The Yucatán? It was strange to think of all the places Sam had been, all the things he had done in the years they'd been strangers. He had gone to the Yucatán while she had raised his son.

"You're probably going to see a scar," he concluded.

"So is there an alternative?" she asked.

"I could clamp the wound, and then you could take him to Missoula. There's a great face guy there."

"The plastic surgeon wouldn't come here?"

Sam hesitated. "Not this guy."

"So you want me to decide."

Sam regarded her for a long time. She wondered what was going on in his head, what it was like for him to have his wounded son lying here yet to have no say in his treatment. She thought of all the times she'd had to make a decision about Cody, wishing for someone else to talk it over with. She'd felt so alone on those occasions.

"I've given you the options, Michelle."

"I don't want to know the options. I want to know what to *do*."

"Chances are excellent that a trip to Missoula won't do him a bit of harm—"

"Quit being such a . . . a *doctor*. I want you to tell me the right thing—"

"Just stitch the damn thing up." A small, annoyed voice crept out from under the draping.

Both Sam and she looked down at Cody. "Really?" she asked.

"Yeah. I want to get it over with. A drive to Missoula doesn't exactly sound fun."

"How big a scar?" she asked Sam.

"You can see where it'll be. A thin line. Red at first, and eventually it'll fade to white."

A shiver eddied over her. It was an accident, yes, but Cody was going to be marked by this incident, marked for life. He'd never be the same.

"Go for it," Cody said miserably.

"All right." Her voice was soft. "Go ahead and finish, Sam."

He held himself very still for a few moments. He didn't move, though she sensed an odd calm settling over him. It was invisible, yet she could see it happening, like some new sort of medical Zen.

True to his word, he took tiny stitches, working with a needle and silk so fine she had to squint to see it. During the procedure, she sat holding Cody's hand as he lay silent and still.

Despite what Sam said about not being a specialist, she could tell one thing for certain. He was a good doctor. He worked smoothly with the nurse. The two of them had a comfortable rapport as if they'd known each other a long while. From time to time the attending clerk came in, and he answered her questions without so much as glancing up or breaking his concentration. His hands moved with a precise, mesmeric rhythm.

Through it all, Cody lay motionless and admirably calm, his hand in Michelle's.

As Sam was finally finishing up, she decided to say what was on her mind. "So I guess this means you know about my father."

"I'm a family practitioner."

"But you know about his illness."

"My partner, Karl Schenk, is his primary-care physician. Gavin didn't tell you?"

"It's all I can do to keep up with the nephrologists and surgeons."

Sam tied off a stitch. "He's getting good care in Missoula."

"He's getting one of my kidneys."

He hesitated for a beat, then took another stitch. "That's really something, Michelle. I figured they'd eyeball him for a transplant."

"How did you figure that?"

Without even looking up, he seemed to sense her getting defensive. "Now, don't turn all prickly on me. Gavin's general health is excellent. Nonsmoker, nondiabetic. Physiologically, he couldn't be a better candidate. That's all I meant. No doctor I know would use Gavin's fame to make a transplant poster boy of him."

He removed the draping. Cody looked pale but relaxed, his eyelids heavy.

"Okay, cowboy?" Sam asked.

"I guess." He took his hand away from Michelle's. He seemed embarrassed that he'd been clinging to it the whole time.

Sam beamed a pen-sized light in Cody's eyes, first one, then the other. "You're not going to kick me in the head like your last patient did to you?"

"I'll decide after I see the stitches."

Michelle liked Sam's ease with the boy. He'd only known him two days, yet his manner was open and natural. Sometimes she wished Brad would—

Alice, the nurse, held up a hand mirror.

Sam grinned. "Take a look, Frankenstein."

Cody grimaced. "Nice haircut."

"You can have Hazlett fix it. He's the local barber, does house calls at the hospital. Or you could wait until you're discharged," Sam said.

"Hey," said Cody. "Do I have to stay?"

Sam's gaze was level and direct. "Yep. Just overnight, okay?"

Michelle studied Cody's dubious face, then Sam's. Dear God, she thought, they look alike. The similarity was apparent now that Cody's long hair had been cropped. He looked almost exactly like Sam did, back when Sam had been the beginning and end of her world.

She got up quickly. "I'll stay with him."

"Oh, no you don't, Mom," Cody said. "I can handle spending one night in the hospital."

She patted his leg. Again she felt that dark hollow of loss, as if her little boy had disappeared before her eyes. "Tonight's going to be a lot harder on me than on you."

"Don't worry about me, Mom."

"I'll always worry about you." The lump in her throat swelled. "Thanks for holding my hand through that."

He lifted half his mouth in a crooked grin. Sam's grin. "Right, Mom."

Chapter 13

When Sam left the hospital, he found Michelle sitting in the dark outside, cradling a Styrofoam cup of tea and crying.

The sight of her on the concrete bench, looking so small and alone, stopped him in his tracks. "Hey," he said, easing down next to her. "Have a Kleenex."

Nearby, the door opened and Alice O'Brien came out, a duffel bag slung over her shoulder. She had that weary sort of prettiness common to a lot of nurses, and she regarded him with more kindness than he deserved, given their history together. "'Night, Sam," she said.

"See you tomorrow, Alice."

Michelle's gaze followed her until night cloaked her in darkness. "She doesn't call you doctor."

At some point he'd have to explain about Alice. But not now. There were other things to discuss now. "To these folks I'm just Sam McPhee. One of them. One of the tribe." He turned to her, noticing the silvery track of a tear on her cheek. He wanted to touch it. Taste it. Make it go away. *Christ.* He shoved his hands into his jacket pockets. "You okay?"

She wiped her face with the tissue. "A little overwhelmed, I guess. It's been a long day."

"You held together like a champ in there," he said, and he meant it. If she was like other mothers of injured kids he'd treated, her insides were a train wreck. Yet outwardly, like so many of those steel-spined mothers, she had been calm and efficient while helping Cody get settled into his room. She'd bought him a paperback Anne Rice novel and a kit of toiletries from the gift shop, sat with him for a while, then left after dinner was served and a Bruce Willis movie came on.

"I can always hold together for Cody," she said.

"He's never seen you lose it?"

"No." She scrubbed away the last of her tears. "I told myself right from the start that I'd be the Rock of Gibraltar for him."

His heart heard what she would not say. That she had been all alone. That in two-parent families, one had the luxury of the occasional breakdown while the other took over. That during all her parental crises, no one had ever been there to hand her a Kleenex.

He couldn't help wondering what it would be like to be in that picture with her. Couldn't help wondering what this strange grown-up Michelle was like. Did she still cry when she heard a sad song on the radio, still get the hiccups when she laughed too hard? Did she still make that funny sound in the back of her throat when she came?

He stood up, his head spinning with anger, frustration, loss—and a lingering fascination with this woman who, despite years of separation, had never quite left him. "Let me buy you dinner."

"No." Her refusal came swiftly, automatically.

"Wrong answer, ma'am. Remember, I'm your ride home."

"But—"

"No buts. Stay right there. I need to change out of my scrubs, and then I'm taking you out to Trudy's for a steak." He walked toward the automatic doors. "People from Seattle eat steak, right?"

She lifted her face to him, the parking lot light carving graceful shadows on her cheeks. And finally, fleetingly, she smiled. "I guess people from Montana would be insulted if we refused, right?"

Sam tried not to make too much of her acceptance as he headed inside, but the light warmth in his chest was the most pleasurable thing he'd felt all day. He went to his locker in the lounge, thinking how unreal it had been to treat his own son. To know that the fragile flesh and bone beneath his hands belonged, at least biologically, to him.

He thought about the day he'd decided to become a doctor. He'd been eight or nine years old, riding in a beat-up old car along a straight, flat road. It was a Valiant with a fake Navajo rug covering the torn upholstery. A bag of Cheetos and a bottle of something red lay on the seat beside him. His mother was smoking a cigarette and singing with the radio.

His mother knew the words to all the rockabilly songs, because for one amazing year she had been the vocalist for a Denver band called Road Rage. Sam was too young to remember it, but she claimed it was the best year of her life. They'd traveled all over the country, and their hit single, "Dearly Departed," had rocketed to number one on the *Country Billboard* charts.

Finding success even harder to deal with than failure, the band had broken up, its members scattered. Still, his mom sang along with the radio, her voice harsh with the static of drinking and cigarettes.

Sam had sat silent, watching bugs squishing on the windshield. After a while, he told his mother he had to pee, so she pulled off at a rest stop. By the time he finished in the men's room, Tammi Lee was asleep in the car. So he climbed on top of the hood to wait.

There he was, a towheaded little kid sitting alone on the hood of a beat-up old car, watching people pull off the highway to rest. Whenever he saw families, he felt a funny tugging sensation in his gut. A mom, a dad, two or three kids, a dog. Doing stuff as simple as having a game of catch or sitting at a concrete picnic table, eating sandwiches and pouring Kool-Aid from a plastic jug. These things—these simple, unremarkable rituals—were things he wanted so bad he ached inside.

On that particular day, he twisted around on the hood of the car, stared at his mother, and wished for some magic spell to make her wake up, smile at him, ruffle his hair, ask him if he wanted a glass of milk.

Her eyes flickered open and just for a second, he thought the spell was going to work. Then she wiped the back of her hand across her mouth, dug in her pocket, took out some quarters. She held a trembling fist out the car window and said, "Get me a Tab, will you, hon?" in what he thought of as her tired voice. Later he figured out it was her hungover voice.

And even though she wasn't like the mothers pouring Kool-Aid, he loved her. Kids, he found out later when he became a doctor, loved their monster parents, no matter what.

On the way back from the vending machine—cold can of Tab held in both hands—a boy and his dad ran past, tossing a softball back and forth. The kid almost slammed into him, but sidestepped at the last minute. He never looked at Sam. Just sort of moved on by. They drove a nice car with M.D. plates. Sam was on the road so much he knew about M.D. plates.

His mom was acting funny when he got back to the car. Her face was white and shiny with sweat, her eyes glazed and rolled back in her head. She arched her back against the seat of the car and a thin, terrible noise crawled from her throat. Sam dropped the cold can on the ground and raced for the man with the softball. "Hey, mister," he yelled. "Are you a doctor?" When the man nodded, Sam said, "My mom's sick."

The doctor came over to the car and put his hand on her forehead, lifting her eyelid with his thumb. "Ma'am?" he asked. "Ma'am, can you hear me?" His wife came over with a bag. The doctor asked some questions—what had she been drinking, how long had she been like this—and Sam babbled out the answers. Rummaging in the bag, the doctor went to work. A short time later, Tammi Lee lay groggy but calm, acting sheepish as she spoke with the doctor, assuring him she'd seek help in the next town.

Sam decided right then and there he wanted to be a doctor. He wanted to be the kind of guy who drove a nice car and played catch with his son and when someone got sick, fixed her.

That little kid seemed a distant stranger now, and many years passed before Tammi Lee kept her promise to get help. Sam hurried, getting into his street clothes in record time, worried that Michelle might change her mind, disappear like a bursting bubble from his life.

Sort of like he'd disappeared from hers.

He shoved his feet into his boots, combed his hair, and slammed his locker shut. When he got outside, she was gone. He stood there, a curse forming on his mouth.

She came out of the hospital behind him. "I went to check on Cody one last time."

He exhaled, the curse unspoken. "And?"

"He's sleeping."

"Good. Best thing for him."

She bit her lip uncertainly. Sam took her hand, feeling the shape of it through her winter glove. She pulled away, and he didn't try again. "He's going to be fine. I'm on call all night, and Raymond's on duty."

"Raymond?"

"Raymond Bear, the head nurse. We call him the Shaman. He can sense a patient in distress even before the monitors, I swear it. Damnedest thing you've ever seen."

"Is he the guy reading *Soldier of Fortune* magazine at the nurses' station?"

"That's him. If he's reading a magazine, that means he's not worried." His hand flexed, remembering the shape of hers. "Come on. My truck's over here."

Only four of the eighteen tables at Trudy's were occupied, but that wasn't unusual for a cold Monday night. With its red vinyl tablecloths, gold plastic tumblers, and longhorn salt and pepper shakers, the place resembled a garage sale from the seventies. What it lacked in elegance it more than made up for in good, simple food.

"Just stick with the straightforward stuff, and you can't go wrong." Sam opened his menu.

"I see the wine list is a no-brainer." She cracked a

smile that did funny things to his insides. "Red, white . . . I assume Rosy means rosé?"

"Welcome to Crystal City."

Her smile lingered. "Still pretty provincial around here."

She was a stranger to him. She was a vast, uncharted continent. Mysterious, but something he wanted to explore.

"You can find all the glitz and sophistication you want in Kalispell and Bozeman. Your old man was one of the first to move up here from Hollywood, but he sure wasn't the last. In downtown Whitefish you can buy a Tiffany bracelet and millesime cognac."

"You could have made a lot more money setting up your practice in one of those towns." She closed her menu.

"Why do people always assume doctors are in it for the money?"

"All the doctors I know are."

He thought of Karl, and of Dr. Brower in the Yucatán. "Then you know the wrong doctors," he said. "There used to be three of us in the practice here, but one defected to Kalispell." He didn't say so, but the third partner made a fortune writing prescriptions for Valium and Zoloft.

"So why didn't you follow the money?"

"I belong here. Karl and I work for the tribe up at the Flathead reservation. It's not about money, Michelle. If it was about money, I could make fifty grand roping calves for a week in Vegas."

"You're not only a doctor, but you're noble."

"Is that what you think?"

"I think you came back here just to give everyone an inferiority complex."

He laughed. "Right."

"Why *did* you pick this particular town?"

No one had ever asked him that before. His credentials were good enough; he'd gone through a six-year combined degree program, and his training from UT was first-rate. He could have gone anywhere.

"I started thinking about a small-town practice when I was working in the Yucatán, mainly with Mexican Indians. I learned more than medicine there. A child is born with a cleft palate? You fix it, and the kid has a better life. A man suffers from hepatitis? You treat him, he survives, and you immunize his family. That's the beauty of working in third-world countries."

"So why not stay in a third-world country?"

"Because we have those right here in our own backyard. Small towns, Indian reservations, depressed areas that can't support a lucrative practice." He studied Michelle, noting the understated elegance of her gold watch, the French designer earrings. "I know what it's like to have money—I had that in my rodeo days. Well, some of the time, at least. I know what money can and can't do for a man."

"See? You are too noble."

He thought about the early days when he'd slept in his horse trailer or the back of his pickup truck, and how he'd lie awake nights on fire and in agony from wanting what rich folks like Gavin Slade had. It had been a sickness with Sam, that need to feel he could measure up, and it probably explained why he drove himself so hard, both in the arena and in the clinic. Only time, and the deep self-knowledge that came of healing people, had cured him of the sickness.

"I'm not noble, Michelle," he said. "I'm just a guy."

They ordered steak dinners and a bottle of wine from a waitress who knew Sam by name. When she departed, Michelle watched her from the corner of her eye. "Are we fueling gossip?"

"In a place this size?" he asked. "Are you kidding? You'll probably read about this dinner on the front page of the *Towne Tattler*."

"I didn't know the paparazzi were so vicious here." She smiled with an old mischievous sweetness he remembered well. Too well. He was getting dizzy gawking at her. It should come as no surprise that the daughter of Gavin Slade turned out to be even more of a knockout at thirty-five than she had been at eighteen. But then again, she had always surprised him.

She watched him with an expression that made his gut churn. Dewy eyes and moist lips. Total absorption in what he was saying. "And so you chose Crystal City," she said.

"Yeah. I knew Edward Bliss from the circuit, he needed a partner for Lonepine, the town needed a doctor, so it all worked out." What the hell, Sam thought. He might as well level with her. He wanted to be in the place where he had been with Michelle, where his dreams had been born and where hope had lingered in spite of everything. "And I figured I'd see you again."

She had no reply to that, but contemplated it with a silence he couldn't read.

While they ate, he thought about the night he'd left. The old Valiant had puttered through the quiet streets of Crystal City, passing the Truxtop and the feed store and the Lynwood Theater, the one-screen cinema where he and Michelle had sat holding hands in the dark. He remembered the yellowish beam of the headlights, the cigarette smell of the blanket covering the seat, the tinny sound of the radio playing a cowboy song, the too-quick rasp of his mother's breathing.

She was nervous, even though Sam, full of outrage,

had wanted to stay and fight his accusers. "I didn't steal a thing," he insisted. "Not a damned thing."

"I know that," his mother had said with weary resignation. "Do you think that matters? Gavin Slade doesn't want you hanging around his daughter. This is his way of telling you that."

"Let's not run away, Mama. It's a free country—"

"Gavin Slade owns this town. If he wants us gone, we're gone." She had looked at him sideways, peering through the darkness. "You're not the only one they've decided to pin something on."

He braced himself. "What do you mean?"

"I had a little visit from Deputy O'Shea this evening. Seems he suddenly discovered a couple of hot checks, a couple of parole violations, and at least two outstanding warrants in Colorado. And that *wasn't* a set-up. I'll have to do time, son. Is that what you want?"

"What I want is for us to quit running."

"Well, we sure as hell can't afford a lawyer. And I sure as hell don't want to be a guest of the state for the foreseeable future. So off we go." Tammi Lee had reached out to punch in the cigarette lighter. "I guess it won't help much to tell you I'm sorry," she said. "I screwed up. Again. Just when you were starting to like living around here."

He had a fierce urge to fling himself out of the car. For years he'd been fleeing with her, but now he had someone to fight for. Michelle. And his own innocence. But he knew he had to stick with his mom. Tammi Lee Gilmer would never survive without him.

Michelle would.

"At least let me stop and say good-bye to her," he'd said.

Tammi Lee grabbed his arm. "This is serious, son. It's

the real world. People like us can't take a risk like that. We set foot on that property, and we're toast."

Sam knew what she wanted him to say. *It's okay, Mama. We'll find someplace else. Something will work out for us.* . . . That's what he always said to her, every time they left a town on the lam. Well, not this time. This time, he wasn't going to tell her everything was okay.

The full moon rode high in the cold November night, and he could see Blue Rock Ranch on the way out of town, a snug compound in the distance, lights twinkling from the windows, a twist of smoke coming from the chimney of the main house.

'Bye, Michelle.

Knowing her had taught him something medical school never could—that the human heart could sing. He had vowed that night to come back to her once he and Tammi Lee settled down somewhere. But there was no time to call the next day, or the day after that, and when he finally scrounged up a handful of change to call from that pay phone in Oklahoma City, he was too late.

"I left Blue Rock the day after you disappeared," she said softly, after her long silence. "My father wasn't terribly understanding about my pregnancy."

Now, that didn't surprise him. Gavin Slade was a man devoted to his own image. The perfect acting career, perfect stock to parade at rodeos, perfect daughter . . . until she had turned out to be human and flawed. After that, she couldn't be part of his image. He had excised her swiftly and cleanly from his life.

"I wish I'd known that," he said quietly.

She sipped her water, a droplet gleaming on her lower lip. Sam tried not to stare. "There's probably a gloat factor involved in my coming back, too," he admitted. "Maybe

on some level I wanted to say 'screw you' to guys like—"
He broke off, catching himself.

"Guys like my father."

"Yeah, okay."

"He should have told me you were living here. But I can't seem to get all worked up over old business like that. His illness makes everything else seem so petty." Michelle set down her water glass with a nervous rattle of ice. "So tell me how you did it," she said. "Tell me how you became a doctor."

"Rodeo."

"What do you mean?"

"I used rodeo money to put myself through school."

"You're kidding."

"No, ma'am." He took a bite of his steak. "I passed my G.E.D. and got into a combined degree program, so I could get my bachelor's and M.D. in six years. It was a pain in the butt, living on the road, sleeping in a horse trailer most nights. I lived on autopilot for a lot of years. Didn't look left or right, didn't let myself falter. I stayed focused on that one and only goal—to get through school and residency, and I didn't let up until I made it." He picked up a breadstick, snapped it in half. "Sometimes I wonder what I missed in those years." A shadowy wave washed over him. "The birth of my son, for one thing." He took one look at her face and said, "Aw, shit. I didn't mean to—"

"I want to know the rest. What about your mother?"

"She's okay. On the wagon, living over on Aspen Street." It sounded a hell of a lot simpler than it had been. With Sam pushing, sometimes bullying her into rehab, she'd fought every inch of the way. But each time she stumbled, he picked her up, checked her back in to rehab or sent her to yet another AA meeting. Sometimes he had to be harsh with her, because sometimes that was the only thing that worked. The experience had given him an edge of ruthlessness he didn't particularly like.

Finally, after years of battling Tammi Lee's addiction, sobriety stuck. She had been sober for five years.

"Really? That's great, Sam."

"She works at LaNelle's Quilt Shoppe in town." Ah, Christ, he thought. He was going to have to tell Tammi Lee about Cody. He had no idea how she'd take it. She was sober, but she'd always be fragile. You never knew what might set her off. "So what about you? I'll bet you've got paintings hanging in the Met."

She stared down at her salad plate. "Maybe the *rest room* of the Met. I work for an ad agency."

"Functional art, then." He immediately wished he could reel his words back in.

She laughed, but the sound was brittle and forced. "Oh, yeah. Pictures of scrubbing bubbles and industrial extrusions."

He felt a sinking regret. She had been so vibrant, so damned talented that people caught their breath when they saw her paintings. She had loved art the way most folks loved food or air. "So is painting a hobby for you now, or—"

"I don't paint, Sam." She stabbed her fork at her salad. "I never had the time. I was busy with Cody."

Shit.

"You should have found me," he said, an edge in his voice. "Should have made me help."

"Oh, right. In between roping championships? Clinical rotations? Trips to Mexico?"

"I want those years back," he said brusquely. "All those years I didn't know I had a son."

"You weren't there. I couldn't find you."

"How hard did you look, Michelle? It wasn't like I was in hiding."

"Neither was I," she snapped.

"But I wasn't keeping anything from you, god-dammit."

"If I'd tracked you down, would it have mattered? Would you have given up rodeo and medical school for us?"

"Why would I have to choose? We could have done it all, Michelle."

"You're dreaming. I tried doing it all, and it's too hard."

He thought of the drawings and paintings she'd turned her back on. Was it because her passion was gone, or because she just didn't have time? "Okay, so I missed my son's childhood. We can't get back the years we lost. But maybe we can go on from here."

Even as he spoke, he wondered why he thought he could succeed with Michelle, who was infinitely more complicated, more demanding, more challenging than any woman he'd known.

"I don't understand."

"Damn it, Michelle, I'm not going to apologize for my goddamned life. You got the kid, I got the career. Which one of us should be gloating?"

She winced. "Sam. Please."

He reminded himself that her son had been injured while in his care, and that she'd been in Missoula all day with a transplant team questioning her, poking at her. "What say we change the subject?"

She relaxed against the back of the red Naugahyde booth. "Think we have anything in common after all these years?"

A son. A boy I never knew. He forced himself not to say it. "Keep talking, and we'll see."

The tension eased up a little. Never in a million years did Sam think he'd be here, with her. Watching her pick at her meal, he wondered what she thought about, what she wished for, these days. When he'd first come back to Crystal City he figured he might see her now and again when she visited Gavin. But local gossip had put that expectation to rest. Everyone in town knew Gavin Slade and his daughter were estranged. But no one knew the reason.

"So where do we start?" he murmured.

She set down her fork. "You mean, telling Cody about us?"

He wasn't sure what he meant. But he nodded, because it made sense. "Yeah. Do you want to tell him yourself or together or what?"

"Um, I guess I thought I'd do it myself. I'm not used to consulting with anyone on decisions that have to do with Cody."

"Whose fault is that?"

"Oh, Sam. I'm not trying to hurt you. I'm trying to be realistic here. I raised Cody alone. I made some good choices and some bad ones for him, just like any parent. I never expected to have to deal with *this*."

"You say *this* like it's a case of VD or something."

"That's not what I mean. Damn it, Sam. You jump on everything I say. Just like—" She shook her head in bewilderment. "Just like Cody does."

"How do you think he'll take the news?"

"After today?" There it was again, that soft smile that drove him crazy, reaching across the years to remind him of how well he used to know her. "He'll be amazed."

"Yeah?"

"He's a complicated kid. Used to be a pretty great

kid, actually. You'd never know it to look at him now, but this is a boy who used to bring me the paper in bed every morning. He'd sit in my lap and fiddle with my hair while I read him the funny pages."

Sam closed his eyes. And he saw the picture so clearly it nearly choked him. *Why couldn't I be there? Goddammit, why couldn't I be in the picture?* He felt a jolt of anger—heated, irrational.

"Anyway, he's not so warm and fuzzy anymore," Michelle said.

Sam opened his eyes. "Hell, I noticed."

"Some days I don't even think I know him. But I believe he'll be . . . glad to learn you're his father."

"Glad. What do you mean by glad?"

"Just . . . glad. Wouldn't you, if you finally met *your* father?"

"Assuming my mother knew for sure who he was. But yeah. Maybe I'd be glad." He cleared his throat. "Once we—once you tell him, what do you think about asking him if he'd like to stay with me for a while?"

She reared back in her seat. *"What?"*

"You heard me, Michelle."

Her hand closed into a fist. She seemed to grow in stature, a lioness defending her cub. "Out of the question."

"Why?"

"We didn't come back here for good. We live in Seattle."

"You said yourself he was giving you a rough time—"

"That doesn't mean I'm willing to give him up. He's not a dog you take back to the pound because he turned out to be a pain in the neck. Jesus, Sam, what can you be thinking?"

"That I have a son you never bothered to tell me about. I want to find out what he's like, what his plans are for college." He hesitated. "I intend to contribute to that and everything else."

She pressed her palms on the table. How clean her hands and fingernails were. They used to always be smeared and spattered with paint. He remembered that about her, remembered her paint-smudged hand touching his cheek, his chest, lower . . . *Damn*.

"Child-support payments? I don't expect it, Sam. And I certainly don't need it."

"Too bad. I intend to contribute anyway."

She stared off into space. "That's the kind of father I had. The one with the checkbook."

He glared at her, but the truth echoed through him. He wasn't sure Cody was something he wanted or needed or was ready for right now, but one thing was certain—if he wanted a place in the boy's heart, in his life, he'd have to earn it. And he sure as hell couldn't do that in a few weeks.

Tuesday

Tuesday

Chapter 14

When the phone rang, Michelle jerked herself out of the restless half sleep that had tormented her all night. Fumbling for the receiver by the bed, she felt a swift revival of every fear and nightmare that had plagued her since leaving her injured son in the hospital.

She clutched the receiver with both hands. "Yes?"

"Mom?"

"Cody!" Her heart shot straight to her throat. "What's the matter? Are you all right? Did something—"

"Hey, Mom, slow down. I'm okay. Sam said I should call and let you know."

Her chest sagged like a deflating balloon. She felt as if she had been holding her breath, bracing herself, for hours. "Wow, Cody. It's good to hear your voice."

"Sam says I'll be discharged today. No sign of concussion."

She glanced at the clock: 6:45 A.M. For all his teenage bravado, Cody probably hadn't had a great night, either.

"I'll come right away." She sat up against the headboard.

"Okay. Sam wants to talk to you for a minute. See you, Mom."

During the pause while she waited for Sam, she let her mouth form a tremulous smile of relief. Nothing, absolutely nothing in the entire universe matched the terror of a mother's fear for her child. When the fear was alleviated, it left in its wake a powerful euphoria, almost a giddiness.

"Hi, Michelle." Sam's voice raised the giddiness to a windstorm in her chest.

Get a grip, she told herself. This is Cody's doctor. *Doctor.*

"Thanks for letting him call. I earned another four hundred new gray hairs last night."

"So wear a hat."

Not even a smart remark could dim her mood. "As soon as I let my dad know what's going on, I'll be there."

A scant ten minutes later, Michelle had put on wool leggings and an oversize Irish sweater, and she was considering the array of hats on the hall tree. She knew she should take the time to call Brad and fill him in on all the drama, not to mention letting him know how the appointment in Missoula had gone.

But she couldn't phone him yet. It was too early in the morning, and Cody was waiting.

There was another reason she was reluctant to phone Brad, but she refused to ponder it right now. Feeling guilty was just something she had learned to do—must be a mother thing. Or a woman thing.

She snatched a heather wool cap from the hall tree, jammed on her boots, and trudged outside. Faint dawn veined the mountaintops in the east, drawing a stark, fiery line over the highest peaks and sending shadows of pink down the ridges and valleys. Snow had dusted the area in the night, and it was cold enough to squeak beneath her boots as she walked across the compound to the main house. Steam wafted gently from the pool on the patio.

A single light burned in the kitchen, sending a fan of gold across the new-fallen snow in the yard. Before mounting the steps to the front porch, she stopped, spying her father inside.

He stood at the counter with the robe half open as he did something with the dialysis apparatus he'd been so reluctant to discuss. It was a private moment, and she couldn't intrude; she knew she mustn't. She took a step back. Gavin turned his head slightly, and she saw him in profile.

Just for a second or two he fell still, bringing his hand to his forehead and leaning the other hand on the counter.

Her throat constricted as she forced her gaze away. For the first time since learning of his illness, she felt the thudding reality of the disease, and it was strange to feel the truth while standing out in the cold fire of dawn, looking in at a scene so painful and private that she nearly choked on her own breath.

Her father was sick, dying, desperately in need of the operation. Urgency pumped through her like adrenaline. She wanted to have the surgery *now*, not next week. Dear God, if she could pluck out the organ with her own hand and give it to him right this moment, she'd do it.

Hurrying back to the guesthouse, she scribbled a note

of explanation to her father and left it at the front door. On the porch she hesitated. Maybe she should go in, say good morning, ask him if he needed anything. What if he wanted Michelle, her company, the comfort she could offer?

But she couldn't go do it. Couldn't go in there, intrude. Couldn't be the daughter he needed. They were strangers in too many ways.

As she drove into town, she grabbed the cell phone and punched in the renal specialist's number. The doctor's answering service asked if there was an emergency. When she admitted there was not, she was advised to call during regular office hours.

"I need to speak to her now," she said.

"Ma'am, I'd be happy to take your number—"

"My father is sick now, not during office hours."

"The emergency number is—"

"I know the emergency number." She dragged in a long breath. "What about Donna Roberts, the transplant nurse. Is she in?"

"She's on duty at nine o'clock."

"Temple, then. Damn it, is he taking calls?"

"I'll forward the call, ma'am."

Simple as that. Temple, the psychologist, knew people didn't get neurotic on a schedule.

"This is Dr. Temple." He sounded crisp and alert, considering the hour.

"It's Michelle Turner, remember?"

"Of course. What can I do for you?"

The words came out in a rush. "Look, I want the transplant to happen sooner. I'm not willing to work around the surgeon's ski trip or whatever's holding it up. This morning my father—I saw—" She broke off, picturing Willard Temple at a Corian breakfast counter in his suburban tract mansion, drinking coffee and looking out over the golf course that backed up to his yard.

"Anyway, I can't stand seeing him like this. Why can't I do the rest of the tests today and the surgery tomorrow?"

A pause. An ominous, doctorlike pause. "Actually, Ms. Turner, I was going to recommend that your surgery be postponed until you and your father could go through some more counseling about the procedure."

A silent scream echoed through Michelle. Her knuckles whitened as she gripped the receiver. "Um, wait a minute. Run that by me again?"

"I don't have your records in front of me at the moment, but there's some concern that there are issues that need to be explored and resolved before we proceed."

Devastation and rage had a taste, she realized. They tasted rusty and bitter, like blood.

"Just a goddamned minute." She tried not to shout, but it wasn't working. She didn't care if her voice blasted him out of his brick McMansion onto his ass in the snow. "After all these weeks of testing, after meeting all those difficult physical criteria, you're telling me we have 'issues'?"

"Ms. Turner, your relationship with your father is unusual. You've spent very little time together—"

"What the hell do you want from me?" she raged. "Do you want me to have some big confrontation with him? Do you want me to accuse him of never being a daddy to me, for chrissakes? Should I accuse him of not seeing me as a daughter, but a donor? Not wanting anything from me except to harvest a few more years? Are those the sort of fucking 'issues' you're getting at?"

His next silence was so long she started to get embarrassed.

"Very impressive, Ms. Turner."

"I'm trying to impress you," she forced out through her teeth. "I'm trying to impress you with the fact that we've waited too long already. I want the surgery now—"

"There is nothing simple about this surgery. It's not a rare procedure, but it's a serious one."

"You're damned right it is. Because—" She shut her mouth, realizing that she was about to threaten Willard T. Temple with death. Not a wise way to dazzle him with her sanity. "Listen. I'm calm now, Doctor. But I don't want any further delays."

As she turned off the phone, she checked the speedometer. Her speed had climbed way out of control. Easing her tense foot off the accelerator, she tried to force the rest of her to slow down, too. It was hard, though. She felt as if she was running from one crisis to another.

Natalie, her best friend, often told her the benefits of slowing down, of being "in the moment." Easy for Natalie to say. She could live "in the moment" as much as she pleased. She flitted from one day to the next with nary a care in the world. She was Michelle's polar opposite, yet they had been best friends for years.

"Okay, Nat. I'm trying to be in the moment." Her breath fogged the air of the still-cold Range Rover. "I'm going to pick up Cody. I've got nothing else going on today, so I can bring him home and make him soup and mother him all day long. I'll see if Sam can figure out a way to get the transplant done sooner. How does that sound?"

Like she was losing it, talking to herself while driving along the highway. But somehow, taking the day step by step calmed her. By the time she walked into the hospital, she had most of her sanity back.

She stopped at the desk, manned this morning by a

different clerk. "I'm Cody Turner's mother. He's being discharged today."

The clerk tamped a stack of file folders together and set them in a metal tray on the counter. "So he is. I think he's getting dressed now. Here are a few forms for you to sign."

"I'd like to see the bill, please."

The clerk opened a folder and handed her a pen, then clicked at a keyboard. A long sheet drifted out of the printer. She studied the itemized bill and pointed to a line. "Does this mean the doctor waived his fee?"

The clerk nodded. "Appears so."

For some reason, this made her mad. She turned the page, spotting the financial liability sheet. Another unwelcome bit of charity leaped out at her.

"It says here the balance has been paid in full."

"That's right, ma'am."

"By Gavin Slade."

"I understand he's the boy's grandfather." The clerk smiled with the dreamy admiration Michelle remembered from Gavin's fans years ago. "Must be something, having him for a father."

She scrawled her signature beside all the Xs. "Oh, it's something, all right." Be in the moment, she reminded herself. She would confront Gavin about the bill later. And Sam waiving his fee. Damn them both. She had a good job with benefits. She didn't need either of them to come blasting into her life, taking over.

"Morning, Mrs. Turner." Nurse O'Brien looked crisp and pretty in pink slacks and tunic, a cardigan draped over her shoulders. "Your son's looking good."

Michelle summoned a smile. "I didn't have a chance to thank you yesterday. I appreciate everything you and Sam did for Cody."

"You're more than welcome."

She didn't seem to be in a hurry to go anywhere. To make conversation, Michelle asked, "Have you worked with Sam long?"

She hesitated, giving Michelle the strangest look. The desk clerk stopped typing, and from the corner of her eye Michelle saw her lean forward. "Nearly five years, since he came on at County," Alice O'Brien said.

Michelle sensed there was a lot more the nurse could tell her about those five years, but not now. Hiking her handbag strap securely on her shoulder, she hurried down the hallway. The door to Cody's room stood slightly ajar. She knocked. "Cody? It's Mom."

"Yeah, I'm ready."

She was unprepared for the sight of him. The pony-tail was gone. A thick white bandage covered the stitches. There was an actual, recognizable style to his hair. She remembered the way it used to grow when he was tiny, in gorgeous swirly waves as if his head had been licked all over by a friendly golden retriever.

He looked at her and his cheeks colored up, and all she could think was *thank God*. The pallor was gone. He actually had blood flowing to his face. A good sign.

And even though she felt like crying, she forced her mouth into a momlike smile.

"Love the haircut, son."

"Some guy came in at the crack of dawn and said he'd just even it out, and look what he did."

"It's fine, Cody. Really."

"It sucks."

It was creeping back over him, she saw. The attitude. After an injury or a bad sickness, a kid usually had a period of perfect sweetness. Cody had been that way yesterday while Sam was stitching him up. He'd been that way on the phone with her. But now things were getting back to normal.

Did he do that on purpose? she wondered.

He held up a white plastic bag with MERIDIAN COUNTY HOSPITAL printed on the side. "Here's all my stuff. Can we go now?"

"I have to see Sam first," she said, her mouth tasting the name, tasting wonder. "I've got some questions for him."

Cody handed her a pink slip. "He already gave me this prescription."

"Watch two hours of MTV and call me in the morning," said a voice from the doorway.

Michelle turned, and there he was, leaning with one shoulder propped against the doorframe. Sam McPhee in scrubs. Yesterday she'd been too worried about Cody to appreciate the sight. It was so different from the way she remembered him, the way she'd always imagined him.

This was the man who wanted to barge his way into Cody's life, she reminded herself.

"Take that prescription for the pain." Sam came into the room. The photo ID tag hanging from his pocket—not to mention the stethoscope and drug-company pocket protector—gave him an air of authority that made her feel strange. "Use as directed, and he should be all right." He propped some films in a lighted display box on the wall. "He checked out fine this morning." With a pencil, he pointed out some areas that reminded her of Rorschach figures, symmetrical paint blobs that shrinks used to see how the mind works.

"This one's from yesterday, and here it is this morning. Head trauma was minimal."

For some reason, she felt like crying. She studied the film. Did it show where the sweetness was hiding? Did it tell you why Cody was so hateful all the time? She bit her tongue against asking.

Sam grinned at Cody. "You've got a thick skull, kid."

"You've got a lame barber," Cody grumbled.

"Hazlett? We're lucky we've got someone who makes house calls."

Cody shuffled toward the door, his jeans dragging at the heels. "I'll be in the car, Mom."

"All right." She waited, biting down on her lower lip, because she knew what she wanted him to do, but she didn't want to tell him to do it, because it wouldn't be the same. *Turn around, you little shit. Turn around and tell Dr. McPhee thank you.*

He didn't. She was not surprised. She didn't think Sam was, either. After only a couple of days, Sam knew good and well that Cody was a surly kid, dancing on the edge, too cool for his oversize jeans.

"Anything else I should know?" she asked.

"The usual. Take it easy for the next couple of days. Stitches come out on Friday or Saturday."

She nodded, looking down at her hands. She was suddenly and unpleasantly conscious that she'd barely slept all night, and here she was unshowered, no makeup, in clothes she threw on in five minutes.

"You waived your fee," she blurted out.

"The kid was in my care when he got kicked in the head. You've got a dandy lawsuit here if you care to pursue it."

Oh, that would be fun, thought Michelle. She could see the tabloids now. *Celeb Mom Sues Dad for Injury to Love Child.* "Don't even think about a lawsuit, Sam."

"I wish everyone had that attitude."

"I have another question."

"Shoot."

"It's about Gavin and the transplant." Her insides twisted into knots. "Um, there might be a glitch."

"A glitch?"

"A postponement."

His face didn't change, but something about the quality of the light in his eyes did.

"Is Gavin having trouble?"

She shifted from foot to foot. The room felt overly warm. "Well, not specifically. It's just that . . . I got up this morning and saw . . . I realized this has gone on too long already, the stuff with the dialysis and all the meds. So I spoke with Dr. Temple, the psychologist from the transplant team. I told him that every single moment of waiting is cruelty." She took a deep breath, feeling tears of exhaustion and frustration pressing to get out. She willed them away. "And the son of a bitch said he's not sure we're ready."

"Ready. You mean they need to order more tests, or—"

"No, the renal angiogram's the only thing left. He's playing head games, Sam. He doesn't think Gavin and I are ready *psychologically*."

"And you think you are?"

"I know I am, goddammit. My life has stopped, and nothing can start again until this is done. And he wants me to determine whether I'm acting out of guilt or loyalty or God-knows-what? How can that matter, Sam?"

He was quiet for a long time. Too long. She was starting to think it was a doctor thing. A conspiracy. Torture the patient until she's over the edge, then collect your fee.

Finally he said, "I'll offer a personal reference."

The bones in her legs turned to water. "Oh, Sam. Would you? Please?"

"I'll do what I can. I've met Maggie Kehr. I could

give her a call." Her business card said "Dr. Margaret Kehr," but Sam called her Maggie. "She's the best," he added.

"That's good to hear." *So what's this about you and Maggie?*

"Anyway, I'm sure she told you how complicated this procedure is. It's got to be orchestrated down to the last second. Everything's got to come together at the right moment. The scheduling can be a nightmare."

"I'm trying to be patient. But it's so damned hard."

"A few more days aren't going to matter, not with Gavin. Like I told you before, he's in great shape. That's not likely to change."

Michelle caught herself putting her hands on her hips. No, not on her hips. At the back of her waist, in the vicinity of the kidneys. She had been doing that a lot lately.

"All right," she said, suddenly self-conscious. "I'll take the reference. Just tell them I'm not a psycho trying to earn cosmic brownie points by giving my dad a kidney."

His eyes twinkled. "I can do that."

"Thanks."

"And Michelle, I meant what I said last night. About Cody."

He couldn't have planned his stealth attack better. He'd waived his fee, offered to intervene on her behalf with the transplant team—and now this. "Are you blackmailing me?" she asked. "A personal reference if I say it's okay for you to steal my son?"

"I don't aim to steal a damned thing from you, Michelle. Do you think it'll damage him to hear the truth? That knowing who I am could harm him?"

She slumped against the doorframe. "I don't know

what I think. I haven't even had my first cup of coffee yet."

Eerily lit by the glow from the light boxes behind the films, he was both strange and painfully familiar to her. The white of the light accentuated his features—the fine nose and high cheekbones and Val Kilmer mouth she remembered from so long ago. Yet she also saw the lost years imprinted on his brow, the maturity put there by Lord-knew-what, and somehow he looked totally alone.

"Sam, I'm going to tell him."

"When?" His response was instantaneous, as if it had been balanced on the tip of his tongue during the entire conversation.

She made herself hide the fear. "I'll do it today."

"How do you think he'll take it?"

Lord, but she wanted to touch him, right now. Take his hand and give it a squeeze. Because for the first time, she finally realized that he was scared, too. Knowing the vulnerability that lay at the heart of this mysterious, familiar man made him so much more to her than a memory.

"I couldn't say, Sam. Really. Cody is . . . unpredictable lately. I never know if something's going to please him, annoy him, anger him."

"Doesn't he still ask?"

Michelle felt as if she was balanced on the blade of a knife. Did it matter what she told this man? Sam was not in their lives now. But . . . how could she lie? What would it serve?

"He used to every once in a while after he started school." Before that he had no idea a two-parent family was the norm.

"And . . . ?" Sam held himself stiffly. She could see the taut cords in his neck and part of her exulted in his suffering, because she had struggled, too, raising her son alone. But another, softer part of her still wanted to touch him.

"I said you were someone I met when I was too young to make good decisions. I told him you were a cowboy, following the PRCA. I explained that I never heard from you again after a brief . . . affair." She almost said love affair.

A muscle tensed in his jaw. "Made me out to be a real prince, did you?"

"There was no point in telling him more. It was dangerous because of the press. Because I'll always be Gavin's daughter. I didn't want them writing things . . . about us, about Cody. If I'd told him your name, given him details, some snoopy reporter would have found out. That's not fair to a kid."

She wished Sam would say something, but he just kept looking at her, and suddenly she was remembering how it used to be between them. His silences, her ramblings. How he'd pretend to be mad at little things, like when she wore his chambray work shirts, but she could tell he was secretly pleased. How those shirts smelled exactly like him.

She had taken one with her the day she'd left Blue Rock Ranch in disgrace. When she was pregnant, she used to take it out and hold it wadded up against her chest, letting the texture of soft faded cotton soothe her skin as she inhaled the scent of him. She had never laundered that shirt, because she was terrified the smell would wear off and it would just be a shirt. When that happened, she told herself, Sam would be gone from her life, finally and irrevocably.

Something very unexpected happened with that old blue shirt. She might tell him about it some time, but not now.

"All Cody knows about the past," she said, "is that I was a statistic, an unwed mother who had to grow up too fast." A shadow crossed his face, and she hurried on. "I didn't tell him in those words. I'd never make Cody feel guilty simply for being born. He is the greatest blessing in my life." There was a little hitch in her throat, because that part was true. "I would lie down and die for that child, and he knows it. I've loved him more than I ever thought possible. I've given him the best life I could. Kept him out of the camera's eye and kept him in school. And . . . that's about it." She was running out of steam, and the thought teased a wry smile from her.

His beeper went off, startling her. He checked the number. "We'll talk later. I'll see Cody later in the week about the stitches."

"All right."

As he walked away, long tails of his surgical coat belling out behind him like a cape, she thought about the task ahead, and she shivered. Not with cold, but with fear. Some small, icebound part of her lived in terror that Cody—her angry, beautiful, troubled boy—would leave her if he had a place to run.

Chapter 15

Sam and his partner, Karl, each spent one day a week at the reservation about twenty miles from Crystal City. They served as medical advisors for the Confederated Salish-Kootenai tribes. There, in a trailer adjacent to the tribal elementary school, he practiced the type of medicine he was best at—direct, hands-on care. The doctoring was frustrating, often sad, sometimes infuriating, and every once in a while, rewarding.

For his troubles, he received a minuscule stipend from the BIA and, if circumstances permitted, an hour of athletic, no-strings-attached sex with a woman named Candy who lived at the north end of the settlement in a Pan-Abode cabin.

Today at the free clinic he'd done a four-month well-baby checkup and booster shots on a perfect baby boy. Moments later he'd seen a diabetic seventy-year-old who wouldn't stop drinking. He had delivered the usual warnings and produced the usual pamphlets and brochures, he'd written a prescription and sent the old guy, who moved with a curious dignity, on his way. If the man lasted the winter, it'd be a miracle.

He treated a shame-faced teenage girl for chlamydia, and extracted a pinto bean from the nostril of an inquisitive three-year-old. He'd seen Linda Wolf, not for the first time and certainly not for the last. She claimed to have a problem with clumsiness. Sam could tell she was too weary and in too much pain to work hard making up a lie. She'd mumbled vaguely that she'd fallen; then she'd wept silently as Sam taped her up and prescribed something for the pain. It was torn elbow cartilage this time, but over the years he had treated the funny, caustic, and ultimately pathetic woman for cracked ribs, lacerations, a detached retina, countless contusions.

When he questioned her, she always gave her usual reply. "I'm a big girl, Dr. McPhee. I know what I'm doing."

And there it ended. Her husband would abuse her until he stepped over the line and committed murder, or until she wised up and left him.

Each time he saw Linda, Sam did everything short of kidnapping the woman to convince her to leave her husband. He talked to Social Services, urged the tribal police to pick up the scumbag on another charge—running a red light, illegal waste disposal, expired tags. But Randy Wolf was, oddly enough, a model citizen, working in the timber industry. His only crimes were against Linda, and she refused to press charges. Once, a few years back, Sam had confronted him. And Randy had gone home and beaten the crap out of his wife.

At the end of the day, Sam parked at the back of a cabin north of the village. Candy opened the door, letting out a herd of cats as Sam stepped inside. She wore a smile and a hand-painted silk kimono. "Hey, Doc," she said. "Long time no see."

He grinned, nodding his thanks as she handed him a cold beer. "Ditto," he said, taking a swig and then setting down the bottle. He kissed her hard, walking her back to the bedroom without lifting his mouth from hers. In a matter of minutes they were naked, straining together, twisting the bedclothes every which way. He liked her softness, the beer-and-perfume taste of her, and the way she used her hands and mouth.

But afterward, he never wanted to stay for long. He got dressed in a hurry, handed Candy her kimono, and went out to his truck. Wrapped in a wool coat, she stood watching him, her face thoughtful. "You're in a hurry today, Doc."

"Uh-huh. I've been busy."

"You want to stay for supper? I got a pot of beans on."

"Not tonight, Sugar-Candy. I'd best be going."

"You take care now," she said, shivering as he got into his truck. Her cats darted in from the woods, swirling around her ankles as she stood watching him.

Sam waved and pulled away, vaguely disgusted with himself for being able to dismiss her so casually, vaguely annoyed at her for letting him. He came away from the encounter with a hollow sense of futility. Sam knew he was deliberately shying away from commitment, even though a part of him ached for it. He snapped on the radio for the drive home. He thought about the four-month-old. Even now he could feel the creamy texture of the baby's skin, the downy fluff of his black hair. He could picture the crooked toothless wet grin when the baby focused on his face.

His gloved hands tightened convulsively on the steering wheel. What had Cody been like as a baby?

Just start where you are, common sense told him.

Start with an angry teen who was probably more at risk than his mother dared to believe. Start with a kid who was well past the age of giving a rat's ass who his father was. Start with a kid Sam knew he'd have to work at liking.

Christ. What sort of father had to work to like his own kid?

Sam stopped his truck in front of the yellow-trimmed bungalow at the edge of town. Late-afternoon sunlight spilled across the ripples of snow in the small yard. He knew she'd be waiting for him inside. She always was on Tuesday afternoons, her half day off. Ever since he'd moved to Crystal City, he'd saved Tuesdays for her.

He sat at the steering wheel, unloading the invisible burdens, mentally leaving all the baggage from the long, trying day inside the truck. Then he slammed the door behind him and walked across the yard to the front porch.

He knocked lightly and let himself in. The familiar smells of vanilla-scented candles and cigarette smoke greeted him.

"Hey, Mama," he said, stomping the snow from his boots onto the doormat.

"Hiya, son." Tammi Lee Gilmer tucked a bookmark into the paperback novel in her lap. Late in life, she had discovered something she enjoyed almost as much as she used to enjoy drinking and partying. She read voraciously: detective novels, romance novels, thrillers, memoirs, and her beloved *National Enquirer* and *Country Billboard*. Sam had no memory of books among their possessions. It was as if Tammi Lee was making up for lost time.

She got up from her lounger and crossed the room,

giving him a brief hug and a kiss on the cheek. Her scent of cigarettes and Charlie perfume clung to the sweater she wore. She was a thin, angular woman whose body had miraculously survived years of self-abuse. Though attractive in an old-fashioned Patsy Cline way, her face bore a delicate webbing of lines and creases, a busy road map of her past.

"You doing all right, Mama?" Sam asked her.

"Sure." She went to the kitchen and poured two cups of coffee, handing him one. "Just made it fresh."

"Thanks." He had a seat at the table as she rummaged in the refrigerator for something to feed him. Though he wasn't hungry, he knew better than to stop her.

This was the woman who had raised him in a beat-up Plymouth Valiant, who had parked him in a playpen while her band laid down the tracks of her one whiskey-voiced hit, who had taught him to buy cigarettes from a machine before he was old enough to count, who had used him to wrest suspended sentences from disapproving judges, who had made him leave the only girl he'd ever loved. She had taken from him any chance of a normal upbringing.

Yet when Sam looked at his mother, he felt only one emotion, a feeling that radiated out from the middle of him and reverberated through his soul. And that emotion was love.

Because in the middle of all the travels, the running, the ducking, the hiding, the arrests, the arraignments, the shouting and the pain when he'd grown old enough to force her into treatment, she had loved him with all that was in her.

Sometimes that wasn't much. Sometimes looking for love from her was like going to the auto-parts store for milk. But during her brighter periods, she'd managed to give him enough to get by on. She used to touch his cheek, tell him she was sorry for missing a parent-teacher conference or forgetting to buy groceries or running out of money when he outgrew his clothes. Without really intending to, she had taught him to dream.

These days, at LaNelle's shop, she listened to the local gossip and snipped fabric for curtains and quilts. It was a quiet life compared to her raucous past, but she didn't complain. She did a lot of serenity work with her AA sponsor, and it seemed to sustain her.

She set down a plate of processed cheese and crackers. "So how are things with you? How's my son the doctor?"

"I'm having an interesting week. Started off by winning a rodeo purse Saturday night."

Tammi Lee wrinkled her nose. "I don't understand why you keep on with that, hon. You're going to hurt yourself."

"Going to? Mama, I've hurt myself in so many places, there's nothing left to hurt." He spread his arms. "Rodeo's my sport."

"Doctors are supposed to be into golf and skiing."

He laughed. "Now, where did you read that?"

"Some magazine I found in your office."

"I reckon I'm not that kind of doctor." With his practice, his service in a public hospital, and the indigent patients he treated, he'd never get rich.

His mind flashed on Cody. The kid's leather jacket alone was probably worth a week of malpractice insurance. Everything he wore was expensive. Was it just his age, or was he the sort of kid to whom status symbols mattered?

Tammi Lee drummed her fingers on the table. He knew she wanted a cigarette, but she tried not to smoke too much around him. As a kid, he'd probably inhaled enough secondhand smoke to choke a moose. He ate a cracker, sipped his coffee. "I ran into someone at the rodeo," he said carefully. He'd learned early to insulate his fragile mother whenever he could, but this wasn't something to hide from her.

Tammi Lee's hands fell still, and she regarded him with a sharp-edged, penetrating look. "Yeah? Who?"

"Michelle Turner, Gavin Slade's daughter."

His mother leaned back in her vinyl-covered chair and let out a low whistle. "Theda Duckworth was in the shop this morning, and she mentioned something about that. She here because Gavin's sick?"

Sam nodded. He didn't want to discuss details with his mother. In a town the size of Crystal City, Gavin's illness could hardly be kept a secret, but it wasn't Sam's place to divulge the progress and treatment of the disease.

"So . . . how'd your old girlfriend turn out?" Tammi Lee asked. She'd known Michelle only vaguely as the blond actor's spoiled daughter Sam had been seeing as a teenager. He suspected his mother knew how far the relationship had gone, but Tammi Lee had never said much. Once, he recalled, she'd tried to warn him about Michelle.

"That girl's going to be nothing but heartache for you, son," Tammi Lee had said.

He remembered the day she'd said it. She'd come home from waitressing all afternoon at the Truxtop Café. In her white polyester uniform, she'd sat in a stained easy chair and unlaced her white leather Reeboks, massaging her aching feet as Sam got ready to meet Michelle at the boathouse. He'd been in a great mood.

"You hear me, son?" Tammi Lee had repeated. "Nothing but heartache."

"Give me a break, Mama," he'd said, toweling his hair after his shower. "We have a great time together."

"You do now. But you can't let yourself forget who she is, and who you are."

Sam's patience had worn thin. "I'll see you later." He'd left her sitting in the rickety rental house, an old wood-frame dwelling on the wrong side of the tracks, with a caved-in garage attached by a shotgun corridor to the main house. It was all they could afford on Tammi Lee's tips and Sam's paycheck from the ranch.

When Sam had first returned to Crystal City to start up his practice, he'd driven past the house, finding it abandoned. The windows had been blown out, probably by kids with BB guns. The roofline sagged like the back of an ancient horse, and the siding had weathered until it was the color of the dusty, sage-choked yard. He'd battled an urge to set fire to the place and watch it burn to the ground.

"Well?" his mother prompted. "How'd she turn out?"

"She's a commercial artist in Seattle."

"I recall she was some kind of artistic prodigy."

"And . . . a single mother."

Her tweezed eyebrows lifted. "Guess she and I have something in common after all."

Sam thought about that for a moment. Like Cody, he too had rarely asked about the man who'd fathered him. "Some old guy," Tammi Lee had always replied, pulling a name out of thin air. "Some old guy, name of . . . McPhee."

Sam had made no attempt to learn more. Because when he'd grown old enough to know how to track someone down, he'd also been old enough to understand just how little it took for a man to father a child. And because, in Sam's mind, no man could equal the fantasy dad he'd created for himself.

He wondered if Cody had done that. Lacking a father in his life, had he fashioned the perfect dad out of wishes and whimsy? Had he imagined someone big and strong, someone who laughed and tossed a football to him and took him fishing? Someone who turned on the hall light at night and checked on him?

The elusive father had been a powerful figure in Sam's life, and he had been wholly imaginary. Sam tried to decide how he'd feel if he had the chance to know the actual guy.

He was bound to be disappointed.

"Michelle's son is sixteen, Mama. She was pregnant with him when she left Crystal City that winter."

Tammi held herself very still, though her pale gray eyes filled with amazement. Finally, she said, "He's your son, then."

"Yes."

"And you never knew about him?"

"No. We left town before Michelle told me."

"She never tried to contact you?"

"No." Sam didn't want to get into it with Tammi Lee. Didn't want her to feel guilty for dragging him along her rocky road. Her sobriety had been hard won. She had gone off a few times before; an emotional upset could push her unmercifully toward that next drink.

"So what do you make of all this?" she asked.

"I'm still getting used to the idea. The kid's name is Cody, he's sixteen, and pissed at the world."

"Sounds like a typical sixteen-year-old."

"When I was sixteen, I don't remember being pissed at the world."

She stared down at her lap. "You were too busy trying to hold down a job and stay in school, son. And you had to give up school when we kept moving. I'm sorry for—"

"Don't be sorry, Mama," he cut in. "You kept me from being a rebellious little shit, so I ought to thank you for it."

"So this guy's a rebellious little shit?"

"Pretty much, yeah."

"What's he think of you?"

"Michelle never told him I fathered him. But she said she'd tell him soon, maybe today. And then . . . we'll see."

"Any boy'd be proud to call you his dad," Tammi Lee said. She credited him for saving her life, dragging her kicking and screaming into rehab again and again. No matter how many times he explained it was her strength, not his, she insisted on giving him credit.

"He might want to meet you," Sam suggested, and he couldn't resist adding, "Grandma."

Tammi Lee froze for a moment. Then she stood up. "I need a cigarette." With quick, jerky movements she grabbed a pack of Virginia Slims from a cupboard and lit one, turning on the exhaust fan over the stove and leaning against the counter.

"He'll hate me." She blew out a stream of smoke.

"If he does, it won't be your fault. I told you, the kid's trouble. Michelle's dealing with it the best she can."

Tammi Lee eyed him through a thin veil of bluish smoke. "Any chance the two of you will start seeing each other again?"

Even though the possibility was as remote as the moon, Sam had been seared by it from the moment he'd seen her in the arena parking lot.

"No way," he said quickly. "She lives in Seattle, and she's . . . involved, I guess. My life is set, Mama. I don't gamble. I tried marriage once, and you know what happened. I'm not about to screw around with an old flame."

Tammi Lee nodded. "Nobody ever ends up with their childhood sweetheart. Or if they do, they wind up dead, like Romeo and Juliet."

Sam laughed. "I guess you're right, Mama."

"So what happens next?"

"I suppose, next time I see Cody, he's going to know I'm his father."

She ground out her cigarette in a fluted aluminum ashtray on the stove. "You scared, son?"

"Hell, yeah, I'm scared, Mama."

Chapter 16

It was insane, thought Michelle, mooning over Sam McPhee like a lovestruck schoolgirl. But she couldn't seem to stop herself from thinking of him, picturing his big hands, and how delicately they had handled Cody's stitches. She couldn't keep from remembering the color of his eyes or the look on his face when he was watching her from the hospital-room doorway. She had an almost-grown son, a sick father, a significant other in Seattle. She had no business speculating, even to herself, what it would be like to know Sam again.

"So you never did tell me about the foaling," she said to Cody on the ride home, as much to distract herself as to get him to talk.

"It was way cool. There was a dys—dyst—um, a difficult presentation, and the vet couldn't make it on time, so we all pitched in. Sam, me, and Edward. The mare kept getting up when she wasn't supposed to, so that was kind of bad. I had to get my hand right up inside her to bring the foal around."

"I'm getting this incredible mental picture. So you didn't gross out?"

"Nope. Like I said, it was kind of cool."

Maybe it was the blow to the head. That had to be it, Michelle thought, because no son of hers would think sticking his hand up a mare's birth canal was cool. But on the other hand, horses had once filled her life and made it beautiful. She wondered if a horse could do that for Cody.

Dooley had been four years old the summer she'd moved to Montana. A trim quarter horse with a splash of white on his forehead, he had snagged her interest when she'd seen him kicking up his heels in the paddock. Her father, eager to spoil her during the year she'd given him, had offered the gelding to her.

Everyone at Blue Rock Ranch must have thought she was a snooty city girl, with her tight buff-colored riding pants and tall English-style boots, an array of dressage ribbons and trophies spread out on her bedroom bureau.

Dooley had no patience for a dressage rider who wanted him to skip over little ivy-covered jumps and arch his neck and trot prettily around a ring. It took a lot of spills—and a lot of coaching from Sam—for her to figure that out.

They rolled up to the house and she cut the engine, turning to Cody. That haircut! She tried not to smile, looking at it, but it made her ridiculously happy to see the last of that obnoxious dual-colored ponytail hanging down his back.

"How do you feel?" she asked him. "Can I fix you something to eat?"

"I'm thrashed, Mom. I think I'll zone out for a while."

She resisted helping him out of the car. When he shrugged off his jacket and flopped down on the sofa, flipping on the TV, she resisted grabbing the afghan and tucking it around him. He used to be hers to tuck and touch and mother as much as she pleased. Now when she did it, she felt as if she was trespassing.

Okay, so tell him, she urged herself. Tell him about Sam.

But as soon as she opened her mouth to speak, he picked up the phone on the end table and punched in a long string of numbers. "Is Claudia there?" he asked. "Hey, Claudia. It's me. You won't believe what happened . . ."

Feeling like an intruder, she left the guesthouse with her coat still on, and crossed to the huge barn at the end of the main drive. It resembled the set for a sentimental movie, the sunlight on the snow, the weathered cranberry-colored structure too perfect to be real.

In the barn, she ran into Jake Dollarhide. The sight of him startled her; she never expected that he'd still be around.

"Jake? It's me, Michelle Turner. Gavin's daughter."

"Welcome back, Michelle. Good to see you." He was only a couple of years older than Michelle. His father used to be ranch foreman, an important and lucrative position on a spread the size of Blue Rock. Jake looked a lot like he did seventeen years ago. Thicker, more weather-beaten. He had the big, callused hands of an experienced horseman, the limp of a longtime cowboy, and the reserved manner of a man who felt more at home with animals than with people.

"Is there a gelding called Dooley here?" A long shot, but she had to ask him.

"Oh yeah. The old man's still one of the boss's favorites."

She didn't want Dooley to be an old man. She wanted him to be as young and quick as she remembered.

Jake led her down the middle aisle of the barn. She wondered if he remembered what happened all those years ago and what part he played, but she knew she wouldn't ask him. They stopped at one of the stalls. A long, paint-splashed chestnut head came out over the half door.

Dooley. Her best guy. She didn't ever remember loving a horse the way she had loved Dooley, and now he stood there in front of her, chewing indolently on a mouthful of alfalfa, the steam puffing gently from his damp nostrils.

Dooley.

They said horses, like elephants, never forgot. She believed that. She believed it with all her heart, because the minute she said his name aloud and hugged herself up against his long, hard skull, he whickered and blew gently into the quiet of the barn.

And Michelle, for no reason she cared to name, burst into tears. She supposed it was because this moment was the culmination of everything that had been building up inside her. In a world that had gone crazy while her back was turned, Dooley lived his life and chewed his alfalfa and stood patiently in this stall. Now he was old, and he was glad to see her.

Jake stepped back, probably embarrassed by her display. Eventually she looked up, wiped her face on her sleeve. "Sorry, Jake. This is my favorite horse in the world, and it's overwhelming to see him again."

He stared at her intently. He used to do that when they were young. It always gave her the creeps, because there was a quiet hunger in his look. "You ought to take the old man for a ride," he said, making her feel foolish for her suspicions.

Michelle knew she should protest, object, think of a bunch of reasons she shouldn't be out riding Dooley for an hour when there was so much else going on, but when she opened her mouth, the only word that came out was "Yes."

In the tack room they took down reins, a curb chain, a Twickenham bit, and a Flores saddle she remembered from years ago. Her father might be one of the Hollywood upstarts Montana loved to hate, but he was a serious upstart. Blue Rock Ranch gave every attention to the animals. The success of a rodeo stock contractor depended on the quality of his livestock. Each piece of tack and saddle was perfectly scrubbed down and oiled. She thought someone must vacuum the blankets; they were that clean.

Dooley stood patiently—she fancied willingly—in the crossties while they saddled him.

"He's fat," she said, grinning as she pulled up on the girth.

"Doesn't get much exercise. This'll be good for him."

"Is he okay, then? No lameness?"

"He's just slow. Lazy. But he'll do what you ask him to do."

She walked him out into the yard where the snow was deep and feathery light. The sunshine and sharp cold nailed her, and Dooley arched his neck in exactly the way she remembered. He knew the route to the vast, covered arena. Her leg cues were superfluous. She started him off slowly, an easy walk around the arena. As he loosened up, he naturally rolled into an easy canter, a smooth-as-wind gait that matched her own heartbeat.

Out of respect for his age, she didn't ask him to extend into a gallop. She just listened to the thud of his nimble hooves against the soft earth, the rhythmic huff of the horse's breath, and the steady creak of leather.

Like windblown leaves, bits and pieces of the past tumbled through her mind. The first time she ever rode Dooley, she'd put an English-style saddle on him and tried to coax him over jumps. He'd balked mulishly, and in the battle of wills that followed, neither horse nor rider won. Then one day Sam came along. She had been bashful and defensive when he came to the fence, wedged a foot up on the rail, and said, "You ought to try barrel racing that horse. That's what he's been drilled on."

She told him she knew how to ride, thank you very much, but he just laughed and waited her out. When she was about to quit in frustration, he gave the horse a break, then set a Western saddle on him and put him through his paces around the barrels.

From that moment on, she was hooked. To hell with prissy ribbons and plastic bouquets bordering fake fences. She gloried in the speed and agility of barrel racing— never in competition, just for the joy of it. Dooley must have been born with the pattern imprinted on his memory, because he did it perfectly, with all the heart she could wish for. A lightning gallop out of the alley, clockwise around the first barrel, counterclockwise around the second, and then finishing with a gallop so swift she felt as if part of her got left behind each time.

And always, flowing with the bits of memory, Sam was there, his loose and long frame a friendly presence at the edge of the arena.

She had thought, that summer, when Dooley and Sam filled her days and nights, that she had found a perfect happiness.

She had thought it would last forever.

Dooley wasn't stupid, he felt her mood slump, and he

took advantage, slowing his pace to a rocking-horse gait. It soothed her; she wondered if he sensed that. He sweated so much that steam rose from every inch of him, so she slowed him to a walk, letting him cool out.

"You both look great," said Gavin. He was no longer the vulnerable invalid she saw in the kitchen early that morning. Looking deceptively hardy and vigorous, he wore a sheepskin jacket and wide-brimmed hat, the tips of his ears and nose red with the cold.

How long had he been there? She'd been so absorbed in riding that she couldn't say.

"I hope you don't mind." She dismounted and led Dooley in a long oval a couple of times around the ring.

"Hell, no, I don't mind. It's good to see him getting some exercise."

"I think he remembers me."

"Wouldn't surprise me. That's one of the smartest horses I've ever had."

Things were quiet and easy between Michelle and Gavin as she put Dooley up, taking the time to grain him, curry him out, paint a bit of red disinfectant on his hock, where she had noticed a small cut. She cleaned the tack while Gavin looked on approvingly.

They checked on Cody to find that he had fallen fast asleep, so they went for a drive out to the small local air park. Gavin greeted people by name there, and showed her into the hangar where he kept his two planes—the vintage biplane, and the P-51 Mustang, his prized possession. The Mustang still had its original D day invasion stripes. It was one of the few surviving WWII planes. Most were in museums these days.

"As soon as your license is reinstated," she said, "I'm going to expect the ride of my life, Daddy."

"You're on," he promised her.

It was early twilight when they returned and walked over to the guest quarters to see Cody. He was curled up, still asleep on the sofa, the TV on but the volume down. Seizing the opportunity to do what he wouldn't let her do when he was awake, Michelle covered him with a knitted striped afghan and brushed a curl of hair off his forehead.

"He all right?" Gavin whispered as they left.

They started across to the big house. "He's doing fine."

"I can't say I'm sorry to see some of that hair disappear."

They stomped the snow off their boots, leaving them in the mudroom. Inside, they sat staring at the fire. Tadao brought cocktails—Dry Sack for her, watered-down cranberry juice for Gavin, a bowl of salt-free pretzels neither of them touched.

"I had a chat with Dr. Temple this morning." She sipped her sherry. "He said he might advise postponing the surgery."

"Yeah?"

"I told him he was full of shit, that I wanted to go ahead right now."

Gavin shook his head. "I've been living with this for a long time. Another week or so isn't going to kill me."

She stiffened against the back of the leather sofa. "I wish you wouldn't talk like that." When she looked at his face, she wanted to think that she was seeing what all daughters saw when they looked at their fathers. But the memories simply weren't there. Maybe that was what she was seeking now. If not history, then at least something dear, something precious. They didn't have that. Maybe there was still time. Would having the transplant bring a new intimacy?

It seemed a fanciful notion. A kidney was just an organ. A spare part, as Cody liked to call it. There wasn't any sort of mystical power in a kidney. And yet she kept thinking, because of what she gave him, he'd be healed.

He clearly had no inkling of her thoughts, because out of the clear blue he asked, "So what does Sam think of the boy?"

"Of Cody?" she asked stupidly.

"That would be the one." Gavin spoke with exaggerated patience and humor.

"He thinks Cody is angry and rebellious."

"So is this a phase the boy is going through, or is there a problem?"

She gazed at her father incredulously. "You really don't know, do you?"

"About raising a teenager? I don't have any experience at it, Michelle."

And she felt it again—the anger, the resentment. "It's both a phase and a problem."

"Maybe getting him together with Sam wouldn't be such a bad idea," Gavin suggested.

"Um, I haven't told Cody that Sam's his father." She swirled the ice in her tumbler. "Why didn't you ever tell me Sam moved back to Crystal City?"

"I didn't think you were interested in hearing that or anything else from me."

She sensed something more beneath his words, some judgment or evasion. She couldn't quite put her finger on it. "I could have done with a word of warning," she said.

He combed a splayed hand through his white hair. "Hell, honey, I guess I was afraid you wouldn't come if you knew Sam was here."

"I would have come anyway," she insisted. "I'm going to let Cody know about Sam this evening." Helplessly she watched the flames leaping in the grate, reflecting against the iron fireback. "I have no idea what he's going to think when I tell him."

"So how's Sam taking all this?" he asked.

"He says he wants to get to know Cody, but that's what's making me so insane. You can't know a kid in a few weeks. You have to raise a child from birth to truly know him."

"You believe that?"

"Yes."

"Then I don't know you? I can't know you?"

She gulped the rest of her drink. "We're talking about Cody."

"Fine, so talk."

"I just . . . don't understand what Sam expects. What if he wants something I can't give? Like more time with Cody?"

"Are you willing to allow that?"

"Of course not." The refusal flew from her, surprising her with its swiftness. Was she that settled in her ways? Certain that nothing unexpected could ever happen to her? Like a middle-aged matron, was she so inflexible that she couldn't imagine straying from a path she'd mapped out long ago?

"Brad and I have goals." She tried to convince herself as much as her father. "We've made commitments. We're building a life together, and I'm not about to change that just so Sam McPhee can get used to the novelty of having a son."

"Honey, believe me, it's not a novelty."

Something in the tone of his voice tugged at her, and she set down her glass. The mica lamps overhead cast radiant heat down into the gathering shadows of the room, and she couldn't help but think they resembled stage lights, showering over his broad shoulders, his magnificent hair, his face craggy with living and troubles. Was she looking at Gavin Slade the actor, or Gavin Slade the man?

"What do you mean, Daddy?"

"Knowing you've got a child somewhere in the world is like carrying a tube of nitroglycerine around. You're scared stiff all the time, scared you're going to drop it, or someone's going to jostle you and the world's going to explode."

"I'm not sure what this has to do with Sam."

"Maybe you should cut him some slack. Let him spend some time with Cody while you're here and see what happens."

"I was sort of hoping you'd spend time with Cody, too."

He wouldn't look at her. "He's not interested. What do I have in common with a sixteen-year-old kid?"

"You never know. Your airplanes?" She remembered the problem with Gavin's license and quickly changed the subject. "He likes the movies. You ought to give him a tour of the Lynwood."

"Okay, maybe I could screen an old movie or two for him."

The whole idea was, her dad should sit in there with him. But she stopped short of suggesting it.

"Always thought it'd be nice to renovate and reopen the place," he went on, surprising her. "I own the adjacent retail space, too. Seems a shame to let it all just sit there."

"It sounds like quite a project," she said. "But first things first," she said. "We'd better concentrate on getting both you guys well in this next week."

They were silent with their thoughts during dinner, perfectly prepared and served by Tadao. Eyeing the young man as she helped him clear the table, she wondered if

he was good company for her dad, if he was more than
an employee. As a teenager, Michelle had enjoyed the
folksiness of the ranch help. Though it was always clear
her father was the boss, there was a casual ease at Blue
Rock she'd never known at her mother's house in Bel Air.
At the ranch, they were like a big family. Though she had
only lived a short time at the ranch, it was the only place
she had ever really fit in. Despite being born in Southern
California, she had never quite belonged there, never quite
lived up to her mother's high style and standards. Once,
long ago, she had asked her father why he had moved
away from California, and he had said simply, "For the
breathing room." One of the few things they had in common, she thought. There might have been more if Gavin
hadn't—

She stopped herself. Vowed she would not dredge up
all bitterness, old regrets.

After dinner, Tadao gave her a covered tureen of soup
and a turkey sandwich for Cody. She thought she had done
a pretty good job playing it cool in front of her father, but
when she said good night, the last thing he said to her
nearly made her drop the soup.

"Don't put it off any longer. Tell the boy tonight,
okay?"

Chapter 17

Cody's mouth tasted rank when he woke up to find the evening news flickering in his face. He stared unseeing at the TV for a few minutes, trying to decide if his head hurt. Barely. When he held perfectly still, not stirring except to breathe, he didn't feel any pain at all.

Sam McPhee had given him some pills. The little brown bottle was on the counter. Maybe he'd take a couple tonight.

No, he told himself. Those were for Claudia. When he'd told her about his injury, her first question had been to ask what kind of pain pills the doctor had given him. She liked getting high on pills. Cody had done it with her once or twice, stealing some Darvons from Brad's sample kit. Brad was so lame, with his designer clothes and big plans, he never even noticed. Clueless, too, but that worked in Cody's favor. He could get away with a lot when Brad was around.

Last Friday, right before a school dance, he and Claudia had swallowed a couple of pills with mouthfuls of beer. The world had turned blurry and bright, and everything he said made Claudia laugh. He loved the way she laughed, shaking back her head with all those red curls and her voice going up and up with each syllable. She had a sexy laugh. He'd walked her home after the dance—his mom was a pain in the butt about not letting him drive unaccompanied at night.

On a storage bench in the darkened mudroom of Claudia's house, she had let him go almost all the way. Cody got a hard-on just thinking about those soft curves and soft lips. She had this amazing way of sucking his tongue that made him nuts. Her spicy-smelling perfume and her taste of Zima and Lifesavers got him higher than any pills could.

Inside the house, someone had flicked on a light, interrupting the magic. He knew Claudia would let him go all the way the next time. They just needed a little more privacy.

But he never got the chance. The very next day, Cody's mom had dragged him all the way out here to the middle of nowhere so he could work his butt off on some guy's ranch and get kicked in the head by a horse.

By the time his mom came in from the main house, he'd worked himself into a lousy mood. And she, of course, put on that chirpy smile of hers. "Tadao sent you soup and sandwiches. You hungry?"

He was starving after that nap. "I guess."

"Stay there. I'll bring your dinner on a tray."

"Okay."

"How's your head?"

"Hurts when I move it."

She banged around in the kitchenette for a few minutes, then walked into the den with a tray of soup in a mug, a sandwich, and a glass of milk.

"Thanks." For some reason, it annoyed him that there was a sprig of parsley floating on top of the soup and that she'd cut the sandwich into triangular halves. His mom was always doing stuff like that, trying to make a nice thing nicer.

Maybe it was because she was an artist. Once, when they'd moved to the new town house next door to Brad, Cody had taken a look at some of her old paintings and drawings. Incredible, wild stuff, tons of it, nothing like the ad layouts she did for work. He couldn't believe his own mother used to paint stuff like that. It was almost scary.

While he ate, his mom had the news on, but she didn't seem to be paying much attention. In fact, she seemed jumpy. Scared about the transplant thing, he figured. It was too gross to think about, but from the second she'd heard about her dad's sickness, she'd insisted on going through with it.

"I have to do this. I *want* to," she'd told him and Brad. "The transplant works best from a living, related donor—a blood relative."

Deep inside Cody lay the knowledge that his mom wasn't Gavin Slade's only blood relative. But when he thought about surgeons cutting him open, taking out a whole organ, for chrissakes, he couldn't even speak, much less volunteer as a donor. So he kept his mouth shut and let his mom be the martyr.

"You want seconds?" she asked.

"Nope, I'm full."

"Dessert? There's ice cream in the freezer, and a bag of cookies—"

"No *thanks*." His voice had a rude inflection, and she flinched, but he didn't care. After telling him to save her some of his pain pills, Claudia hadn't found much to talk about, and their long, awkward silence echoed in Cody's ears now.

His mom took the tray away and returned to the living room. Cody reached for the remote to turn the channel to MTV, but she intercepted him, grabbing the device and killing the power.

He glared at her, surprised and affronted. "What gives, Mom?"

"I need to talk to you about something."

"Yeah?" He was starting to feel bored already. Maybe she was feeling nervous about the surgery, and she wanted to say how much she loved him and all that shit in case something went wrong during the transplant. It was the last thing Cody wanted to discuss.

"Yes." She tucked one foot up under her in the chair and picked up a throw pillow, her right index finger fiddling with the tassels. "This is serious, Cody. I need you to pay attention."

He lifted both hands in an exaggerated shrug, even though it hurt his head. "Do I look like I'm going anywhere?"

"I, um, I need to talk to you about the man who fathered you."

Holy crap. Cody felt himself come to full alert. He forced himself to stay still on the sofa, his face expressionless and his voice bland when he said, "Yeah? You said he was just some cowboy, and you'd never seen him again."

"That's true. I mean, I thought it was true. But he's living here, Cody. In Crystal City. I had no idea where he was until I saw him Saturday night."

Oh, man. He didn't know what to do with himself, with his hands, with his eyes, with his mind. So his mouth said a lazy, "No kidding."

But his brain went into overdrive. He tried to picture the crowd at the rodeo arena. All he remembered from Saturday night was the girl named Molly Lightning. And a mass of people who looked like hicks and hillbillies.

"I wouldn't kid about this, Cody."

"So who's the guy?"

Her finger kept twirling the tassel, faster now. "It's . . . Sam. Sam McPhee."

"Whoa." The exclamation escaped him before he could stop it. His heartbeat sped up. A father. He had a father. Sam McPhee was his goddamned father.

It was too weird, knowing now, after all the years of imagining, who he was. Stranger still knowing Sam and his mom had been bonking each other as teenagers.

"Thanks a lot for never telling me, Mom."

"I didn't know how to tell you. It was a shock, seeing him so unexpectedly." She hugged the pillow up against her chest. "And really, we've been so busy, this is the first chance I've had."

Suddenly, in the place in his life where there had been a blank picture frame, a face showed up. A cowboy's face, tan and lean, some guy dressed in a plaid flannel shirt and Levi's. A guy with big hands and a screw-you attitude. A guy who made his voice go all serious while he was sewing Cody up with the same big hands he'd used to heft a wheelbarrow full of manure.

Christ. Sam McPhee. His father. There was an earthquake heaving up inside Cody. The world was rearranging itself, and he had no idea what it would look like when things settled.

"Cody?" His mother's voice was light, quavery. He

hoped like hell she wouldn't start bawling or trying to get him to talk about his feelings. "Is there anything . . . you want to say?" Her voice kept wobbling.

He wanted to say everything, and nothing. He wanted to yell at her for keeping this huge secret from him. He wanted to ask what was so goddamned wrong with him that he didn't deserve to know his father. He wanted to hide behind a wall and wait for the world to return to normal.

But most of all, he wanted to know the answer to one big burning question.

"So does he know . . . who I am?"

"Yes."

"Shit, you told him before you told me? Thanks a l—"

"I didn't tell him. He figured it out based on your age. Or, I guess it was your age. Might have been something else."

"What else?"

"You're alike in . . . subtle ways. The way you hold yourself sometimes, I suppose. Certain movements. It's hard to say." She started picking at the tassel. It was driving him crazy, the way she kept fidgeting. "But I imagine it was your age. He realized you were born just a few months after we . . . after I—"

"After he fucked you," Cody exploded.

He heard his mom draw in a breath, but he didn't look at her. Gripping the arm of the couch, he pushed himself up. Battling a wave of dizziness, he stalked down the hall to his room and slammed the door as hard as he could.

Damn it. Goddamn it to hell. *Now* what was he going to do?

Chapter 18

Oh, *that* went well, thought Michelle. With a savage tug, she jerked the stupid tassel off the stupid pillow. Then she tossed both pillow and tassel aside.

Her cheeks were on fire. Her insides—stomach, heart, throat—were all on fire.

After he fucked you.

Cody's words hung in the room. She couldn't hide from them. She couldn't make them not be true. She couldn't make them not hurt. Sure, he had much worse problems than using foul language, but the moment seemed to crystallize all their issues into a single, sharp hammer blow of a syllable.

She wanted to go to him, sit at the side of his bed, tell him she knew, she understood what a shock this must be, yet it didn't change anything between them—

But it did. It already had. She couldn't put things back the way they were.

Pulling her knees up to her chest, she stared at the blank screen of the TV, then at the wall shelves filled with old novels and knickknacks. She wondered if the knickknacks had any meaning, or if Martha Stewart had been a guest here, putting dried flowers in rusty horseshoes and making an umbrella stand out of an old cowboy boot.

Cody's furious reaction had thrown the universe out of whack for her. He'd been rebellious lately, but in a strange way it had seemed like a manageable anger, not some out-of-control dark substance that hardened, like coal into diamond, into indestructible hate.

Dry-eyed, she forced herself to assess the situation. Minimize the problem. He was in shock over finding out about Sam, but the shock would fade, and he'd be back to his old self again. She and Cody would be here only a short time. After that, there would be no need to come back.

I just stopped by to drop off a kidney and save my dad's life. Then I'm out of here.

Sam claimed he wanted to know his son, to get involved, but his involvement ended the day he skipped town seventeen years ago. The only reason she had told Cody was that it felt deceptive not to. She didn't owe Sam a thing. He didn't owe her a thing.

And really, she had no business thinking about him.

She picked up the phone and dialed Brad's number. He needed to hear this, too. Would he worry? Feel threatened?

Early on in their relationship, he had asked about Cody's father, and she'd told him exactly what she always told Cody—a youthful mistake, they'd never been in contact, she had no idea where he was.

That had all changed now.

Sam McPhee was real and rock solid. He had a career and a ranch and a business partner and the respect of a town that had once kicked him in the teeth.

He had large gentle hands and a way of watching her that brought warmth to forbidden places inside her.

She hung up the phone when Brad's answering service picked up. He'd always hated answering machines, so he paid strangers to take his messages for him. She couldn't imagine telling a stranger what had just happened. What would she say? "Tell Brad to call me, because I just told my son who his real father is, and now he hates me."

The phone rang, startling her. She grabbed it, praying it would be Brad. He'd never been the sort of guy who popped up just when she needed him, but she kept thinking he would be one day.

"Hello?"

"Michelle, it's Sam."

God. Oh, God. "I don't want to talk to you right now."

"Is this a bad time?"

"The worst." Her heart pounded. Her throat ached with the things she wanted to tell him.

"Cody's all right, isn't he?"

"Of course he's not all right—" She broke off. Sam meant the injury. "His head's fine. He had a nap, and a pretty good dinner, and he's in his room right now."

"Then why did you say he's not all right?"

She swallowed hard, and it hurt, as if something enormous was stuck halfway down. "I told him about us. I told him you're his biological father."

Silence. In the background on his end, a dog barked. The Border collie. The morning she'd gone out there, she had noticed that Sam had an unconscious, affectionate way with the dog, idly stroking her head and ears without even seeming to know he was petting her. He was probably doing that right now.

"How'd he take it?" Sam finally asked, his voice low.

"He's not a happy camper. After he said the word 'fuck' to his mother, he walked out and closed himself in his room."

"I'm coming over."

"No, Sam, you can't—"

His end of the line went dead. She couldn't stop him now. She felt helpless. Should she tell Cody that Sam was coming over? No; then he might barricade the door, or worse, run off somewhere.

She settled for straightening up the bungalow, doing the most mundane of chores. A fresh hand towel in the bathroom. A light on over the front door. Minutes dragged by, and she ran out of things to do. Restless, she took out her sketchbook and favorite pencil—a Primacarb Number One. Accustomed to bringing her work with her from the office, she never went anywhere without a sketchbook. Even though she had given up painting, she still thought in pictures, and she never knew when an idea for an ad design or concept would hit her.

Her pencil swirled and danced over the page, and she felt a tug of sensation, something she hadn't felt in a long time. Nerves, she told herself. That's what it was. And when she saw what had emerged onto the paper, she knew it was nothing more. The image she had outlined was icy cold, a vineyard everyone had seen before on a dozen wine labels. It came from her mind's eye but not from her heart. Perfect for one of their big winery accounts.

She shut the book and put it back on the table. A few minutes later, a knock sounded at the door. She went to Cody's room and said, "Sam's here."

No response. He probably had his Discman on, fitting the headphones over the dressing on his head.

Sam took his boots off at the door. He didn't smile when he greeted her. He just sort of stared, those eyes probing, seeing her in a way she didn't think anyone else ever had. Finally, he said, "You look awful."

"Thanks. I'm having a swell evening." She gestured at the fridge. "Can I get you something to drink?"

"Not right now, thanks. Where's Cody?"

"In his room." She indicated the door.

Sam didn't hesitate; that was the first thing she noticed. She had always hesitated when it came to dealing with Cody. She tended to stop, weigh the options, rehearse the scenario in her head, and proceed with caution. Sam plunged right in. Of course, he had a lot less to lose than Michelle did. Sam couldn't lose what he'd never had.

He knocked on the door and said, "Cody, it's Sam. Your mother and I want to talk to you."

Your mother and I.

Michelle had never thought she'd hear those words, not in the context of her own life. There had never been a unit known as "your mother and I." The phrase conjured up images and yearnings Michelle didn't want—a partnership, a union . . . a dream she once had.

Cody's reply put the sentimental thought into perspective: "I got nothing to say to either of you."

At this point, she generally let him be, let him chill out. But Sam didn't know Cody's implacable moods. He put his hand on the knob. "I don't recall giving you that option. Now, you can either come out here or I'll come in there. Either way, it happens in the next five seconds."

"Or what? You'll spank me?"

Sam twisted the doorknob, and Michelle was surprised it didn't come off in his hand. He looked perfectly calm as he strode into Cody's room. The bedroom was done in muted plaids and stripes, like an upscale resort hotel. Cody lay on the bed, his hands clenched into fists, his eyes full of hate as he watched Sam.

Michelle stood in the doorway and held her breath.

"I'd never hit you." Sam kept his voice soft and low, the way he always did when he was angry. That was one of the things Michelle remembered about him. The madder he got, the quieter he got. "I'd never hit anyone. But I also don't take no for an answer. So why not get up off your butt and get into the living room?"

"Maybe I don't feel like it."

A small, evil part of Michelle took pernicious delight in this exchange. In the past she had been the one on the receiving end of Cody's defiance. Finally, someone else had to hear it. Sam stood like a shield between Cody and Michelle, absorbing the boy's contempt as if it were nothing.

"So you want us to camp out in here?" He moved Cody's suitcase off the luggage bench and had a seat. "Fine with me."

Cody didn't say a word, but levered himself up from the bed, marched out of the room, and plunked himself down in an armchair in the living room. He didn't look at either Sam or Michelle. She was amazed that Sam got him to come out.

"I guess I'll start, then." Sam lowered himself to the sofa, and she did the same, folding her arms, unconsciously protecting herself.

"First of all, you've got to know this, Cody. Finding out about you is the biggest thing that's ever happened to me."

This was a man who had been a six-time national rodeo champion. A man who had saved lives, delivered babies, told people a loved one had died. And yet he could still say this was a bigger deal.

Cody stared straight ahead, stone-faced. And Lord, even now, startlingly good-looking, a fallen angel with a mended head.

"Second thing," Sam continued, "is that if you ever talk to your mother like that again, you'll be sorry you ever found me."

Cody turned to her, contempt written in hard lines around his mouth. "Great, Mom. Already running to him and telling him private stuff."

"I don't blame you for wanting to keep it private. I'd be ashamed, too, if I said stuff like that to the woman who raised me." Though Sam's voice was mild, there was an edge to his words, an edge that was sharp with warning.

Watching Cody, she could see that he sensed the sharpness, too. He was out of his league here. Sam had grown up fighting his way through the rodeo, through school, through seventeen years of battles she could only imagine. Cody's attitude might have the power to hurt her, but to a man like Sam it was nothing.

"So what are you doing here, anyway?" Cody asked.

"Same thing as you are. Trying to figure out what to do next." Sam crossed one foot over his knee. He wore flecked gray thermal socks. Bits of snow still clung to the cuffs of his jeans. "I have figured out what not to do. And that's mouth off to your mother. I won't tolerate it, Cody. Do you understand?"

Their gazes locked. From the very start, there was no question who was going to win. Within a few seconds, Cody shrugged and looked away. "Whatever."

"Your last outburst was just that," Sam said. "Your last. Believe me, I know what you're thinking. You're thinking I'm just some old guy. I have no authority over you."

"You don't," Cody pointed out.

"You know what?" Sam leaned back congenially. "You're absolutely right. I won't take you over my knee. But I can tell you this. Don't be such a little shit to the person who's put in sixteen years and nine months raising you."

Cody did his best to look bored, but she could tell he was fascinated by all this. "Why not?"

Still maintaining a relaxed pose, Sam nailed him with a stare that would wither grass, and he spoke softly, with deadly control. "Don't ask me that again."

Michelle unfolded her arms and studied them both, and in a flash, she saw an uncanny resemblance. They looked so much alike she was surprised the whole town hadn't figured it out by now.

"All right," Cody said at last, keeping his chin up despite his capitulation. "Whatever."

"Well," Michelle said, trying to dissipate the tension. "I suppose we have to decide what's going to happen next."

"You're going to finish this operation thing and then we're going back home," Cody said.

"It could happen that way," she conceded. "Is that what you want?"

"Why would I want anything else?"

"No reason, maybe," Sam said, and she was glad he spoke up, because she couldn't think of anything more to say. "But then again, maybe there is a reason."

Silence. And sadness. Sam's words filled Michelle with a huge ache. Because in her heart she knew they had both made cocoons of themselves. And somehow, it had diminished them. No strings, no connections. *Safe from love, safe from hurt.*

"So what are you talking about? You think I want you to take me to baseball games and buy me stuff and all that crap?" Cody demanded. "I'm a little old for that."

"Good. I can't stand baseball. Hate shopping." Sam drilled him again. That stare was powerful. Where did he learn to do that? Michelle wondered.

"So here's the deal," Sam continued. "If you feel okay in the morning, and it's all right with your mom, you come out to my place. See how that foal's doing. Maybe we'll talk some, maybe we won't. We'll just see."

Cody sat stiff and silent for a while. "What if I don't feel like it?"

"Then you don't come." But Michelle and Sam had both seen it. The spark in the boy's face when Sam mentioned the horse. "You stay here and . . . do whatever it is you do."

More silence. Cody was as still as a stone, but she knew a battle raged inside him. Finally, he said, "Can I go to my room now?"

Sam's face turned hard with a silent demand.

Finally, reluctantly, Cody added, "Um, please?"

Wonders never cease, thought Michelle. He asked permission.

Sam looked at her. "Michelle?"

"See you in the morning, Cody," she said. "You can let me know then if you need a ride to Sam's place."

Chapter 19

S am watched Cody leave the room, noting the studied slouch, the hands jammed in his pockets. Despite the attitude, he was still a good-looking kid, and Sam had thought so even before he'd figured out who fathered him.

He wanted to ask Michelle what Cody had been like as a baby, a toddler, a little boy, but each time he thought of all those lost years, he nearly choked on rage and frustration. Those years were gone and there was no way to get them back. But that didn't stop the hunger in him to know.

"What's going through his head right now?" he asked softly.

"In a minute, probably Marilyn Manson on his Discman. I hate his music. And I hate it that I hate his music, because I love music."

"Believe it or not, I understand what you're saying."

That coaxed a fleeting, weary smile from her. Sam knew he should go, but he didn't want to. Leaning forward, he picked up a sketchbook off the table. "May I?"

"Sure. It's work, though. I doubt you'll find it very interesting."

He'd always liked looking at her drawings. When they were young, she'd had the sort of talent that made people do a double take. They'd look, then look again, and then the low-voiced comments would start.

But when he opened the sketchbook, he didn't see the wild, emotional abstractions he'd been expecting. These were studies, mostly of inanimate objects—furniture and running shoes and grapes and shower nozzles—and a chilly, anatomical study of a winter merganser in flight. Each was rendered with remarkable control and perfection, as if a computer had done it.

Michelle shifted on the couch, tucking her feet up under her. "I told you, it's work. I'm a graphic designer."

"You're damned good," he said with total honesty. "I can't believe you quit painting. You were so passionate about it."

"Sam, I was eighteen years old. I was passionate about everything—about my art, about horses . . . about you. The trouble was, life outlasted passion. Some people call it growing up."

Her statement thumped into him like a dull blow. The firelight flickered off her cheek, illuminating a haunting sadness in her face. He didn't like seeing this wistful melancholy in her. But he sure as hell didn't know how to make it go away.

"Aw, damn it, Michelle." He moved closer to her on the sofa. "I didn't mean to upset you." And because it was late and he was on autopilot, he did the next thing quite naturally. His arm extended across the back of the seat and went around her.

In the space of a second, she softened against him, and he couldn't believe the rush it gave him to feel her like this, pliant and giving. But only a heartbeat later, she seemed to realize what she'd done and pulled away. He let out his breath in relief. His life was finally on track, and getting involved with Michelle Turner could cause a train wreck. Nobody in his right mind wanted a train wreck.

"I'm all right, really," she said with a quaver in her voice. "Things've been difficult lately."

"That's putting it mildly. But you and your dad are strong. You'll do great with this procedure. I had a talk with Maggie Kehr today, and she accepted my personal reference. The surgery's going forward as scheduled."

She shut her eyes for a long moment. "Thanks, Sam." Then she opened her eyes and looked at him. "And . . . thank you for coming over tonight."

"So is Cody what parents like to call a 'handful'?"

"Oh, yeah. Year Sixteen has been a real picnic."

"I got that idea."

"Let's see. He came home the first week of school with a pierced navel and a cigarette habit. He didn't even try hiding either one from me. I think he liked seeing the effect self-mutilation had on me."

"I imagine he did. What's the point of piercing something if no one notices?"

"And your suggestion would be?"

"I guess I'd ignore it until he injures himself zipping his pants. Then let the wound heal over."

"And the smoking?"

"That's tougher. Maybe the smell will gross out some girl and he'll quit."

"Cigarettes are one of his girlfriend's major food groups."

"He needs a new girlfriend, then."

"Oh, and my telling him so is going to work? Sam, you're not that naive."

He *had* been once, long ago. He'd believed in a love so strong no outside force, certainly no parental disapproval, could interfere. It had taken Gavin Slade precisely one evening to lay waste to that belief.

Sam pushed away the thought and concentrated on Cody. "Does he play any sports?"

"Skateboarding and snowboarding. Even a smoker's lungs can handle both. Here's the deal, Sam. I haven't been the most perfect parent in the universe, but I haven't been awful, either. Something happens to a kid who's growing up, something the Dr. Spock books don't mention. The kid becomes his own person. And sometimes that might be a person who does things that drive you nuts, and nothing you can do will stop him."

"Is it possible he *wants* to be stopped?"

"You mean is he looking for limits? Of course. Do I draw the line? Of course." She stood up, went to the window, stuck her hands in her back pockets. "Does he step over the line, of course."

Clearly this was familiar territory to Michelle. But there were hidden facets she wasn't seeing.

"You know, I reckon it's none of my business, but it appears to me that you're so concerned with making the kid happy, giving him some kind of life that looks good on paper, that you're forgetting something."

She turned to face him, defenses going up like an invisible wall. "And you've figured this out based on knowing us three days?"

He sent her a lopsided grin. "Hey, it's a gift."

She rolled her eyes.

"Seriously, Michelle, it's my job to figure out somebody's problem based on a fifteen-minute office visit. Sometimes that's all I get—it happens a lot around here, where most people don't pay regular visits to the doctor and don't follow up. I have fifteen minutes to work on a patient's trouble. In the past five years I've had a lot of practice."

She folded her arms beneath her breasts and eyed him warily. "All right, you have my attention. Tell me your expert opinion, Doctor."

Shit. Why was he doing this?

He planted his elbows on his knees. "My opinion as a doctor is this—Cody's like a lot of kids I see. The more rope you give him, the more ways he finds to tangle himself up. He needs a shorter rein."

"He didn't come with a how-to manual," she said. "That's the thing about raising a kid, Sam. You have to figure it out as you go along."

He felt himself teetering on a precipice. Common sense told him to pull back. His heart made him dive in. "You know as well as any doctor that kids who have unhappy parents wind up a lot more troubled than kids whose parents are relatively content. It doesn't have anything to do with how much money they earn or the sort of house they live in. It has to do with their perception of their place in the world."

"Oh, you're good, Sam. Let's make it my fault."

"Damn it, Michelle—" He was talking himself into deep shit, so he stopped and studied her, petite and slim, unsmiling and coldly beautiful as she stared at the black squares of the window. Then he glanced at the sketchbook on the table. And finally, he stood, taking a wad of keys from his pocket.

"Michelle, get your coat. I want to show you something."

"But Cody—"

"We won't go far."

She pulled on a jacket and boots while he did the same. The night wind slashed at them as they stepped outside. A high three-quarter moon spread a frozen blue glow over the area, and lights from the main house fanned across the yard. Sam led the way along the darkened drive past the cluster of bunkhouses. At the last one, he turned and waded over the unshoveled walk to the front door.

Angling his wad of keys toward the light, he selected one, old and worn, nearly lost in the mass of other keys. "Wonder if it still fits."

Michelle stood silently by as he inserted the key. It stuck, but that was mainly from the cold. Then it turned, and he opened the door, stepping into a room he hadn't seen in seventeen years.

Ghosts haunted this moonlit place. The presence of sheet-draped furniture heightened the eerie effect. He flicked a switch, and the light came on. "Remember this?"

"What would you do if I said no?"

"Call you a liar." He plucked a sheet off a threadbare chair, and one off a nearby table.

"Sam, I don't see the point—Oh."

He watched her take in the scene, wishing he knew her better, wishing he knew what she was feeling. He'd counted on Gavin Slade having a hidden streak of sentimentality, and he'd been right. The old man had left this place alone, a shrine to the daughter who had walked out of his life.

"It's exactly the way it was when I used to work here." Michelle's words made little frozen puffs in the air.

Gavin had equipped the bungalow especially for her.

It had a drafting table, easels and clipboards, tons of canvas and jars of brushes, tubes of paint. Everything was still there, left to atrophy with time and neglect. Sam removed another sheet to reveal an old-fashioned sofa, covered in flea-bitten velveteen.

The sight of it gave him a flash of memory so hot that he nearly shoved Michelle down on the musty cushions. He remembered the feel of her beneath him, the way her legs went around him, the sound of her breath in his ear. He remembered what it felt like to be buried to the hilt inside her. He remembered what it was like to feel a love so pure and strong that it burned like a flame that would never go out.

Jesus. It was eighteen degrees in here, and he was starting to sweat. He cast a furtive glance at Michelle to see if she noticed.

She was blushing red to the tips of her ears.

"I wonder if it happened there," he said softly, recklessly. "I wonder if that's where we made Cody."

She caught her breath with a little hiccup. "No. It was the boathouse. It . . . happened at the boathouse."

The place by the river had been their secret retreat, where they could steal away and find privacy together. Suddenly Sam was inundated with memories of that summer. It was the one time in his life when he saw everything with perfect clarity, when he felt absolutely certain he was going in the right direction, absolutely certain he knew what the outcome would be.

Funny thing about life. It had a way of spinning you around, shooting you off in a totally different direction, like a wild ride on a greenbroke horse. You had no idea where you were heading until you landed ass-first in the dirt.

"Sam, why did you bring me here?"

I keep remembering what it was like to be with you. He gritted his teeth to keep from saying it. Instead, he said, "There's a lot of waiting around involved in transplantation and recovery. You could be painting while you're here."

"No." She spoke swiftly, decisively. Almost defensively.

"Why not?"

"I draw and paint for work. As long as I have this enforced sabbatical, why would I do anything that resembles work?"

He wanted to say that the paintings she used to do were so different from the sketches in her book that they didn't resemble work at all, but a gifted mind and eye and hand creating something extraordinary.

He didn't say anything. She was hard to read, this grown-up Michelle. One thing was certain—she was in a skittish state, and he didn't seem to be helping matters.

He could feel himself moving fast toward a conviction that there were things he and Michelle should explore. What would it be like to get to know her again, to look at her through adult eyes? He could see the yearning in her eyes, the shadows of unfulfilled dreams, and he knew he couldn't dismiss her from his life when the transplant was over.

"Besides," she said, picking up a frozen paint tube, "the supplies are spoiled."

"You could replace them easily enough. Next trip to Missoula, you could lay in a bunch of paint and brushes."

"I'm really not interested, Sam."

He let her words sink in. "We'd better get out of here before we freeze to death."

He walked her back to her door and stood there for a moment, studying her in the glow from the porch light.

Suddenly he felt like a trespasser. "I've got to go, Michelle."

"'Night, Sam."

"'Night." His hand, without consulting his head, came up and cupped her cheek.

She didn't move. "Your hand is cold."

"Your cheek is warm." He leaned down and kissed it, soft skin and a subtle fragrance of perfume and snow. "I guess I'll be seeing you around . . . or not," he added. Then he walked to his truck, resisting the urge to whistle.

Chapter 20

When Michelle rushed back inside the house, she pushed aside the kitchen curtain to catch a last glimpse of Sam. The moon, a cold white smile, threw a stream of light over him, and he held up one hand in farewell. Embarrassed to be caught, she dropped the curtain and leaned against the counter. She was shaking all over. Shaking with memories and wanting and, most of all, with fear. Sam McPhee was part of her past, part of a past she had traveled far, far away from, and she shouldn't be having this explosive chemical reaction to him. But he was so bound up in things that were important—Cody and her art and Montana and Gavin—that she felt both wildly attracted to him and terrified of him.

She checked on Cody, finding the door to his room firmly closed. Then she brewed a cup of tea, using two bags to make it stronger, and when she sat down on the sofa, her hand went to the phone.

After two rings, she was tapping her foot with impatience. He picked up on the fourth ring. "Brad Lovell."

"It's me."

"Hiya, babe." He sounded warm and comfortable.

She smiled, her insides watery with relief. "What are you doing? Are you busy?"

"Going over some papers. Looks like we'll be able to afford a condo on Kauai after all—"

"Brad?"

"Yeah, babe?"

"I have to tell you something."

"What, you'd rather find a place on Maui?"

"No, nothing like that." God. When did he get the impression she wanted a condo in Hawaii in the first place?

"What is it, Michelle?"

She blew on her tea, took a sip. "It's about Cody."

"Shit. Is he in trouble already?"

It bugged her no end that Brad's first assumption was that Cody got in trouble. It bugged her even more that, basically, he was right.

"Well, there's trouble . . . and there's trouble."

"So you want to tell me, or are we going to play twenty questions?"

She took another sip, then set her cup down. "It's about his . . . about the man who fathered him."

"The cowboy."

"Yes. Um, he lives in Crystal City now. The other night I . . . ran into him." She made a swift decision not to explain the details.

"So did he recognize you?"

She was a little insulted by the implication. "Yes. And

it didn't take him long to put two and two together and figure out about Cody."

"Silence.

"Brad?"

"I keep waiting to hear you say you're going on *Oprah* with all this."

She smiled in spite of herself. "Right. Anyway, we— I told Cody tonight. He wasn't thrilled, but I think he's still getting used to the idea."

"What about you, Michelle? Are you thrilled?"

She felt a sting of guilt, because she wanted to be able to say that seeing Sam again meant nothing to her. That she felt nothing.

"I was shocked, I guess. Surprised. I never thought I'd see him again. But it turns out he did all right for himself, became a doctor, and he's a partner in a horse ranch about ten miles from here. His name is Sam McPhee."

"Do you think he wants something from you?"

She thought about the way Sam had touched her, the way he'd said good night. A shiver passed over her. "Like . . . what?"

"Like visitation rights or something."

A terrible chill touched the base of her neck. "I have no idea. It all came about so fast. He hasn't asked for a thing." *Yet.* But tonight she had seen the questions in his eyes.

"Well, if he gets some idea that playing the dad is all fun and games, remind him of what college tuition costs these days."

"It's not a matter of finance."

"Sweetheart, everything is a matter of finance."

"Not this. I'm going to let Cody get used to the idea and . . . see what happens. Oh, God, Brad, what if he wants to be with his father more than he wants to be with me?" She poured her fears into the receiver.

"Why would he want that?" Brad sounded genuinely baffled. "Look, don't worry. You're good to Cody. He loves you. He's just having a tough time right now, like any kid." Brad changed the subject easily enough, and she let him, grateful for once to hear him ponder the merits of Kauai over Maui. After making the appropriate murmurs, she said good-bye and hung up.

The conversation left her with a vague, ineffable sense of dissatisfaction. Why can't Brad be as decisive about us as he is about vacation property? she wondered.

Restless, she finished her tea and made a second cup, knowing the caffeine would keep her up, but she was past caring. For a long time, she gazed at the small framed picture of her mother, which she carried in her briefcase everywhere she went. Sharon Turner stood swathed in a Dior gown, her hair and makeup perfect as she blew a kiss to someone behind the camera. "Miss you, Mom," Michelle whispered. "I sure as heck would like to hear your voice right now." She drummed her hands on the phone. She knew who she was going to call. She knew she'd probably regret it, but she was going to do it anyway. She punched in the number and waited.

On the third ring, a voice said, "Hello?"

"Natalie, sorry to call so late. It's me."

"Michelle!" she squealed in unfeigned delight.

"Are you busy?" Michelle asked, though she knew that whatever Natalie was doing would come to a halt, because she was that sort of friend.

"I've been practicing arpeggios on my cello. Very exciting. But I love house-sitting at your place. Awesome hot tub. Now *you*, sweetie! What's happened? How's it going?"

Aside from Cody and Brad, Natalie was the only one Michelle had told about the transplant. It wasn't the sort of thing to be discussed with casual work acquaintances. And with Gavin Slade for a father, Michelle had learned to keep quiet lest the media sense a story.

"I'm all set to go into the hospital Saturday for one more procedure. If that checks out, we'll get a thumbs-up for surgery on Monday."

"When's Brad going over? Will he meet you at the hospital in Missoula?"

Soft leather creaked as she shifted position on the sofa. "Brad and I had a long talk about this before I left. I can't decide what I need from him. Maybe I don't even need him to come at all."

"Oh, for Pete's sake. You're taking this I-can-cope-on-my-own crap too far. Of course he needs to come."

"If Brad's around, I'll worry about what he's doing and thinking, pacing the halls of a hospital in a strange city. I'll go nuts wondering if he and Cody are getting along. It might be better to let him stay in Seattle, keep him posted by phone. Anyway, he's on standby. He promised that if I decide I want him with me, he'll drop everything and come."

"Brad's never dropped a thing in his life. Except maybe hints that I should take a hike."

There was a grain of truth in that. Brad and Natalie drove each other insane. "My dad and I are prepared. Everything will be fine."

"You're going to save your father's life. I'm getting a rush thinking about this."

"Don't knock yourself out, Natalie. It's just a surgical procedure."

"Just? *Just?* Not hardly, sweetie. I know you don't believe in this stuff, Michelle, but it's real. You've got to think about the spiritual aspect of it. You're giving life to the father who gave you life."

"I'm giving a kidney to the father who gave me a monthly check."

"No, listen, you have to listen." Michelle could picture Natalie sitting forward in that in-your-face way of hers. She wondered what color her friend's hair was tonight. Natalie had discovered hair mascara and hadn't been the same since. "There is a deeper meaning to this. It's not just plumbing."

"Natalie, it *is*. And thank God that it is, because that means it can be done at all. If it required magic and miracles, we'd be in big trouble."

"Okay, at least think about this. Physiologically, it *is* just plumbing. But you have to stay open to the possibility that something more is going to happen to you. Something amazing. You're going to connect with your father on a *cellular* level."

Michelle laughed, trying not to spray tea. "Yeah, Nat, that's the part I'm really looking forward to."

"You wait and see. How are you and your dad getting along?"

"I hate to disappoint you, but we're like a couple of cordial strangers. He's embarrassed and apologetic about the whole thing. Like he committed a faux pas by getting sick. And now that we're together again, it's . . ." She paused, feeling a sting of regret. "Let's just say there's been no cellular connection."

"There will be. I bet he went bananas over Cody."

This time she almost choked. "Natalie," she gasped into the phone, "you're killing me."

"What? Your dad's never seen Cody. It must be wonderful, bringing them together."

"It's like bringing together Johnny Depp and Charlton Heston. Cody's being horrible, my dad doesn't know what to make of him, and they're both inches from exploding."

"Oh, Michelle. I'm sorry. Let me talk to the Codyboy." She had known him since the day he was born—literally. As Michelle's birthing coach, Natalie was the one who, sobbing as hard as Michelle was, had cut the umbilical cord. She decided then and there that she loved him, and her love hadn't wavered since.

"He's asleep. He had a little accident."

"*Accident?* You bitch, why didn't you call me?"

"It was minor. He cut his head."

"How?"

"On . . . a horse's hoof."

"Hold the goddamned phone, Michelle. You're telling me he got kicked in the head by one of your father's horses?"

"Actually, he got kicked in the head by one of *his* father's horses."

"Michelle!" She could picture Natalie now, totally agitated, pacing up and down in her designer living room, shrieking into the phone. "Do you mean to tell me the cowboy's there?"

She had never told her any more than she told Brad or Cody. "He lives in the area now."

"*Get out.* Did you know he was there?"

"No, it was a complete surprise. He's actually a physician now."

Silence. Complete and utter stunned silence. It was rare, a totally quiet Natalie, and Michelle grinned, enjoying the novelty of it.

"Holy goddamned horseshit," she said at last. "So let me get this straight. The no-account cowpoke who knocked you up came back to town and is now a respected citizen and doctor?"

"That's about it."

"And your dad never thought to tell you?"

"We never spoke, Natalie."

"Okay, get to the good part. Is the cowboy doctor married?"

"No."

"Involved?"

"I don't know."

"If he was, you'd know. What did he and Cody say when you told them?"

"It's . . . complicated."

"Fine. I'm coming."

"What?"

"Probably take me a day and a half in the Volkswagen."

"Natalie, you can't—"

"I said, I'm *coming*." She slammed down the phone.

Though she knew it was fruitless, Michelle hit redial a couple of times, but she got the expected voice-mail pickup.

"Nat, I've got enough going on without you showing up," she said, knowing her friend was ignoring her as she flew around the town house, flinging mismatched, inappropriate clothes into a woven Costa Rican shoulder bag. "I think," Michelle said, speaking to the tape, "there's such a thing as being *too* good a friend." She went on in this vein, trying to dissuade Natalie, but she knew it was useless.

When she hung up the phone, she felt strange and sort of disoriented. She was happy Natalie was coming. She was dismayed that Natalie was coming. She couldn't make up her mind how she felt. But one thing was certain. Natalie was the sort of person who got everything out in the open. And she knew Michelle better than anyone else in the universe.

Natalie would take one look at Michelle when Sam was around, and she'd *know*. Natalie would know that Michelle couldn't stop thinking about him, and that she had no idea what to do about him.

Michelle kept reminding herself that she had a life. She had Cody and Brad and her career. That was what she needed to focus on. That, and getting through the surgery.

She lay down on the sofa, shut her eyes, and suddenly the ideas started coming. There was a part of her, a wild, out-of-control part, that had some very explicit ideas of what to do about Sam McPhee, and if she knew what was good for her, she'd ignore them.

sofia was the sort of person who got in trouble out in the open. And she knew Michelle better than anyone else in the universe.

Natalie would tell... she... at Michelle, when they were... and she... now, Natalie would know that Michelle wanted to stop thinking about him, and that she had no idea what to do about him.

Michelle kept spinning herself until she had a little... She had only wanted to find out... and her... except that when she... it wanted to focus on them, and going through the journey, she let go of the thoughts until her guard and suddenly the ideas started rushing. There was a part of her, a wild, crazy, reckless part that had many very cynical ideas of what it saw about Sam McGhee, and I sure knew what was good for her, like it gave in to them.

Wednesday

Wednesday

C ody was glad his mom didn't demand some big explanation when he said he wanted to go to Sam's in the morning. All he had to tell her was that his head felt fine, he'd wear a hat, and he wanted to see the foal he'd helped deliver.

Her face took on that tight, nervous expression she got when she suspected he was up to something, but she drank her coffee in thoughtful silence. He wondered what she was thinking. Then he decided he didn't really want to know.

Cody waited, stiff and apprehensive, while she called Lonepine. But she didn't talk to Sam. She talked to that Indian guy, Edward Bliss. Edward was okay, kind of goofy but not too bad. He said it was fine to come, so by nine o'clock Cody was jumping out of the Range Rover and heading for the barn. The dog—Sprout? No, Scout—came churning across the snow to accompany him.

He heard his mom calling stuff after him—keep his hat on, call if he started to feel bad, all that crap—but he simply waved without turning. It was rude to blow her off, but if he didn't walk away, she'd sit there for an hour telling him be careful of this, watch out for that, and he wasn't up for maternal lectures this morning.

"Hello," he called as he stepped into the barn. Scout trotted around, sniffing loudly, acting important. The central breezeway was dim and a little warmer than outside thanks to some heat lamps hanging from the rafters.

He poked his head into the cluttered office. "Anyone here?"

No one in sight. He figured Sam was probably at work, and Edward was either out on the range somewhere or still in his cabin across the way. The Border collie found a heap of old blankets by the wood-burning stove and curled into a ball for a nap.

"Excellent," Cody said under his breath. It felt good to be alone, away from everybody. He didn't like people hovering over him.

Outside the office, he put on the boots he'd worn the other day. He picked up a set of tan coveralls and stepped into them. Stomping his feet to warm them, he was glad there wasn't a mirror around, because he was sure he looked like a complete dork. As he pulled on a pair of gloves, he quit thinking about how he looked. He wanted to see the mare and her foal.

The birthing stall had its own set of heat lamps in all four corners. The light from them fell at an angle over the mare and the baby, and for a second Cody gawked at them with a hitch in his throat. Sylvia stood calmly in the middle of the stall. She made a noise, like someone clearing her throat, when she spotted Cody. It was a friendly sound. At least, he was pretty sure it was friendly. Then she used her big muzzle to nudge at the foal, which was sleeping curled up like a kitten near her feet. The little one lifted its head, then staggered up, all wobbly. First it splayed out its front legs, then its hind legs, and after a minute it figured out how to get up on all fours. Cody was tempted to help, but Sam had said it was best to let the baby get up on its own.

It lurched against its mother, lips nibbling comically at her belly. She nuzzled it some more, twisting back to guide it to her udder. After a while, the foal stuck its head in the right place. Cody had never expected the sound of nursing to be audible, but it was—sucking, swallowing, gurgling. He'd probably be embarrassed if anyone else was around, but he had the moment all to himself, so he leaned on the stall door and grinned.

The soft morning light, the little drift of steam from the mare's nostrils, the funny sucking sound made by the foal and the way its skinny legs splayed out. Aunt Natalie—she wasn't his real aunt but his mom's best friend—would get all gushy at this point. But hell, Natalie got gushy over Hallmark commercials on TV.

When he'd talked to Claudia last night, he'd tried to describe what it was like seeing a foal being born, but she'd just said "Gross" and started nagging him about the pain pills. He sort of wanted to tell her about finding his father, but he couldn't figure out a way to bring up the topic. Sometimes he wished Claudia was the kind of friend he could tell this stuff to, but the fact was, she never really seemed interested in heavy personal stuff. She was too into having a good time, and when Cody was with her, that's what he wanted, too. But sometimes he wondered what it would be like to have someone he trusted, someone he could really talk to, because some days, like today, he had news burning a hole in him.

Maybe he couldn't unload about Sam, but he'd try to find a camera somewhere, take some pictures of the horses to show Claudia. The filly was so goddamned cute, how could anyone not want to see it?

His mom used to draw awesome pictures of horses. He thought of the paintings stacked in the closet of her study at home. The large, flat folder was filled with old sketches and watercolor and acrylic studies. When he was little, he had asked her about them, paging reverently through the stack and regarding the horse drawings with astonished admiration. "What are these, Mom? Did you do these?"

"Years ago, baby." She always used to called him baby, sometimes even slipped and did so now. "I don't have time for that kind of drawing anymore. I'm too busy drawing for work."

"I like these better than work."

She'd looked at him with big, sad eyes and tousled his hair. "So did I, baby. So did I."

She had never said much more about those pictures, but Cody used to look at them in secret sometimes. Now that he'd seen his grandfather's ranch, he knew where those drawings came from. Horses and mountains and a rushing river. A tall fir tree next to a salt lick. A nest of loons in a marsh, the still water mirroring a snow-peaked mountain. They were all pictures made while she was at Blue Rock Ranch.

Sam's mare and foal would have fit right in with those pictures. His mom could have made a hell of a drawing of those two. But she had given up painting when he was a baby, and he had no memory of her doing anything but agency work. Still, she kept her old pictures.

One Fourth of July when he was about ten, Cody had been awakened by the boom of fireworks over Elliott Bay. He'd gone looking for his mom, and he'd found her in her home office, the drawings spread out on the floor. She was drinking a glass of wine and silently crying. Disconcerted, Cody had crept back to his room.

Now he knew the source of her memories and her sadness. When she had lived at Blue Rock Ranch all those years ago, she'd met Sam McPhee.

His father. His goddamned father.

Cody scowled the thought away. He actually did some work, cleaning the lines and pans of the watering device. The contraption served all the stalls, filling with fresh water when one of the horses pressed its tongue against a bar in the center. He filled the wheelbarrow with manure from empty stalls and hauled it outside. He kept stopping to check on the mare and foal.

After a while, the filly quit nursing. The mare started doing motherly things, like sniffing it all over, giving it a lick here and there. Cody wondered if he'd be welcome in the stall. The kick in the head had been an accident. A reflex. Even with his limited experience, he knew that.

When he lifted the latch of the stall door, his hand trembled a little, surprising him. He didn't think he'd be afraid. That was stupid. He made himself open the half door and step inside, boots sinking into the soft layer of straw. He made a smooching sound with his mouth, the way he'd heard Edward and Sam do.

The filly shied, but the mare looked up, nodding her head in a funny way that made him smile. "Hey, Sylvia," he said softly. "How you doing, girl?"

She grunted, then stretched out her neck so her big soft muzzle nudged his shoulder. And Cody, the most self-conscious kid ever born, forgot to be self-conscious. He rubbed her nose, and her bristly chin, and her neck, murmuring soft nonsense. She sighed with contentment when he scratched her between the ears.

The foal kept watching them, tail flicking, ears pricked forward. Cody held out his hand, low with the palm open. "C'mere, little one. I won't hurt you. C'mere . . ."

The foal lurched to its feet. Cody went down on one knee, moving slowly so he wouldn't startle her. She sniffed his hand, nose twitching, and jerked her head back. He held his hand steady, keeping up a low-voiced monologue. The foal sniffed and pulled back a couple more times. Finally, she allowed Cody to give her a rub between the eyes. She pressed forward in clear acceptance, letting him rub her muzzle and head. He laughed out loud when her small pink tongue came out and licked his hand. She latched on to his finger, sucking away. She was so damned cute, shiny as a new penny, cuddling up to him like a regular pet. Completely lost in the moment, he looped his arms around the foal's neck and pressed his cheek to her warm, smooth face.

He heard a noise behind him. The mare, thumping her foot on the floor, he told himself. Please let it be that.

He stood up and turned, knowing goddamned good and well it wasn't the mare that he'd heard. Someone had just caught him red-handed at his most ridiculous.

"Hi, Cody," she said. "I came to see the new foal."

"Um, Molly, yeah." He could feel his face filling up with a blush like a thermometer rising. "That's your name, right? Molly?" As if he'd forgotten. As if she'd be fooled.

She grinned at him, and the sun through the skylights seemed to get brighter for a second. She was amazing, her long straight black hair so shiny it was like water. Her face was the type of face you never wanted to look away from.

"That's my name."

His ears were on fire. He could feel the flames rising from them. "I was, um, making friends with her myself."

She let herself into the stall, expertly stroking Sylvia to put the mare at her ease. But her eyes never left the foal. "Ooh, she's such a little beauty." She dug in her pocket and pulled out a treat for Sylvia. "It's okay that I saw you doing that," she said as the mare crunched down the carrot.

Cody nearly choked with embarrassment. "I was just—"

"I usually kiss 'em on the lips," she stated, then squatted and held out a hand to the foal.

He stood back, feeling a tad superior that the filly wouldn't have a thing to do with the girl. He didn't care how long she spent trying to coax it. He'd be happy to stand here all day staring at Molly. Barn clothes looked just right on her. At his school in Seattle, the tight leggings and paddock boots, oversize sweater and puffy down vest would draw comments of dork and dweeb. But here in Sam's barn, she looked natural and comfortable. He found himself wondering what it would feel like to hold her slender form close to him. He wondered what her hair smelled like, and if her cheek was as soft as it looked, and if her lips—

Whoa. His thoughts were way out of control. He owed Claudia his loyalty, not this skinny backwater stranger. Claudia was the one who had pulled him out of obscure mediocrity at school. Because Claudia was his girl, he was suddenly someone, suddenly important. People knew his name when he walked down the halls at school.

The trouble was, when Molly Lightning looked up at him with shining eyes, she made it real easy to forget all that stuff.

"She's a perfect filly," Molly said. "Just perfect. I knew she would be."

"How'd you know that?"

"She's by Calyx, out of Sylvia. The perfect combination."

"By Calyx. You mean that's the father?"

"Uh-huh. Or the stud, you could say. Breeder talk, I guess."

"Whatever." Awkwardness stole over Cody. "Um, do you want to get a Coke or something?"

She stood. "Sure. We should leave the baby alone, anyway."

It turned out she was right. Practically the second they left the stall, the foal curled up and fell asleep. They raided the beat-up old refrigerator, filled with shots and wormer and soft drinks. The Border collie thumped her tail, then went back to sleep. They stood in the barn office, sipping from the cans as unease settled over them again.

"So my mom heard you got kicked in the head." Molly eyed the knitted gray cap Cody had pulled on that morning.

He felt a little swell of pride as he touched his forehead where the edge of the bandage showed. "Yeah. I got in the way of Sylvia's hoof at the wrong time."

She regarded him with such admiration that he felt inches taller. "I'm glad you're all right."

He liked the way she sipped her Coke from the can. He liked the way her fingernails were cut, short and plain. Claudia painted hers a different color practically every day, and on special occasions she painted tiny designs on each one. He had never seen the point of it, but it was a girl thing, he supposed.

"So how'd your mom hear about the accident?" he asked.

Molly rolled her eyes comically. "My mom hears everything. She teaches English at the high school. I bet Edward Bliss told her."

"Did he tell her the other stuff?" Cody felt a strange lightness in his chest, as if he'd inhaled cigarette smoke and was holding his breath.

"What other stuff?"

"About . . . Sam McPhee."

"What about Sam?"

"That he's my dad." He made sure he sounded totally blasé. "My biological dad." He didn't look at her, but he felt her stillness, her dawning amazement.

"Wow," she said at last.

"So I guess your mom doesn't hear *everything*."

"Guess not. Did Sam know about you?"

Something that felt uncomfortably like shame touched Cody. It pissed him off that he had been conceived so carelessly and then dismissed, no more important than a foal to a stud. "Nope. He and my mom lost track of each other."

"Do you have a stepdad?"

He thought of Brad, with those clean hands and that fat wallet. And those eyes that didn't trust him. "Nope." He poked the toe of his boot at a coil of rope on the floor.

"So are you happy about it or what?"

"He's just some guy my mom used to know. It doesn't change anything."

Molly put her empty can in the recycle bin. "Are you sure?"

"What, you think they're going to pick up where they left off and fall into each other's arms?"

"What if they do?"

"They won't," he said quickly, fiercely. "We live in a different state. We're here temporarily."

"I really like Sam. Everybody does."

"I don't even know the guy."

She paused. "He was seeing my mom last summer."

Cody's head jerked up; he narrowed his eyes. "Yeah? Are they still together?"

"Nope. They're good friends and all, but they don't really go out. I heard he sees a lot of different women." Her cheeks glowed pink. "That's what I heard, anyway."

"What about your dad?"

She shrugged. "Ditched us when I was little. I barely even remember him."

"I guess you know Sam a lot better."

"I guess."

Cody waited, wishing she'd say more. Since learning about Sam, he'd been on fire with curiosity. There was so much to wonder about. Where was Sam from? How had he grown up? Did he have any brothers or sisters? What did he eat for breakfast?

Why didn't he come looking for me?

He slammed his can into the recycle bin and stalked out of the barn office. "I better get to work," he said, growing short-tempered with all the thoughts swirling through his head.

"Want some help?" Molly asked.

"Nope."

"I could—"

"No." He turned and faced her. She stood in the doorway, backlit by sunlight. He wished she'd leave in a huff, but she stood her ground. "There's not much to be done," he said lamely.

"See you around, then." She walked out of the barn. A tall Appaloosa with a shaggy winter coat stood tethered to the paddock rail. She untied the horse and swung up into the saddle, turning him and walking him away with unhurried dignity.

Chapter 22

The illness was the enemy. The moment he had been diagnosed, Gavin had envisioned it as a living thing, a monster stalking him through the dark. Initially, he'd wasted a lot of time in denial and rage. Humiliated by the disintegration of his body, he had cursed the universe, embraced a death wish. A binge of drinking and tomcatting had nearly brought him to his knees. He had awakened one morning in an emergency clinic in Kalispell to find that they'd dragged him back from the edge of a coma—temporarily. The rest was up to him.

He went home and got down to the business of survival. He waged a battle against his disease, planning strategy with the precision of a film director blocking out a scene.

Yet he was losing ground. Hiring a special nutritionist, participating in special therapies had only postponed the inevitable. His kidneys were useless. Dialysis wasn't getting the job done. He was slowly poisoning himself. If the transplant didn't work, he'd be dead in a matter of months.

Driving down the highway away from town, he flexed his hands on the steering wheel. Part of his strategy for dealing with this was to act as if everything was fine, as if he didn't carry around a bag of dialysis fluid connected by a tube sticking out of his side. He still went to the feed store, still placed his stock orders and gossiped with the cow buyers and rodeo directors who came through town. Still stopped in at the diner for a cup of tea—coffee had been banned long ago.

He was a fixture in Crystal City. Even now, years after his last film, he was regarded as the town celebrity. People liked coming up to him and saying hi. They liked telling their kids he was the guy on all those tapes at the video store.

They kept his movies in the Classics section.

He drove along the empty road, thinking about Michelle and wishing like hell for some alternative to the surgery. Christ, she didn't owe him a thing, least of all a frigging *kidney.*

But the minute she'd figured out the score, she'd latched on like a tick, and she wasn't about to let go.

Why was that? Filial love and devotion didn't explain it. A sense of duty—maybe. The trouble was, they were doing this ass-backward. Forgiveness should come first. *Then* the transplant. Sad to think it took a crisis to bring them both to the table.

He pondered the long gap in their relationship, a gap that spanned the years of Cody's life.

I'm pregnant, Daddy.

I'm not surprised. Your mother was careless, too.

Christ. What the hell had he been thinking, speaking to his young, frightened daughter that way? Worse, Gavin had made sure she didn't have Sam McPhee to turn to. No wonder she had left, erecting a wall of silence that had endured for years. He didn't blame her.

He had responded to her departure by finding a mistress nearly as young as Michelle and becoming the resident playboy of Crystal City. He threw himself into work, producing a few small-studio independent films and giving the rest of his attention to the rodeo stock breeding program on his farm. There had barely been time to come up for air. And he sure as hell hadn't been inclined to let her know her old boyfriend had made good and moved back to town.

He'd salved his guilt about Michelle in equally typical fashion—by setting up a massive college fund for her child. He knew better than to suppose he could buy her forgiveness, but at least the boy would never have to worry about paying for his education.

Many times since his diagnosis, Gavin had picked up the phone, even dialed the number. It was a terrible thing, a pathetic thing, to use pity and compassion to bridge the gap. He'd held off telling her as long as he could. Michelle caught on when Gavin had set up a new trust fund in Cody's name. Within hours of receiving the papers to sign, she had called.

On some insane level, he was grateful for the illness that had brought her to him so swiftly and unquestioningly. If the transplant didn't work, he'd feel like a failure. But that was asking for a guarantee, and for once in his life, he knew better than that.

The sight of a breakdown at the side of the road startled Gavin from his musings. He recognized the beige Chevy Celebrity parked on the shoulder with its hood propped up. He eased off the road and parked behind the car.

"Car trouble?" he asked the woman bent over the engine.

She straightened up. Instant recognition froze her face. Tammi Lee Gilmer was in her fifties and looked it, with tired skin and overtreated hair teased high. She was slender and pale-eyed, a wary smile playing about her mouth. In the years since she'd moved back to Crystal City, she had lived a quiet life, never showing any signs of the out-of-control partying that had once made her the talk of the town.

She worked in a fabric shop—Gavin had never set foot inside it. On the rare occasions that he saw her, they dismissed each other with a nod and a murmured hello. Now he was trapped.

"It just died on me," she said. "I can't think what happened." Her voice was husky. As far as Gavin could tell, she'd given up drinking, but the habit still haunted her voice.

He opened the passenger door of his truck. "I'll give you a lift."

She slammed down the hood and grabbed her purse off the seat. "Thanks, Gavin. I was on my way out to Sam's. I can call McEvoy's Garage from there."

It was a tall step up into his truck, and he held out a hand to steady her as she climbed in. Her arm felt small and bony, but she was spry enough as she settled into the passenger seat. She smelled of cigarettes and drugstore perfume, and he found the fragrance unpretentious and therefore slightly welcome. He came from a world where women donned formal dress to go to the mailbox. He didn't miss that world at all.

He walked around the truck and got in, easing back onto the highway.

"You know the way to Sam's?" she asked.

"Yeah, I know where Lonepine is. I've been out there once or twice." Gavin had bought a couple of horses from Sam. Beyond that, they hadn't spoken.

Tammi Lee crossed one leg over the other, adjusting the wool cuff of her snow boot. Gavin kept his eyes on the road, but he found himself remembering, almost against his will, one of the meetings he'd had with his transplant team. The psychologist had pretty much guaranteed him he'd have no interest in sex for a good long while—maybe never again. The antirejection meds had a motherlode of side effects.

"But it's life," Dr. Temple had said, his painfully earnest face animated by optimism. "Preferable to the alternative."

Gavin hadn't smiled. "Shoot me now," he'd grumbled, and the psychologist had scribbled something on his clipboard.

Gavin missed Carolyn, who had lived with him until he'd been diagnosed. A former first-runner-up Miss California, her favorite things were riding horses, watching movies, shopping, and having imaginative, recreational sex.

When he told her about his illness, she had looked at him in horror, left that same day, sued him for eight thousand a month in palimony, and sold her story to a magazine.

His attorney had negotiated a much cheaper settlement, and Gavin had set up the second trust fund for Cody.

"I guess you know why I was headed out to Sam's," Tammi Lee said, bringing his thoughts around full circle.

"To see the boy, I imagine."

"I've been told the boy's name is Cody." Her voice held a gentle censure. "Cody Jackson Turner. So it's lucky I ran into you. Now you can tell me all about him, sort of prepare me."

"I haven't seen much of my grandson, Tammi Lee."

"Yeah, well, he's my grandson, too, and I've *never* seen him."

"A word to the wise. Don't expect a bunch of hugs and kisses."

"From a sixteen-year-old boy who doesn't know me from Reba McIntyre? Don't worry, Gavin, I'm not that stupid." She was pensive for a few moments. "When Sam was that age, he acted more grown up than me. Quit school and went to work for you. I took that boy's childhood away from him. No. I never let him have a childhood in the first place."

The frank regret in her voice made him wince. "Hey, take it easy on yourself. Sam's fine. Not every mother raises a boy to become a doctor."

"He did it all on his own. I never forget that. Never."

"You have a right to be pretty proud of Sam," Gavin remarked.

She laughed briefly, shaking her head. "I keep thinking he was left with me by mistake, that he was actually meant for some couple with a nice house full of books and a piano and supper hot on the table every night."

"I bet that would have made him too soft to do everything he's done." Gavin wished she'd drop the subject. He knew what she'd been like when Sam was coming up. Though she'd been his full-time mother, in a way she had been as absent from Sam as Gavin was from Michelle. Because when you were a drunk, you weren't there. Simple as that.

"Okay, here we are." He turned down the drive to

Sam's place. It wasn't a showy spread, not like Blue Rock was. A battered mailbox was the only indication that it had a name; LONEPINE was stenciled on the side and the flag was up. In the middle of the front pasture, the huge old lodgepole pine tree that had given the place its name stood draped in snow.

A slim girl on a tall Appaloosa rode in the opposite direction, leaving the ranch. Gavin recognized her as Ruby Lightning's girl.

"Wonder if she was keeping Cody company," Tammi Lee murmured. "If the youngster's anywhere near as good-looking as his dad, he'll have no trouble in the girl department. How about that daughter of yours?" she asked suddenly. "I hear she's some big-shot ad executive in Seattle."

"Uh-huh. But I didn't have anything to do with that."

"Nice she came back after all these years."

He pulled up to the barn and parked. A Border collie scampered out, barking and leaping in the snow.

Turning to Tammi Lee, Gavin forced himself to level with her. "Michelle didn't come back to be nice."

"Oh . . . ?"

"I've been sick." He hated saying it, nearly gagged on the words. "You probably heard that."

"There was talk of it in the shop."

"I've been on dialysis, but it isn't doing it for me. I could go toxic anytime. I need a kidney transplant. Michelle's going to be the donor."

"My God—"

"I'll never be able to thank her."

"Just get yourself healthy, Gavin. That'll be thanks enough. I know that for sure."

Sam's partner, Edward Bliss, came out hefting an extra

large Havahart wildlife trap. Gavin opened Tammi Lee's door for her.

"Hey, folks," Bliss said, his greeting light, his stare heavy with curiosity.

"Hey yourself, Eddie." Tammi Lee tucked her knitted hat down over her ears. "My car broke down. I'll use the phone in the barn office."

"Sure. Sam's at work today."

"I know. I came to see Cody."

Bliss's interest was so intense it was almost comical. "He's in the barn."

Gavin said, "You want some help with that trap?"

"No, thanks." Bliss shuffled away on reluctant feet. "I've got it." He deposited the trap on a flatbed sled hitched to a snowmobile. "Better be going. We've had a cat prowling around lately."

"Let me know if that thing works. I've had trouble with mountain lions myself the past couple of years," Gavin said as Bliss started the engine and rode off. Gavin stood between the truck and the barn, undecided. There was no need for him to stay, but he didn't feel like going just now either.

Tammi Lee hesitated at the barn door. "Hey, Gavin?"

"Yeah?"

"Maybe you could, um, introduce us."

For the first time since finding her on the side of the road, he smiled. He didn't blame her, feeling nervous about meeting a sixteen-year-old grandkid she never knew about. Cody was enough to make anybody nervous. "Sure," he said. "Of course."

They went into the barn together. The fecund smells of hay and molasses oats and manure filled the air and, somewhere, a radio played terrible music designed to drive people crazy.

"I'm no square in the music department," Tammi Lee whispered to Gavin. "Does this count as music?"

He made an exaggerated show of covering his ears. "Welcome to Cody's world."

They spotted him cleaning a stall. Oblivious to the visitors, he had a pretty good rhythm going with the shovel, bending to load, then swinging up to deposit the load in a wheelbarrow.

"Too bad Sam got to the kid first," Gavin commented, surprised to see him working so industriously. "He would be pretty useful around Blue Rock."

"You should give him some chores," said Tammi Lee, her stare devouring Cody. "I bet he'd work for both of you."

"When I first laid eyes on the boy, I didn't think he'd turn out to be good for much of anything. To me, he looked like every reason I never watch MTV."

Tammi Lee crossed her arms in front of her, leaning against a post. "Then you forgot the cardinal rule of kids."

"What's that?"

"Underneath the most terrible attitude and the most terrible clothes, he's just a kid."

"I don't have much experience with kids."

"Me neither." Apprehensive as a nervous filly, she took a step toward Cody.

"You okay?" he asked, surprised by her hesitation.

"Look, I didn't do so hot with Sam," she said. "I don't want to blow it with Sam's son."

Gavin's heart took an unexpected lurch. Suddenly it struck him that getting off the bottle had been a struggle for her, a battle, a war. And that she was never really safe from a relapse.

Without thinking, he took her hand. "Come on. I'll introduce you."

Reaching for the radio, he switched it off.

Cody's uncertain tenor voice kept singing, then broke off. "Hey, what the—" He stopped himself again when he saw Gavin and Tammi Lee.

"Sorry about that." Gavin grinned in a friendly fashion. But he'd screwed up already, embarrassing the kid.

"You shouldn't sneak up on people like that." Cody set aside his shovel and peeled off one glove, inserting his finger up under his cap where the edge of his bandage showed.

"Your head all right?" Gavin asked.

"It itches."

"I brought someone for you to meet. This is Sam's mother, Tammi Lee Gilmer."

He felt her give his hand a squeeze before she took the final step toward Cody. For someone Gavin barely knew, she was easy to read. The woman was petrified. And moved—he could see that in the tremor at the edge of her smile, in the extra sparkle in the corner of her eye.

"Hey, Cody," she said in her cigarette voice. "This is such a surprise. I couldn't wait to meet you."

He quit scratching. After a second, he held out his hand. She took it briefly.

"Hi," he said.

"I guess you'd better call me Tammi, or Tammi Lee," she said.

"Not Granny or Grandma?" Gavin asked in a teasing voice, trying to lighten the moment.

"I sure wouldn't mind," she said in a rush of honesty that left her flushed. "But 'Grandma' is a name that has to be earned, don't you think? Cody and I have only just met."

She folded her hands in front of her and studied his face. "You're probably going to get sick of hearing this, but you look exactly like Sam did when he was young. Sam was just about the best-looking kid in town."

The boy shrugged. He was a little lacking in the poise department, Gavin observed. Too much time plugged into Nintendo? He didn't know. There was too much he didn't know about this boy.

"Cody," Tammi Lee said, "I don't want to embarrass you. I don't want to push myself on you. But if you don't mind, maybe we could spend a little time together sometime."

"I have to work," he said bluntly.

"Oh," she said. Her fingers knit together. "I make a mean homemade pizza," she added.

He nodded noncommittally and pulled on his glove. "I'd better get after it then."

"See you around, maybe," Tammi Lee said.

"Maybe."

Gavin walked away with her. The music came back on. They stopped to look in on the mare with the new baby, leaning against the half door and admiring the little one. Gavin chanced a look at her, and wasn't surprised to see a tear tracking down her cheek.

"Hey, he's just a jerky little kid," he said, handing her a bandanna from his pocket.

"I didn't expect him to fall into my arms. But Jesus Christ, I wanted to hold him." Her hands shook as she grasped the top of the stall door. "How I wanted to hold him."

Her stark, honest yearning touched Gavin. "I think we both missed out on that stage with Cody."

She blotted her cheeks and handed back the bandanna. "I guess what makes me so sad is that I missed out on a lot of that with Sam, too. Some things you just learn too late."

An old twinge nagged at Gavin. Seventeen years ago, he'd made up his mind about Tammi Lee and Sam—and he'd been wrong.

"I better go call about my car," she said.

As they reached the barn door, the loud music cut off. Tammi Lee and Gavin turned back. Cody stepped out into the breezeway.

"Hey . . . Tammi Lee." He sounded uncertain as he spoke her name.

"Yeah?"

"What kind of pizza?"

A smile broke across her face. "Whatever you like, hon. Whatever you like."

Chapter 23

Sam's snow tires crackled on the drive as he turned into his farm. He was surprised to see Gavin Slade's Ford 350 parked outside the barn. Damn, what was Gavin doing here?

Sam pulled up to the house and spotted a light on in the kitchen. He stopped on the back porch, amazed to see his mother offering a steaming mug to Gavin Slade.

Sam paused to collect himself. His first meeting with Gavin Slade had set in motion events no one could have predicted. When Sam was seventeen, his mom's car had died in the parking lot of the Truxtop Café in Crystal City. The owner, above average in the decency department, had arranged a tow to McEvoy's Garage and had given Tammi Lee a job. A few inquiries steered Sam to Blue Rock. Good reputation, rodeo stock contractor. The kind of operation a cowboy dreamed of.

Gavin's foreman had taken one look at Sam in the saddle and summoned the boss. Sam's physique had always worked in his favor. He was tall and rangy with long hands and a relaxed way that gave people—and horses—confidence.

"Well, you look like a cowboy. Can you ride like one?" Gavin had wanted to know.

Digging in his heels, Sam had demonstrated on the borrowed quarter horse.

"How'd you get here?" Gavin had asked.

"Walked."

"From town? That's six miles."

Sam made no comment. Gavin hired him on the spot.

Sam had been quietly fascinated by the parade of glitterati that came to call on the famous actor. He recognized faces from old movies, late-night talk shows, celebrity game shows. Beautiful women and well-dressed men came seeking favor, for after retiring from movies, Gavin Slade became a respected producer, picking and choosing his projects with care.

Gavin had entered Sam in a few local roping events. The purses at the small shows didn't amount to much, but Sam had a taste of something he hadn't sampled before—possibility.

Fate had worn a yellow ponytail, expensive riding clothes, and a soft-eyed, dreamy look that made him forget his place in the world.

Damn. The boss's daughter.

Could he have been more stupid?

Sam yanked open the kitchen door. Gavin was a charmer, a ladies' man. What the hell did he want with Tammi Lee?

"Hey, Mama." Sam took off his hat, holding out his hand. "Gavin."

"Good to see you." Gavin flashed a smile, but his eyes stayed cool, wary.

"I had car trouble," Tammi Lee explained. "Gavin gave me a lift out here."

Sam relaxed a little. That seemed innocent enough. But he didn't kid himself about Gavin Slade. The old man had considered him ranch-hand scum, not good enough for his daughter. That in itself might have been forgivable, but Gavin had played hardball. Even the ruse with the missing money had been understandable, if not forgivable. What Sam couldn't ever forget, though, was that Gavin's schemes had knocked Tammi Lee in the dirt when she was already down.

"I wanted to meet Cody," Tammi Lee continued.

"He was feeling well enough to come to work." Pride touched Gavin's voice. "Frankly, I was glad to see it. A little work sure can't hurt the kid."

"So you met him, Ma?" Sam studied the lined and faded face, and he sensed the sadness that always seemed to linger at the edge of her mood. For as long as he could remember, he had felt responsible for that sadness. He knew it wasn't his fault, but he'd give anything to banish it.

"Gavin introduced us," she said. "I won't bullshit you, Sam. We're not the Waltons."

"I hope he was civil, at least."

She waved her hand. "I don't think we'll find much in common, but I'm glad we met. He's a good-looking boy, Sam. Reminds me of you at that age."

Sam wondered if he'd had that same screw-you attitude. Maybe he had. Maybe bonking the boss's daughter had as much to do with his attitude as his hormones.

"Speaking of Cody, we'd better head out." Gavin picked up his hat from the rack behind the door. "It's getting dark."

Sam shot his mother a look. Had she been hanging out with Gavin Slade all afternoon? Telling himself it was none of his business, he went out to the barn. While Gavin warmed up his truck, Sam found Cody standing at the far end of the row of stables, his shoulder propped against the door. Sam was pleased to see all the equipment had been washed down and put up. He was a lot less pleased when he saw that Cody was smoking a cigarette.

He tried to sound casual as he remarked, "Those things'll kill you."

Cody turned quickly. A rebellious look shadowed his face. "It's just something I do sometimes. I can quit any-time."

"How about now?"

"I'll choose the time."

"Well." Grabbing a water hose, Sam twisted the spray nozzle and doused both Cody's gloved hand and the cigarette. "I choose now."

"Hey!" Cody jumped back, shaking water from his hand. "That's cold as hell."

"So don't smoke around here anymore."

"I'll do what I—"

Sam held up the hose. "Don't push me. I'm armed."

Cody flung off his glove in disgust. "You could have just asked me to put it out."

"I'm *telling* you to quit."

"And I'm *telling* you to get off my case."

They faced off, glaring like a pair of rival dogs. Sam refused to flinch, but so did Cody.

"How's your head?"

"Itches. I better get going. 'Bye." He stalked away, muttering under his breath.

Welcome to parenthood, Sam thought. Christ, how did Michelle do it?

Thursday

Thursday

Chapter 24

Waking up was hard for Michelle at home. She had done her bedroom in soft aquas and golds, spent an absurd amount on bedding from Nordstrom's, and invested in an imported eiderdown, the kind you sink into like a cloud. Her bedroom exuded comfort and luxury, and she responded by sleeping too long and too hard there.

In Montana, she woke up at the crack of dawn and hurried like a child to the window to look out at the long fields and pastures of her father's ranch. The sides of the mountains corrugated by the blue ripples of glaciers. The fall of light from the rising sun.

And God knew what was going to happen each day.

She got a clue when the early light glinted off a car parked in the circular drive in front of Gavin's house.

There was probably only one lime green Volkswagen bug in the Northwest.

Michelle paused to check on Cody—dead asleep, a benefit of hard physical labor—then pulled on her old gray sweats, stuffed her feet into boots, and hurried across the compound to the main house. She entered through the kitchen, greeting Tadao in passing. The aromas of coffee and kidney-friendly roasted green tea wafted over her, but she was not hungry, just on fire to know what the hell was going on.

Gavin and Natalie sat in the sunken living room before a roaring blaze. Gavin spotted Michelle first; he was in the middle of laughing, and the smile on his face lifted her heart. He stood up. "Hey, Michelle. Morning."

"Hi, Daddy. I see you've met Natalie."

"I certainly have."

"At about five o'clock this morning." Natalie's bangle bracelets and hoop earrings, silken head scarf and tie-dyed leggings, and especially her warm smile, were familiar and dear to Michelle.

"Hey, you," she said, holding out her arms.

"Hey, you," Natalie said back, standing up to give her a hug. "I tried to get here last night, but the old Volkswagen wouldn't cooperate. I had to take a breather in Coeur d'Alene."

"You should have called, Nat."

"We talked, remember? You knew I was coming."

"Yes, but—" Normal logic didn't work with Natalie Plum. Michelle sat down on the big leather sectional with them.

Natalie's eyes twinkled. "I acted as though I'd never seen a movie star before—"

"You haven't," Michelle reminded her.

"Well, that explains why I kept staring and stammering." She sipped from her mug of coffee. "Your dad got all squirmy on me. You'd think he's never been awakened at five in the morning by a crazed fan before."

Her father leaned back, crossing his booted feet at the ankles. "I admit it's been a while."

He was loving this, loving every minute of it. His need to put his face in front of millions of people was nearly as strong now as it had been at the height of his career in the movie business. There were those who hungered for recognition, even though it didn't necessarily mean anything to them except recognition. She thought it was true in her father's case. Anyway, he was far from annoyed by Natalie's breathless admiration.

"So we've been up talking for a couple of hours." Natalie sent him a look of melting sympathy. "You should go back to bed now. I feel so guilty getting you up."

"I'm an early riser. And this visit was worth it." He patted his hand on a stack of fat photo albums on the coffee table.

"You brought those from Seattle," Michelle said, sounding slightly accusing.

"You bet I did, girlfriend." Natalie sent her a smile. "I can't believe you forgot them."

Guilt stained her cheeks. To be honest, Michelle had never even thought of bringing the photo albums to show her father. Never even thought he'd be interested in snapshots of Cody's first birthday, or the bike Santa brought him one year, or his first day of school.

"I loved the pictures, Michelle," her father said quietly. "More than you can know. I'm proud of you for the life you've built for yourself and Cody."

She blinked, startled. Since she arrived at Blue Rock, they had avoided talking about certain topics. Dr. Temple and the social worker on the transplant team had been saying how important it was to discuss personal stuff, family stuff. They gave Michelle and Gavin some little blank books for writing down thoughts and feelings. Michelle's was still blank. She bet Gavin's was, too. So his statement about being proud of her took her by surprise.

Putting his hands on his knees, he got up, his thick heather gray sweater looking warm and comfortable on his big, lean frame. The bulkiness of the knit camouflaged the dialysis bag. "Chores," he explained. "I've got a meeting with the arena director."

"See you around, pardner," Natalie said in an exaggerated, corny drawl.

"Jake turned on the heat in the bungalow next to Michelle's. If you need anything, holler."

"It's all perfect, Gavin. Thank you for welcoming me."

"My pleasure, ma'am." He went out through the kitchen, and Michelle drummed her fingers on the arm of the couch, trying to figure out if he was flirting with her best friend or not.

Natalie and Michelle sat alone in the living room, watching morning sunlight steal across the hand-painted tile floor. Michelle picked up a plaid pillow, tossed it at her, saying, "You bitch."

She caught the pillow, laughing. "You have no idea."

Suspicion stole into Michelle's radar range. "I don't?"

Natalie propped her sock feet on the leather-bound albums. "I figured your dad would want to see the old family photos. But I really brought them for you to show Sam McPhee."

"God, you really are a bitch."

"You have to show him. You have to let him in on Cody's whole history."

"I don't have to do squat."

"Legally, probably not, unless he sues for visitation."

A chill skittered down Michelle's spine. "He wouldn't dare."

"Who knows? But he'll want to see the pictures."

"You know what makes you such a bitch?"

"What?"

"It's that you're right."

She grinned. "I know. So when are you going to show him?"

"I guess I could today, when I drop Cody off to work at his ranch. Sam's on split shift." It was amazing how quickly Michelle had memorized his schedule. He'd explained how he split the clinic duties with his partner, how his on-call situation worked. He'd only told her once, yet she had absorbed it like a sponge. Funny.

"You don't have any more . . . appointments and stuff with your father?"

"It all starts Saturday." She took a shaky breath, silently blessing Sam for intervening with Dr. Temple.

Natalie held Michelle's cheeks between her hands. "Do you know how special this is?"

Michelle swallowed a sudden painful lump in her throat. "I can't seem to look at it as anything more than a fairly complicated surgical procedure."

"It's so much more than that." She stood up, tossing a glance outside at her car. "I've been naughty."

Michelle picked up the heavy leather albums. "True."

"I mean, not just the photos. For once in your life, you've got time to get back into painting."

Not you, too. Michelle got the feeling Natalie had colluded with Sam about this. Or maybe her secret wish was absurdly obvious. "Give me a break," she said flatly.

"As if." Outside, Natalie lifted the front hood of the Volkswagen, revealing the trunk. In addition to her luggage, there were shopping bags from Madrona Bay Art Supply in Seattle.

Michelle's heart lurched. Madrona Bay was a Mecca for fine artists all over the West. The store was one of the first things she had discovered when, newly pregnant, she'd moved to Seattle. She used to save every last scraped-together dime to buy art supplies. It was a magical place, filled with all the things she needed to give life to the images burning inside her.

She hadn't been there in years, though.

"You bitch," she whispered, her eyes glazing over with yearning and frustration. "I don't need any of this."

"Oh, honey." Natalie grabbed her flowered bag and hefted it over her shoulder. "You do. You absolutely do. What else are you going to do while Gavin recovers?"

"I—" Well, really, thought Michelle. Natalie had a point. The studio was still there, untouched, as Sam had showed her the other night. "I guess I could mess around in my spare time."

"Good girl. So let's get a move on. We've got to bring poor Camille in out of the cold."

Camille was her cello, a 1968 Juzak concert instrument from Hungary. She never went anywhere without it. She kept it in a hard shell case plastered with stickers from all the places she'd visited—places like Sri Lanka and Lake Lucerne and Montreal and Rio de Janeiro.

They walked across to the bungalows, and Michelle stowed the photo albums in the Rover. She wondered if she would dare to show them to Sam. Natalie was right, Michelle conceded reluctantly. He needed and deserved to see what Cody's first sixteen years had been like.

They toted the paints, brushes, and Belgian linen canvases into the studio. Then Michelle helped Natalie carry her stuff into the guesthouse. It was already warm and cozy inside, and Natalie sighed with satisfaction. "Let me freshen up a little, and we'll go together."

"Go where, Nat?"

"To Sam McPhee's. Didn't you say Cody's working there? He needs a ride, right?"

"Yes, but—"

"Do you think I could stay away?" Natalie rummaged in her bag and found a brush, which she used to draw upward through her spiked hair. "I'm dying here, Michelle. You're my best friend, and you've got a scarlet past I know nothing about. Do you have any idea how crazy that makes me?"

In spite of herself, Michelle grinned. "I sort of like this."

"Bitch," Natalie said, and gave her a hug.

Chapter 25

S am walked out onto the front porch with Edward
Bliss as the Range Rover pulled into the yard.
Sam felt a now-familiar lurch in his chest when
Cody got out of the car.

My son. I have a son.

Yet other than stitching his wound, Sam had never
touched him.

"He's doing a little better in the wardrobe department."
Edward sipped from a mug of coffee. "Starting to dress
for the weather and the job, eh?"

Cody still appeared a little ragged, though he had abandoned the studied slouchiness of his city garb in favor of
old jeans, work boots, a fleece-lined denim jacket. A warm
hat covered the new haircut and the bandage.

"Who's that in the car with Michelle?" Edward asked.

Sam squinted, but the glare of the sun off the windshield blinded him. "Not sure. Gavin again?"

The passenger door of the car opened and out stepped the strangest woman Sam had ever seen. She resembled a butterfly, wearing a long multicolored shawl, crazy purple boots, and a Sherpa mountain guide's alpaca hat. With her skirt and shawl flowing, she skimmed over the snow toward the house, gabbing with Cody the whole time. Michelle went around to the back of the car, lifting the rear cargo door.

"*Ai caramba,*" Edward said under his breath. "Who's the babe?"

". . . so unbelievably cool of your mom," she was saying to Cody as they reached the porch. Barely pausing for breath, she tilted her head back, revealing earrings in unexpected places, and said, "Okay, Cody, shall we play *What's My Line?* Which one's your dad?"

She took off her hat to reveal spiked hair with purple and green streaks. She had slightly uptilted eyes and the face of a pixie—impish, animated, and sly. Tinkerbell on acid.

Red-cheeked but clearly enjoying himself, Cody said, "Sam and Edward, this is—"

"Wait, wait!" The imp held up a hand, impractically covered in fingerless black lace gloves. "Don't tell me. Let me guess." She grew very serious, looking from Cody to Sam to Edward to Cody. "No contest," she said. "It's the tall one. So introduce us, numb-nuts." She elbowed Cody in the side.

"This is my mom's friend."

"Not your friend?" Tinkerbell looked wounded.

"Yeah, mine too." Cody stuffed his hands in his pockets. "Natalie Plum."

"Actually, I'm his fairy godmother." She stepped up onto the porch. "He didn't tell you about me?"

"I better get to work," Cody said, hurrying toward the barn.

Sam was gratified by his haste to check on the mare and foal. He wanted to believe the kid could get interested in the horses. Maybe that way they'd find some common ground.

Natalie stepped up onto the porch and shook hands with Edward, then Sam. "You'll have to excuse me," she said. "I've had about nine gallons of coffee. You might find me a tad talkative. Hope you don't mind."

"We don't mind a bit," Sam said.

Edward put the full force of his charm into a comical bow. "Welcome to Montana."

Natalie's face lit up. "Thank you."

Michelle arrived, lugging an armload of large, thick books.

"Here." Sam jumped down from the porch. "Let me help you with those."

"Michelle, you bitch," Natalie burst out, turning on her friend. "You didn't tell me he was George Clooney!"

Sam took the top two books from Michelle. "I'm not George Clooney."

Natalie Plum raked him with a frankly assessing glance. "Close enough."

"But I'm friendlier," Edward cut in. "And I have better work hours."

"Perfect," she said with a dazzling smile. "Then you can show me around the place. Cody wouldn't shut up about the new baby."

Edward took her hand and led her toward the barn. "My pleasure."

As they walked off, Sam heard her say, ". . . every last thing, do you hear? I want to know absolutely *everything*."

Michelle watched them go. The morning light was soft on her face, nose and cheeks tinged by the cold. She held two of the books against her like a shield. "And does Edward know everything?" she asked.

"If he doesn't, he'll make it up."

"I'm serious, Sam."

"Okay, he figured out about Cody even before I did. The second he saw him. But he didn't say anything until I told him. Edward doesn't lie, and he doesn't hurt people. Ever." He indicated the books. "So what's all this? Photo albums?"

"Uh-huh. You got a minute?"

"I'm guessing this will take more than a minute. But as a matter of fact, I've got all morning." He glanced down at the pager clipped to his belt. "So long as the beeper stays quiet. Come on in."

In the living room, he added a couple of golden larch logs to the fire crackling in the woodstove and cleared a spot on the coffee table. "Can I get you something to drink?"

She didn't answer. He glanced at her to find her staring at the painting over the mantel.

"My God," she said. "I had no idea what happened to this."

The picture had occupied a place of honor over the mantel ever since he had settled in Crystal City. It was the only gift Michelle had ever given him. The painting had a life of its own; it glowed with the sheer wonder expressed in every brushstroke, echoing the underlying tenderness of a very young, very talented artist.

"I'm glad you kept it," she said, her voice soft, husky. "It's a good picture."

"I've always thought so. Everyone who sees it says so."

She shivered, though it wasn't cold. "I thought I had so many more pictures in me."

"I still can't believe you don't paint anymore."

"Painting took more out of me than I had to give. Life comes first, then art."

"I bet your pal Natalie doesn't agree."

"Natalie's different."

"I noticed."

Her manner became brisk, almost businesslike as she seated herself, as if her show of vulnerability had embarrassed her.

"You should still be painting, Michelle."

Her chin came up. "What, in all my spare time?"

"You make time for what's important."

The anger that flashed in her eyes was new to him. The Michelle he'd known years ago had a temper, sure. But her anger had never been cold like this. Or strangely directed at herself.

"What's with the books?" he asked, changing the subject.

"Natalie brought these from home."

Sam lowered himself next to her. His heart thumped; until now he wouldn't have thought a moment like this was important, critical. "Pictures of Cody growing up?"

"Yes. You interested?"

Here it was, then. The past, staring him in the face. Here in these four fat books lived the history that had left him out. The years he had lost with his son.

"Hell, yeah, I'm interested."

She picked up the top one. "I haven't had time to go through these and edit them, so what you see is what you get."

"What would you want to edit?"

"You'll see when we get there." She took off her shoes and tucked her feet up under her on the sofa. Sam, who had seduced a decent number of women on this very sofa, found the gesture almost unbearably sexy. He forced himself to focus on the photo album.

She flipped open the front cover. "My first apartment in Seattle. Natalie and I shared a place on Capitol Hill when I first moved there." Unremarkable, a snapshot of a sunny room with sliding glass doors and overstuffed furniture. Neat, nicer-than-average student housing.

"I studied painting while I was pregnant," she said. "I tried to keep it up after the baby was born, but life just got too hectic."

His gaze dropped down the page to a picture of Michelle. It wasn't a very good shot, but it moved him. She stood at the rail of a ferry boat painted white and green. Blue water and forested islands and a distant mountain range in the background. She wore her hair in a silky blond ponytail, and she had on a denim jumper.

A breeze plastered the blue dress against her round, ripe abdomen. She was the picture of a healthy young woman in the last trimester of pregnancy. Sam stared, fascinated by the knowledge that only months before the shot was taken, he had held her in his arms. He had planted that baby in her.

He lightly rubbed his thumb over the girl in the photo. "I hate it that I missed this."

"Right." She seemed to be working to keep her voice in control. "I was fat and cranky all the time. I think this is the only picture of me pregnant."

"Who took it? Natalie?"

"Yes." She turned the page. "Ah. Here we go."

The next photo showed a black-haired imp with thickly mascaraed eyes peering over a surgical mask.

"Natalie again?" Sam asked.

"She was my birth coach."

He set his teeth. Then, when he could trust himself, he said, "Should've been me."

Michelle shook her head. With the motion, a light drift of her fragrance hit him, and his body heated with the need to touch her.

"Sam," she said, "you were eighteen. You weren't ready to go through childbirth—"

"You were only eighteen, too. Were you ready?"

"I didn't have a choice."

"I wasn't *allowed* a choice. I would've stuck with you, Michelle. You know damned well I would have."

"I didn't know a thing. You were gone so fast, I didn't even have a chance to tell you I was pregnant." She pointed to a poorly focused photograph. "And there he is, hot off the press."

There was nothing unique about the picture. As a physician, Sam had seen his share of moments-after-birth shots, and this one wasn't particularly well done. But because it was Michelle, holding his son, his mouth dried. He couldn't speak; he couldn't even swallow.

Cody's wet red face lay against her chest, clad in a dotted hospital gown. The baby's tiny foot flailed, and Michelle wore a look of complete, exhausted relief.

"You had the glow," he remarked.

"The glow?"

"The new-mom glow. Some people deny its existence, but it's a very real thing." Gently he outlined the shape of her face and the baby's.

"Very scientific, Dr. McPhee," she said, though a soft edge diluted her sarcasm.

And then, step by step, page by page, she took him through the lost years. It was like opening a door and stepping into a world whose existence he hadn't even suspected. A parallel universe, hidden from him for seventeen years.

He saw Cody as a round-faced baby, doted on by Natalie. A toddler in overalls and a Seattle Mariners cap waved at him from a wrenching distance of years.

"See that blue thing in his hand?" Michelle rubbed her finger over the photo. "He never went anywhere without that thing. It's one of your old work shirts."

Sam felt a powerful jolt of emotion at the sight of his shirt, clutched in that chubby little hand. "Yeah?"

"When I left here, it was one of the few things I brought with me. Your—" She broke off and bit her lip.

"Your what? What were you going to say?"

"Your smell. It had your smell on it."

He put his arm around her. This was why things never worked out with him and women. He couldn't handle their softness, their fragility, the way his heart twisted in a knot when sentiment struck. "Aw, Michelle, damn it—"

For a moment she leaned into his shoulder. Then she seemed to get a grip and turned her attention back to the album. A first-day-of-kindergarten shot revealed a kid who was becoming his own person as he stood by a redwood fence with a Power Rangers lunch kit and a Looney Tunes backpack. Sam viewed school portraits, Little League team photos, excursions to the zoo, the aquarium, ski trips, summers at remote beaches.

What struck him about Cody was the kid's smile. It was the kind of smile that made the sun look dim—it covered his whole face and lit his eyes. Joy radiated from every photo of him.

Cody didn't seem to smile much anymore.

Natalie Plum appeared in a lot of the pictures. Every so often, there would be a picture of Cody with a guy.

"So who's this?" Sam indicated a man in a Hawaiian shirt, roller-blading with a six-year-old Cody.

"Someone I used to date. I haven't seen him in years."

Sam hoped she didn't hear him let out his breath. He found a couple more interlopers—Cody's third-grade teacher: "He was the gentlest man. Cody really loved him."

"And you? Did you love him?"

"He wanted a full-time wife. I had no idea how to be that, so we stopped seeing each other."

"And this other guy?"

"Someone else I used to see. We met at a commercial-art convention."

"Did he want a full-time wife, too?"

She gave a humorless chuckle. "As it turned out, he preferred several part-time lovers. What a jerk."

"So did you date a lot?"

"Did you?" she shot back. "You're digging for dirt, Sam. And trust me." She drummed her fingers on the photo album. "You won't find it here."

Sam spotted a good shot of Cody at about twelve, frozen in the midst of executing a perfect soccer kick. His face was intent, his gaze focused like a laser on the ball.

"He scored a goal with that kick," Michelle said.

Sam would have traded anything—*anything*—to have seen that kick in person. "Looks like he was a good little athlete."

"He was, but he lost interest in team sports."

"Do you know why?"

"Because he turned sixteen?"

"Plenty of sixteen-year-olds go out for sports."

She drew a quick breath. "I told myself I wouldn't get defensive. I'm working really hard not to."

"Sorry." He touched the photo. It was a five-by-seven, covered with the gluey cellophane of the album page. "This is a good shot."

She hesitated. "Brad took it."

"Ah. Brad."

"The year I met him. He was a community sponsor for the soccer club. His pharmacy franchise was, actually. Med-Plan Pharmacies." She flipped ahead a couple of pages. "Here we are at our ski place in Whistler."

It showed the three of them in front of a modern condo. Cody smiled his winner's smile. Michelle's gaze seemed curiously off focus, as if she was searching for something beyond the camera. The guy called Brad was tall, probably six-two, and thick-set, with a tanned face and a white-toothed grin, designer logos splashed across his ski outfit.

Sam had no doubt this was a decent guy, well-heeled, caring.

But as he regarded the picture, he felt such a stab of complete hatred that he had to look away.

As Cody grew older, the pictures of him were sparser, taken at infrequent intervals. "I think that's always the way," Michelle confessed. "When they're little, you want a picture of them every time they sneeze. But by the time they're in high school, a Christmas picture is about all you remember to take. Here he is with his girlfriend," she said. "Claudia Teller. They didn't want me to take their picture, but they figured it was the only way I'd get out of their hair."

"What are they dressed for, Halloween?"

She laughed. "A school dance. This is formal attire."

The girl was somberly pretty, with anorexic shadows under her eyes and cheekbones. Her hair was too red to be natural, her smile too sly to be genuine. Standing next to her, Cody looked tall and fiercely proud.

"Is she still his girlfriend?"

"As far as I know. Her parents are upper management at Microsoft, and she's supposedly the most popular girl in the school."

"She looks like a barrel of laughs."

Michelle grinned. "I'm glad it's not just me, then. But—" She looked away.

"What, Michelle?"

"It's awful."

"So be awful. I won't tell anyone."

"I'm hoping our stay here will cause his relationship with Claudia to chill. Is that awful?"

"Cody would think so."

She pressed her hand down on the picture. "I want him to have a girlfriend. Just not *this* girlfriend."

Sam studied the pale girl in the photo. From the perspective of years, could he still blame Gavin?

"Face it, Michelle," he said, "the days of arranging your kid's social life are past."

"But I *know* she's bad for him. He's completely blind to that. He thinks they're totally in love. Just like—" She stood up quickly. "We'd better see what Natalie's up to. She's a bit unpredictable."

"Finish what you were saying."

She went to the front window and stared out at the long white fields and mountains. He stood behind her. He wanted to clamp his hands around her shoulders, draw her back against him.

What did her hair smell like? What would her hips feel like, cradled against his?

"Were we wrong, too, way back then?" she asked softly. "Were we blind?"

"Your father thought so."

She turned to him, worrying her lower lip with her teeth. "My father never knew about us. At least, not until I told him I was pregnant." She moved past him. "You were gone by then."

"He knew, Michelle." Sam couldn't believe she thought otherwise.

"He never knew, not until I—that last day. We were careful," she insisted.

"You ought to ask him sometime."

Something like panic flickered in her eyes. Her relationship with her father was complex, unfathomable to Sam. He sensed that she was afraid it might crumble under scrutiny.

"It's lunchtime already," she said in a rush. "I'd better get Natalie out of Edward's hair." She went to the door and got her jacket from a hook. "I'll leave those albums here in case you want to look at them some more."

The moment had twisted, turned, changed. He had connected with her briefly, but she was slipping away again, eluding him. She seemed agitated as she stuck her arm in her jacket and fumbled with the zipper. "Damn," she swore between her teeth.

Sam took hold of the zipper and pulled it up. "Easy, Michelle." When the zipper reached the top, he didn't step away, but placed two fingers under her chin, holding her gaze to his. Her skin was as soft as it looked. Maybe softer. "Thanks," he said, his entire awareness fixating on her lips. "Thanks for bringing those pictures. It meant a lot to me."

"Thank Natalie." She ducked away, bending to put on her boots. "Why are you looking at me like that?"

"Maybe I still carry a torch for you, even after all these years."

"Men like you don't carry anything that long."

"You don't know me, Michelle."

"No, I don't." She went out onto the porch. "I guess that's my point."

"We can fix that," he said.

"If something in my life needs fixing, I'll take care of it myself." She seemed flustered, disconcerted by his attention.

It made him mad, the way she held him at a distance. "Oh yeah? From what I can tell by looking through those photo albums, you sure as hell haven't found what you want with . . . what's his name? Brad."

"How would you know that?"

"It's obvious. You're like this picture-perfect icon—a lover he doesn't really have to love, a partner who carries more than her share of the weight, a Barbie doll that looks good on the arm of his Armani tux."

"You don't know anything about me and Brad."

"Tell me I'm wrong."

"You're trivializing us. Trivializing a relationship that's been building—"

"Building toward what, Michelle? A marriage, or a business merger?"

"Oh, and you're the expert on relationships, right?" She marched outside without waiting for him to reply.

He felt a stab of guilt because maybe she had pegged him right. Certainly his track record bore it out, more than she could possibly know. *Tell her. Tell her now about the marriage.* But the moment passed, and he followed her outside.

Against the unrelieved white of the snow-draped paddock, Natalie Plum's tie-dyed skirts and leggings made a wild splash of color. She and Edward stood at the loading gate. She was talking a mile a minute, making fluttery gestures with her hands. When Cody came out of the barn leading the mare, even Natalie fell still. Sam and Michelle hurried over, stopping at the opposite side of the paddock. "What's going on?" Michelle asked.

"Edward and I decided the mare and filly could come out today," Cody answered.

"That's the one that kicked Cody in the head," Michelle told Natalie.

"She's dangerous," Natalie said, aghast.

"All females in labor are. But she's fine now. Watch."

Edward must have been giving Cody pointers. The bridle was buckled on correctly. Cody walked the horse with the proper amount of lead, her steam-puffing nose at his shoulder. She followed him like a big docile dog. Across the paddock, Natalie's coos of admiration carried on a light, cold wind.

The foal stood on stick legs in the open breezeway, whickering nervously as Cody led its mother slowly away. Unwilling to let its mother out of its sight, the baby took a tentative step into the snowy yard, then another. Its front legs splayed apart and it stumbled, then righted itself. Its muzzle came up covered in snow. It sneezed, shaking its head. Cody looked back and laughed, a ringing sound that made Sam think of the pictures he'd just seen, of a younger Cody. A happier Cody.

It made Sam's heart hurt to watch them. His son and his favorite horse, and the foal they'd helped bring into the world. There was something special and right about the fact that they were all here together.

"She's a beauty, Sam," Michelle said. "A perfect little filly. No wonder I can't keep Cody away."

Cody unhooked the bridle lead to let the mare walk around at will. The foal stuck close by her side, though it veered over to inspect Natalie, probably drawn to her flowing garments.

"I hope he doesn't get too attached," Michelle said softly.

"Would that be so bad?"

She lifted her face to his in a way he remembered from many years before. No other face, no other eyes had that particular softness, that vulnerability. "He'd never get to see the filly."

"Never?"

She blinked, long lashes sweeping down with a tragic knowing that chilled Sam to the bone. "After the transplant, I don't see us coming back here too often. Before long, Cody'll be off to college, and I'll—" She broke off and her gaze slid away from his.

"What'll you be doing, Michelle?"

She was quiet for a long time. The only sounds came from Natalie and Edward's chattering and the occasional blowing of the mare.

"When I first came out here," she said, "I had some wild notion that my father and I would finally connect. That we'd finally get to know each other the way a father and daughter should know each other. Maybe I bought into some of that cellular memory stuff, thinking that if we shared our own flesh and blood, a perfect relationship would surely follow." She loosed a small, bitter laugh. "Instead, I think we're proof that there's nothing particularly special about a living related donor except maybe a few antigens in common."

"You're making up your mind about a lot of things in a short period of time," Sam pointed out. "Slow down, Michelle. You—" A snowball exploded square in the middle of his chest. "Hey!"

Edward and Natalie were both armed, hurling snowballs as fast as they could make them. Cody jumped the rail of the paddock and joined the attack. "Be careful of your head," Michelle called.

Cody barely acknowledged the warning. Sam aimed low with a snowball, missing. The kid was quick, a hard target.

Michelle took one in the shoulder before ducking to make some snowballs of her own.

The war drove off all thoughts of lunch. Natalie's wild squeals filled the air. Sam got in a few good shots, glad to ease the tension. Michelle, complaining of snow down her neck, grabbed his shoulders and held him in front of her like a shield.

"Wait a minute," he said, though her grip on him felt eerily right. "What's wrong with this picture?"

Cody took advantage, pelting him in the face and laughing so hard that Sam laughed, too.

Sam scooped up another handful of snow. The pager clipped to his belt went off.

"What's that?" Michelle held up her hand to signal a truce. Her face was wet from snow and beautifully flushed. Sam felt a strong surge of desire. If they were alone, he knew just where he'd kiss her, taste her. . . .

He checked the digital readout on the pager. His skin chilled at the code. "Michelle, your father's gone to the hospital."

Chapter 26

I hate it that I know the way to the hospital," Michelle said as the landscape whizzed past. She ran a finger around her collar, feeling the damp spots from the snowball fight. "It's sort of ghoulish, knowing the way to the hospital."

"Not if you work there." Sam's voice was calm, doctorly.

She pressed her knuckles to her mouth to keep the questions in. *What happened? Why? Does this mean the transplant has to be postponed?*

She didn't want to ask those questions yet. She was not ready to hear the answers. She wanted to see her father. Wanted to hear his voice again, take his hand in hers. Wanted to let him know she loved him.

I love you, Daddy.

How hard was that to say? Why hadn't she said it before? Because she wasn't sure she meant it, or was she afraid it would be one-sided?

"Almost there," Sam said, his truck veering around the snow-covered Salish statue in the middle of the town square. They arrived at the hospital, and under the awning she jammed her shoulder against the car door and opened it, feet racing as they hit the ground. The electronic doors hissed open.

"Gavin Slade," she told the clerk, the same one who was there for Cody's accident. "I'm his daughter, Michelle."

"In the exam room."

She rushed in to find her father with a stocky, gray-haired physician. Gavin looked haggard, a yellowish cast to his skin and the whites of his eyes.

"I'm Michelle Turner," she told the doctor, not taking her eyes off Gavin.

I love you, Daddy.

"Hey, Michelle. This is my doctor, Karl Schenk." His voice was gravelly, tired, thin.

"What happened?"

"Toxemia. The dialyzing fluid failed."

"But it's going to be fixed, right? He's going to be fine?"

Schenk stayed busy with the monitoring equipment.

Sam walked in, bringing the smell of snow and wind with him. She thought about what he'd said to her earlier, that her father had known about them as kids.

Is it true, Daddy? Are you the reason Sam disappeared?

She cast away the thought. This was hardly the time or place. She wanted to touch her father, but she didn't know where. He had an IV stuck in the top of one hand and another in the crook of the opposite arm. Tubes snaked from his midsection. She settled for laying her hand on his leg, covered in a thin aqua-colored sheet.

Time for the questions. She took a deep breath. "Will this have any effect on the transplant?"

Schenk regarded her with a level look. "I've got a call in to his nephrologist."

"And?"

"If Gavin stabilizes, he can proceed."

She looked her father severely in the eye. "So stabilize."

He tried to smile. She could tell he felt crummy, but the attempt encouraged her. "I'm trying."

Then Sam took charge. It didn't surprise her. In the past few days she had come to realize that the attractive, serious boy she'd once known had turned into a calm, decisive—still-attractive—man. So when he started going over the tests Schenk ordered, then switched to making sure someone called Edward to tell him to send Natalie and Cody home in the Rover, and then called her father's nutritionist, Tadao, she just stood back and let him work.

It felt good. Sinfully good. To have someone else in charge for a while. To have someone else say, "This is how it's going to be," was a luxury.

She watched Sam with a phone cradled on his shoulder and a metal clipboard in hand. Why did it feel so good when he took charge?

She felt vaguely disloyal, having such thoughts. Brad was a take-charge guy, too. But the things he took charge of were . . . different. The vacation plans, his next real-estate investment, country-club dues. He never burdened her with that sort of thing, because he knew it wasn't that important to her.

But there were burdens she had never asked him to share.

The sorts of things Sam was helping with, and she hadn't even asked.

As the afternoon headed on toward evening, she stood back in a daze of dissipating worry. Gavin's tests came back, indicating that he was stabilizing. Orderlies arrived to take him to a private room, and she stood by his bed while attendants checked all the monitoring equipment.

"Don't scare me like this again, Daddy." She tried to sound stern.

"Go on home to supper. I'll call for Jake when they decide to release me."

"I'd rather stay—"

"Michelle, I'm trying to tell you politely that I'm tired as hell, and as soon as you leave, I'm going to sleep. Okay?"

She peered at his thin face. It was a wonderful face, full of character and experience. He had such a stunning aura of charisma that even lying sick in bed, he still qualified for *People* magazine's "most beautiful" issue.

"Okay." It was awkward to kiss his cheek because of all the tubes and monitors. The cool, medicinal smell hung thick in the air. "'Bye, Daddy. See you tomorrow."

"First thing in the morning, I'm out of here."

"I hope so."

Sam was waiting in the corridor as she came out, quietly closing the door behind her.

"Never a dull moment," she said, trying to lighten the mood.

"That's Crystal City, all right."

They walked outside to find that it was sunset already. A glaze of orange tinted the mountains, and the temperature had dropped a few degrees. A gleaming black sport-utility vehicle drove by, slowing down as it passed the hospital. "Someone you know?" she asked Sam.

"Nope. Car's too new. Probably a rental." He opened the truck door for her. "You'd be a great candidate for primal-scream therapy."

"Why do you say that?"

"The tension. You're so damned tense even I can feel it. I think it's contagious."

"Sorry. You think it'll affect my kidney tests if I drink myself into oblivion tonight?"

"Most definitely."

"That's what I was afraid of."

"I'm not a big fan of drinking to oblivion on any night."

She climbed into the truck, shivering against the chill vinyl seat. "Sorry, Sam. I know it was awful for you, dealing with your mother's problem."

The streetlights blinked on, just a few along Main and Aspen. There was a certain coziness to this town that tugged at her. Some people thought it would be oppressive to live in a place where everyone knew everyone else's name. But after years in the big city, she understood the appeal.

"Cody mentioned meeting your mom," she said, uncomfortable with Sam's silence.

"Yeah?"

"He's curious. I think he wouldn't mind getting to know her."

"She'd like that. No idea what they have in common, though."

They passed the movie house. When they were teenagers, they had gone to the movies there. She remembered sitting in the popcorn-flavored darkness with Sam, holding hands and watching *An Officer and a Gentleman.*

"Too bad the Lynwood folded," she said, bothered by

the sight of the unlit marquee. The movable letters gaped like rotting teeth, spelling out the imperfect message, "CL SED."

"I think it had its last season about three years ago."

"My father wants to reopen it, but everything's on hold until after the surgery."

Sam pulled around to the side of the old building. "Want to go in?"

"Can we? It's not locked?"

In the lowering light she could see his smile as he rummaged in the glove box for a flashlight. "I've sneaked into a few picture shows in my day. Come on."

She felt a little furtive as they headed for the back of the building. She saw the gleam of headlights on Main Street, but no one was likely to notice the truck parked in the alley by the theater. As Sam had predicted, the rear fire exit wasn't locked. They went in, and he switched on the flashlight.

The shifting beam illuminated an eerie scene straight out of *Phantom of the Opera*. Michelle gazed at the old-fashioned chandeliers draped in cobwebs, peeling fleur-de-lis wallpaper, the shirred-velvet curtain over the screen in shreds.

"Creepy," she said, her breath making frozen puffs.

"You want to leave?"

"No, let's look around."

Floorboards creaked as they walked up the aisle. The box office and concession stand were dusty and deserted, the lobby empty, lined with vintage movie posters. The ones featuring her father bore his autograph. Sam beamed the flashlight on *Act of God*, a disaster epic that set box-office records and blasted her father into the ranks of the highest-paid stars of his day.

In the thirty-odd years since the poster had been printed,

Gavin Slade had changed very little. He had a classic, time-less bone structure that weathered well despite the years.

"I've always been ambivalent about his career," she confessed to Sam. "On the one hand, how could I look at something like this, or watch his performance in *The Face of Battle* and *not* be proud? On the other hand, he put his career before me—at least, until he needed something only I can give him. How can I not resent that?"

He was silent, and she hugged herself against a chill. "I'm a terrible person. I shouldn't think things like that."

Sam touched her shoulder. "You're not a terrible person. I figure it's pretty normal to feel that way, given the circumstances."

"Now you're sounding like Temple. The one who thought we had too many 'issues' to sort out."

An electric heater hung over the concession stand. Sam plugged it in, and Michelle was gratified when the coils took on a comforting red-orange glow. Evidently her father still kept up the utilities on the old place. Within a few minutes, the overhead heater bathed the lobby in faint light and a pleasant heat. She remembered the funky old furnishings from long ago: a musty club chair and chaise, marble ashtrays yellowed by the years. She took a seat on the old velvet-covered chaise lounge with rolled ends and fringe. Its springs creaked as she settled in.

"The way I figure," Sam said, turning to her, "your 'issues' will work out a lot better after the surgery's behind you."

So simple. She felt as if someone had taken a forklift and moved the weight that had been pressing on her chest. Why hadn't she thought of that? Why hadn't she made herself look beyond the surgery and understand that the real healing would take place if she simply let it happen?

"Thank you," she whispered as he sat beside her on the chaise. "Thank you for saying that."

"Feel better?"

She sensed the warmth from the heater and the comfort of Sam's presence and the dry odor of the abandoned building, and a strange and unaccountable feeling of peace and safety came over her.

"Much better."

"Good." He grinned. "It's what I live for."

Michelle drew her knees up to her chest, watching him. "I can't get over that you're a doctor."

He lifted his hand, skimmed his thumb over the ridge of her cheekbone, and everything inside her fell still, waiting, totally focused on the spot he was touching.

"I can't get over that you're a mother," he said.

He reached a place inside her no one had ever reached before—except the boy he had been so long ago. How could she have known, when they were eighteen, that he would be the only one? How could she have known that when he left her life, he'd leave a gulf of emptiness and loneliness no one else would ever fill?

"Damn it, Michelle," he said, dropping his hand, "I wish you'd told me."

She heard his anger, too, echoing her own, and the problem with this sort of anger was that it was fueled by regret—for what they didn't do, for the road they didn't take. And the problem with regret was that it had no place to *go*. It just stayed inside, turning dark and bitter.

"I tried to tell you," she said softly, picturing herself that day, frightened and excited and oh, so very young. It was November, the sunset dull in the sky, and she was wearing her riding clothes—buff-colored leggings and a big cable-knit Aran sweater. "You didn't show up for work that day."

He held himself very stiff, as though every cell in his body had come to attention. She could tell he knew which day she was talking about. She borrowed a Jeep from the ranch, and she drove slowly, terrified because of what the home pregnancy test had just revealed and nervous because she had never gone to Sam's home before.

It was a weathered, wood-frame shotgun house on the east side of town, one of a row of dwellings built for migrant cherry pickers to use in the summer. She had not missed the symbolism of having to drive over the railroad tracks to reach his house.

No lights burned in the windows, and the driveway was empty. On some gut level she could already sense the desertion, could already predict the silence that would greet her knocks upon the door. But she knocked anyway, at the front door and the back, ducking under a clothesline with a single forgotten sock hanging frozen from it. She called out, and then tried the back door, not surprised when it opened. Crystal City was a small town where people left their doors unlocked—particularly if there was nothing in the house to steal.

She had shivered, walking through the four rooms, picturing Sam there with his mother. Sagging furniture with holes in the upholstery, a dinette set from the fifties, swaybacked beds in the tiny bedrooms. No wonder he'd never invited her over.

"You were gone," she said after a long silence. "Your house was empty. I drove up to the café to see if your mom was still working there. Earl Meecham said she took off, hadn't even left a forwarding address for her last paycheck."

"Forwarding addresses are always a problem," he said, "when you don't know where you're going."

She stared into the ripening glow of the heater. "What would it have cost you to tell me good-bye?"

He was quiet for a long time, so long that she got suspicious and studied his face in the light from the heater. She didn't know him anymore, couldn't read that lean, serious face. He seemed tense, his eyes turbulent as if he was at war with himself.

"Sam?"

"I don't know why I didn't say good-bye," he said at last, his voice quiet and controlled. "It was a long time ago."

"Everything was a long time ago."

The anger drained away and brutally soft memories crept up to seize her. There was a time when they stood at the center of the world, and everything seemed possible. She remembered the laughter, the passion, and the utter belief that all their dreams would come true. She remembered the love everyone thought they were too young to feel.

He rubbed his thumb over her cheek. "I've never been good at good-byes."

She knew he was going to kiss her. He had his hand in the right place, cradling her cheek, and he had their eyes in the right place—they were both staring at each other's lips—and, most of all, he had the moment in the right place. She was not thinking of anything beyond the here and now, and how badly she wanted him to kiss her, hold her.

He leaned forward and she moved her knees out of the way, and neither of them hurried, because every heartbeat, every breath, every second was important. Their lips touched, and the taste of him rushed through her with a powerful force, memories exploding across the years, and the passion between them was fresh, alive, yet as old and familiar as something they had carried around for decades.

They didn't speak. They knew better than that. Because if one of them spoke, they'd start to rationalize, and if they rationalized, they would know this was insane, and in a tacit agreement they decided to explore the insanity. Their coats came off, then boots and sweaters and jeans, and his hands were everywhere, and so were hers, sensations tumbling faster than thought. Hard muscle, soft flesh, his mouth mapping the topography of her body until instinct and remembrance converged and they knew each other again. Finally, the hurrying started, because there was an urgency, a need that wouldn't wait. She leaned back against the curve of the chaise and he braced his arms on either side of her, and he came down and she came up, and there was a moment of union so perfect that she saw stars.

Afterward he stayed on top of her, and she wanted to keep him there forever, because as soon as one of them moved or spoke, life had to start up again. She felt his back warm beneath her palms, listened to his heightened breathing, touched her lips to the pulse in his neck.

"What are you thinking?" he asked, and he remembered that thing with her ear, the way it made her tingle all over when she felt the heat of his intimate whisper.

No one but him had ever discovered that about her.

"That we shouldn't move or talk," she whispered back.

"Good idea."

But after a while, she couldn't help it, and she asked, "What are *you* thinking?"

"Oh, honey. Dirty thoughts. Really dirty thoughts." And he told her in explicit detail, shoving her back against the chaise, whispering into her ear in the way only he knew how to do, and all of a sudden they were making love again, his kisses and the strokes of his body harsh the way she needed them to be, bringing her to a soaring climax that had her crying out, her voice echoing through the gloom of the empty building.

"*Now* what are you thinking?" he asked, long afterward.

"That I'm glad for the dark." She kissed him briefly— that inventive mouth that had just done such unspeakably exquisite things to her—and forced herself to sit up, pull on her sweater.

"Why?"

"Because—" she stood up, hurriedly pulling on panties and jeans "—I'm not an eighteen-year-old girl anymore. I'm thirty-five, and I look it."

He laughed in disbelief, zipping his jeans. "You're worried I'll be disappointed in how you *look?*"

She fumbled with the buttons of her fly. "Well, maybe not worried, but—"

"Listen." He took her busy hands and put them against his bare chest, his unbelievably muscular, sexy bare chest.

"I'm listening."

"Of course I remember the way you looked back then. How could I not? I was eighteen, too. Your body used to drive me nuts. Yeah, I remember that." He traced his finger down her throat, over her breasts, waking them up again. "But what I was thinking about when I was holding you just now was how I used to love you."

She felt dizzy, suddenly, sick and dizzy with guilt and confusion. "We'd better go."

He hesitated, as if he was going to say something else. But then he buttoned his shirt, turned and unplugged the heater, and flicked on the flashlight.

They left through the door they had come in. It had started to snow, big thick flakes, the kind pictured on

Christmas cards. In the sodium vapor glow of the corner streetlamp, the swirling snow looked glorious, magical.

Halfway between the door and the truck, a shadow fell across the alley.

Sam put his arms around her, catching her against his chest. "What the—"

A flash exploded in their faces, and although Sam didn't realize it, she knew exactly what had happened.

They'd found her. The dirt diggers. The paparazzi. The kidney-patient stalkers. The princess-murderers.

Tires spun on the salted and sanded road, and then the sport-utility vehicle sped away, leaving Michelle and Sam frozen like a pair of coyotes caught in a bounty hunter's searchlights. The familiar glowing ache from the flash filled her head. She should have recognized them. She had seen their Explorer pass the hospital earlier this evening. She should have known the buzzards were circling.

"What the hell was that all about?" Sam asked.

"You'll read it in the papers," she said dully, feeling her insides coil up with dread. "Could be as early as tomorrow." Digital file transfers had made the process as swift as a phone call.

"I don't read that kind of paper."

"You'll be amazed when you see who does."

Friday

Friday

M ichelle stood in the hall of the hospital feeling weak with relief. Her father had stabilized and he was back on the pre-op meds he'd been taking in preparation for the transplant. Barring any other crisis, they were back on track for the procedure. In a few minutes, he'd be discharged.

But she felt as if all the other parts of her life had careened off in different directions. Last night, in the mysterious darkness of a half-forgotten place, she and Sam had made love. She'd wanted him with a wildness and a hunger so uncharacteristic of her that she had begun to think she was becoming someone else entirely. A stranger to herself. A traitor to the life she had built so far from here. She should be feeling shame, regret, guilt . . . but she couldn't.

Restless with her thoughts, she wandered to the small

waiting lounge by the reception area. No one was around, so she helped herself to coffee. Nurse O'Brien came in, smiling a greeting.

"Michelle, right?" she asked.

"Michelle Turner. I'm spending way too much time at this hospital."

The nurse sat down on a vinyl-covered sofa and gave a weary sigh. "Tell me about it. There's a flu going around, so I've been working overtime for the past week. Your boy doing all right?"

"He's fine. But that head wound was a big scare." She paused, wondering how much the nurse knew about them. Everything, probably. This was a hospital, after all. "Did you happen to notice a reporter or photographer snooping around last night?"

"Uh-huh. I'm afraid your father was seen checking in yesterday." She sent Michelle an apologetic look. "We didn't let anyone in to see him."

"Good. It's a constant worry," she admitted. "I've tried to keep Cody anonymous for years." She took a deep breath. "Um, so are people here talking about it? About Sam and Cody?"

"That they're father and son?" she said easily. "Oh, yeah."

"I was afraid so." Michelle was dying to ask what they were saying, but she was not sure she wanted to know.

"I never could picture Sam with a kid of his own."

Something in Alice O'Brien's tone, in the deep knowing of her observation, caught Michelle's attention. "Have you worked with Sam long?"

Alice O'Brien lifted her eyebrows in surprise. "He didn't tell you?"

Michelle felt a strange shift in the atmosphere and instinctively braced herself. "Tell me what?"

The nurse waited, clearly weighing her options. Then she said, "Sam and I used to be married."

The atmosphere silently exploded. "Oh." *God*.

"It appears you and Sam must have a lot of catching up to do."

"He should have told me," Michelle said, mortified by the situation he had put her in.

"It's all old history, but it's no secret." Alice O'Brien spoke straightforwardly. "When he came here five years ago, I took one look at him and fell like a ton of bricks." She grinned. "Most of the staff did. Sam and I got along great, decided to get married. I think Sam just drifted into the relationship, and I was fool enough to mistake it for love." Tugging her pink sweater close around her shoulders, she added, "I have the classic nurse personality— nurturing, caretaking—and he wanted love and sex and a woman."

"Alice," Michelle said, "you don't have to explain this." *Sam should have*.

"I don't mind. You're bound to hear the story from somebody or other. It wasn't too dramatic. I fell hard, and Sam—well, he sort of came along for the ride, I suppose. When I said I wanted to start a family, that was my wake-up call." She pushed back the sleeve of her sweater, checked her watch. "He had a bad reaction to that. Said he saw enough unwanted kids in his practice. And I realized he was never going to give me what I needed. Hell, what I *deserved*. So we split up." A tolerant smile tilted her mouth. "He felt bad about it, but I stuck to my guns. It's better this way. We're still friends, colleagues."

Michelle leaned back in her chair, her thoughts spinning. Though younger than Michelle, Alice spoke with the wisdom of a much older woman, and her words reverberated in the silence. *He was never going to give me what I needed.*

"In his way, I think he loved me for a while. Just wasn't meant to last," she concluded, standing up and checking her watch again. "He's a complicated guy, had a rough life. He learned to love fast, he learned to love hard, and he learned to let go. No one ever taught him how to hold on."

Mounted on a line-backed dun mare named Daisy, Michelle rode along a track that wound to the south and west of Lonepine. She felt the cold slice of air in her lungs, the numbing lash of the wind on her face. The afternoon sky was overcast and tinged bronze by a stingy leak of sunlight.

After Alice's revelation, Michelle had taken her father home; then she drove straight to Lonepine. Sam had gone off on horseback to check a wildlife trap. "He'll probably stop at the hot springs on the way back," Edward had informed her. "He generally likes to do that when he's in a mood."

In a mood. She didn't ask Edward what he meant by that. She'd find out for herself soon enough.

The trail was easy to follow, just as Edward had said it would be. She rode up past an abandoned slash pile from an old logging operation, then angled down toward a low field where the snow had melted away to reveal steaming mudflats. A herd of elk shied away as she approached. At a rock-bound natural pool, a tall roan horse was tethered, but she couldn't see Sam. Dismounting, she wound the reins around a low alder branch and climbed up to the pool. Thermal springs abounded in the area, and the wispy steam softened and obscured everything, adding a faint tinge of salt and sulphur to the air.

"Fancy meeting you here," said a disembodied voice.

Michelle peered through the steam, and there he was, sitting chest-deep in the pool, wearing nothing but a smile. She tried not to think about that smile, or the way the dampness curled his hair, or the beads of water on his shoulders. "I had a little talk with Alice at the hospital today," she said.

His smile disappeared. "Then I guess you'd better have a seat."

"Maybe you could get dressed, Sam—"

"Or you could join me." The smile sneaked back across his lips.

She sank down on a flat rock, covering her face with her hands. "I can't believe you didn't tell me you were married."

She heard a trickle of water, and suddenly he was gliding toward her, taking her hands away from her face. She should leave now, just get up and ride away, but she felt stuck here, unable to move.

"I would have told you, Michelle, but we haven't had that much time to talk."

"We've had time to do a lot more than talk."

"Yeah." His hands—damp, warm, insistent—peeled off her gloves and unzipped her jacket. "Yeah, we have."

The rising steam and the heat and his touch filled her with a strange and helpless lassitude, and everything she'd planned to say simply evaporated. With slow and deliberate care he removed her boots and socks.

"It's my fault my marriage to Alice didn't work out." His whisper rasped in her ear, and then he kissed her in a leisurely way, imprisoning her by her own desire. It was a powerful drug, the taste of him, the taste of passion.

"She claims her needs . . . weren't met." She forced the words out even as she surrendered, peeling off sweater and jeans, letting the delicious shock of cold air and hot water race over her bare skin.

"She's right. I couldn't give her what she needed." Long slow slide of his hands down over her body as he drew her deep into the silky water, secretly heated in the heart of the earth. "Because I gave it all to you."

Sam had always been one to think on a matter before deciding what to do. But the thing was, all the thinking in the world never seemed to do a damned bit of good. He always came around to what his gut told him to do in the first place. The second he had figured out the truth about Cody, he had been consumed by fascination. He wanted to know the boy, be near him, be with him. Circumstances had handed him a way to do that—if he could get Michelle to agree to it.

Still sitting in the thermal pool and squinting through the thick wisps of steam, he watched her getting dressed. His body reacted as fast as it had when he was eighteen— maybe faster. Because now he knew from experience that sex like they'd just had didn't come along every day.

He figured he ought to be dressed when he broached the topic of Cody, so he made himself chill out, waded to the shore, and dried off before the numbing cold hit him. Yanking on jeans, socks, and boots, he kept stealing glances at Michelle. She was beyond beautiful, always had been, but now that he was coming to know her again, he saw something more in this woman. Years ago, he had seen the promise. Now he saw the way time and caring and motherhood had molded her, softened her. Though she was slender, her breasts and belly had the sweet roundness common to any woman who had ever given birth and nursed a baby. It didn't seem to matter how much time passed. The mother-shape was always there.

"What are you smiling about?" she asked, slightly suspicious, still flushed from the hot springs and from their lovemaking.

He tugged a gray UT Athletic Department sweatshirt over his head. "Do you have to ask?"

She sniffed, but not before he caught a flash of amusement in her eyes. "I didn't come out here looking for sex. I came looking for answers."

"So the sex was just sort of a bonus, I guess," he said.

"Very funny." She put on her boots and started walking toward the horses.

"Michelle, wait." He followed her, jumping from stone to stone to keep clear of the steaming mud. A few elk, only slightly perturbed by the presence of humans, sidled off toward the woods. "There's something I need to ask you."

His tone must have touched off her suspicions, for she turned to him with her eyes narrowed and her arms folded across her chest, unconsciously protecting herself. "What is it?"

He figured he'd best just get it said. "When you and Gavin go in for the surgery, I want Cody to stay with me."

He knew she was going to object before she even said a word. It was there in her narrow-eyed, guarded expression. He didn't wait for her to speak, but went on, "I've been thinking about it for days, and it's a good plan. He can—"

"I already have a plan for Cody," she said. "He's staying at Blue Rock. Tadao and Jake are there, and now Natalie. They—"

"They are not his family." Sam tried to keep his temper, his desperation, in check. "His flesh and blood. He's got me and my mother. He needs a chance to know us. The timing's right, Michelle."

She took a step back. "No."

"What are you worried about?" he asked. "I want to spend some time with my son. How can you object to that?"

"Because I don't think you know what you're asking." She spread her arms. "You just dismissed your marriage to Alice with a shrug, more or less. You split up with her after a year. And now you want to take on a son?"

The barb dug deep, but Sam wouldn't let his pain show. He knew what she was doing. She was trying to make him mad, hurt him, so he'd back off. Suddenly, he saw her so clearly that he wanted to hug her. "Aw, Michelle, you don't need to be afraid."

Her chin came up. "I'm not afraid."

"You are. You're scared Cody and I will become best friends and he'll forget the person who walked the floors at night with him, and fixed him birthday cake, and stood in the rain at all his soccer games." Sam walked over to her, took her hand, pressed his lips to it, and kept hold. She tasted of the mineral springs. "You don't need to worry. A kid will always choose his mother. Trust me on this."

He stepped away and jammed on his hat. He hadn't meant to say something so revealing. "Come on, Michelle. You've had sixteen years. I'm asking for a week."

She unlooped the lead rein of her mare, then raked her fingers through the horse's thick winter coat. "Where are we, Sam?" she asked him. "I need to know that before I decide."

He knew she wasn't asking for directions home. They had come to a place where there were no more secrets, no hesitation. But with their new closeness came vulnerability on both their parts. He didn't know for certain he could become a family man overnight. His experience with his mother had taught him the tender hurts of commitment and responsibility. But he wanted to try. They were opening themselves to trouble—but also to joy, if they could make this work. Sam was sure of it.

"Well?" she asked, waiting. "Where are we?"

He held her horse's head while she mounted and stood looking up at her. "At the beginning, I guess."

The restaurant called Trudy's was one of the few good things about Crystal City, Cody decided. His meal of a giant cheeseburger and fries, followed by chocolate cream pie, had been a welcome change from the macrobiotic stuff his grandfather's nutrition specialist served.

Too bad his parents had ruined it by dropping a bomb on him right after dessert.

He scowled into the darkened display window of the Northern Lights Feed Store. He had asked to be excused after dinner, and for the past fifteen minutes had been wandering down Main Street, which was basically the only street in town. At one end lay city hall and the library, which appeared to be the only place other than Trudy's that stayed open after dark. At the other end was an old movie house with an abandoned shop adjacent to it, the glossy windows practically begging for someone to throw a rock through them.

His mom said Gavin owned the Lynwood and might do something with it one of these days, but for now it was as empty as a Sunday afternoon. A few kids came and went from the library, and the sight of them—guys pushing and jostling each other, girls with schoolbooks hugged to their chests—only lowered Cody's mood. Day after tomorrow he would be starting school, which added insult to injury.

Hunching his shoulders up, he moved along, passing the shop where Tammi Lee Gilmer worked. His mom and Sam were probably wondering where he'd gone. He pictured them sitting across the table from each other at the restaurant, maybe holding hands and looking worried. Hell, let them worry. He had promised to stick around, said he just wanted to get out for some air. Fat chance—the Greyhound bus was idling across the street, puffing diesel fumes into the night. The lighted header over the bus bore enticing destinations: MISSOULA-SPOKANE-SEATTLE.

Man, what he wouldn't give to hop on that sucker right now. Digging in his pocket, he found a flattened pack of Camels. Two left. When those were gone, he didn't know what he'd do. How did kids get their smokes in a town where everyone knew everyone else? He lit up, letting the match burn for a minute while reading the matchbook cover: "Alone? Scared? Broke? Dial 1-800-RUNAWAY . . ."

"I should be so lucky," he muttered under his breath, then took a deep drag of the cigarette. Around the first of the school year, he had taken up smoking in order to hang out with Claudia, and it had worked. She'd noticed him, bummed a cigarette, and within a few weeks they were going out. He wondered what she was up to now. They'd only been apart for a week, but he was already worried she wouldn't wait around for him. The thought pissed him off so much that he nearly plowed down a couple of kids coming out of the library. He said a brusque, "Excuse me" and propped his hip on a cold steel bike rack in front of the building. There were only a couple of bikes chained to the rack. Must be hard to ride on these pitted, icy streets. Why did people live in Montana anyway? he wondered, blowing out a stream of smoke.

"Hey, Cody," said a familiar voice.

He looked up to see Molly Lightning, her arms laden with books. He held his pose at the bike rack. "Hey."

Her gaze fell to the orange-tipped cigarette in his hand, and he felt stupid all of a sudden. Stupid and self-conscious, the way he had when he'd first learned to smoke. Trying to act nonchalant, he dug for the nearly empty pack. "You want a smoke?"

"No."

He'd known without asking that she didn't smoke. Ah, well. At least she wasn't going to be all sanctimonious about it.

She seemed ill at ease as she glanced up and down the street.

"You waiting for someone?" he asked, trying to be discreet as he dropped the cigarette and ground it out in the damp snow. Good move, he thought peevishly. Half of a perfectly good smoke, and now it was gone.

"My mom's supposed to pick me up at eight." She gazed at him with unmistakable interest. She might have a crush on him, he thought, and the idea pleased him.

At the other end of the block, three guys in baggy pants and big parkas made a racket, laughing and shoving each other. One of them picked up a rock or a chunk of ice and hurled it at the marquee over the awning of the Lynwood, punching the air in victory at the sound of shattering lightbulbs.

"Jerks," Molly said softly.

Cody felt a little better to hear her echo his own thoughts. "Who are they?"

"Guys from school. Billy Ho, Ethan Lindvig, Jason Kittredge." The threesome crammed themselves into the cab of an old El Camino and roared off into the dark. "Everyone thinks Billy is so cool, but I think he's a jerk.

He was on juvey probation last year for stealing, but that only made kids think he's even more cool. He didn't even get kicked off the football team." She fell silent, looking worried, as if she had said too much. She shifted uncomfortably from one foot to the other.

"Um, can I take those books from you?" Cody asked, hoping he didn't sound too dorky.

She smiled the way she had the first day they'd met. Sort of shy, but also a little bit sexy. "Thanks," she said, transferring the stack of library books to him. "I didn't want to put them down in the snow." She smelled really good, like soap and fresh air. Cody hoped the cigarette smell didn't cling in his jacket. "So what are you doing out here?" she asked.

He nodded toward Trudy's in the middle of the block. "My mom and . . . Sam McPhee took me to dinner. I just wanted to walk around a little." She didn't say anything, but listened with an expectant quality. "My mom's going into the hospital to donate a kidney to my grandfather," he blurted out.

He braced himself for her shock and disgust, but she surprised him. She simply smiled again, and said, "Cool."

"I guess." For the first time, Cody started to think maybe it *was* kind of cool. "But," he added, his rush of candor continuing, "while they're in the hospital next week, they want me to stay at Sam's. They sort of left the decision up to me."

"So what are your choices?" she asked.

He liked it that she seemed genuinely interested. He had planned to call Claudia tonight and get her take on all this, but she didn't know the people involved. It was easier standing around talking to Molly, face-to-face. "I can stay at Blue Rock with Jake and Tadao—they work for Gavin." He rested his chin on the top book. "Or I can go to Lonepine."

She grinned and put her hands on her hips. "Are you kidding? Like there's a decision to be made? Sam's your dad, and he's got a horse farm. It's a no-brainer."

Saturday

T ammi Lee Gilmer didn't usually get Saturdays off work, but she had arranged to be off in order to pick up her car at McEvoy's Garage. Setting a freshly lit cigarette on the cluttered bathroom counter, she took a round brush and teased some loft into her hair. No one teased their hair anymore; she knew that. Hell, no one smoked anymore. But that sure didn't stop her.

She knew Sam didn't like her smoking, but he never said a word. He had stood by her, helping her break so many other habits that the cigarettes probably seemed minor in comparison. She picked up the cigarette and took a drag, scowling at the amber burn mark it had made on the edge of the faux marble countertop. It was disgusting, really. She should quit.

Tomorrow.

Today, she wasn't going to beat herself up over it. This

was something it had taken her years of AA to learn. She had to forgive herself, to avoid sinking into regrets about the past. It was an everyday battle for her.

She did her makeup and put on a pair of jeans and a loose sweatshirt. She still fit into her size-eight Wranglers, and she was proud of that. Yet deep inside her dwelt a strange longing that seized her at the oddest of times. It was a longing to be soft and doughy, maybe like LaNelle Jacobs, who owned the quilt shop. She secretly dreamed of being like LaNelle: plump and bespectacled, with forearms that jiggled and a double chin, wearing a housedress and a bib apron and sensible shoes. Smelling of talcum powder and Jergens lotion and freshly baked bread.

Tammi Lee walked outside, lifting her face to an overcast sky and feeling the tingle of the nineteen-degree temperature on her face. Yeah, it was insane, but she wanted to be one of those plus-size blue-haired women. Because when you looked like that, it told folks you knew your place in the world. It meant you'd raised a family, making pancakes for them on the weekends and reading bedtime stories to the kids. It meant you'd made a house into a home, putting up curtains and picking out the right color for the walls and buying flats of petunias for the garden every spring. It meant you had grandkids who came running up the walk to the front door because they couldn't wait to see you. It meant you had a husband who had several annoying habits, but you loved him anyway because he was your whole world.

God, what she wouldn't give to fit into a life like that, instead of into her size-eight Wranglers.

She felt a familiar buzzing heat inside her and started walking down the street toward the center of town. The buzz was a warning; it was the craving, the dark desire that had consumed her for so many years. One drink, that was all it would take. One drink, and the buzzing would quiet and she'd feel normal again.

She quickened her pace, clenching her hands into fists inside her jacket pockets. Maybe she'd better give her sponsor a call. This was a weak moment; it had come out of nowhere. They always did.

Yet as she walked, the cold had a calming effect on her, and the sick, thirsty moment passed. She had the life she had. God knew it was more than she deserved. By the time she got to the garage, the craving had settled to a dull roar. "Hey, Tom," she said, stepping into the overheated, grease-scented office. "Am I all set?"

"New water pump did the trick," he said.

She paid him in cash. She used cash for almost everything these days, because writing checks had never brought her anything but trouble. Sam had given her a debit card drawing on his own account, but she avoided using that. Giving her her life back was enough; she didn't want to take more from him than she already had.

A block from the garage, she pulled into Ray's Quik Chek to get a cup of coffee and the latest *Enquirer*, hot off the press. Sam gave her grief about all the gossip rags and movie magazines she bought, but she loved them.

The new *Enquirer*s were still wrapped in plastic binding. As she poured herself a cup of coffee, Ray opened them up and sold her one, along with *People* and her own reserved copy of *Country Billboard*. She went to her car and sat there sipping the coffee, waiting for the blower to heat up and paging through the magazines.

A giant picture of a 108-year-old *Titanic* survivor occupied the front page of the *Enquirer*, but a small inset at the top caught her eye.

"Ho-ly shit," she muttered, nearly dropping her coffee. Her hand shook as she set the cup in a holder and opened the paper to page two. A file photo of Gavin Slade and Michelle, looking as golden and fit as Peter and Bridget Fonda, caught her eye. Next to that was a blurry shot of someone on a stretcher being wheeled into County Hospital. On the same page, a grainy black-and-white picture showed Michelle Turner and Sam, caught in an embrace in the middle of a snowy street. The headline read: *Daughter of Dying Movie Idol Seeks Solace with Lonesome Cowboy.*

The Chevy fishtailed out of the parking lot. One of the few good things about her rambling lifestyle was that she had probably driven more miles than a long-distance trucker, and she was good at it. Negotiating the icy patches on the highway, she raced home and picked up the phone.

Sam was on duty today, but his service took the message. "No emergency," Tammi Lee said, "but it's important."

Next, she tried Blue Rock Ranch. The guy who answered the phone said Mr. Slade was "unavailable." Tammi Lee had no choice but to try the hospital. Maybe the *Enquirer* was right about something for a change.

She reached the hospital in five minutes, and the first thing she saw was Cody Turner sitting hunched on a concrete bench outside the attached professional building where Sam's office was. He wore a knitted black cap and little wiry headphones. His foot jiggled in time to the music only he could hear.

My grandson. That's my goddamned grandson, she thought wonderingly.

He looked cold, sitting there, restless and sulky. And a bit like Sam.

She got out, boots crunching on the sand-and-salt surface of the parking lot. "Hey, Cody. Remember me? Tammi Lee Gilmer."

He took off the headphones. "Hi."

"So what's up?" She kept her voice casual.

"My grandfather drove me over to get my stitches out. And he had some kind of checkup."

"So how's the cut?"

He took off his black knit cap. "Okay, I guess."

She studied the curved wound. "Some week, huh?" she said. "All this hospital stuff."

"Yeah, it sucks."

She indicated his Discman. "What kind of music do you like?"

"Alternative, some heavy metal. And some older stuff," he said vaguely.

"Ever heard of rockabilly?"

"Sure." He put his hat back on.

"I know something about rockabilly. Used to sing in a band."

"Nuh-uh," he said, regarding her with dubious interest.

"I did. A group called Road Rage. Had a big hit single called 'Dearly Departed.'" She hummed the melody line.

His eyes grew wide. "No way. I've heard that song."

"A lot of folks have. It was on a Dodge truck commercial." She steadied herself. "Listen, maybe you could come over for a while today."

He was quiet, scuffing his toe against a lump of ice on the sidewalk.

"If you get bored, you can go right home, promise."

He looked her straight in the eye, and she realized he had a great face, a beautiful face, the face of a boy who was turning downright handsome. But in addition to handsomeness, Tammi Lee could see insolence, difficulty. Michelle Turner must be having quite a time, raising this kid.

"I saw that thing in the paper," he said.

She forced herself not to drop her gaze. "I was hoping you hadn't."

"Sam saw it, too. All the nurses were waiting to show it to him when he got to work this morning."

"The paper's a rag. They print lies and innuendo." She took a deep breath, wishing for a cigarette. "That picture doesn't mean a thing. Your mom probably slipped on the ice and Sam grabbed her so she wouldn't fall."

"Maybe," he said. "I hate those damned tabloids."

"Me, too," she lied.

"When I was little, my mom was always worried they'd come after us because of Gavin."

"And did they?"

"No, but she'd always say, 'Look at Lisa Marie Presley. You want to end up like that?'" His mouth hinted at a grin.

"So what do you say? Want to come see where your old grandma lives?"

He hesitated. "I guess."

"Wait here, then. I need to make sure it's okay."

He replaced the headphones and Tammi Lee went to the clinic entrance of the brick building. She usually got a big kick out of seeing Sam in his long white coat, but today she was worried. "Got a minute, Sam?" she asked him quietly.

He held open the door to the staff lounge. It was empty, a clutter of coffee mugs and well-thumbed medical manuals and clipboards on the table.

"So how much truth was there in that tabloid story?" she asked. No point in beating around the bush. "Are you taking up with a girl you went nuts over seventeen years ago?"

It was hard to read her son's mood. He had always been a stoic. In one of her many recovery sessions, she had admitted to taking shameless advantage of his calmness, his willingness to forgive her, no matter what. When she'd said so to his face, he had given her a sweet-sad smile and said, "You are who you are, Mama. You don't forgive the clouds for raining."

The memory touched her, and she took Sam's hand. "So is this just a fling," she asked, "or—"

"It's not a fling," he said.

She wished she could be the kind of mother you saw on TV, the one who could pat his arm, say a few wise words, and make everything work out fine before the next commercial. "Well, I'm no expert, but you'd better be sure you know what you want out of this. Because there are three of you involved, and one's just a kid."

"I realize that. Cody's going to stay with me while Michelle and Gavin go in for surgery."

"Yeah?" She rinsed a coffee mug at the sink and poured herself a cup, trying to picture her son being someone's father. "So are you excited?"

"Sure. Nervous, too. He's got to start school on Monday. I never heard of a sixteen-year-old starting mid-year in a new place and actually liking it."

She sipped the slightly stale coffee. "Builds character." She set down the mug and glanced at the door, making sure they were alone. "What are you going to do about the tabloid story?"

"Ignore it."

"Is Michelle ignoring it?"

"We haven't had a chance to talk." His face looked taut with frustration. "She and Gavin just left for Missoula to prep for the surgery."

"Maybe you'd better get on down to Missoula and talk things over with her." Something—fate, destiny, pure chance—had brought Sam and Michelle together again. Lord knew, they'd never had much of a chance as kids. "Don't second-guess her, Sam. You know, this morning I was having regrets, wishing I'd done things differently, made better choices. I don't want you to do that. I don't ever want you to have regrets."

"I can't get away until tomorrow morning."

"Then go tomorrow morning," she said. "I swear, for a doctor, you're pretty dense sometimes."

He sent her a fleeting grin. "Okay. I'll offer to drive Cody down in the morning."

Cody was quiet on the way to her house. As she let him in the front door, she wished she had put out some potpourri. The house smelled of stale cigarette smoke and yesterday's coffee. She wouldn't blame the kid if he turned and walked out.

He stepped inside hesitantly, looking around.

Tammi Lee couldn't stand it anymore. She grabbed a cigarette from a pack on the counter and lit up. Belatedly she asked, "You don't smoke, do you?"

He shrugged. "Sure."

"Well, I'm not offering you one. Your dad would kill me. How about a Coke?" She went to the fridge. "I understand Monday is the big day. For the transplant."

He popped open the can. "Yep." He drank his Coke while a long, awkward silence spun out. Tammi Lee finished her cigarette and lit another one. Cody's gaze wandered around the room like that of a trapped animal looking for escape. And suddenly his expression changed from wary to wondering.

"Wow," he said under his breath. "Is that a Stratocaster?"

"Yeah. Just like Dick Dale used to play." She took the vintage electric guitar from its stand in the corner. The old instrument was a classic. She'd pawned and rescued the thing countless times, and in the end she still had it. She rarely played these days, but she knew she'd kept it for a reason.

As she looked at Cody's face, she finally figured out what that reason was.

"Do you play?"

"A little," he said. "Do you?"

She took the guitar, adjusted the tuning, strummed a few riffs, her fingers surprisingly nimble. Glancing at Cody, she laughed at his expression. "What, you didn't believe me?" She stuck a cassette tape into the console. "This is a demo tape called 'Hand-Me-Down Dreams.'"

She hadn't heard it in ages, and the sound of her own playing and singing startled her. She remembered laying down the tracks in a Reno studio they'd rented by the hour. She'd left Sam wailing in a playpen in the control room. After the final cut, they'd all gone out to get wasted, Sam sleeping in his carseat under a table in the dim, smoke-filled club.

"It's a good song," Cody said when it was over.

"You think so?"

"Sure."

"Feel like making pizza?"

"I could eat, I guess."

Amazing. A teenage grandson who actually wanted to spend time with her.

And she didn't even have to wear a housedress and sensible shoes.

Sunday

Sunday

Sam had no privileges at St. Brendan Hospital in Missoula, but he used his credentials to inquire about Michelle's procedure, and learned that everything was still on schedule. She was staying at an old Arts and Crafts–era hotel built for timber barons early in the century. Now, because of its proximity to the hospital, it was always occupied by families of patients and visiting doctors. Early in the morning, he stood outside her door, trying to collect his thoughts, but they refused to be collected so he knocked.

"Who is it?" Her voice was small, but not sleepy.

"It's Sam."

"Come on in," she said, opening the door. Bathrobe. Bare feet. A look of apprehension on her face. On the bed lay a paperback novel and several newspapers spread across the rumpled covers.

"Hi." He bent and kissed her, aiming badly, his lips grazing her temple. She smelled of toothpaste and pHiso-derm disinfectant.

"Is Cody all right? Did he drive down with you?"

"He's fine. I left him downstairs in the coffee shop with Gavin, eating pancakes."

"So you think this arrangement—him staying with you—is going to be all right?"

"Sure, Michelle. We agreed."

"If he gets to be too much for you, I want to know right away."

"Your confidence in me is so gratifying."

She sent him a fleeting smile. "I think you believe it's easier than it is."

So far, it *had* been easy, but he and Cody had only been together one night. Cody had been quiet, probably thinking about the surgery and school. Sam almost felt sorry for the kid. "How did your angiogram go?" he asked, deliberately changing the subject. The procedure was the last and most physically invasive of all the testing done on a living donor. He knew it to be a fairly scary and un-comfortable procedure. She had been treated to a mild sedative. Through a small incision, a tube was inserted into a vein and a dye injected so the transplant team could study her kidneys and all the related connections.

"It was great. A barrel of fun. Natalie and I laughed for hours."

"Ah, a sense of humor. That's always a good sign."

"That's what the nurse who shaved my groin said."

"You feeling all right now?"

She sat down on the bed, leaning back against a bank of pillows. "I felt all right five minutes after the proce-dure, but they made me lie motionless for six full hours. They picked out a lovely kidney for my father, so I guess everything worked out. They're going to take the one from my left side."

She paled a little as she spoke, and Sam's heart constricted. Who did she tell her fears to? Her hopes and her dreams? Natalie? The elusive Brad? Was Cody old enough to understand?

"So do you want to talk about it?" Unable to ignore the issue any longer, he indicated the paper on the bed.

She picked it up by her thumb and forefinger. "I've seen worse. When I was twelve, they printed a photo of me dancing with one of the Kennedy cousins at a wedding, with a caption about a child bride."

The paper was folded open to the story. The headline and text were filled with blatant suggestions and outright lies, but the camera had caught . . . something. The falling snow softened the focus, and there was a suggestion of movement in the way Sam's arm went around her and her head was tucked against his chest. It was a picture of two alone, absorbed in each other. The invasion of privacy made him sick.

"When I saw this rag," he said, "I wanted to hurt somebody."

"Welcome to Gavin's world." She gave an unapologetic shrug. "You get used to it by learning to ignore it."

He didn't want to get used to this. Didn't want to ignore it. But he felt himself being drawn to her, just as he'd drawn her into the hot springs. The first time he'd lost Michelle, he had built a hard wall around his heart, and that wall had protected him from the very things he was starting to feel now.

She worried her lower lip with her teeth. "So did Cody see the story?"

"Yeah."

"Did he say anything?"

"Not much. Just that you made out better than Lisa Marie Presley."

"So you don't think . . . he's reading anything into it?"

"I don't know. He didn't say much about it to me or my mother."

Her eyes widened. "He was with Tammi Lee? By choice?"

Sam felt a twinge of annoyance. "What, you don't approve of my white-trash mother?"

"Oh, Sam. Damn it, you know that's not what I meant. I have trouble picturing Cody hanging out with anyone over sixteen. I hope he was civil to your mother."

"They seemed to get along okay. Talked about music, I think."

She drew her knees to her chest. "I guess I don't really know her myself."

"She's changed a lot," Sam said.

"We've all changed a lot."

"Some things don't change at all." He took a deep breath. "After all these years, I still want you."

"Sam—"

He gestured at the papers. "There's something going on between us."

"Don't believe everything you read," she shot back, her pale cheeks turning red.

He stepped closer to the bed, touched her shoulder. "I didn't have to read it in the paper. But you know, I'm kind of glad it's out in the open."

She shifted away from him. "Do you know how incredibly bad your timing is?"

"What, because I didn't show up at a soccer game when you were feeling lonely?"

"Screw you." She glared at him. "I never thought I'd

see you again, Sam. Ever. And now I'm just supposed to make room in my life for you?"

"Why are you so testy?" he asked.

She took a deep breath, closed her eyes briefly. When she opened them she appeared more composed. "It's nerves," she admitted. "I've never been much good at dealing with . . . unforeseen circumstances. I'm letting Cody stay with you this week. What more do you want? What?"

He paused. Put away his frustration. "It's not just Cody. I want to know you again. I want . . . what we had Thursday night, and Friday at the hot springs."

"We got carried away. It's not like me to lose my . . . perspective like that." Her hands twisted into a knot of nerves in her lap. "I have a good job, I'm up for partner, I have a perfectly fine life in Seattle. Shall I chuck all that because you've got those great eyes?"

"I never knew you thought I had great eyes."

"There's a lot you never knew about me. If you knew me, you'd understand that I can't have a fling with you for old time's sake."

"What makes you think it's a fling?" He watched the agitated pulse leaping in her neck, and he traced it with his finger. Soft. So soft, like dry silk.

"We have no business getting involved no matter what our hormones are telling us."

He threaded his fingers up into her satiny hair. The years swept away, and everything he had felt for her, everything he had kept inside him all his life, rose up, seeming to push the air from his lungs. "Michelle, I'm not listening to my hormones. I'm listening to my heart."

Her lower lip trembled, and she caught it in her teeth, looking away. "What on earth," she asked with tears in her voice, "makes you think this could work?"

He drew her around to face him. "What makes you think it can't?"

A sharp knock on the door interrupted them.

"Michelle," a voice called. "It's me."

"Oh, God," she whispered. "Brad."

Chapter 30

"D on't get up." Sam walked over to the door, cool and calm, as if he had not just turned Michelle's world inside out. He opened the door, and in walked Brad.

He was good-looking in a clean-cut J. Crew way. He had a "yachty" air about him. One of the things that first attracted her to him was that settled refinement. There could be no chaos in the life of such a man.

"Brad." She tried to compose herself. "I wasn't expecting you." She was dying to know why he was here. Earlier they had agreed he wouldn't come unless she asked him to. But he was here. Was it because of the tabloid, or had he decided she needed him?

Her voice deserted her as he and Sam regarded each other like a pair of rival stags about to tangle their antlers. Then he brushed past Sam and came over to the bed, bending to kiss her forehead. Expensive aftershave and a shirt that crackled with starch. Altoid mints. *Brad.*

"Hi, babe." He stood back, regarding her critically.

She shifted nervously on the bed. Was she blushing? Could he see where Sam had been touching her cheek, her hair—

"So how'd it go? You okay?" Brad asked.

"Great. We're all set for tomorrow. Brad, I want you to meet Sam McPhee. Sam, this is Bradley Lovell."

"You're the guy," Brad said, his voice controlled. "The guy in the paper." He patted the side of his Louis Vuitton flight bag, stuffed with folded newspapers. "Michelle told me all about you."

"Yeah?" Sam looked over at her, lifting an eyebrow. "She didn't tell me squat about you." There was nothing— *nothing*—J. Crew about his looks. It was obvious he hadn't shaved today. He had on time-worn jeans that had custom-tailored themselves to his long, lean body. A gray athletic sweatshirt and a baseball cap. And he was asking her with his eyes: *What did you tell him, Michelle? Did you tell him we made love? Did you tell him you saw stars? Did you tell him you cried yourself to sleep that night?*

"Michelle said you used to be . . . what, some sort of hired hand at her dad's place?" Brad spoke nonchalantly, as if it really didn't matter to him. A small muscle tensed in Sam's jaw.

"That was years ago, Brad," she said, breaking in. "Sam's a physician now. I told you that, too."

"So what are you doing here?" Brad's gaze was blunt and challenging as he glared at Sam.

"Wondering why a guy would let Michelle go through this alone."

The testosterone was getting thick, she thought wryly. "I'll tell you what he's *not* doing. He's not getting into a pissing contest with you." She scowled at Sam, then at Brad, daring them to defy her. "In case you've forgotten, this is about my father."

Sam went to the door. She knew he was not retreating. It was clear on his face that he wasn't through with her yet. "I have to get back. I'm on call this afternoon. So I guess . . . I'll see Cody after school tomorrow." He stared at her for a moment, and she felt strange soft echoes of the way he had touched her when they made love. He adjusted the bill of his baseball cap. "Your transplant team's the best. Everything will be fine."

Michelle felt compelled to explain to Brad, "Cody's going to stay with Sam this week."

Brad let out a low whistle. "More power to you. Don't let him pull the wool over your eyes. The kid's bad news."

Sam's eyes narrowed. "My son is the best news I've ever had. See you around, Michelle."

Brad turned to her before Sam was even out the door. "Hey, I didn't expect a three-ring circus," he said. His easy grin relaxed her. This was the Brad she knew, the one who charmed her clients at office parties, the one who took her out to dinner every Friday night, the one who attended swing-dancing lessons just because she asked him to.

Even as she welcomed his familiar presence, she felt Sam's absence, a dark and gaping hole in the day. A sense of unfinished business. And the terrible, wonderful words echoing through her: *I'm listening to my heart.* She should have let him go on, but she hadn't dared.

"God, what a week it's been." She deposited the papers and magazines on the floor.

One week. In that short span of time, the world had been transformed. Everything she used to believe was being challenged, pushed, reshaped. Everything she thought she had planned out was starting to unravel.

Even the idea of family. When she was growing up, "family" was something she and her mother lacked. When she was bringing up Cody, it was something she insisted they define for themselves. "Family" included Natalie, who was the sort of aunt every kid wanted, the sort of sister every woman should have, related by something much more potent than blood. And it was Brad, who tried to get along with Cody because of her, an effort she knew not many men would make. Cody hadn't been making it easy for him.

Now the circle widened to encompass her father, and Sam, and even Tammi Lee, who—wonder of wonders— had spent the day with Cody yesterday. She had to fit them into her life now. She *needed* to.

"So did he spend the night here, or what?" Brad asked bluntly.

For a second, she was too stunned to answer. "I can't believe you asked me that."

"I can't believe I showed up at your hotel room at ten in the morning and found some guy with you."

"He's not some guy. He's Cody's father."

"Then he should be with Cody."

"He was worried about the bullshit story in that tabloid. He wanted to talk to me about it."

"Yeah, he looked real worried to me." Brad took a tin of Altoids out of his shirt pocket and offered her one. She shook her head, and he said, "You didn't answer me, Michelle."

"Answer what?"

"Did you sleep with him or not?"

Sleep? She could safely deny that. No sleeping had taken place. "I had a surgical procedure yesterday. I ordered a tuna sandwich from room service and watched

HBO last night." She folded her arms defensively in front of her. "Why did you show up without calling first?"

"I wanted to surprise you. Wanted to do something spontaneous."

"You've never done a spontaneous thing in your life."

"Okay, so maybe that tabloid thing made me curious."

As he lowered himself to the bed and put his arms around her, she realized she had a lot of things to explain to Brad. A huge confusion swirled through her. She knew she should confess, but she had no idea how to begin.

"Have you had breakfast yet?" she asked him, chickening out.

"A cold bagel and weak coffee on the early flight."

"We could join Cody and my father downstairs, or maybe call for room service."

"Room service sounds good." He went over to the desk, picked up the hotel guide with the menus in it.

While he was reading off the selections, the divider door to the adjoining room opened. Natalie, who had driven down to be with Michelle during yesterday's procedure, waltzed in. Her bright hair was damp from a shower, her skirts and shawl shimmering around her. "Beat you to it, buddy." She crossed the room to give Brad a kiss on the cheek. "I already ordered breakfast." Her smile was full of mischief as she winked at him. "But I'll let you buy it, okay?"

"God, it *is* a circus," he said, standing back to look at Natalie. "We've got the tattooed lady and everything."

She touched a spot just above her left breast. "You're not supposed to know about my tattoo."

"You weren't supposed to go topless in my hot tub, either," he reminded her, laughing.

Michelle laughed, too, remembering that night last summer. Natalie had come over, weeping because she'd just dumped her current boyfriend, a timpani player named Stan. A few tequila slammers later, they had stripped down and jumped, giggling, into the hot tub on Brad's deck. Michelle hadn't realized back then that he'd noticed the tattoo.

Natalie stuck her tongue out at him and came bounding over to the bed, sitting on the end. "Okay, so give me a report."

"I'm fine. Had a great night," Michelle told her.

"Really?"

"Really. I'm dying for a shower."

"I thought you weren't supposed to get that incision wet."

Brad rifled around in his bag. "I'm way ahead of you, babe." He brought out a packet of DermaSeal, something from the pharmacy to keep wounds dry during bathing.

"You're a lifesaver." She hiked up the hem of her nightgown. "Have at it."

"This is too kinky for me," Natalie declared, hurrying to the window and looking out.

In the shower, Michelle took longer than she should, standing in the steamy tub, feeling the water needle down on her neck, shoulders, back. After a long time and plenty of soap, she got out of the shower and put on leggings and a loose sweater, wrapped a towel around her head. When she walked out to the bedroom, there was Natalie in the lotus position on the floor, her eyes closed and her lips moving soundlessly. It was a bizarre start to a day that promised only to get more bizarre.

Beginning with the breakfast Natalie had ordered— cheese blintzes, fruit compote, scrambled eggs, smoked salmon, and a pot of herb tea. Michelle sat on the edge of the bed, nibbling a croissant, and it hit her. Brad had barely mentioned Cody. The kid had just found the father he never knew, and Brad hadn't even asked about what the experience had been like for Cody.

She wondered why. Was it because he felt threatened?

"So I was talking to the concierge, and he gave me a list of recommendations for tonight." Natalie passed her a folder with the hotel logo on it.

"What's tonight?" Brad asked.

"The night before the big event, numb-nuts." She sampled a spiced apple from the fruit compote. "I decided we need a party."

"A party? You can't just have a party—"

"Watch me." She rolled her eyes. "God, Mr. Wet Blanket, can't you for once in your life be spontaneous? I bet you schedule your bowel movements."

"You're a real charmer, Natalie. You really are."

"Just listen, okay? Tomorrow, Michelle and her dad are going to make a miracle. Don't you think it would be good karma to mark the occasion in some way?"

Michelle expected him to argue, but instead he softened. "A kidney party. It would be a first for me."

"Wait till you see the menu," Michelle warned him, giving Natalie a hug.

Monday

Monday
13

Michelle stared at the glowing red digits of the hotel-room clock: 4:45 A.M. She was supposed to be asleep, resting up for the big event that loomed only hours away.

The truth was, she had barely slept at all. Natalie's party had been as strange and wonderful as Natalie herself. The group, consisting of Gavin, Brad, Cody, Natalie, and Michelle, had occupied a corner of the restaurant. Somehow, Natalie had managed to get Dr. Kehr, Donna Roberts, both surgeons, and Dr. Temple to show up. Natalie and Cody hung up balloon people with incisions drawn on them. Some of the balloons bore terse instructions: *Please close carefully after opening. Did you leave anything behind? Please check in the overhead compartment for personal belongings.* Lave los manos.

The laughter and toasts ranged from silly to sentimental. Her family, Michelle had thought, regarding them with a powerful surge of affection. They were not exactly a Norman Rockwell painting, but they were hers, and her love for them burned strong and steady. The doctors, acting officious, broke up the party by eight o'clock, sending Gavin to sterile isolation and advising everyone to get a good night's sleep. Michelle wanted to feel grateful for Brad's closeness, for the familiar feel of his arms around her as they lay in the dark of the hotel room. But it felt awkward being with Brad again. In Seattle, she had become accustomed to a predictable schedule, making plans together, letting herself in and out of his house at will, confident of her place in his life. Now she didn't know anything at all.

She moved restlessly in the bed. Brad awakened, squinting at the clock. "Hey, stranger."

"I didn't mean to wake you," she said.

"I sure wouldn't mind making love to you," he whispered.

She froze, her throat locking shut. Dear God.

"But we need to watch that incision." Brad's pronouncement rescued her from having to answer. "Besides, I bet that's the last thing on your mind."

Had he always done that? Made up her mind for her? Idiot, she told herself. He was a stable, responsible man who knew her well. Most women would kill to have that.

He turned over, mumbling, "Go back to sleep, Michelle."

Sleep. He was telling her to sleep when she needed him to listen. Really listen—to her fears and apprehensions about the surgery, her guilt and confusion about Sam. She sat up in bed, looped her arms around her drawn-up knees, moving gingerly to protect the incision. "Brad?"

A long-suffering sigh. "Yeah?"

"If something goes wrong with this surgery——"

"Hold on," he said, reaching over and snapping on the lamp. "We've discussed this. As a donor, your risk is completely within reasonable limits."

"Of course," she agreed. "But I thought you should know. If anything happens to me, I'm leaving Cody in the custody of Sam. I had the papers redrafted yesterday."

"Makes sense, since he's the kid's father. But it's a moot point. You're not in any danger. You'll be home before you know it, and all this will be behind you."

"No." She barely spoke above a whisper. "I don't think it's going to turn out like that."

"So do you want me to stay?" he asked.

She knew he'd wait through the surgery if she asked him to. But was that what she had been doing with Brad the past couple of years?

Making him stick around?

"No," she said. "Everything is going to be fine. You don't need to stay."

He was quiet for a long time. Then, with a small, curious smile on his lips, he got out of bed and slowly, deliberately got dressed.

She got up, feeling ill at ease. "Do you want to talk about it?"

"Michelle." His voice was quiet, firm. "I know what you're going to say."

It had been a long, strange week, she was an emotional wreck and a ball of anxiety, but she got it. She finally got it. They'd had a good run, she and Brad, three years of a relationship that went no deeper than the epidermis. And they didn't even have to discuss this. Just by watching his face, she could see that they had come to the same conclusion independently. But it was time to move on. He deserved more. She deserved more. Sam hadn't made her any promises yesterday, but she didn't need promises. She simply needed to be free.

"I feel like crying," she admitted.

"I hate when you cry."

"I know." A very slow smile formed on her lips. "That's why I never do it around you." She sat quietly on the bed while he finished packing and phoned to check on the early commuter flight to Seattle. A brief, awkward peck on the cheek, a wish for luck, and then he was gone.

After Brad left, she crossed to the glass doors that led out onto a second-story balcony. The heavy drapes were shut, but she could hear the sounds of the road outside, trucks' air brakes hissing, the scrape of snowplow and sander.

There was a table in front of the window, and on the table was a telephone. She could take it outside, sit in the cold predawn, and call Sam on the pretext of last-minute instructions about Cody.

She hated it that she wanted to call him.

Fighting the impulse, she stared at a narrow gap in the curtains. The sky was getting lighter. And something started to happen in her head. She couldn't look away from that space. Almond-shaped, it framed nothing but the sky, yet her mind transformed what she was seeing. The slender gap in the drapes became a round, ripe, pregnant shape. Or an eye. Or a raindrop. Or the space between two praying hands.

It was a space that she suddenly wanted—*needed*—to fill.

On the table lay the flat folio box with the art supplies Natalie had brought from Seattle. Almost without thinking, Michelle grabbed a pencil and began drawing in the half-light, her heart guiding her hand. Something inside her had come unstopped, and it gushed over the paper, and she filled page after page, her hand barely able to match the speed with which the images and emotions overtook her.

By the time the sun tinged the sky with a pink blush, she sat at the table with tears streaming down her cheeks. Maybe it was only for a moment, maybe it wouldn't last, but for the past hour she had glowed with an inner light she thought had burned out. She didn't know what had sparked the change; it was probably a combination of everything that was happening: being back in Montana, saying good-bye to Brad, facing the surgery, finding Sam again.

With shaking hands, she looked at what she had done. She had no judgment. Trash or treasure, she couldn't tell. But the work was hers. She knew where it came from, and it was a place more honest, more deep, than anything she had recognized in herself in more years than she could count.

She felt a certain quiet reverence as she gathered up the drawings and slipped them into the zipper compartment of her suitcase. And for the first time as she faced the surgery, she thought, I can do this. *I can do this.*

When the radio clicked on at precisely 6:00 A.M., she was ready.

As ready as anyone could be for an organ transplant.

The final preparations felt almost surreal. Forms being checked and double-checked. Signatures in triplicate. Meetings, IV drips, paper gowns and caps. Cody and Natalie hovering, chattering nervously. Michelle looked in on her father and found him waiting with a patience and a stillness that broke her heart. When an orderly came to take her away to her private room, Gavin turned to her.

Neither of them said anything. Gavin put his hand on

his heart. She did the same, afraid to speak, afraid she might cry. *What do I do?* she wondered. If she said her good-byes, did that mean she was afraid something would go wrong, that she'd never see him again? If she said nothing, what would they have to hang on to if something *did* go wrong?

In silence, with all the unsaid things screaming inside her, she walked away, following the orderly to her room.

She hovered wildly between acting like this was the most mundane of procedures and feeling convinced, as Natalie was, that it was a spiritual event. Natalie and Cody came in. Each bent to kiss her, to murmur "I love you," and to hear her whispered echo of the phrase. Cody looked pale, unable for once to cover his apprehension with attitude. She hadn't said much about Brad—just that he'd taken the early flight to Seattle. Explanations would come later.

She was glad Cody was starting school. He needed the distraction. Rather than pacing the halls during the procedure, Natalie would be driving him back to Crystal City in time for first bell.

"It's going to be all right, Cody," she said from her hospital bed.

"What if it's not?" he asked, his voice breaking as it sometimes still did.

"You have to believe it'll be all right." Michelle watched his face, loving him with all the fullness of her heart. "For months the doctors have been telling us that attitude is everything. That includes your attitude."

"You didn't answer my question. What if something goes wrong?"

"Nothing will—"

"Mom, cut it out."

She took his hand, noticing with mild surprise that he

had calluses from working at Sam's. "All right. Yes, there is a risk that something could go wrong. But it is a tiny, calculated risk that's hardly worth considering when you think of how this is going to help my father live again."

"Why wasn't I tested?" he demanded suddenly, anger pushing through his fear, redness rising in the pallor of his face.

"What?"

"When you started in on all these tests to find a donor, why wasn't I tested?"

"Right from the start, it looked as if I was the best match, Cody. There was no need."

"You didn't even bother testing me."

She was stunned. He actually resented her for overlooking him as a donor.

"Hey, sport." She forced herself to sound calm. "I did you a favor. How'd you like to be in my position right now?" She gestured at the thin, printed gown, the wheeled bed, the cold tile walls.

Natalie came hustling in. "We'd best get going, kiddo. School today."

"Aw, man," he said, genuine distress in his face. "Why can't I go back to Seattle with Aunt Natalie—"

"Hey," Natalie cut in, her voice uncharacteristically sharp. "We went over this last night. You're going to school today. You'll knock 'em dead."

"Yeah, right."

Michelle's heart sank at the misery in his voice. She had never felt more helpless in her life. Cody had to go to a new school, and she was too out of it to be of any use at all.

He glared at her. "You should have tested me for the kidney."

"I love you for saying so, Cody. Remember that. I love you."

A pair of orderlies came in. "Time to go to pre-op," one of them said.

"One more kiss, for luck," she said to Cody.

He kissed her cheek and squeezed her hand, and she closed the sweetness of the moment into her heart. "I'll see you soon," she whispered.

"'Bye, Mom." His eyes flooded with brightness, and then she lost sight of him as they wheeled her around a corner of the corridor.

"You got a nice kid, ma'am," an orderly said.

A gentle cottony calm, augmented by the sedative she was given, washed over her. Doing the sketches this morning had been cathartic, and the last moments with Cody had set a seal of serenity upon her. The orderly had called her kid "nice." What a concept.

They reached the pre-op area, and she was amazed to see a second gurney there.

"We've got to stop meeting like this." Gavin winked at her.

Reaching out, they could touch hands. "I didn't know I'd see you here, Daddy."

"Me neither."

Their respective anesthesiologists came in and chatted with them, telling them what to expect.

Then the oddest thing happened. The orderlies and the anesthesiologists left. Gavin and Michelle found themselves alone for long, quiet minutes.

"They gave me a pre-op sedative," she said. "You?"

"I'm not sure. They've been prepping me all night." He rubbed his finger over hers. "So here we are, just the two of us."

"Here we are." She didn't know what to say. They'd

had plenty of time to express their regrets, proclaim their commitment, acknowledge the love that lay at the center of everything. But had they said it? *Had they?*

Michelle's mother had died during surgery. She tried to keep her mind from going there, but she couldn't help herself.

"Daddy?" The word came out on a high note, sounding juvenile, but she didn't care.

"Yeah, honey?"

"I'm scared."

She could feel him smile, could feel it somewhere in the region of her heart. He squeezed her hand. She had forgotten they were still touching.

"Me too, Michelle. I'm scared, too."

"I don't think it's something we're going to get over, do you?"

"Not likely. But we'd better not let Temple hear us. He'd put the brakes on this whole thing."

"He was a pain in the ass, wasn't he?"

"Yeah. Listen, I know I only showed up in your life every once in a while." He took his hand from hers and touched his chest. "But you've always been here, right here in my heart."

She wanted it to be true so badly that she held her breath.

"Michelle?"

"What?"

"You're giving me my life back. I wish I could tell you what that means to me."

Emotion came in a warm rush, driving away the chill of the tiled pre-op. They lay side by side, helpless in their hope and love and fear. She swallowed hard and tried to keep from crying.

"Don't cry, sweetheart. I don't ever want to make you cry."

She felt it flowing, the smooth warm river of light that she had felt earlier, and she finally believed that maybe there was some merit in what Natalie had said about this bond, this invisible connection between father and daughter, between mother and son.

"I don't mind crying for you, Daddy."

"Everything's done, Michelle. I fixed my life as best I can. I played my hand the best I know how. I don't know what more I can do."

The doors swished open. "Showtime, folks," someone said. "Ladies first."

Michelle kept thinking she should say one more thing to her father, something hopeful and profound, but the only words that came out were, "See you around, Dad." Then they were both wheeled away, passing the glass-enclosed scrub area where surgeons and nurses readied themselves like postulants in some strange cleansing rite.

The operating room looked smaller than she had pictured it in her mind. Too many doctor shows on TV. In the real world, operating rooms were chilly and crammed with monitoring equipment. Blue-green tile and stainless steel. Glare from the observation dome overhead—dear God, she thought, someone might be watching this?—and the transplant team assembled in a semicircle around her. Masked and capped, miner's headlamps strapped to their heads, plundering hands in skintight gloves. The nurse stood on a stool to tower over the rest.

Their questions came fast, floating disembodied from behind the anonymous masks: Did she remember them from the meetings? Did she feel all right? Did she know each person's role and what was happening? Did she have any more questions?

Michelle shook her head, mute with terror. Now it was real. Now it was happening. No turning back.

The mask came down, the sharp lemony taste of the drug invaded her air passages, and images swam and stuttered before her eyes—the blue-green tile, the monitors and masked team, and then all that was gone and she saw faces tumbling through her mind: Cody and Gavin and Sam and finally the slender space formed by a gap in the draperies, a hole in the world, a shape she had to fill in, had to fill and fill with everything that was in her.

Chapter 32

Q uit driving yourself nuts, son, and go on down to Missoula."

Sam kept shoveling. It had snowed last night, and he was clearing his mother's front walk and driveway. "I'm not driving myself nuts."

Tammi Lee sat down on the porch step and regarded him with a knowing sympathy. "Well, you're driving the hospital down there batty by calling every fifteen minutes."

"I'm not calling every fifteen minutes."

"Yes you are. And Karl's on call, Cody's at school, and if you shovel any more snow, you'll end up having a coronary right here in my front yard. So get your butt in the truck."

"I should be around when Cody gets out of school. See how his day went." It felt strange thinking about a kid's school schedule. He had never imagined himself in such a role. The thought led to a flash of memory. When he was a kid, riding the school bus home, he used to observe kids getting off at their stops, eagerly awaited by their smiling mothers. Watching them used to make Sam sick with envy.

"You can get to Missoula and back before school's out," his mother said.

"I'm not needed in Missoula," he said after a long, ponderous silence. He kept telling himself that. Maggie Kehr had promised she'd page him the minute each surgery was over.

"How do you know that?"

He sliced the blade of the shovel into the new-fallen snow and thought about Brad Lovell. Serious, sure-of-himself Brad Lovell, who had a 401(k) plan, who had seen Cody play soccer before Sam even knew his son existed. Lovell was the perfect example of someone a woman *needed*, pure and simple. He was steady and clean-cut, practical and predictable. A regular bachelor of the month.

How did a guy get like that? Sam wondered, deliberately ignoring his mother's question. He wished he knew, because he ought to try it himself. Try listening to common sense. After surviving a chaotic childhood, struggling through school, and failing at marriage, he'd finally put his life in order. His mother was sober. He had his practice, his horses, a respected place in the community. Did he really want more than he had? He was wary of taking on more. He didn't know if he had what it took.

Michelle Turner had only been back for a week, and already people were starting to talk.

He shoveled at a furious rate, scraping the driveway down to bare concrete. He was fighting to stop the knowledge building inside him, but he couldn't run from it, couldn't hide from the truth.

In all the years he'd lived and all the miles he'd traveled, he'd never loved anyone the way he loved Michelle.

When he had taken her into the empty theater, he'd felt a harsh desperation to possess her, even if it hurt them both. At the hot springs the harshness had softened, reminding him that he still had tender places deep inside him, places only she could touch. In that moment, he'd known with a certainty he hadn't felt in years that they needed a second chance. They needed to get to know one another, to look at one another through adult eyes and see if the passion they shared as teenagers really meant something.

At least, that was what he'd thought.

Now he had no idea what to think.

When his pager went off, he stabbed the shovel into the snow and pressed the readout button.

His mother stood up on the porch step. "Any news?"

"The surgery's over."

Chapter 33

"Michelle. Michelle, wake up." A woman's voice reached like ghostly fingers through a fog.

"Mmm." Her mouth felt welded shut. Taste of rust and clay. She supposed what she was feeling was pain, but it was so huge, so overwhelming, that she couldn't call it pain. It was a vast red cloud, pulsating in the middle, holding her in a grip of such power she couldn't think.

She moved her jaw from side to side. "'S'it over?" No saliva in her mouth. Completely dry. The crimson fog throbbed, intensified, punishing her for her effort.

"You're all done. You did great, just perfect." Donna. That was the woman's name. Donna Roberts, the nurse.

Michelle didn't feel perfect. She felt inches from death. The pounding in her head blotted out all sound. She forced her eyes to focus on the nurse's mouth, made herself listen carefully.

Donna checked a green-and-black monitor. "We'll be transferring you to your room pretty soo—"

"My father. I want to see my father."

"He's all right, Michelle. He's in post-op, too."

I want to see him. But she couldn't get the words out. The pain surrounded her, clouding her brain, lifting her up and swirling her far, far away, and she couldn't see anything except that tiny slit of space opening up to the paintings she hadn't done. Two hands, parting a curtain. Giving her a glimpse of something she hadn't created yet. Now it was clear to her. She had to learn to do it anyway, even though it hurt.

She sank deeper and deeper into the formless red morass of pain, and she let herself go, a victim of slow drowning, too weak to fight her way back to the surface.

Chapter 34

There was something wrong with the clocks in this frigging school, Cody decided.

They didn't move like normal clocks. They must be from another dimension where a minute equaled an hour and a day lasted forever.

Because that was how long his first day at Crystal City High School had lasted—forever.

And it was only lunchtime.

Feeling like a complete dork, he had shown up in homeroom with a "New Student" folder under his arm and this enormous zit on his forehead. He hadn't had a zit since September, and he'd woken up that morning looking like he was about to sprout a unicorn horn.

No sympathy from Aunt Natalie, who had driven him up from Missoula. "Nobody will notice. It just feels obvious to you. Act like it's not there."

"Oh, right, like no one's going to notice Mount Vesuvius in the middle of my face."

"Sweetie, if this is the worst thing that ever happens to you, consider yourself blessed." In his mom's absence, Aunt Natalie played the part of the expert on all things.

At least Brad had gone back to Seattle. Cody had been worried that he'd hang around asking a bunch of questions. Brad liked to act all buddy-buddy, and Cody didn't feel like answering stuff like how did it feel to meet his father and all that crap.

Coming in new mid-year was a special torture that should be reserved for convicted felons. First there had been the homeroom teacher's "Class, we have a new student" routine. Then the issuing of books and supplies. The stack of forms to be signed.

The Assignment of the Seat.

The teachers all thought they were doing him this big favor, putting him right up front in the middle so he wouldn't miss a second of their fascinating lectures on the Voting Rights Act or phytoplankton. What they were actually doing was making him vulnerable to the whispers. This was the equivalent of blindfolded torture, because he could hear bits and pieces of the conversation, but couldn't see the speakers.

". . . like some skater from the inner city . . ."

". . . he's got a pierced *what?*"

"Well, *I* think he's cute . . ."

". . . acts like hot shit because his grandfather's a movie star . . ."

". . . wait till you hear who his *father* is . . ."

The hissed speculation, through civics, trigonometry, and science, had hit him like spitballs to the back of the neck. When he'd try to get a look at the speakers, dropping a pencil or something and twisting around, he was met by mute, blank stares.

Losers. Everyone in this frigging school was a loser.

After third period, he had trouble with his locker—of course—and once he got it open, couldn't cram all his books in along with his coat, so he kept the coat on even though he was sweating like a hog in the overheated building.

Lunchtime. In his regular school it was his favorite period of the day, because he sat at the table where everyone was cool and where everyone else only *wished* they could sit. Claudia would be at his side, eating like one potato chip and then saying she was full, and talking and laughing the whole time.

He was a long way from that lunchtime, a long way from Claudia.

Shit. Shit. Shit.

He went through the fast-food line and ordered a burger and a Coke. Safe choices. Picking something different for lunch was risky, even at his school in Seattle. If you had something like tofu or Thai noodles, you were in danger of being Different. There was a guy named Sujit at his other school who brought the weirdest stuff because of his religion. During certain times of the year, he couldn't eat meat or dairy products or anything normal. The kids had made a big deal of it, holding their noses and gagging when he walked by, sometimes playing keep-away with his falafel burger or hummus. One time, Sujit had lost it totally, calling them all pig-eating infidels, which had only made them laugh harder.

Cody wasn't laughing now. He wished he hadn't teased Sujit. Because now *he* was the one surrounded by pig-eating infidels.

He took a long time getting his napkin and straw, lingering at the counter while letting his gaze dart frantically around the busy, noisy cafeteria. Where to sit? *Where to sit?*

Though fewer in number, the tables were segregated exactly as they had been at his old school. The popular kids occupied the middle. Just as in Seattle, these kids were uniformly good-looking, relaxed, laughing while the whole school revolved around them. Nearby sat the football players and cheerleaders. The jocks were like jocks everywhere—food fights erupting, body noises followed by a chorus of "eeeeuw . . ."

Around the busy inner sanctum tables, there was a neutral buffer zone of regular kids with no distinguishing status. And of course, on the fringes of all the activity were the dweebs, geeks, and losers.

They had plenty of room at their tables. Some hid behind comic books or thick-lensed glasses. The fat ones ate furtively, pretending they didn't eat but were just fat because they had unlucky glandular activity. The totally clueless ones acted as if they had no idea they were dweebs. They just gabbed away and had lunch—lots of nerdy thermoses and Tupperware kits. These kids didn't give a rat's ass that they were the scum-sucking bottom-dwellers of the school population.

Maybe he could just hunker down at the end of a geek table, scarf his burger, and slip out to the Commons, an outdoor spot for hanging out during break.

But man, a *geek* table.

If he didn't do better than that, he'd be a goner for sure.

He sucked in a deep breath and went to one of the neutral zone tables. Like all of them, it was crammed. He spotted one possibility. A gap at the end of a table of mostly boys who were talking loudly about snowboarding. Hey, he could talk snowboarding. Keeping his eyes focused on the empty spot, he moved in, trying not to hurry, determined to make it look as if he'd arrived there almost by accident.

"Sorry, that's my spot." A kid scooted in fast, grabbing the seat.

Cody felt his face redden, though he shrugged nonchalantly. But now he was trapped, standing like an idiot with his tray in the middle of the lunchroom.

Somebody jostled him from behind, sloshing his Coke on the tray.

"Hey, look out," he muttered, but not loud enough to be heard.

The bun of the burger was soggy with Coke. If he didn't find a place to sit in a minute, people were going to notice. But the only seats he could see now were at the geek table. Sweat trickled down his back. Damn, he wished he'd taken his coat off. A feeling of impending doom pressed at him, and he felt as if he was about to lose it. The geek table. The goddamned geek table.

"Hey, Cody!"

At the sound of his name, he looked up, and there was Molly Lightning.

It was like seeing an angel, watching her stand up with one knee propped on a bench, waving her slender arm at him.

"Hey, come have a seat." She was at a neutral table where the kids weren't particularly geeky or particularly cool. Just regular.

He nodded, nonchalant as you please, but inside he was exulting. She'd saved his butt, no doubt about it.

*　　*　　*

Feeling like an ex-P.O.W., Cody exited the loud, gym-bag-smelling school bus and stood at the side of the highway. Breathing. A survivor after a disaster. Man, he felt as though he'd been holding his breath all day, expecting an ambush. They'd promised to get him out of class if anything bad happened at the hospital, but there had been no interruption of the slow torture of school. He had to feel grateful for that, at least.

Swinging his backpack over his shoulder, he trudged up the frozen gravel drive toward Sam's house. Another bonus, he thought sourly. On top of everything else, he had to stay here all week.

In spite of his thoughts, his heart lifted when the Border collie came careening down from the field and leaped at him, long pink tongue reaching for his face. For a minute, Cody couldn't help himself, and he laughed aloud. Then he saw Sam coming out of the house.

If he asks me how school was, I'm going to hurl, I swear it.

"Hey, Cody." Sam swung a canvas bag into the back of his old pickup truck. He put a cooler of drinks and a bag of tortilla chips in the cab. "I guess you want to get on down to the hospital right away."

The guy had read his mind.

They were both quiet as Sam pulled out onto the highway and headed south. The old Dodge truck smelled of timothy hay and motor oil, and the column shift rattled with the bumps. Sam McPhee sure wasn't like any of the doctors Brad played golf with, Cody reflected. But then again, he pretty much wasn't like any other doctor, *period*. Or maybe Cody just thought he was weird because he was his dad.

"My mom taught me to ride a bike when I was five,"

he said suddenly, for no particular reason. His breath fogged the window.

Sam flexed his hands on the worn, shiny steering wheel and kept his eyes straight ahead on the road. "Yeah?" Another long silence. And then, "We're a little short on bikes around here. Plenty of horses, though. You could do some riding."

Cody felt a spark of interest, but forced himself not to show it. The truth was, he really did want to ride a horse, but he thought he'd feel stupid. Most of the kids at Crystal City High had been born knowing how. They were all goat ropers and cutters and stuff. "Maybe," he said guardedly.

"You could fool around on a snowmobile, too."

"That'd be cool, I guess."

"Can you drive a standard shift?" Sam asked. "A car, not a horse, that is."

Cody's mouth twitched. "Sure. I learned on one."

"There's an old Jeep in the pole barn I could let you use for getting to and from school. That way, you wouldn't waste time waiting around for the school bus. You'd have more time for chores in the morning."

Cody carefully weighed the merits of the offer. It was really no contest. The bus that smelled like a locker room or chores and his own wheels. "That'd be good," he said. Then, reaching through reluctance, he said, "Thanks."

Sam acted like it was no big deal. He opened the chips and passed the bag to Cody. They were silent again until Cody spoke up without even thinking. "This morning really sucked," he said, feeling stupid but unable to keep quiet.

"The transplant, or school?"

"The transplant. School—well, that sucked all day. At the hospital, everybody was like, really nervous." He made a face in the side mirror. "I kept thinking how totally gross the whole thing was."

"Gross, huh?"

He stared out the window at the scrubby landscape swishing past. "You must think I'm really selfish." He immediately wished he hadn't said that. It was none of this guy's business what was going on in his head. But it was so strange. Cody just kept wanting to *talk*.

"Why would I think that?"

"Because I didn't make them test me to see if I could be the kidney donor."

"I suspect they would have tested you if your mom hadn't turned out to be a near-perfect match."

"Nobody even asked me."

"And that's a problem?"

Cody scrubbed the side of his hand at the fogged-up window. "They should have checked me out instead of treating me like I didn't exist."

"Did you say you wanted to be tested?"

"My mom didn't even tell me what was going on until a few weeks ago. And then it was like, 'Well, we're moving to Montana so I can give this guy a kidney.'"

Sam cleared his throat. Cody thought he might be grinning. For some reason, Sam was pretty easy to talk to. He didn't push, didn't try too hard. He was just . . . there. Quiet. Cody's mom was always nagging him about "opening up." She didn't seem to understand that he was not going to open up if she kept talking all the time.

"So anyway," he said, "it was like, really intense. They had my mom in this room with one of those paper hair things on her head and a bunch of tubes and wires all hooked up to her, and I had to go in and say good-bye, like she was going to another planet and I wouldn't ever see her again. And all that was *before* I had to go to Hicksville High."

"I can see how that would suck."

Though Sam didn't take his eyes off the road, Cody could feel the full force of his attention, his fascination. It was a new experience, having an adult be this interested in what he had to say. Why? Because Sam was a doctor? Or his father, or just a guy? Or because he'd been hanging out with Cody's mom and they put that stupid picture in the *Enquirer*?

"Since nobody called from the hospital while I was at school, I guess everything went okay. But I was wicked nervous all day."

"Uh-huh," said Sam in that lazy way of his. "So was I."

Chapter 35

"M om. Hey, Mom." *Cody*. More powerful than any drug, her child's voice drew Michelle out of the fog.

"Cody . . ." She could feel her lips move, but only a whisper of sound came out. She had the sense that time had passed; she remembered hearing that her father was all right. The pain-cloud still surrounded her, but this time she wanted to fight her way out of the fog.

"Where . . . am . . ."

"In your room, Michelle." A deeper voice. A man's voice.

"Brad—" No. Sam. *Sam*. "Hurts," she said.

"She's miserable." Sam spoke to someone in a clipped voice. "I want her to have a self-administered morphine pump."

Bless you, Sam.

"Yes, we've ordered one—"

"Now, okay? Not in a minute, but now."

Typical doctor. That aggressiveness, that obnoxious, abrasive personality. His staccato order worked. She couldn't open her eyes or count the minutes, but in a short while she felt the drip, and someone guided her thumb to the button that would deliver the gentle, numbing surge of narcotics to her system. She pushed the button, and almost instantly felt the wavelike swish of morphine curling in, then rolling back out, taking some of pain's fury with it.

"'S'working," she said. Dry. Mouth was so dry.

"That's good, Michelle," Sam said. "You rest now."

She couldn't remember if he'd touched her or not since she awakened. Probably not. Doctors didn't do that so much, not anymore. She tried to recall what had passed between them the last time they'd been together. Hotel room. Something big, important, interrupted. She couldn't think.

"School." She formed the word carefully with her lips. "Cody. How was school?"

"I survived," he said simply.

She wanted to hear it all, every detail, but she couldn't stay focused on one subject. "You've seen . . . my father?"

"I'll take Cody in a minute," Sam said. "Gavin's on this floor, different wing. He has to be quarantined in ICU for a while, but we'll look in on him."

Michelle drifted in and out of pain and consciousness. Heard the TV news, and smiled when she felt Cody come over to the bed and awkwardly, hesitantly, touch her head.

Floating in the morphine fog, she listened to them getting ready to go back to Crystal City. She mouthed *I love you* and when they left she turned her face to the wall and wept for no reason she could name.

When she woke up again, the room was empty except

for the drips and equipment. The space between the drapes showed a night sky.

She pressed the button on the morphine pump. Gentle swish of drugs.

The sky grew red around the edges as if it had caught fire.

Later, someone put something around her ankles. Helpless but resentful, she mumbled, "What's that?"

"Air cuffs. You'll hear the electric pump come on about every twenty minutes."

"Too loud. Won't get any sleep at all."

"You have to keep these on until you can get out of bed."

With that powerful motivation, she was up at sunup, clinging to the arm of a nurse's aide as she took one step, then lowered herself gingerly to the chair by the bed.

"Okay," she said. "Off with the cuffs already."

The aide touched a buzzer. "You win. Your husband warned us that you were a fighter."

Husband. Sam. No way. He wasn't her husband. He was . . . too damned complicated to explain to the nurse's aide.

Later she forced herself to get up again and wait patiently, staying in the chair, even eating something. Rice pudding. Too sweet, not enough nutmeg. Then it was back to bed, feeling as if she'd run a marathon. At one point Donna checked in on her, face wreathed in smiles.

"Just wanted to be sure you heard—your kidney is working great."

Michelle squeezed her eyes shut and felt a powerful rush of gratitude.

We did it, Daddy. We did it.

Tuesday

Tuesday

"God, these are incredible. When did you do these?" Natalie's voice pried into a strange dream Michelle was having. In the dream, she floated through the wisps of steam that curled off the surface of the hot springs where she and Sam had made love. Only she was alone in the fog, searching, calling out, but no one could hear her.

"Michelle?" Natalie was insistent. "I was asking about these drawings."

She gave up on the dream and dragged her eyes open. "What . . . drawings?"

"Here." Cody held a plastic bottle with a flexible straw to her lips.

Michelle drank gratefully. "Thanks. What drawings?"

"I found them in your suitcase." Natalie held up one

of the sketches Michelle had done before the surgery. "These are wonderful."

"They're pretty cool, Mom."

She took another drink. Didn't want to think about the drawings and what had happened the morning of the transplant. Truthfully, she had no idea if the experience meant anything at all. "I feel as if I've been away forever," she said. "What day is it?"

"Tuesday."

She studied Cody. He seemed . . . different. She supposed that working outside a lot added color to his usually pale face. He might be eating better, too. He looked bigger. Filled out. When had that happened? she wondered with a clutch of apprehension. Changes don't happen overnight. Why hadn't she noticed?

"Is school going all right?" she asked.

"Yeah."

She didn't believe him. Someone had probably coached him not to say anything to upset her. "Are you and Sam getting along okay?"

He shrugged. "I guess."

"I've been keeping tabs on the situation," Natalie reminded her. "They're getting along fine."

"He doesn't know me," Cody pointed out. "He's just some guy. Ow! Quit kicking me, Aunt Natalie."

"Now the big question," Michelle said. "How's school going?"

"Sucks," he said predictably, then winced as Natalie kicked him again. "I'll survive, Mom. But I really want to get back to Seattle."

"Speaking of getting back, I have to leave, sweetie," Natalie said. "That is, if you'll be okay without me."

Michelle smiled, feeling her lower lip crack with the

effort. "I'll be okay without you. Just not nearly as entertained."

"Call me, all right? Anytime, night or day."

"Sure, Nat. You've been a peach."

"Take care of yourself. I'll keep the home fires burning."

After visiting hours were over, the nurses let Michelle walk in the hallway, wheeling her IVs. She made them take out the catheter at the first opportunity. Pain flamed through her, but she kept walking, concentrating on the scuffing sound of her slippers on the linoleum tile floor. She found her way to Gavin's room.

Her father was asleep, zippered in a sterile cocoon of clear plastic. He looked terrible, a waxen corpse. *No.* She wanted to scream it. *Daddy. Oh, Daddy.* We're not finished, she thought frantically. We just found each other again. The very air around her suddenly felt unnatural, noxious. Everything was broken.

But his coloring was remarkable—a healthy flush to his cheeks, hands and fingernails pink. Everyone assured her that the transplant was a success, the kidney was working.

Please let it be true. Please please please let it be true.

She lifted her hand, pressed her fingertips lightly to the plastic bubble, and said, "I love you, Daddy." Her words sounded muffled and small in the machine-snarled room. His chest gently rose and fell, rose and fell.

As she shuffled slowly back to her bed, she wondered if she'd ever told him that when he was awake.

She hadn't.

But if he didn't know it after this, he'd never catch on.

Sam cleared away the Styrofoam remnants of Trudy's takeout. Never much of a cook, he felt lucky Cody had taken a shine to Trudy's burgers and pizza. Cody picked up his backpack and headed for the stairs. The two of them had been circling each other like a pair of wary dogs, giving a little here, taking a little there. In some moments, Sam felt a connection, but usually they were strangers. He kept telling himself to be patient. Most fathers had years to get to know their kids. He had only days.

"There's a Sonics game on tonight," he said. "You a Sonics fan?"

Cody paused at the bottom of the stairs. "Sort of."

Sam went into the den and flicked on the TV, filling the room with bluish light and the rapid-fire monologue of a basketball commentator. Without looking at Cody, Sam took a seat and gave his attention to the game. Cody sat on the end of the couch, poised to spring up and flee any minute. When a beer commercial came on, his attention wandered, touching on the stack of journals Sam didn't have time to read, the beige drapes, the photos of horses. Alice had tried to spiff the place up when they were married, but Sam had never put much effort into it. He didn't know diddly about fixing up a house to resemble a home.

Then Cody's gaze fixed on the large painting that hung over the fireplace. "Did my mom do that?" he asked.

"Uh-huh." Sam reached up and turned on the mantel light. "Have a look."

Cody stood with his hands dug into his back pockets, studying the winter scene. Sam kept his face neutral, remembering the day Michelle had given him the painting. They had done everything teenagers are lectured *not* to do. They had unprotected sex, they believed love would be enough, they dared to cross the invisible-but-rock-solid barrier of class and privilege. The result had been a pair of broken hearts . . . and this boy.

"It's pretty awesome," Cody said, staring at the signature and date in the bottom corner.

Sam tried to imagine what was going through the kid's head just then as he stood looking at something his mother had done before he was born. He wondered if Cody was able to picture the girl she had been, to think of her as someone other than his mother. Probably not. That just wasn't the way a kid's mind worked. "Your mom says she doesn't paint anymore."

"She does stuff for work, mostly on the computer." He sat back down on the sofa. His expression gave no clue to his thoughts.

The game came on again, and Sam couldn't think of

anything else to say. But he wanted to fill the silence, so he asked, "Did that Jeep run okay?"

"Yeah, it ran fine." Cody hesitated. "I gave Molly Lightning a ride home after school today."

Sam wasn't sure how to respond to that. Should he commend the boy for giving a ride to a friend? Admonish him to drive carefully and wear seat belts? Chastise him because he hadn't asked permission to give rides to passengers?

He said, "You should have checked with me before offering rides to people."

Cody stared him straight in the eye. "Why?"

"Because I'm responsible for you."

Cody snorted. "Right."

"This week I am, damn it—" Sam stopped, amazed to find that his pulse had sped up. This kid had a killer instinct when it came to pushing buttons. "Okay, look," Sam said, pressing the mute button on the remote control. "I should have told you not to take on passengers unless you check with me first."

"So why didn't you?"

"Because I'm new to this, that's why. I'm making it up as I go along."

"That's obvious."

"You're not making it easy, Cody."

"Why should I?"

Sam clenched his teeth until he brought his temper back in check. In a slow drawl, he asked, "Are you enjoying this?"

"What, being here? Hell no," Cody said bluntly. "You're not having any fun, either, so maybe you should just send me back to Seattle to stay with Natalie." He patted his shirt pocket. "I have a copy of the bus schedule."

"Not an option," Sam said, his gaze flashing to the painting over the mantel. "I said I'd look after you this week, and that's what I'm going to do. We could probably have an okay time together if we could get past the bickering stage. What do you say?"

Cody picked up a thread on the arm of the sofa. "I don't see the point."

"Maybe there doesn't need to be a point. Look, you're a teenager. It's your job to question every rule and push at every boundary. It's my job to tell you the rules and boundaries. By not telling you about passengers in the Jeep, I fell down on the job. So here's the rule—number of passengers cannot exceed the number of seat belts. Got it?"

"Yeah. Whatever."

"It's your job to tell me where you're going when you leave and what time you'll be back."

"I don't see why—"

"So if you don't show up, they'll know where to look for the body," Sam snapped.

Cody got to his feet. "Jeez, I didn't mean to start World War III. I just mentioned I gave a girl a ride home. She likes me. Is it so hard for you to believe someone likes me?"

"Christ, no, Cody. *I* like you. I want you to be safe. I want us to get along, okay?"

"Whatever," he muttered one last time, stooping to pick up his heavy backpack and heading for the stairs. "I've got some homework to do."

Crossing his arms across his chest, Sam scowled at the TV screen without really seeing it. The conversation had exposed glaring inadequacies he never knew he had, and it bugged the hell out of him. As a parent, you had to figure out when to say yes and when to say no. When to praise and when to upbraid. And getting it right was harder than it seemed.

Wednesday

I t wasn't until he pulled up to the barn at Lonepine after school the next day that Cody realized he'd forgotten to call Claudia—again. If he didn't keep in touch with her better, she was going to think he'd died or fallen off the planet or something.

But the days kept rolling along, the distance between here and Seattle seemed endless, and time got away from him.

Still, he should have phoned her. But he'd been so eager to get away from that frigging school that he'd roared off in the old Jeep without even remembering he'd meant to stop at Blue Rock and call Claudia. He didn't want to use Sam's phone for long-distance. Sam would probably let him, but Cody didn't want to ask.

He just didn't know where he stood with Sam. It was so weird being in his house, knowing the brand of shaving cream he used and what magazines he subscribed to, learning personal stuff about a stranger. Sometimes they had normal conversations and everything seemed fine, and then they'd rub each other the wrong way and argue. Cody kept trying to tell himself it didn't matter. He kept telling himself he didn't want to know this guy. He'd done fine without a father and he didn't need one now.

Sam McPhee was a hard guy to know. He sure as hell wasn't a guy Cody wanted to ask favors from, like phone permission.

Ah, well, he thought, swinging down from the driver's seat, he'd call Claudia tomorrow.

The Border collie came racing across the yard, barking her foolish face off. She knew Cody by now, having slept at the foot of his bed the past few nights. She launched herself like a missile at him. He caught her in his arms, staggering back a little with the motion, and laughed as she licked his face. It felt good, having someone greet you with this level of enthusiasm.

When they got back to Seattle, he'd talk his mom into getting a dog or a cat, maybe.

"That's loyalty for you," Sam said, ambling across from the house. "The minute I turn my back, I find my best girl in the arms of another man."

Cody tried not to grin as he set down the dog. "How's the new horse doing today?"

"Come on back and see for yourself." Sam didn't spend a long time looking at Cody, studying him. He just turned, totally casual, and ambled away.

Cody wondered if Sam was just naturally cool, or if he didn't care, or if he didn't want to get involved with a kid he didn't know. Maybe Cody was trying to read too much into Sam's attitude. It was hard as hell not to ask a bunch of questions, but he'd be damned if he'd make the first move.

Seeing the filly wiped out all his worries for a while. She acted as if she was happy to see him, frisking around the stall and thumping the walls, butting up against the mare. When the mare tried to eat, the filly kept trotting back and forth in front of her. With a quick, exasperated motion, the mare shoved the filly bodily away.

"Hey, why'd she do that?" Cody asked.

"The filly got in the way of what the mare wanted. She didn't hurt it." Sam drummed his fingers on the stall door, catching the filly's attention to distract it while Sylvia ate. "I was thinking she'll need a name one of these days. I have to register her papers."

"Yeah?"

"What do you think we ought to call her?"

Cody looked at the horse, and everything that crossed his mind was hokey and cute. Brownie. Blaze. Socks. He shrugged. "I don't know. Whatever."

Sam crossed his feet and propped his shoulder on the side of the stall. "A good horse might be around for twenty, thirty years. You have to make sure you pick the right name."

"So pick one."

"How about you pick it?"

"Why me?"

"You brought this animal into the world. I thought you might like to be the one to name her."

Cody shrugged again. Shit. He didn't know how to act. How did kids act around their fathers, anyway? "I can't think of anything."

"Maybe something will come to you. You let me know, okay?"

"Yeah. Okay."

The foal got tired and curled up in the straw for a nap. The mare fussed and licked at it for a while. It was amazing how she seemed to know exactly what to do.

"Do you have homework?" Sam asked. Then he shook his head. "Feels strange asking that."

You think you *feel strange,* thought Cody. "I did it in study hall."

"Okay, then you can get started on chores." Before Cody could reply, Sam held out a shovel and said, "It's good having you around."

Cody glanced at him sharply. What was good? His company? Or his manure-shoveling skills? Sam didn't say, and Cody didn't ask. They went to the tack room, put on quilted coveralls and gloves. Cody was mildly pleased to see Sam pick up a shovel, too. After the usual stall duties, today's task was to clean out the oat bins, getting rid of the moldy stuff on the bottom, scouring the galvanized metal bins, and replacing the oats.

"Ever given any thought to what you want to do after high school?" Sam asked.

"Some. I haven't made up my mind, though."

"You interested in college?"

"Sure. Most people go to UW. That's probably where I'll end up."

It helped that they were working as they talked. For some reason, it felt more natural to talk during the rhythm of the shovels. This week had to be the strangest time of Cody's life, starting a new school while his mom and grandfather did the kidney transplant. Talking didn't make things any better, but it didn't make things worse, either.

"You'll probably like college," Sam remarked. "I liked it a lot."

Cody wondered what it had been like for Sam and his mom, years ago, making a baby together and then never seeing each other again. He pushed away the thought and got back to work. Even though the chores were a drag, Cody sort of liked being out here, messing around with the horses and going all over on a snowmobile.

"What do you think of horse ranching?" Sam asked, reaching for a hose.

Cody snorted, chagrined that he even *looked* as if he might be enjoying himself. "It's a barrel of laughs." He stabbed his shovel into a mound of manure. The strange dance of uncertainty between him and Sam McPhee made him nervous.

At sunset, Sam and Edward were in the pole barn, replacing the spark plugs in a snowmobile. Two car doors slammed. Sam walked out to the drive to see Cody and Tammi Lee going toward the house.

"Almost suppertime," Tammi Lee called. She gestured at the two pizza boxes Cody balanced in his hands.

"We'll be in shortly." Sam grinned with the fine pleasure of seeing his mother and his son together. Family had always been in short supply for him. This was a new sensation for him. Did he like it, or was it something a guy like him was better off without?

"I think he likes it here," Sam said. "I think he even likes my mother."

Rummaging in a tool box, Edward regarded him sharply. "So you getting attached to the kid?"

"He's my kid." The wonder of it still swept through Sam each time he said the words. "What, I'm not supposed to get attached?"

"I didn't say that. But what happens when they leave?"

A blunt question, one that had been nagging at Sam. "It's not like they live on another planet," he said.

A faint yelp echoed down from the hill beyond the paddock. Edward shaded his eyes. "Hey, check this out."

Sam followed his gaze and felt a cold churn of fear in his gut. It was Scout, hurrying toward them—but not with her usual swift and joyous abandon. "She's hurt," he said, breaking into a run. He reached the collie halfway down the hill. A smear of blood marked her trail. It came from a long slash down her foreleg. Four scratches furrowed her muzzle.

"Hey, what's the matter with Scout?" Cody asked, jumping down off the porch and hurrying toward Sam.

Scooping up the dog, Sam hurried to the tack room. In one corner was a stainless-steel table and a couple of exam lights. He set her down, eyes and hands scanning her injuries.

"She need the vet?" Edward asked.

"Let's have a look." While Sam took off his gloves, Cody went around the other side of the table and murmured the dog's name, stroking her. Sam met the boy's eyes. "Keep her calm. I need to check out this cut." Edward opened the large first-aid wall station, stocked with instruments and supplies, and Sam used the clippers to trim away the long white-and-black hair, exposing a wicked gash.

"What happened?" Cody asked. "Is that from barbed wire?"

"Cat, more likely," Sam said. "A mountain lion. See the scratches across her nose? Scout's been known to tangle with a big cat if it wanders too close."

"Is she going to be okay?"

"Yeah, we'll fix her up."

Cody looked at the indigo sky through the small square window. "Are there a lot of mountain lions around here?"

"A fair number," Edward said, bringing some medicine from the office fridge. "We put out a trap, but they're street-smart. Last season we caught three, sent them down to Yellowstone to be turned out in the wild." Muffled thumps came from the stalls, the horses settling in for the night.

Sam snapped on a pair of surgical gloves. He and Cody worked together, Cody soothing the dog while Sam disinfected the superficial scratches. Edward stood back watching them thoughtfully.

"Hand me that syringe of lidocaine," Sam said to Cody. "Don't break the seal until I tell you." He cleansed the site and injected the topical anesthetic. The dog whimpered, and Cody hushed her. While he waited for the lido to work, Sam caught himself studying his son's hands, gently splayed across the collie's silky fur.

Wow, he thought, the kid's got my hands.

"You okay?" he asked Cody. "This is on the gory side."

"I can handle anything after pulling that foal," Cody assured him.

Sam used a double-ended needle and surgical thread to stitch the gash. At one point he glanced up and caught the boy looking at him, and the expression on Cody's face nearly bowled him over. Having a son was a fine thing. Having a son who admired you made you feel like a god.

"Go ahead and spray her with the Furex," he said, nodding at the plastic bottle. "That's right, up and down the wound." With intense concentration, Cody applied the yellowish antiseptic.

"Ever give an injection?" Sam asked.

"No."

"Want to learn?"

"I guess."

Sam prepared a dose of anti-inflammatory and penicillin, then coached Cody through the injection. As he worked, Cody's face wore an expression of complete absorption. Scout whimpered and took advantage of the extra attention she was getting. Walking tall with a sense of accomplishment, Cody carried her across the yard to the main house, putting her down gently in the kitchen.

"You guys make a pretty good team," Edward said, as they washed up at the sink in the mudroom. A certain quiet ease pervaded the atmosphere, and it felt good to Sam. A hell of a lot better than coming home to an empty house.

That evening after supper, Tammi Lee hung on Cody's every word as he described the treatment. She made a good listener, and he responded to that. Absently, he kept his hand on the dog's head as he spoke, and the sight evoked echoes of that rare warm feeling that had come over Sam earlier. Then Tammi Lee glanced at the clock.

"Better go," she said. "I've got some videos to return before closing time. You know what folks say." She winked. "Crime doesn't pay."

Sam was pleased to see that Cody stood up when she did, out of courtesy. She turned to him. "You looking forward to your mom and granddad getting home?" she asked.

"Yeah." Yet the reminder seemed to agitate him. He lifted a shoulder, just this side of insolent. "The sooner they get better, the sooner we go back to Seattle."

"You miss your friends?"

"Sure."

"I figured you'd make new ones here," said Tammi Lee, heading for the door. "Nice kid like you."

Cody looked startled. He was probably trying to recall the last time someone had called him a nice kid.

Thursday

Thursday

Chapter 39

With a weary motion, Cody shrugged his backpack over one shoulder and made his way to the main door of the school. Somehow, another endless day had ended.

Somehow, he had survived another day at this armpit of an institution.

He was sort of glad to be going to Sam's rather than the hospital this afternoon. His mom was lots better, but that meant she'd ask the usual questions about how his day went, and what were his teachers like, and did he make some more friends, and all that crap, and he didn't want to talk about it.

The only bright spot in this godforsaken place was Molly Lightning. She was great, not making a big deal of him but making sure she introduced him to a couple of her friends each day. They were way different from his friends in Seattle. Who would have thought he'd be sitting around at lunchtime talking about goat roping and 4-H Club?

At least it wasn't the geek table.

Maybe he'd call Molly tonight, pretend he needed a homework page or something.

"Cody?"

A voice behind him. Female, but not Molly.

He stopped at a heavy door with wire mesh through the glass. He recognized the girl from homeroom, the one he was already thinking of as the Blond Bombshell. Shiny yellow hair, huge tits.

He smiled. "Yeah?"

"It's Cody, right? Cody Slade?"

"Turner."

"Oh." She stuck her thumb in the top of her jeans pocket, tugging the waistband down to show a little of her bare stomach. "Someone said you were related to Gavin Slade."

"I am, but I've got a different last name." He pushed the heavy door open, stood to one side to let her pass. She smelled like bubble gum and shampoo. Her sweater was tight. Really tight. "He's my grandfather. I'm staying at his place."

Her face lit up, pretty and bright. "I think that's so cool." She ducked her head and looked up at him through long eyelashes. "I'm Iris York. We're in homeroom together."

"And English." Color flooded his face. "I noticed you in English class last period." He'd noticed her in the lunchroom, too, at the inner sanctum table, but she hadn't called out to him.

She made a face. "I can't stand the teacher, Mrs. Lightning. She's picky, picky, picky. I can't wait until the term's over and I can take drama instead."

Cody had actually thought Mrs. Lightning—Molly's mom—wasn't too bad. She was the only one who hadn't made him sit in the front, and she didn't act all chummy with him just because she was friends with Sam McPhee.

"Can I give you a ride somewhere?" he asked boldly, gesturing at the Jeep.

"Um . . ." She looked from side to side, then shrugged. "I don't see my usual ride, so I guess I'll take you up on that. I live up in Windemere Hills, on the golf course."

"Great." They headed across the parking lot.

"So tell me about your grandfather. I think his old movies are sooo bitchen—"

A Bondo-colored El Camino came around a corner and lurched to a stop in front of them. Cody jumped back, flinging out his arm in an instinctively protective gesture. Slush from a filthy puddle sluiced over his feet. Ice-cold water trickled into his shoes.

"Hey, Iris." The driver got out and came around the car, opening the passenger door. "I thought I'd missed you, but here I am."

Iris bit her lip. "Hi, Billy. This is Cody Turner. Cody, this is Billy Ho. The guys in the back are Ethan Lindvig and Jason Kittredge." Gangsterlike, they nodded at him from the rusty bed of the truck.

Billy was one of the coolest guys in school; Cody could tell. Good-looking in a Native American way. Outside the library Molly had pointed him out, said he was big trouble. But he was just cool. Molly probably couldn't see that.

"Cody offered me a ride home," Iris explained. "I thought you'd left without me," she hastened to add, pushing out her lower lip.

"Today's your lucky day." Billy opened the door wider.

When she hesitated, Cody knew it was now or never. Speak up now and get the cutest girl in the school on his side, or forever hold his peace . . . and sit at the dweeb table.

"The offer's still open," he said.

Billy didn't speak, but his glittering black eyes and go-to-hell expression said it all. Cody was trespassing, and Billy didn't like it one bit.

"Maybe another time," Iris said.

"Maybe never," Billy snapped.

Billy grabbed for Iris's arm. Cody didn't think, he just stepped between them.

"Maybe she can make up her own mind," he said.

"Out of my way." Billy shoved him. Hard. Cody stumbled back, putting out a hand behind him, but there was nothing to catch him, so he plopped, ass-first, into a puddle of muddy, half-frozen slush.

He came up swearing, ready to fight, but it was a stupid move. He wasn't cut out for fighting, and Billy Ho was built like a dump truck. Cody laughed and hoped he sounded convincing. "Hey," he said, trying not to let his teeth chatter. "No big deal, right?"

At that moment the El Camino coughed and died.

"Balls." Billy reached in and tried the ignition. "This has been giving me trouble all day." He tried several more times, but the heap wouldn't start. "We better push it out of the way."

Iris got behind the wheel. The guys went around to the rear. Billy tossed his long black hair out of his eyes. "Yo, Cody. You gonna stand there, or you gonna help?"

Cody threw off his backpack and his anger. Here was his chance to get in good with these guys. Being one of their crowd might even make school bearable.

Once they'd moved the car to a parking spot, Iris pouted at Billy. "*Now* where's my ride home?"

Just for a second, Cody recalled his conversation with Sam about passengers in the Jeep. Only if there were enough seat belts to go around. They were one short, but Cody didn't even hesitate. Screw Sam. He'd never find out. "I'll give all of you a lift,"

"Excellent, man. I need to get to the auto-parts store." They all piled into the Jeep. Cody's jeans felt squishy, making him wish for a hot shower and clean towels. As he pulled out of the parking lot, he heard a faint "Hey, Cody!"

"Who's that?" Billy asked.

"Ugh, Molly Lightning." Iris wrinkled her nose. "The *cowgirl*."

Molly emerged from a knot of students. "Can you drop me by the arena?"

"No!" Billy said, putting his hand on Cody's shoulder. "Jeez, the teacher's kid. Her mom's flunking me."

Cody had a split second to decide. He made eye contact with Molly as she approached the Jeep. Taking a deep breath, he said, "Sorry, kid. Car's full." At least he didn't have to lie. He punched the gas pedal too hard, sending up a plume of mud and slush.

"Good move, man!" Ethan thumped him on the back.

Cody glanced in the rearview mirror to see Molly standing on the curb, shaking out her book bag. He felt something icier than the parking lot slush. Something that wouldn't come off with a shower and a stack of towels.

Friday

Friday

Chapter 40

An old El Camino, pockmarked by rust, came fast up the drive to Lonepine, spitting a rooster tail of gravel and ice in its wake. Favoring her wounded leg, Scout had to dart to the side of the road to avoid getting hit. Annoyed, Sam walked out onto the porch. He was still in his office clothes, having just got home after a long day of clinic visits.

Behind the El Camino came Cody in the Jeep. Patience, Sam told himself as he crossed the yard to the horse barn. No one ever said this fatherhood gig was going to be easy.

But as four disreputable-looking kids tumbled out of the vehicles—the most disreputable of all being his son— he gritted his teeth into a forced smile for the introductions. With a decided lack of grace, Cody gestured at each boy in turn—Billy, Ethan, and Jason. He recognized Billy from providing his school sports physical every year. The kid was wearing a jacket that looked brand-new and unaffordable. Sam grew annoyed at himself for having the thought. He was turning into a pretty judgmental s.o.b. lately.

A throaty screech, far off but distinct, echoed down from the veil of trees above the meadow. Scout growled and crouched in close to Sam, too smart to run off after the predator a second time. Sam shaded his eyes, studying the blue-shadowed distance, but he saw no movement in the field.

"Hey, guys," Sam said to the boys. "How was school?"

They rolled their eyes in unison. "Sucked," Cody said.

"Yeah?" Sam asked, tugging his tie loose. "You might consider the alternative."

"What, no school? That'd be awesome."

Sam shook his head. "When I was sixteen, I was working ten hours a day unrolling frozen bales of hay. Trust me, it's not awesome."

They didn't trust him, of course. Kids never fell for that "in my day" stuff. He ought to know better.

"I brought the guys over to show them the filly," Cody said.

"Fine. Take it easy around the mare. Don't get between her and—"

"I know, I know," Cody waved a hand. "Always face and acknowledge the mare, blah blah blah."

"You got it."

"Can we use the snowmobiles?"

Sam hesitated. "All right. But they're working vehicles, not toys. So don't screw around—" He stopped. Christ, he was talking to them like an old schoolmarm. "Okay, so you're going to screw around. But be careful. Use the helmets."

"We will," Cody said.

Sam nodded to Cody's friends. "Nice to meet you, but I can't stick around. I need to shower and shave." He rubbed his jaw.

"Big date tonight?" Billy Ho asked with a sly wink.

"I guess you could say that." If you counted a hospital visit as a date.

Cody regarded him with narrow-eyed suspicion. He'd made it clear he didn't favor Sam and Michelle getting to know each other again. Probably a natural reaction—kids raised by single mothers tended to feel threatened by any interloper—but it annoyed the hell out of Sam.

"C'mon." Suddenly in a hurry, Cody headed into the barn. His friends trailed after him, and Sam went back to the house.

He had no idea how to judge what kind of job he'd done with Cody this week. He was a difficult kid. They weren't all like that, Sam thought as he got into the shower and raised his face to the hot needles of the spray. Take Molly Lightning, who lived down the road. Bright, athletic, good student. She had prospects. You could look at her and picture her in a good place in ten years. As for Cody, it was hard to imagine where he was headed. Sam sensed that he'd never been tested. Never been forced to the wall, because Michelle had been so concerned about insulating him—from photographers, from hurt, from want. It wasn't her fault, but everything had come so easy to Cody that he had never learned to work for what he wanted. He maintained a sense of entitlement that bugged Sam. It was a hell of a thing.

So far, the father-and-son bond had eluded them both. There had been moments, here and there, when something, some connection, could be felt. Sam supposed that was all he could hope for at first. Deep down, he still wondered if he wanted more, and his own hesitation bothered him. Above the hiss of the shower, he could hear the nasal whine of snowmobiles being ridden fast. Too fast. He had to force himself not to go yell at them to take it easy. They'd just blow him off anyway, he knew. These kids were like creatures from another planet. He felt awkward around them, as if he had never been that young himself.

He scrubbed himself hard and efficiently, cleaning off the remnants of a rough day. Too many patients, too much red tape, not enough time. At least when he went to see Michelle at the hospital, it would be as a visitor, not a doctor. He was just drying off when he heard someone pounding at the door.

Pulling on a pair of jeans, he hurried downstairs.

Billy Ho stood on the back porch, his eyes wide, looking different from the go-to-hell kid who'd climbed out of the El Camino. "Um, Cody had sort of a . . . problem. With the horses."

Sam was already stuffing his feet into a pair of snow boots by the door. He grabbed a parka from the mudroom and put it on over his bare, damp chest. "What kind of problem?"

"Well, the little horse—the foal—got out."

"No big deal," he said, relaxing. "She'll come back in once we put the mare up. A filly that young won't stray far from her mom."

"No, man. I mean *out*. Like outside the paddock. Then it kind of panicked and took off."

Sam broke into a run. Billy trotted alongside him, breathless, trying to choke out an explanation. "We were just goofing around. No one knew the horse would take off. Cody went after her."

"Where's the mare?"

"She tried to follow the foal out, but Cody put her up. She's pissed, man—"

Sam could hear her. Frantic whinnies and stomping hooves echoed down the breezeway of the barn. He could see the snowmobile trails slashing and crisscrossing the broad slope of the meadow leading up to the woods. Shit. A filly that young would never leave her mother or the familiar terrain of the paddock unless she was truly terror-stricken. The boys had probably herded her uphill on the snowmobiles. As he put on a pair of gloves, he tried to remember what Cody was wearing. School clothes. If he got lost, he'd freeze to death in no time flat.

Sam harnessed a utility sled to one of the snowmobiles. He shot out of the yard, following a crooked line of footprints up the rise behind the barn. The panicked foal had traveled fast; he could see the stretch of its stride in the snow. Despite its young age, it could outrun Cody, especially if it was scared and lost without its mother.

The footprints disappeared into a cover of larch and fir trees. Sam drove into the woods, feeling a shower of golden larch needles rain down on him. He had to slow down to dodge the trees. Before long the density of the trees stopped him altogether. The sled behind the machine was too wide to negotiate the forest. Turning off the snowmobile and cursing through clenched teeth, he continued on foot.

In the silence after the engine's rumble, he heard a sound midway between a cough and a snarl. His blood ran cold. It was the distinctive call of a mountain lion. A big cat didn't usually bother things it couldn't easily kill, but if it felt cornered or hungry enough, it might take a swipe at a young horse. Or a kid. The eerie screeching escalated, a deadly rasp that echoed through the winter woods.

Sam climbed to the top of the ridge. There, he spied

a bitten-off section of snow that had crumbled down the opposite face in a small avalanche. Pressed against the curve of the scarp was Cody, waist-deep in snow, the horse floundering, its skinny legs sunk uselessly into the bank.

A livid smear of blood stained the snow.

Crouched on a bare rock above the boy and the foal was the cat. This one was big, maybe ninety pounds.

Its paw slashed out, claws extended, lips peeled back in a snarl. Cody had grabbed a branch and held it out, trying to fend off the reaching paw.

"Yah!" Sam yelled, waving his arms. "Yah, beat it, you old bitch!"

The cat froze and faced him with glittering eyes.

"Stay calm, Cody, and don't crouch down or turn your back, okay?" Sam called.

The boy's face was gray with terror.

"These cats like small prey," Sam said, praying the kid wouldn't panic. "Don't run, or you might trigger her instinct to attack. Keep waving the branch. You have to act aggressive."

He walked steadily toward the cougar, and his gut twisted as she swung her tawny gaze back to the boy and the horse. "Don't look it in the eye," he yelled, cupping his hands around his mouth.

The long tail switched slowly, rhythmically, nervous as a rattlesnake. The horse fell still, its stamina gone.

"If she attacks, you fight back, Cody," Sam hollered, hurrying as fast as he dared. "You hear me, son? Fight back!"

"O-okay," Cody said, his voice thin, snow-muffled. He brandished the branch like a sword.

The mountain lion coiled like a spring. For a sickening moment, Sam feared it would attack. A cougar always went for the head and neck. He reached the top of the bank and waved his arms, kicked up snow. The mountain lion retreated a few steps, turned, snarled. He yelled and waved his arms again, close enough now to see a string of drool drip from her mouth. Sam grabbed a chunk of ice and hurled it as hard as he could. Grumbling low in her throat, she slunk into the woods.

"Cody!" Sam half ran, half tumbled down the bank. "You okay? What's all this blood?"

The kid's bare hand kept its hold on the mane of the horse. "I'm okay. Let's get her up. She's stuck, see?" His face was dull white, his voice shaking.

"What's bleeding?" Sam demanded.

Cody held up his free hand. "Hit it on something on my way down." His chin trembled; maybe it was a shiver; Sam didn't know. "Help me, Dad."

It just seemed to slip out, the *Dad* part. Probably didn't mean a thing, but it had an incredibly powerful effect on Sam. "Okay, keep hold of the mane, you've got it. She's in a panic because she can't get her footing. We'll help her up the bank." Inch by inch, they pulled the foal upward. She was terrified, her eyes rolling, her hooves kicking out every which way.

"Watch the feet," Sam said through his teeth. They had no bridle, no way to control the horse except by brute strength. The minutes seemed to crawl as they struggled up to the top of the escarpment. The snow crumbled beneath them, sending them back a foot for every few feet they gained. Cody was panting, almost sobbing, when they reached the top, then staggered, pushing and pulling the horse to the snowmobile. She flailed every step of the way, twisting and snapping, hooves slashing out, impossible to contain.

"I'll hold her on the sled and you drive," Sam instructed. Using his teeth, he peeled off his gloves and tossed them to Cody. "Put those on. You'll get frostbite." He wrestled the foal onto the sled and Cody held her in place. Off they went, a smooth ride down the mountain, then into the paddock. The El Camino was gone. He wasn't surprised the kids had hightailed it at the first sign of trouble.

Sylvia had practically torn a hole in the stable door. The little one trotted inside and Sylvia was on her immediately, sniffing and licking her from stem to stern. Cody stood in the breezeway, teeth chattering, his nose bright red.

"Thanks," he said in a quiet voice.

"I'm just glad I found you."

The boy hesitated, then looked him in the eye. "I'm glad I found you, too."

And then without even thinking about it, Sam hugged him. It could have been awkward, but it wasn't. It was the most natural thing in the world to let a sudden wave of love for this boy spill out and over, to gather him in his arms in a hug that tried hard to make up for all the years of hugs he'd missed. Sam's throat felt tight as he stepped back. He didn't know if he was cut out for this. He'd never felt anything like the icy burn of terror that had ripped through him when he'd seen Cody in danger. His nerves were shot.

Cody was shuddering violently now. "Are you going to tell my mom?"

"Your mother's got enough to worry about." Sam grabbed his arm, pulling him toward the house. "We need to warm you up, have a look at that hand," he said.

A minute later they sat at the kitchen table, Cody's arm propped on a towel while Sam used tweezers to clean the grit out of the cut.

"When was the last time you had a tetanus shot?" Sam asked.

"Not sure." Cody winced as the tweezers dug deeper. "I had a bunch of shots before going to camp two summers ago. Ow!"

"Sorry. Don't watch. It's making you tense up."

Cody turned his head away. "Who's Alice McPhee?" he asked, focusing on the stack of junk mail on the table. The top item was a lingerie catalog with a label bearing Alice's name.

Sam hesitated. "My ex-wife."

Cody drew breath with a hiss. "Man, I didn't know you had a wife."

"I don't."

"It's bogus not to tell me you were married before."

"I was married before."

"I mean it's bogus that you didn't tell me right off."

"Cody—"

"Does my mom know?"

"She knows." Sam tweezed a sliver of dirt from the wound. "Hey, cut me some slack. I'm new at this."

"Yeah, well, so am I," Cody muttered.

Sam wanted to take the focus off him and Alice. She represented a failure he didn't like to talk about, so he changed the subject. "So what happened?" he asked, concentrating on the deep gash.

Cody shrugged, some of that old screw-you attitude slipping back into place.

"Hold still," Sam said through his teeth. "What happened?"

"We were just goofing around, man. We let the mare and the foal out into the paddock. Then we started riding snowmobiles and . . . the filly got out and took off. The noise confused her, and she went up the hill."

"Because you left the paddock gate open."

"Somebody did. I don't know who."

"Do you think that matters? You were in charge, Cody."

"Everything worked out okay, no harm done. Back off, man."

Sam's hand didn't falter, his gaze didn't waver as he cleaned the cut. But inside, he froze. "Everything *didn't* work out. A valuable filly almost died or broke a leg. Sylvia could've injured herself going ballistic in her stall. You almost got killed. What if I hadn't been around to come after you?"

"Man, you haven't been around for sixteen years, and I survived." Contempt dripped from his voice.

Sam stopped working. He set down the tweezers and regarded the sullen, defiant face so like his own—and yet so strange to him. "Well, I'm back now. And the bullshit is over. I figured putting you in charge of the filly would be good for you. Don't prove me wrong, Cody."

"Yeah, well, maybe you *are* wrong about me."

Sam got out a bottle of disinfectant. "This'll sting."

"Ouch. Hey, man." Cody tensed the muscles in his arm.

"Maybe you'd better choose your friends more carefully. You could use a few more responsibilities—"

"Hey—"

"—don't interrupt. You screwed up, and there are consequences. If you thought the work around here was hard before, you—"

Cody snatched his hand away before Sam was finished. "You're not my frigging jailer." He stood up fast, his chair legs scraping the floor. "What do you want with me?" he demanded.

Sam didn't have an answer for that. *Did* he want a

kid, or was it a concept he liked better in the abstract? No matter, he told himself. The reality was, he had a kid—and a difficult one at that. He had no idea if he knew how to be a good father. He picked up a length of gauze. "Let me wrap that wound."

Cody grabbed it from him. "I'll take care of it myself." He backed away, pausing in the kitchen doorway. "I know what you want with my mom, and I can't do anything about that, but stay the hell away from me."

Saturday

Chapter 41

It seemed like half the population of Missoula found some reason to stop by Gavin's room. They were timid at first, asking if he needed anything, making small talk. As the week wore on and he was moved from the SICU to a private room, their numbers increased. Nurses, aides, orderlies, residents, volunteers. The timidity fell away and then finally, on a rush of hard-won courage, they started asking for his autograph.

The mistake had been in giving out that first one, to a brown-eyed aide who looked a little like Carolyn.

"You remind me of the last woman who dumped me," he said, scrawling his signature on the back of a work-order pad. "No, on second thought, you're prettier."

She must have alerted the whole ward, maybe the whole floor, because all through the week he had to deal with furtive fans. He'd given the hospital strict instructions that the transplant was to be kept private, but strict instructions only went so far.

"They're wearing me out, Doc," he said to Maggie Kehr when she stopped in. She wore a shamrock in her lapel and a little leprechaun clinging to her scope. "You've got to let me go home and get some rest."

She smiled down at the chart she'd been writing on. "I want to keep you at least a week."

"It's St. Paddy's Day, fer chrissake," he said in an exaggerated brogue. "I've been lying around on my poor arse long enough."

"A week, Gavin."

"Aren't you the one who said it's the best kidney transplant you've ever seen?"

"Yes, but—"

"Didn't you say we set some sort of record, getting the kidney to work? Didn't you remove the catheter forty-eight hours sooner than you thought you could?"

"I did, Gavin—"

"Didn't I just take the healthiest piss you ever saw a man take?"

"Now *that*," she said, "is debatable."

"Only because guys piss for you all the time."

"One of the great perks of my specialty."

"I'm going home, Doc. With or without your blessing, I'm checking out when Michelle leaves here." She was being discharged today, and he was bound and determined to go with her. There was something vaguely horrifying about being left behind while his daughter went back to Crystal City. If he stayed, he'd feel like the loser in some battle or race.

"Never say whining doesn't work," Dr. Kehr said, signing a sheaf of forms.

"What do you mean?"

"You're a free man, Gavin. You've got the luck of the Irish on your side."

"I love you, Maggie, I really do."

"You're an old coot. Take care of that kidney now. They're a little hard to come by."

"My body is now Fort Knox."

"Just make sure that body doesn't miss a single follow-up appointment or a single pill. A pharmaceutical therapist will stop in to go over your meds and your daily log with you."

"Again, huh?" He didn't argue. From the very start, they'd impressed on him the importance of taking the antirejection medications. With a decided lack of sympathy, Maggie had warned him that the drugs would make him itch and sweat and suffer from impotence. He'd probably gain weight, and it would show in the cheeks and gut.

Not a pretty picture. Still, given the alternative, he'd settle for night sweats and chipmunk cheeks. But if this didn't work and he died, what the hell. It had brought him and Michelle together. It was up to them to find the things that mattered. Maybe they hadn't quite found that just yet, but they would. He knew they would.

The discharge was nicely choreographed so that he and Michelle were both wheeled into the main lobby at the same time from opposite wings. Smiling volunteers gave them green carnations for St. Patrick's Day. Gavin looked around suspiciously, thinking maybe the media had managed to barge in. He'd hate having this moment captured by some shutterbug who'd get five grand for the photo.

But what a moment it was.

Michelle. His daughter. She had always been incredibly beautiful, blond and luminous, with a way of looking at the world that was completely original, completely unique. It was something he had seen even in the cray-oned Father's Day cards she'd dutifully sent him as a small child. Seated in the wheelchair, smiling at him, she touched his heart.

He felt his throat fill with thick emotion, and the act-ing skill that usually came so naturally deserted him. He held out his hand. "Thank you, honey," he said, suddenly reaching forward to touch her cheek. "You know, you're the best thing I ever did."

For a moment she just blinked at him, almost comi-cally speechless. They'd seen each other now and then through the week, visiting, talking quietly, but this was different. They had done what they'd set out to do. They were going home now.

She took his hand and pressed it against her cheek. "All set, Daddy?"

"Yes. I want to tell you, I haven't felt this good in two years. I'm not sick anymore. No matter what I'm doing or thinking, I just stop in the middle of it and say to my-self, 'I'm not sick anymore.'"

"That's the point." Her smiled widened. "Ready?"

"Past ready." He signaled to the orderly pushing the chair and put on an English accent. "Driver, to the eleva-tors."

"Feels good to be going home."

Gavin wondered what she meant. "Home" as in Blue Rock, or "home" as in Seattle? He didn't know much about her life there, had only met two of her friends. Natalie was great. Brad Lovell was . . . adequate. The sort of solid guy you'd want for your daughter. Except that you wanted a guy to look at your daughter with worship, pure and simple. Not pride of ownership, which was what Gavin had detected in Brad's manner.

Gavin's burgundy Cadillac pulled up beneath the

awning. He expected his foreman, Jake, to get out, but instead, it was Cody. He sent Michelle a questioning look, narrowing his gaze suspiciously. "Did you know about this?"

She laughed. "Uh-huh."

He gave a low whistle. "I think I'd rather wheel this chair home."

"Be nice, Dad. The drive's nothing. A straight shot up the highway. It hasn't snowed, so the roads are clear. And he's worked really hard. Sam said he was practicing all week."

Gavin saw her knuckles tighten on the arms of her chair. "So how did the week go, him staying with Sam?"

She watched the suitcases being loaded into the trunk. "I don't know. He hasn't said much." Finally, she turned to him. "Daddy, what if he does better with Sam than he did with me?"

Gavin wished he was close enough to touch her. "It's not a competition." It was all he had time to say, when she needed so much more from him. She needed the years he couldn't give back to her, when pride and anger had kept them apart. "We'll be all right," he said, and vowed to make it so even if it killed him. "We're going to be fine."

The doors swished open, and out they went. Cody looked a little out of place, but very determined behind the wheel. Probably gave the kid a charge, driving Gavin's Caddy. Something about driving two people who were full of stitches and drugs probably made him feel particularly important.

"Here goes nothing," Gavin pushed himself up out of the chair.

The electric doors opened, and he stepped out into the bracing cold air. He wore a shirt and slacks that hadn't been cut to fit over a dialysis bag, and his blood sang. He wasn't nervous about the kid's driving. How could he be? Something magical had happened to him in the hospital, and now he was going home.

"I do love the occasional miracle," he said.

Sunday

Sunday

Chapter 42

Cody was pretending he wasn't nervous about school in the morning, Michelle observed that evening. It made her nuts that she'd been so out of it the past week, unable to be there for him every second, helping him through the ordeal of starting a new school. She had been there for every moment of his life, big and small, but last week, he'd been on his own.

And—wonder of wonders—the world had not come to an end. She was thankful he'd survived that first week, but she could tell he was anxious about the days to come. She knew that look, the shifting of his eyes, the jiggling of his foot against the chair as he ate dinner—a feast prepared by a beaming Tadao. They had eaten in the huge den of the main house, with Gavin and Michelle reclining like Romans on sofas. She had asked Cody if he liked his classes, if he'd made any friends, how he'd liked stay-

ing with Sam, but he'd only given her one-syllable answers. That was all she'd heard all week. She'd questioned
him about the bandage on his hand, but all he'd said was
he'd cut himself working at Sam's.

Gavin drank a glass of wine, his first since he was
diagnosed, and he got almost teary-eyed as he tasted the
Jordan Cabernet. With both Tadao and Michelle supervis-
ing, he took his evening meds and noted them in his daily
log. Though he didn't whisper a word of fatigue, Gavin
excused himself to go to bed early.

After an extralong shower, Cody went to his room,
leaving Michelle lying on the sofa, fiddling with the TV
remote. She was oddly manic and restless on her first night
away from the hospital. She felt fragile and vulnerable
from the lingering pain of an invasive procedure. She worried about bumping into things, worried about sleeping,
worried about her father, worried about how she'd feel
seeing Sam again.

But when she looked out and saw the snow begin to
fall, her worries seemed to have no more substance than
the weightless snowflakes settling over the yard. That
was the gift that had been given back to her the morning
of the surgery. She hadn't recognized her old friend at
first, but it was just as Joseph Rain had said, so many
years ago. *The gift comes to you in secret. If your heart
and your mind are not open to inspiration, then it passes
you by.*

Now, finally, in the midwinter of her life, she understood. It was the space she had glimpsed between the two
parting curtains. That was the offer. What she did with it
was up to her.

She didn't allow herself to think. Ignoring her doctor's orders, she bundled up and walked through the blowing snow to the small dwelling at the end of the compound,

the studio she had abandoned seventeen years before. There, she turned on the heat, rubbed her hands together, and took a deep, steadying breath. Physically, she felt dead tired. But she couldn't quell the restless need inside her. Time enough later for sleep, she decided.

Natalie—bless her—had set up stretched and gessoed Belgian linen canvases and laid out new paints and brushes. But even if these had been the crudest of supplies, it wouldn't have mattered, because at last she was ready. She lowered the legs of the easel and positioned it in front of the old red couch so she didn't have to stand up. Then she rolled up her sleeves and began.

She worked at a fever pitch from a vision that had been hidden inside her for years. It was a painful emergence, a birthing of sorts. For someone so conditioned to look outside herself, to emulate the hard lines and precise angles of that which could be seen and quickly grasped by someone paging through a magazine, it was a difficult transition. But for once that didn't stop her. After enduring what she had endured this past week, nothing could seem hard.

The transplant, confronting mortality, and coming face-to-face with her past had forced her hand. From her slumbering subconscious emerged the inspiration, the sense of awe and wonder, that had once meant everything to her.

The shapes and colors of her soul exploded onto the canvas. She didn't think, didn't evaluate. She just worked. And inside her, something happened. Something magical and true and luminous. She felt free, racing above the earth, elation pouring over her, out through her hands and her heart, becoming something wholly original, wholly her own.

She had no sense of time passing. She simply sank

into a strange beta state where nothing mattered except the painting, where the colors and emotions came from, and what the images were. The urge was sensual, predatory, dangerous, seductive, and in a leap of faith, she gave herself to it utterly.

When Sam McPhee walked into the studio, she should have been surprised, but she was not. It made a terrible, wonderful sense that he would come here alone, searching for her.

He stood in the dim foyer, his shoulders dusted with new snow, his face unsmiling, his eyes filled with a look she recognized from long, long ago.

"I saw the light on," he said.

Suddenly nervous, she grabbed a linseed rag and wiped her hands. "I . . . couldn't sleep."

"You sure as hell ought to be. You're recovering from surgery—"

"I'm all right, Sam. Don't doctor me. I've had enough doctors hovering over me, okay? I'm on the couch, see?"

"You're supposed to be flat on your back."

"That would make it hard to paint."

"Worked for Michelangelo." He studied her, and she braced herself for further argument, but he didn't pursue it. Taking off his coat, he hung it on a hook behind the door. He wore jeans and a thick flannel shirt.

"You're staring," he said.

"Am I?" One Christmas, she had bought Brad a shirt exactly like that. It was still in his closet, still folded with the pins in it.

"Michelle. Are you feeling okay?"

It was a question from Sam the doctor. Not Sam the ex-boyfriend. Not Sam the father of her child.

"Yes." She settled back on the old sofa. "I'm fine, really. My father and I are fine. We had a nice dinner to celebrate coming home. And I'm glad you came over. I want to thank you for keeping Cody last week."

He lifted the corner of his mouth in a half grin. "He's a barrel of laughs. We're going to have to do something about him being so accident-prone."

We. Did he really mean that? "He never did explain how he hurt his hand."

He tucked his thumbs in his back pockets. "Barn chores," he said dismissively.

"It was sweet of you to take care of him, Sam."

"I didn't do it to be sweet." He crossed the room and sat down beside her, very close, and the unique smell of him was achingly familiar. He touched her chin. "So you're fine."

"Uh-huh."

"Been painting."

"Yes." She held her breath while he regarded the tall, spattered easel with the halogen lights shining down. "It's not finished."

She watched him, still not daring to breathe. She saw the impact of the painting go through him as if he'd touched an electrified fence. His arms, legs, shoulders, neck stiffened; then he turned to her quickly.

"Wow," he said.

"Is that good wow or bad wow?"

"You mean you don't know?"

"Sam, the paint's still wet. I barely know my own name."

He held out his hand. She hesitated, then took it, studying the broad canvas. She saw an abstraction of pure emotion. It was no use. She had no objectivity.

"It's the first time in years I've done a painting that wasn't for work," she admitted.

"It's about damned time, Michelle."

"But what do you *think*, Sam?"

"Hell, I'm no art expert. To me, it's amazing. I look at this, and it makes me think differently. Makes me want to stare, fall into it, I don't know. I don't have the vocabulary or the expertise."

She tried to see the picture as he saw it. The composition was classical, straight out of Art 101. But so were van Gogh's compositions. The principal motif in the middle came from her vision—the mysterious space between the parted curtains. Within that space dwelled an abstract study of color, light and shadow. She saw pain and passion and depth, and realized she was looking at a painting that expressed precisely what she wanted it to express. Whether or not that had any particular value didn't matter.

"You know what?" she said suddenly. "You don't have to tell me if it's good or not. It's the painting that came out of me."

"I think it's incredible."

"Do you think it could be the drugs? I'm on Percocet."

"It's not the drugs, Michelle."

They sat together for long, silent moments, staring at the painting. She felt drained in a good way—the tension had flowed through her. She was the crucible. All the feelings, emotions, good and bad, had melted down inside her and then emerged in a new form, a thing of power and beauty, this painting.

She looked out the window, weighing her thoughts. What if she asked him about Cody's week? Then Sam would know Cody had barely spoken to her. But then she remembered her father's words: *It's not a competition.*

"What?" Sam asked, regarding her reflection in the blackened window. "Are you all right?"

"Just . . . thinking. I'd like to hear how last week went from your perspective. With you and Cody."

"It was fine, Michelle. Not every second, but we got along all right." Lord, just like Cody. He wasn't telling her a thing.

"What does he think of school?"

"Sucks," Sam said, emulating Cody's sullen manner. "But what else is he going to say?"

"Has he made any friends?"

"Hard to say. He was hanging with some guys. I don't know if you'd call them friends. He spent some time with Molly Lightning, too."

It felt . . . normal, talking over her son with Sam. Maybe this was what married couples did. She recoiled from the thought. "I feel so bad, making him go to a strange school."

"You ought to try to get over feeling bad on the kid's behalf."

"I'm a mother. It's what I *do*." She fell silent.

After a while, Sam said, "I was surprised Brad didn't stick around for the surgery."

Michelle felt a stab of defensiveness. She didn't know how to tell him about Brad. It was too . . . embarrassing. And he might read something into Brad's departure that wasn't there. *Would* she have broken off with Brad if Sam hadn't been in the picture? She wanted to believe she would have, but the truth was, she didn't know for certain.

"His job is incredibly demanding," she said evasively. Color heated her cheeks. She had let Sam make love to her. Did he understand that she hadn't given herself to him lightly? Did he understand she had never done anything remotely like that before? Did he understand that she'd been swept away by yearning and nostalgia and a passion that she needed more than air?

Or were those just excuses?

"If you're so committed to some other guy, then why is he in Seattle while I'm sitting here doing this?"

"Doing what?"

"This."

He cupped his hands over her shoulders and kissed her long and searchingly just then. His embrace caught her, supported her, and imprinted the texture and taste of his mouth on her, and when it was over, she felt stupid and dazed.

She wanted to speak out, to stop him, but she held a hush in her throat, trusting the knowing tenderness of his hands as he caressed her. He drew from her a shameless and powerful wanting.

"We can't do this, Sam." Guilt shuddered through her. If she let him make love to her again, she was a goner.

He pulled back and gave her a look. "Only because you're still recovering. Otherwise, we'd make friends with this old couch again."

Laughing at her blush, he helped her turn off the lights in the studio and walked her back to the guesthouse. At the front door, he kissed her again, like a suitor dropping her off after a pleasant date. She went inside and stood at the window in the darkened living room, watching his headlights illuminate the snowy night and letting the tears come, feeling her heart shatter. What sort of life would she have had if they had stayed together?

If only.

The big burning issue in her life.

If only she had believed in Sam, if only she had worked harder to find him and tell him about the baby, her life would have been so different. They might have supported each other through the hard years, and now they'd be a family.

No. If Sam had known about Cody, there would have been no rodeo circuit for him, no medical school, no Yucatán. Burdened with a family, he might not have become a doctor at all, and all the lives he had saved would be lost, all the wounds that he'd healed and all the illnesses he'd cured might have gone untreated. Perhaps everything happened for a reason. Perhaps their estrangement was some sort of preordained event, designed to make their lives work out the way they had.

The thought nagged at her. She was back in Crystal City, wasn't she? Beyond the obvious, what could be the reason for that?

It was idiotic to speculate. Gavin's illness wasn't part of some cosmic plan. It was something that had just . . . happened. Meeting Sam again was pure coincidence. She shouldn't make any more of it than that. Certainly she shouldn't be having these thoughts just because Sam McPhee had a way of kissing her until she couldn't see straight, because he made love like a form of worship.

She had failed with Brad. Sam had failed with Alice. Maybe the two of them just weren't cut out for the long haul.

The thought followed her to the edge of sleep.

Monday

Monday

M ichelle spent the day lost in thoughts of Sam. Her father was in bed, on the phone trying to arrange the renewal of his pilot's license, and Cody was at school. Michelle tried reading, watching television, sketching a plan for a painting, but after a while she simply gave in to memories of Sam. She felt herself being sucked back into the past, dredging her heart through memories that burned. He was the first boy she had ever loved, and that one long-ago summer stood out vividly as a magical time. Each sunset burned brighter, more beautiful than the last. Each moonrise glowed with a promise she had felt certain was meant for her, only for her. She had been so naively young back then. She thought her love was like a river, ever flowing, never ceasing; nothing and no one could stop it—not even the granite boulders that divided the stream. She used to tell Sam her wildest dreams, and he would confess his deepest secrets. They were so open with each other, so trusting. She had thought she would remain in that dream-state of bliss all the rest of her life. She hadn't understood that those golden days were rare, never to be lived again.

The hours passed so quickly that she felt startled when she heard someone drive up. Getting out of bed, she saw Cody getting out of the Jeep Sam had lent him. It was a cranky old thing, one that would have caused Cody acute embarrassment to be seen driving in Seattle. But here it was different. Her son was different, she thought, observing his assurance as he hefted his backpack over one shoulder and headed for the barn complex.

She put on a jacket and went outside, finding him with the farrier and a bright sorrel horse in the crossties. The hot smell of the blowtorch pervaded the air.

"Howdy, ma'am." The farrier spoke past the wad of snoose that bulged in his lower lip.

"Hey, Mom." Cody sat with a box of shoeing nails in his lap.

She couldn't help smiling. "I guess this is something you don't see every day."

The farrier aimed a stream of tobacco juice into the waste trough. "Hand me one of those sixes," he said, all business.

Michelle was surprised that Cody could distinguish a six-nail from a five or an eight. When the horse shied, she was even more surprised to see her son help out while the farrier worked.

"Let's see what's going on in the arena," Michelle suggested when the shoeing was finished.

They stood at the rail, watching some of the hands work with the broncs. The horses wore flank straps to irritate them so they'd kick up their back legs, the higher the better. Raising rodeo stock was serious business. A good bronc or bull could become famous in its own right, and many Blue Rock animals had, but it required constant care and training.

"Until we came here, I never even knew they trained bucking broncs," Cody said, lapping his elbows over the top rail. "I just thought they were wild horses."

"Some cowboys have been known to ride their broncs home after a show. They just take off the flank strap and the horse turns into a kitten."

They watched for a while, and Michelle took in the clear bright air, the sound of hoofbeats and equine snorts, the sharp profile of white mountains against blue sky. The ranch hands and horses worked together with a rhythm that seemed ancient, timeless. And in some way, crucial.

"You were a bit late getting home from school," she said to Cody. "Did you stay after?"

"I gave some kids a ride."

"I'm glad you've been making friends." She took a long, slow breath and stared straight ahead at the jagged line of mountains. She didn't want her expression to sway her son's response in any way. "Hey, Cody?"

"Yeah?"

"Uh, Brad and I aren't going to be seeing each other anymore."

From the corner of her eye, she saw him stiffen. "Yeah?" he said again, this time with a different inflection.

"He's a good guy, but we weren't really going anywhere." She hesitated. Cody didn't seem to have any comment. Michelle asked, "Do you ever wonder what it would be like if we lived here instead of Seattle?"

"Hell, no, Mom," he said, almost panicking as he jumped down from the fence and backed away. He touched the healing wound on his head where the stitches had been. "There's *nothing* here. Nothing! We live in Seattle. It's where we belong." He paced up and down in the snow. "No one moves in the middle of high school. It sucks here." Eventually he slowed down, then stopped, leaning against a fence post. "You're not really thinking about moving here, are you?"

"I've been thinking about a lot of things, Cody."

He picked at the gauze bandage on his hand.

"I wish you'd tell me how it really went last week, with you and Sam," she said, frustrated.

He stuck the bandaged hand in his pocket. "It didn't *go* any particular way. He's just some guy to me. We got thrown together because of you, that's all."

Could it be? No chemistry, no magic, just circumstance between them?

"It's too early to tell."

"There's no point. We're going back soon. Right, Mom? Right?"

She didn't answer him.

Tuesday

Tuesday

Chapter 44

Some days, it was the emptiness that hit Sam hardest. It didn't happen often; long ago he had taught himself to survive without support from another person. Yet every once in a while, it caught him, that emptiness. Especially after having Cody around the week before.

To make things worse, today had been one of those days in doctoring that made him wonder why he thought he could help anyone. First there was the forty-year smoker who had decided to hold Sam personally responsible for his inoperable lung cancer. Followed by a harried mother whose HMO benefits had just been cut—she could no longer bring her asthmatic son in for therapy. She had to lie awake at night, crying helplessly while he wheezed for breath. Then there was a guy with a broken hand—claimed he'd done it on a hay baler, but when, shortly afterward,

Deputy O'Shea showed up, Sam knew the cowboy had done it on some other guy's face. He had seen Mrs. Duckworth for imaginary aches and pains, turned away a drifter who came looking for a prescription for narcotics, and listened as a teenage girl wrestled over whether or not to terminate her six-week pregnancy. Given the recent changes in Sam's life, her dilemma took on a painful, personal edge.

As he drove home, he felt tension building in his neck and shoulders, and he knew it was one of those days when the empty house would echo with the void that existed, usually hidden, in his life. He used to visit Candy on the rez for some uncomplicated sex, but that wasn't what he needed. He had to quit fooling himself. What would it be like, he wondered, to walk into a house that was warm and glowing with evening lights? That smelled of dinner and the presence of another human being?

What would it be like to talk about his day, really talk, not just complain or vent his frustration but to explain what went on in his heart, in his soul, when he had to look a good man in the eye and tell him he had cancer or when he lost a patient to the absurd vagaries of the health-insurance system?

He had attempted, long ago, to create that sort of life. It hadn't worked. He and Alice had both tried, but their marriage had felt wrong, artificial. The end-of-work conversations were strained. The affection felt both false and forced. He was always pulling back when he should forge ahead.

The thing about it was, Sam knew how to take care of a needy person. He'd done it all his life, and never knew any other way. But he didn't know how to love a woman who didn't *need* him. A woman who could stand strong without support. Life had taught him that relationships were hard work, not a quest for joy and completion.

Ordinarily there was nothing Sam couldn't get over by sitting down and having a beer with Edward, tossing a rope at a dummy steer, or taking one of the horses on a long, solitary ride up to the hot springs. But now that Michelle was back, he wanted more.

More than talk.

He wanted a connection, and he wanted it with Michelle. God knew, he'd seen enough other women over the years to understand that it only worked with a certain person.

Christ, she must think he was a maniac, coming on to her while she still had a healing incision. He wondered if she was pissed about that.

He swore between his teeth, and when he reached the turnoff for Lonepine he drove right on by. Kept going until he got to Blue Rock Ranch, its imposing gates and the dark boulders at the entrance as ostentatious as a castle drawbridge.

A glare of lights burning in the window of the studio beckoned him. He didn't pause to think, just parked the truck and walked to the door. Through the sidelight he could see her on the sofa, and he paused, waiting for the nervous energy churning through him to calm down.

She was in another world; he could tell by the look on her face. He knew that look. It was the expression she had worn as a girl, totally absorbed by the images on the big canvas in front of her. Michelle was a beautiful woman, there was no doubt about that. But Michelle in the act of creation was beyond beautiful. As she painted, there was an incandescent quality about her that made him believe in her with all that he was.

He knocked at the door, but didn't wait for her to answer it. "It's me," he called, letting himself in. "Don't get up."

"Sam." She sounded pleased. But cautious.

"Where's Cody?"

"He's over at the main house, doing homework. He needed to do an assignment on a computer, so he's working in my dad's study."

"How's Gavin doing?"

She squirted something on her hands and scrubbed them with a rag. "He's amazing. Stronger and healthier every day. He complains about the medications he has to take, all the side effects, but he's faithful about it. We had a checkup today, and my staples are gone." Drying her hands, she pulled her knees up to her chest. "I'm so glad it's over." She caught his expression. "The doctor in you probably feels compelled to point out that we're not out of the woods yet. The transplant team warned us about rejection episodes, but I've already put my father on notice. He wouldn't dare reject my kidney."

She smiled and spoke lightly, though he could tell she worried. Rejection episodes were always devastating. Between Michelle and her father, more than the kidney was at risk.

"These days, the episodes are treatable," he said. "I recommend you quit worrying about something that hasn't happened and might not."

"Okay. Thanks, Sam."

"Michelle, about the other night—I was damned pushy."

Her face darkened with a blush. "Was that an apology?"

"Well, I'm not sorry I kissed you like that."

She ducked her head and fell silent.

"Can I see what you're working on?" He hung his coat on a hook behind the door.

"Um, sure." She angled the easel toward him. "I'm in advertising, remember? I'm used to people looking over my shoulder. Breathing down my neck, even."

He walked over to the easel. It was the abstract painting she had been working on before. The big, violently emotional images hit him on a visceral level. Maybe he was reading a lot into it, yet he thought he could see the rage and the melancholy, but more than that, the sense of hope radiating through a distorted, two-sided structure near the center. It was a strange and moving work, startling and possibly disturbing.

"Michelle, this is no advertising art."

"I thought I'd work on some things for the firm, but I keep wanting to paint." She shrugged apologetically.

Her attitude bothered him. "Don't apologize for doing work like this."

"I'm not apologizing. I'm just—"

"Don't explain this or rationalize it, either. Not to me."

She glared at him. "I wasn't."

"And don't get defensive on me. It's a bad start, especially when you consider what I came to say."

She eyed him warily. "And what's that?"

He took a deep, steadying breath. Held her gaze with his. "For seventeen years you were dead to me," he said. "I had to live my life as if you'd never existed. Then, out of the blue, you come back here."

Her hands twisted in the hem of her painting smock. "I didn't come to torture you."

"True. But your coming here made something happen. Something new and good."

"Sam, that's all in the past."

"Look, if it was just a youthful fling, we would have

forgotten, would have moved on. I know, because in seventeen years, I never forgot you, and believe me, it's not for lack of trying. It's because I never stopped loving you, Michelle."

She tore her gaze from his, shaking her head. "How do I know I didn't just catch you between 'tryings'? How do I know your sudden interest in me isn't because of Cody?"

"He's a part of this, too. And you know better than I do that he's not an easy kid. But he makes me want to try like hell to work this out."

She went to the long worktable by the easel and started cleaning up, her hands moving nervously as she put the caps back on tubes and swirled paintbrushes in jars of cleaner.

"What is it you want from me?" she asked.

"For starters, I want you to sit back down. You're supposed to be resting."

"I'm sick of resting." She worked faster, finishing her cleanup with an air of defiance. That was her way. Finish one thing before starting another. Finish cleaning up the paints before you give your attention to a man baring his soul.

He waited for her to finish. When she finally did, he said, "I've been thinking about you a lot, Michelle. You don't seem happy, and your happiness matters to me."

She wadded up her smock between her hands. "Don't pretend this is about me and my happiness, Sam. It's about you—"

"Let me finish, damn it." He knew he was stepping out on thin ice, but he'd already decided to take the risk. "You asked what I want from you. Why didn't you ask what I want to *give* you?"

"Why should I think you have anything to give me?"

"You've trained yourself not to expect anything from anyone. You're the giver, Michelle, not the taker. You give Cody every last thing he needs and expect nothing in return."

"It's called parenting."

He ignored that. "You give your friend Natalie a roof over her head when she needs it, a shoulder to cry on. You give your father complete forgiveness for anything in the past, and just in case the world needs a symbol of your daughterly devotion, you give him a damned kidney."

"I think you'd better go. Before we both say things we regret."

He shook his head. This wasn't coming out right at all. "I'll regret the things we *haven't* said, Michelle."

"What hasn't been said?" She stood there, beautiful, challenging, vulnerable.

And he thought back over his life, and the years that had gone by, the path he had taken, and where everything had brought him. In all the places he'd been and people he'd met, he had learned and moved on. But there was one person in his past from whom there was no moving on. Someone he was destined to carry around in his heart for the rest of his days. The truth of it stood out like a scar on pale flesh.

"I love you." The words sounded so inadequate for the size of what he was feeling. "I never stopped."

She sat down and hugged her knees up to her chest as if she'd felt a sudden chill.

His gut churned, and he realized he was scared, scared in a way he hadn't been in a long time. He'd been doing fine, his life had been set, and suddenly she had him walking off the edge of a cliff. "I mean it, Michelle. It's not hard to love you. It's one of the only things that came easy when I was young. And it's still easy."

She looked terrified. "But it can't mean anything. It can't change anything."

He put out his hand, cradled her cheek in his palm. "It already has."

"No, not in the way you're saying. That night at the theater—"

"What, you're saying that didn't change anything? The hot springs didn't mean anything?" He took his hand away. "Does that mean you're in the habit of cheating on your boyfriend?"

"I believe that's my cue to smack you across the face."

He raked his hand through his hair. "It was a shitty thing to say. But you've got to do better than tell me 'it can't work' or 'it hasn't changed anything.' Because we both know it can. And it has."

She sat silent, pale and tight-lipped with anger. And fear, too. He saw that in her eyes, and he hated being the reason for it.

"Just what do you expect from me?" she asked at length.

"I want you to be completely honest. Do you have the life you want back in Seattle? Or is it just something you settled for?"

"I worked damned hard to get my act together in Seattle—"

"That's not what I asked." He gestured at the canvas. "Do you do that in Seattle?"

She waved a hand dismissively. "When I'm home, I *work*. This time I'm spending here, Sam, it's not real. I'm not on a sabbatical from work. I'm on a sabbatical from my life. But that's the thing about sabbaticals. They're temporary. And you still haven't been straight with me. What do you expect? You want me to ditch everything

I've built for fifteen years and move out here? Be your 'woman'?"

"Now you're talking."

"How about the other way around? How about you drop everything here and move to the city?"

"Is that what I should do, then? Sell my place, set up practice in Bellevue or some nice suburb?"

"You'd do that?" Her voice was small, disbelieving.

"Haven't you been listening? This kind of love doesn't just happen every day. Believe me, I know that. Took me a while to figure it out, but now I know. I loved you when we were young, and I lost you. After all these years, we've found each other. I'm not about to lose you again without a fight."

"This is not a fight." Panic flashed in her eyes. "You haven't thought this through. Say Cody and I decided to live out here. I'd turn into some beatnik studio artist selling my paintings at county fairs. Cody would never forgive me for ripping him away from his school and his friends in the middle of high school. The difference is, he'd have two of us to blame for his misery. Two of us to torture."

"I'm not about to let the kid torture either of us, Michelle. Or dictate my life for me."

"Oh, Sam. It's what kids *do*. It's what they're about. Until you're a parent, day in and day out, facing every crisis and triumph and dealing with him moment by moment, you won't get it."

"Then give me a chance. Give me a chance to 'get it.'"

"What if you decide it's not for you? Then you just move on? Send us back to Seattle?"

"You aren't listening. I'm not saying let's give this a try. I'm saying let's do it. Let's be a family, Michelle."

She shut her eyes. "Don't you think we should give this a little more time?"

"Time's not going to change my mind."

"*I* need the time. It's late, Sam. You'd better go."

He stood, forcing himself to walk away from her. "See you, Michelle." He left before she could answer, and stepped out into the cold, clear night. "By the way," he said, turning to see her framed in the warm light of the doorway, "what I said earlier about us being a family—that was a marriage proposal."

Wednesday

Wednesday

Chapter 45

A marriage proposal. Michelle kept her eyes straight ahead, watching the vanishing point of the trail framed between low bramble and bunchgrass trying to push up through the snow. She had gone AWOL. Her surgeon wouldn't approve of her taking a walk so soon, but she couldn't help herself, and she'd picked a day when spring felt like a certainty instead of an empty promise. Physically, she felt fine. Emotionally, she was roadkill.

A marriage proposal. With those three words, Sam had taken her world, her life, and turned it upside down, and then he'd gone home, leaving her stricken by doubts . . . and aching with hope.

After a restless night, she needed to get out into the wild spaces of Montana, to watch spring arrive on a sudden gust of warm chinook wind. Moving slowly and gingerly, she walked a short way to a ridge top. A timberline of towering Douglas firs skirted the mountains. Layer upon layer of snowy peaks stretched out against the endless bowl of the sky. An eagle circled, then dived, and she watched the silent fury of its descent. The mystery and magnificence of the place gripped her. She felt infinitely small and insignificant, yet at the same time a sense of vastness and possibility expanded her soul.

The silence gave way to the sound of a stream. Rounding a bend, she came to a snowbound creek. Awakened by the chinook, the sun beat strongly on the south face of the mountain, and chunks of melting snow and ice littered the trail. Even as she watched, the thaw escalated. The irrepressible power of the flowing water and the relentless glare of the midday sun worked at the stingy trickle. She stooped to drink the icy, numbing water from her cupped hands. The constant, steady swish of the current echoed the flow of blood in her veins.

In the corner of her eye something glittered and instinctively she turned to look. As a trio of hawks spiraled against the blue sky, a ledge of snow gave way above the stream. The avalanche boiled down a natural couloir that curved away from the trail. In its wake, the stream was unleashed. A whitewater cataract sprang from the heart of the mountain, shooting out and down over the rocks, making the sound of someone exhaling after holding a long breath. A rainbow, thrown up by the sun-shot water, dazzled her eyes.

Inside her, something rose up like the rise of the hawks, kettling and then moving off in a different direction.

It was the artist—Michelle recognized her exuberance and her darkness. For years she had kept this creature imprisoned, icebound, but she was free now. She was home.

All her life, Michelle had tended to hide from things

that scared her. Losing her mother and being estranged from her father taught her to avoid facing the rocks and relics of emotional entanglements. But now she had changed; the hurt was still there but not the fear. She let all the feelings in like the cataract tumbling over the rocks, and the exultant pain cleansed her, reminded her that she was alive. Awakened her to old dreams that had never really died. Like the icebound stream, she had been silent, but the current never stopped coursing through her.

Sam's words had hung over her head all night long, and now they nagged at her, unanswered, impossible to ignore. She had been haunted by their last conversation. *A marriage proposal.* He'd left her stunned, speechless, her tongue numb with the inability to reply to him.

No one had ever proposed to her before. She had tried to savor the novelty, but instead it scared her. Brad had never proposed, even though they had been together, neighbors and lovers, for three years. They had both been extremely adept at avoiding that level of intimacy.

But Sam didn't know the rules. He didn't know how she operated. He didn't know she tended to hide from things that scared her, surrendering her dreams in order to keep herself safe.

As marriage proposals went, his was a doozy. It had done everything it was supposed to do. Gave her chills, made her blush, kept her awake at night, stopped her from thinking about anything but him.

His schedule gave her the gift of this new spring day all to herself, to gather her thoughts and steady her nerves. He was working at the clinic and then at the Flathead reservation, so she wouldn't be seeing him until tomorrow night at the earliest. Maybe by then she would know what to say.

Perhaps the reason she hadn't given Sam an immediate answer to his proposal was that on some level she didn't really trust that he'd meant to ask her. It could be a way of saying he wanted to spend more time with Cody.

As for herself, she had to figure out the secrets of her own heart. Watching the spring thaw, she thought she was beginning to hear what her heart was telling her. Sam McPhee made her feel as starry-eyed as a girl again. Yet in the end she had to acknowledge that she was a big girl now. The grown-up part of her knew the truth—that asking was the easy part.

It was what came after that was so hard.

That was why she was still resisting him. She could look beyond the dizzying whirl of passion and see that there was work to be done—and it wasn't the sort of work she and Sam had proven themselves to be good at. After the passion, there was struggle, sometimes disappointment, the daily grind of living—could they survive that, year after year?

She tipped her face up to the dazzling brightness of the sun. In that moment she realized that she knew the answer. She'd always known.

Chapter 46

*T*ammi Lee Gilmer's car reeked of cigarettes, but
Cody didn't mind, because she was letting him
drive it. He'd pretty much slacked off smoking
because cigarettes were too hard to get in this one-horse
burg. The clerks at Ray's Quik Chek knew all the kids by
name—and by age. They were anal about not selling to
minors.

Cody probably could have sneaked a pack or two from
Tammi Lee, but he would have felt too shitty, stealing
from her. She was pretty cool, and he didn't mind hanging out with her now and then. If anyone would have told
him he'd actually *like* having a recovering alcoholic rockabilly grandmother, he would have snorted in disbelief.
But the fact was, he and Tammi Lee got along more like
friends than relatives, and that was fine with him.

He'd had supper with her tonight because the ranch

Jeep was in the shop and wouldn't be ready until McEvoy's Garage closed at eight. It was a gas, driving around here. Cody didn't have to worry about traffic and winos and one-way streets like in Seattle.

Tammi Lee had made fried chicken for dinner, with chocolate mud pie for dessert. After dinner, Cody had to go to the library to get a book on Montana state history for some bogus assignment, and his grandmother had offered her car. She also asked him to return a rented videotape she'd left at the shop. She hated being late. It wasn't just the fines, she'd explained, but the whole idea of being forgetful.

It was kind of spooky, thinking about her lonely existence, and how she stayed up late watching movies and reading paperback novels to keep from wanting to drink again. She'd told him that some days, it wouldn't take much to set her off, make her take another drink.

"While I'm out, I'll get the tape from the shop and return it for you," Cody had offered.

She hadn't hesitated a single second. "Here's the key to my car, and this one's to the shop. I left the tape in the storeroom in the back. Little cubby with my name on it."

Cody was getting too used to this small town. He realized, as he drove along Main Street past the Indian statue in the square, that it was becoming as familiar to him as the palm of his hand. He passed the darkened Lynwood Theater, thinking that a movie house would be a huge improvement around here.

In the library, he found the book he needed and applied for a card, the whole transaction only taking a few minutes. Under "Home Address" he had written Blue Rock Ranch, wincing as he did so. When his mom had asked him what he thought of moving here permanently, he'd instantly hated the idea. If she was just checking, she had her answer.

In the parking lot, he spotted some kids coming out of the library, backpacks on their shoulders, shoving each other as they skidded along the icy sidewalk. One student walked alone, slim and straight. Cody leaned across the seat and cranked down the window.

"Hey, Molly," he said.

She tensed, reminding him of Sam's filly. He didn't blame her. They hadn't spoken since the ride incident because he couldn't figure out a way to apologize. He'd never been big on explaining his behavior or apologizing.

She came to the car, tucking a silky black lock of hair behind her ear as she bent to peer into the passenger-side window. "What's up, Cody?" She didn't look at him the way she had when they'd first met—the sideways, kind of shy-but-interested way he liked. She was neutral now. Guarded.

"I'm running an errand for my grandmother," he said. A ride, yeah, that would do it. He'd offer her a ride home. That would give them a chance to talk. "Hey, you want a lift—"

"Yo, Cody!" a familiar voice called. "Where'd you get the wheels?" Without waiting for an answer, Billy Ho and his sidekick, Ethan Lindvig, jumped in, one in front, one in back. "My El Camino's wasted again. Couldn't get it to start." Billy sent an "aw-shucks" grin to Molly. "You want to come along, cowgirl?"

She shook her head and stepped away from the car. Her face went all hard, her eyes flat and glossy. "See you, Cody," she said, her tone dismissive.

He couldn't very well call her back with Billy and Ethan breathing down his neck. "Where to?" he asked them.

"My house," Ethan said.

"I've got to make a quick stop." Cody eased away from the curb. "Then I'll give you a lift." He glanced in the rearview mirror. Molly stood on the sidewalk, slender and straight as a young tree. She watched the car for a moment, then turned and walked away.

Damn.

He didn't listen to Billy and Ethan yakking away as he drove a few blocks and stopped at the quilt shop. "Be right back. I need to grab something for my grandmother," he said.

He used the key to let himself in. The shop smelled of dry goods and old ladies. A dim light over the counter cast its glow on an old-fashioned brass cash register.

"Cool," Billy said. "I've never been in here before. What *is* all this shit?" He took a bolt of fabric and draped the loose end around him, strutting in the aisle and singing the wedding march off-key.

"Hey, you shouldn't be in here," Cody called. "I just need to get something from the back room."

"Chill out," Ethan said, honking the breast of a mannequin. "We're having a little fun."

Losers, Cody thought as he went to the back room. He didn't know why he put up with them. It wasn't like they liked *him,* they liked who he was—Gavin Slade's grandson, the one with the big allowance and the reliable wheels. He couldn't believe he'd left Molly Lightning freezing on the sidewalk for these two clowns. He'd make it up to her, he decided. He'd ask her out, maybe invite her over to Sam's to ride some of his horses. She'd like that.

He could hear the guys goofing around in the shop while he retrieved the rented video from a cubby with Tammi Lee's name cross-stitched over it. Then, closing the storeroom door behind him, he said, "Okay, let's go. Did you put back whatever it is you were messing around with?"

Ethan and Billy exchanged a glance. "We didn't mess with anything, man," Billy said.

Cody didn't like the furtive glee on their faces, but he was in a hurry. He wanted to get them out of the shop before they wrecked anything.

Thursday

Chapter 47

The way the morning light cut down through the skylight of the big kitchen of Blue Rock reminded Michelle of those old murals in church, the ones she used to stare at when she was little. They went to All Saints on Camden Drive in Beverly Hills, her mother wearing white gloves and Michelle in lace-edged socks, gleaming Mary Janes, and an outfit bought on her father's I. Magnin account. She used to sit beside her mother, studying the little girls seated securely between two parents, swinging their legs and bumping their toes against the soft foam-covered kneelers. Mom on one side, Dad on the other, a pair of bookends to prop her up no matter which way she leaned. Michelle used to lift her eyes to the back wall where a pair of gigantic pre-Raphaelite angels soared, the sun pouring over them like melted butter, and when mass was over, she would go home and draw what she had seen.

Fixing herself a bowl of raisin bran, Michelle realized she hadn't thought about those moments in church for a very long time. Something about the angle of light and the quiet of the house brought back the memory.

And of course, it was easier to think about the past than the future.

She owed Sam an answer, but they hadn't had any time alone together. Yesterday he'd worked out of town, and last night he was on call. He had office hours today, and she had to go to Missoula with her father for another checkup. She supposed they could discuss it on the phone, but this was the sort of thing to talk about face-to-face.

Her confidence faltered. It was fun playing two-crazy-kids-in-love, but when real life intruded, it intruded with a vengeance. Already, outside events were conspiring to keep them apart.

Her father came into the kitchen just as the alarms on both of his wristwatches beeped. Medicine time.

"Hey, Daddy." She got up from the stool at the counter and poured him a glass of water.

"How's my girl?" He grinned, and the flush of health on his face was so welcome it made her want to weep.

But she felt compelled to ask, "You feeling okay?"

"Fine."

"Really? I'm not making idle chitchat here."

"Okay, the side effects of the medicine can get annoying." He held out his hand, and for a second she noticed a tiny, brief tremor. "Cyclosporin does that. Prednisone and immunosuppressants are their own kind of fun." He grinned again. "Enough whining. All I have to do is consider the alternative, and it shuts me right up."

She handed him the water and waited while he took

out a massive plastic pill box with dividers for each day. He swallowed his meds, the radical cocktail of stabilizers and antirejection pills that were so critical after the transplant. So far so good. The transplant team had declared that their speed of recovery was one for the record books.

Gavin set a stack of mail on the breakfast bar and slowly picked up a thick envelope. Michelle saw his hesitation and the slight shaking of his hand as he broke the seal and took out a packet of official-looking papers. He studied them for a minute, then shut his eyes and kissed the certificate with beatific reverence. "My pilot's license has been renewed," he said. "I'm back in the game, honey."

"Daddy, no kidding?"

"No kidding." His legendary blue eyes shone. He poured himself a bowl of raisin bran and then methodically proceeded to pick out all the raisins. Michelle watched for a second, hiding a grin. She and her father were alike in ways that startled her. An occasional gesture, a look, a quirk of taste. She didn't eat the raisins in raisin bran, either.

Her father seemed unaware of his thoughts. He ate some cereal, then drummed his hand on the stack of papers. "This is the second-best thing that's happened since I got sick."

"What's the first best?" She held her breath.

"Finding you and Cody again, honey. Didn't you know that?"

She couldn't speak for a moment. This, she thought as her heart soared. This was the essence of life. A moment of joy and triumph so sweet that her entire being filled up with happiness. How long had it been since she'd allowed herself to feel this much, this deeply? "Ah, Daddy," she said, and something in her inflection made him look up. "I did know."

Simple little words. An ordinary conversation. But she had waited a lifetime to share a moment like this with her father. They finished their breakfast; then he helped himself to coffee, shutting his eyes and smiling as if he had just seen God. "I've missed drinking coffee."

They sat in companionable silence for a while, sipping their morning coffee and watching the play of sunlight over the polished-granite countertops and gleaming copper cookware hanging from the range hood.

"You going to work on your painting today?" her father asked.

"Yep. I have no idea what I'm doing over there, but I'm loving it."

"That painting you've been doing. It makes me damned proud of you."

His words filled her with warmth. Just for a second, she wanted to ask him where that belief in her came from, why he had never expressed it until she gave him a kidney. But the second passed, and she knew there was no answer, and no point trying to get one.

"Thanks." She indicated his clipboard, covered with pink phone message slips. "You've been busy."

"As a matter of fact, I have."

"What is all that?"

He paged through the notes. "Here's one from Carolyn." He winked, though buried in his cynicism was an almost-hidden hurt. "She's ready to kiss and make up now that I don't have a dialysis bag hanging out of me."

"So are *you* ready?"

"I told her to piss off." He crumpled the note. "Pun intended. Here's one from a contractor in Polson. I'm going to reopen the Lynwood on Memorial Day."

"Really?" She felt a rush of excitement. The old theater was filled with memories for her, memories of that long-ago summer, but even more important, memories of a snowy night not so very long ago. "I'm glad. This town's more than ready."

He pushed a fax across the counter to her. "This is what we really need to talk about."

It took her a minute to assimilate what he was showing her. "Daddy?"

"It was on the fax machine when I got up this morning. It's from the same contractor who's going to be renovating the Lynwood."

Michelle swallowed, but she couldn't banish the dryness from her mouth. "Daddy," she whispered, "what the hell's going on?"

He beamed at her. "Keep reading."

It was a bid for restoring the vacant retail space in the shop next door to the old theater. At Gavin's request, the space would be converted into an art gallery. Picturing the vintage storefront, the old plank floors, the hammered tin ceilings, Michelle felt a giddy light-headedness. A buoyant sense of wonder.

"A gallery," she said.

"Might bring some culture to Crystal City." He touched her hand. "You've never had a showing, Michelle, and God knows, you deserve one. That is, if you think this is something you want."

It was something she hadn't even dared to want—until now. Maybe that was what the whole ordeal of Gavin's illness had been about. It was a kick in the pants. A way to jolt her out of the comfortable monotony her life had become. She got up slowly, walked around the counter, and put her arms around him. "Dad—"

The phone rang, and he grabbed it. "This might be the contractor." But then he handed her the receiver. "It's Sam."

"Sam!"

"Did I catch you at a bad time?"

"Um, no."

"I've missed you." His voice was low and sexy.

A shiver ran through her. She could feel her whole body start to smile. "Same here." She stared at the fax on the counter. She thought about what he had said the last time they were together, and all the things they had to talk about. What would it mean if she decided to marry Sam? So many questions. They had so much to discuss. It was too much, too big to explain to him right here, right now. "Have dinner with me tonight, Sam," she managed to say. "I have something to tell you."

A pause. Then she could hear the grin in his voice as he said, "Honey, wild horses couldn't stop me from seeing you tonight."

Chapter 48

I t's okay to grab the apple," Molly said.

Cody looked down at her from the dizzying height of the horse's back. This was a terrible idea. It was the worst idea he'd ever had, inviting Molly over to ride horses at Sam's after school.

"What apple?" he asked, mortified when his voice broke on the last syllable.

She didn't seem to notice. "The saddle horn," she explained. "If you feel a little unsteady, you can always grab hold of the saddle horn, pull a little leather."

"Oh." He clutched it, two-handed, white-knuckled. "I thought that was against the rules."

"Are you competing?"

He liked the laughter in her eyes. It almost made him forget he sat atop fifteen hundred pounds of bone and muscle and hoof, a sorrel gelding called Ace. "No," he said.

"Just try to relax, okay? If you're tense, he can feel it." It was pretty great, the way she instructed him. She had lots of patience and didn't make him feel inferior just because he'd hardly ever ridden a horse. She started him out really slow, and before long he actually began liking the rocking motion of the horse, going round and round the fenced arena, listening to the creak of the saddle and the heartbeat of hooves. Thanks to Molly, he was feeling pretty good, all things considered.

This afternoon during study hall, he'd gone right up to her, looked her in the eye, and apologized for being a jerk. Instead of making him squirm like a bug on a pin, she had forgiven him with more generosity than he deserved. He would always remember her words: "I like you, Cody, no matter what." No one had ever said such a thing to him. When he'd said he'd like to try his luck riding a horse, her smile had lit up the day.

After about an hour, Ace had worked up a sweat, so Cody got off and put him up, carefully hanging the saddle and pad and all the gear. They went into the barn office, where he washed his hands at the sink and got some soft drinks from the fridge. They sat together on an old couch with lumps in the seat, and it felt perfectly natural to put his arm around her. She made it clear that she liked it, setting her head easily on his shoulder. For a while, they just listened to the whistle of the wind through the barn, the flutter of swallows high in the eaves, and the occasional low-throated sound of a horse stomping and muttering. They had the whole place to themselves. Sam was at work, and Edward was doing errands in the city.

He turned on the radio and couldn't find anything but country western. But he didn't mind.

Molly didn't say a word, just took his can and set it on the floor next to him. When she turned her face up, he kissed her, softly at first, then longer and harder. She tasted like Dr Pepper, chilly and sweet, and everything about her was perfect. She pressed close, clearly liking the kiss as much as he did, and when he eased back on the sofa so he was half-lying down, she came with him. He put his tongue in her mouth. His hand strayed. He really, *really* wanted to touch her.

She lifted her mouth from his just a little. "It's okay," she whispered, and undid the top two buttons of her denim shirt. "I've been thinking about this a lot, Cody. I don't mind."

She spoke as if she'd read his thoughts, and her honest desire touched off a forest fire inside him. Yet despite her words and the excitement shining in her eyes, he realized that she probably hadn't done much fooling around at all. But she wanted it, he could tell, and she took his breath away. Her kisses were open and searching and inviting, her hands like a pair of inquisitive kittens crawling over him. Quickly enough, things got away from them— shirts undone, and then the top button of his jeans, and she held him and made a nervous, excited sound in her throat. It struck him then that she was not going to tell him to stop. What happened next was totally up to him. He pulled back and looked down into her face. "Girl, you're driving me crazy."

Her eyes shone. "Really? I wasn't sure you wanted me."

"Hell, yes, I wanted you."

"I'm glad, Cody. I'm real glad about that." She lifted herself toward him, and he couldn't help himself. He kissed her again, opening his mouth over those soda-sweet lips.

She was soft and willing, her touch honest and warm. For the first time since he'd started dating girls, he'd found one who made him feel something tender and new, something that had more to do with feelings than with sex. Amazing.

And so, at the crucial moment, Cody astonished himself. "You're a nice girl, Molly," he said. "But I think we'd better stop."

"I don't want to stop," she said quietly, pressing her open hand to his chest.

"I don't either," he admitted. "I like you, and maybe one day it'll be right for us. Just not now. We should wait. Okay?" Man. It *hurt*. He couldn't believe he managed to get the words out.

"I'm not a baby. I know what I want."

"Then waiting a while won't change that." He ground the words out through gritted teeth. Faintly he heard a car or truck, but it sounded very far away, and he had more immediate concerns. He had Molly right where every guy dreamed of getting a girl—ready and willing—and he was blowing his chance. How stupid was that? Still, it was the right thing to do, and by some miracle, Cody still knew what the right thing was.

As he drove home from work, Sam caught himself pushing hard on the accelerator. Unlike most days, he was eager to get home, to get cleaned up, and go see Michelle. Tonight it would begin. The love that had started more than seventeen years before kept growing stronger every day. It was a scary thing, to love someone like that. But scarier still to think of life without her.

He drummed his fingers on the steering wheel and tried to shrug the day off his aching shoulders and back. He had set a bone this morning—a sheep rancher's tibia. He'd seen four flu patients, an infant in respiratory distress, treated a dog bite, and had gone over a special diet with Earl Meecham, who had an ulcer. The last appointment was with a mentally handicapped ranch hand. Sam had to show him how to use a rubber and he wasn't sure the lesson would stick. The kid was slow, but his body was that of a man. Bad combination. Sam still had some of the rubbers in his back pocket.

The day just wouldn't go away until he filled his mind with Michelle. That was the magic of her. Before she'd come back to him, his bad days and hard thoughts had no place to go. He tried to picture her in this house, in his bed, in his life. And the worrisome thing was, the picture wouldn't form. She was so damned sophisticated. Could she really be happy here, a ranch wife, of all things?

It was almost as ludicrous as picturing himself living in some suburban sprawl outside of Seattle. Then there was Cody, who needed things Sam didn't know how to give.

Details, he told himself, loosening his tie. That's all they were. Details. They'd work things out. He saw a shadow in the sky over the highway and looked up. He thought it might be Gavin Slade's little P-51 Mustang, banking through the breaks and draws of the valley over the country air park. Sam grinned in spite of his complicated feelings about Michelle's father. So Gavin was flying again. He was truly on the mend now.

When Sam pulled up at Lonepine, he noticed the Jeep parked outside the barn, and country music wailing from within. Curious, he went over to the barn and saw a horse from the Lightning place tethered to a loop. Good, he thought. He'd rather see Cody making friends with Ruby's daughter than those punks who had spooked the horse. Sam decided to go in and say hello, let them know he was home.

When he walked into the office, Cody and Molly Lightning were as stunned and embarrassed as he was.

They both jumped up from the sofa, brushing hastily at their rumpled clothes. Molly's hair was mussed, her face red as a beet. She clutched the front of her unbuttoned shirt.

"I, um, I was just leaving," she said in a strained voice. She was gone before Sam could think of a single thing to say.

He swung around to glare at Cody. Still no words. His earlier thoughts mocked him. He was totally unprepared for this situation.

Cody tried to brush past him. "I'd better get over to Blue Rock," he muttered.

"The hell you will," Sam burst out, planting himself in front of him.

"Hey, man—"

"Don't you hey-man me," Sam said, flexing his hand. "What the hell were you thinking, groping her like that?"

"We're both sixteen," Cody pointed out. "And you might not believe this, but I wasn't going to do anything."

"Yeah, sure," Sam said. "I *don't* believe you."

"I wasn't." Cody jutted his chin out. "But that's between me and Molly, not me and you."

"Under my roof, it's my business."

"Hey, I didn't ask to come here. I'll go back to Seattle anytime, just say the word. But if I'm stuck here, the least I can do is try to make friends."

"Looks like you were trying to make more than that. You've grown up thinking you're entitled to every goddamned thing in the world." Sam's anger wasn't rational, the way a wildfire wasn't rational. It flared and flamed with a life of its own. "Smart-ass like you ought to know better than to have unprotected sex."

"We were just fooling around," Cody snapped. "Not having sex."

"Only because I happened to show up before things got out of hand."

"You don't know that. You always want to think the worst of me."

Something inside him snapped, and he blew up with anger. "Did you even think for one second what you're risking? Bringing another unwanted baby into the world—"

Sam stopped himself. Too late, he realized what he'd just said. Too late, he recognized the source of his anger. And the deep red flush on Cody's face meant he recognized it, too. Neither of them said a word, but a silent storm howled between them.

And Sam knew in that moment that he loved his son. He knew, because it hurt so bad to hurt him.

The phone rang, shrilling into the tense quiet of the office. Holding Cody with a raised hand, Sam grabbed the receiver from the wall. "Sam McPhee." He frowned as an automated message instructed him to press 1 to accept the collect charges from the incoming call. With a shrug, he pushed the button.

"Hiya, hon. It's your mama."

He didn't move, but at the unmistakable slur in her voice, he could feel everything inside him curling up, burning down to nothing. "Mama. Where are you? What've you been drinking?"

Cody's pale face sharpened, but Sam couldn't think about the boy now. "Mama? Talk to me."

"Lessee. Made it to Kalispell. They got a honky-tonk here, the Roadkill Grill. Think they'll lemme be in the band? I used to sing real good. 'Member when we cut that album in Reno? You were in your playpen still . . ."

He could hear the lazy slide of liquor through her

voice. Jesus, five years. She'd been sober five years, and now this. "Mama, slow down. What happened?"

"That old cow LaNelle fired me from the shop."

"LaNelle Jacobs fired you? Why?" From the corner of his eye, Sam could see Cody edging toward the door. He pinned him in place with a fierce stare. The boy flattened his lips and squinted defiantly, but he didn't leave.

"They said I stole all the money from the cash register. All forty-two bucks of it. A staggering fortune. Jussst . . . staggering."

"That's absurd, Mama. LaNelle knows you wouldn't steal from her shop."

"Someone saw my car parked there last night. 'S'morning, the cash was gone. 'Course she's gotta blame me. Who else could it be, son? Who the hell else could it be?"

"Mama—"

"You never really outgrow what you are, do you son? Folks' opinions of you never really change."

"I'm coming to get you," he said. "Don't move. Get a cup of coffee and sit tight."

She wasn't listening now. He could hear someone asking her if she wanted another tequila sunrise, could hear her cackle with harsh glee. *Oh, Mama. Not again, Mama.* He slammed down the phone.

"What's going on?" Cody asked, his face strangely still. "Someone's saying she stole from the shop?"

"When I find the son of a bitch who did, I'll kill him, swear to God I will."

Cody paled. "Hey, it's not the end of the world, man."

"I don't have time to deal with you now," Sam snapped. "I have to go." He grabbed his parka and his keys. "Tell your mom I can't make it tonight. Tell her—" He broke off. "Ah, hell. Tell her I'm sorry."

Chapter 49

"How was school today?" Michelle's hairbrush hit the carpet with a *thunk*. Klutz, she thought. She was a bundle of nerves.

"Okay," Cody mumbled into the refrigerator. He stood in the white glow of the interior light, scanning the contents.

Michelle picked up the brush and studied her son. He wore his black jeans and leather jacket, and she felt a frisson of unease. For some reason, it struck her that he looked exactly as he had when they'd first come to Crystal City. He wore gloves, concealing his bandaged hand. A knitted hat covered the scar on his head, so there was no evidence of the wound Sam had mended.

She walked toward him. "Is something wrong?" she asked.

He twisted away from her, ducking his head as if to

avoid getting an unwanted kiss. "Just the usual." He dropped his backpack on the floor and took out a carton of milk.

"Uh-uh," she said automatically as he put it to his lips. "Use a glass."

He eyed her over his shoulder as he got a tumbler from the cupboard. "Can I ask you something?"

"Sure, Cody."

He sloshed some of the milk on the counter. Without thinking, she grabbed a paper towel. Annoyed, he took it from her and wiped up his own spill. "I was wondering. Did you . . . want me? I mean, did you ever think of getting rid of me?"

He had never, ever asked her before. Michelle wondered how long he'd held the question inside him, unasked, festering. Tears gathered thickly in her throat, and she touched his cheek. "Oh, Cody. Not for a single second. You were so wanted. You were my life." She swallowed and hoped she wouldn't cry. He had almost never seen her cry. She remembered, with startling clarity, every sensation of being pregnant, and pain was no part of that sensation, no part at all. She had gone for natural childbirth, and she had felt his entire journey from her womb into the world, and seeing his tiny face for the first time had filled her with a fierce sense of purpose. "Having you saved me," she said. "You were the best part of my life, and you still are."

He seemed a little embarrassed by the display his question had incited. "Cool," he said, and took a deep gulp of milk. "What're you all dressed up for?"

She laughed, wanting to hug herself with glee. "Well, I've got some news."

He narrowed his eyes in distrust. When had he learned to do that? To conclude that her good news meant bad news for him? He leaned against the counter, drinking his milk, waiting.

"You know I've been painting lately." It felt good to voice the notion that had been at the back of her mind for days. Saying it aloud made her heart soar. It was impractical, impulsive, but she was determined to reclaim herself. "Like I used to, years ago. I've been thinking about making some changes. Gavin and I are looking into opening an art gallery in Crystal City." She felt almost fearful about how badly she wanted this. How much it meant to her.

His gaze flicked over her—black cashmere trousers, black angora sweater, her good pearls. "So what's with the outfit?"

"Sam's coming over for dinner." She tried to keep the tremor from her voice as she told him the *real* news. The one thing she wanted more than the next breath of air. "Sam asked me to marry him. I haven't said yes yet, but I'm going to. Tonight."

"*Shit.*" He set down his glass and brushed past her, flopping down on the sofa.

She tasted lipstick as she bit her lip. "I was sort of hoping for a more supportive reaction from you." Don't do it, she wanted to beg him. Don't take this happiness from me. But on the heels of that thought came the thoughts any mother was conditioned to think: How can I do this to my child? How can I rip him out of the middle of his life and plunk him down amid strangers? Isn't there some compromise? Can I have what I want and keep him happy, too?

He was quiet for long, long moments. She was dying to know what was going on in that head of his. Finally, he took a deep breath, looked her square in the eye, and said, "Don't bother waiting for Sam to show up. He took off."

"What do you mean, he took off?"

"He's gone, scram, vamoose."

A chill of disbelief snaked through her. "Gone where?"

"Out of town. He said to tell you . . ." Cody hung his head.

"What? What did he say? What happened?" Disbelief hardened into a horrible dread. She had to know. She needed a reason. She was inches from shaking this kid's teeth right out of his head.

"I guess he didn't want to be my father after all."

"Oh, for Pete's sake, that's ridiculous. Sam loves me. He wants to love you, Cody—"

"Not anymore." His head hung lower. "Something, um, happened."

She pressed herself against the counter until she felt her surgical scar. What occupied the space where the kidney used to be? she wondered irrationally.

"Talk, Cody," she said, fixing her attention on him with a will. "Start at the beginning."

"Molly and I were hanging out at his place this afternoon, and he . . . he acted like I was molesting her or something. We weren't doing anything much, Mom, we weren't."

Michelle took a deep breath, trying to assimilate everything he'd just told her. "Let me get this straight. You and Molly were at Sam's."

"Yeah." He glowered at the toes of his shoes. "I was riding a horse, and it was great, and then we went into the barn office. We were like, fooling around a little bit, no big deal—"

"Fooling around." Her stomach knotted.

"No big deal," he repeated sullenly. "We're not babies. We know the score. We were fully clothed, Mom, every second. But Sam scared Molly off and started yelling at me."

Overnight, she thought. Overnight her son had changed from a little boy with grass stains on his knees to practically a grown man ... with a man's desires. "Look at it from his perspective. She's a neighbor. The daughter of a friend. Can you blame him?"

"I should've known you'd take his side."

"I'm not taking sides—"

"But you don't believe me. You didn't hear the things he said, Mom. He went into this big insane lecture about safe sex and unwanted babies." Cody folded his arms across his chest. "Then he said he ... he doesn't want me for a son."

The pain was sharp, hot. "He can't have said that."

"Call him. Just try it. He won't answer. Swear to God, he doesn't want me, and good riddance, I say. I don't want him either."

She studied his pale, worried face. And deep in the center of her, a core of ice formed, grew bigger, colder. "Why would you say a thing like that?"

"Because I mean it, Mom. Sam has the hots for you, but that doesn't mean he gives a shit about me."

Michelle went through the motions even though her horrified certainty hardened with each creeping moment. She called Edward, who had been in the city all day and had seen neither hide nor hair of Sam. She called Sam's service only to be told Dr. McPhee would return calls when he checked in for his messages. No answer at his mother's. His partner Karl was brusque, telling her to try the service or, if it was an emergency, to go to County.

Her hand was ice-cold and shaking as she hung up

the phone for the last time. A terrible sense of déjà vu broke over her. She remembered exactly how she had felt that long-ago night, sick and exhilarated with the knowledge of her pregnancy, rushing over to Sam's house only to discover that he'd left without a word.

He took off. He took off. He took off. Disappeared into the night just like before.

Friday

Chapter 50

Almost dizzy from lack of sleep, Michelle dressed in the gray quiet of the dawn. Cody's bedroom door was firmly shut, and not a sound came from within. She wondered how well she knew her son anymore. She could only guess at what was going through his head. The emotional roller coaster of finding his father so unexpectedly, then having the big quarrel with Sam, was a lot for a kid to handle. A lot for *anyone* to handle. Yet beneath the hurt and anger, she had detected something a little harder to put her finger on. Evasiveness. Shame, perhaps.

Resolving to talk to Cody about it when he got up, she put on a pair of boots and went over to the main house. She walked into the great room, stood before the fire, and thought of that first night when she and Gavin had sat together in this room. It seemed long ago that they had been so awkward with one another. She'd gone to him because, at long last, he needed her. The irony was that she had needed him just as much.

She pressed a wadded Kleenex to her cheeks. Her father came in, took one look at her, and opened his arms. It felt so right to collapse against him, and the tears spilled again. She knew her father now, and she needed him in a way she never had before. "Sam's gone, Daddy. He and Cody had a fight last night," she said. "It was bad. Cody thinks Sam doesn't want him."

"Cody's wrong. Sam wants his kid. Trust me," Gavin said, bringing her to the sofa and sitting down.

"How do you know?"

Lines deepened in his craggy face. "I did a stupid thing years ago, letting you leave. Before you came to me when your mother died, I didn't think I wanted a kid. I didn't know how to be a father. I sure as hell wasn't much good at it. When you left, I convinced myself it was for the best. But I was wrong. I wanted my daughter. I just didn't know how to bring you back. Anyway, that's how I know Sam wants his son. Whatever went on between them won't change that."

"But if Cody doesn't believe Sam wants him, then we've got problems. And something tells me they won't just blow over."

"If he's gone, there's bound to be an explanation. He's not some no-account drifter. He'll be back this time."

"True. But how can I get Sam's side of the story if he simply takes off at the first sign of trouble? He should have called me."

"Don't jump to any conclusions."

"I'm trying not to. But I just feel so . . . stood up. Maybe I'm not cut out to be with a guy like Sam. People don't really change, Daddy. He took off seventeen years ago, and he's done it again." She felt the chilly ghost of the old feelings of abandonment. In different ways and for different reasons, she had lost her mother, her father, Sam . . . and now she felt Cody slipping away from her. "Maybe," she admitted, "I don't have it in me to love them both in the way they need."

Gavin turned to her on the sofa. "You know better than that. You have the most generous heart of anyone I've ever known, Michelle. You came to me in spite of my failings. You came even though you knew it would be hard for you. Things turned out to be even harder than you imagined, and you stayed, honey."

A long silence stretched out, and the sun broke over the mountains. Michelle turned to her father. "The first time Sam took off, I never even tried to find him." She took a deep breath and finally admitted something about herself, something she wasn't proud of. "There was probably a part of me that saw him as a delinquent, no good, a guy who would never amount to anything. I was wrong back then. The failing was mine, not his. That's what I don't know, Daddy. I don't know if I'm better than that now."

"About the first time." Gavin put his hand on her arm.

His touch made her pause. She looked up into his face, a little puffy now from the meds, but still so expressive, so anguished.

"He and his mother left town because I arranged it," Gavin said quietly.

Michelle stared at him. Her fist tightened around the Kleenex. "I don't understand."

"There was money missing from the foreman's office. Maybe Sam took it, maybe he didn't. I wasn't really thinking about that. I was thinking about you, Michelle. I'd just found out you were seeing Sam, and I wasn't thrilled with the idea. I thought the boy and his mother were trouble, and I didn't want you hurt. So Deputy O'Shea and I confronted him with the missing cash. He denied taking it, of course. For good measure, O'Shea also reminded Tammi Lee of her rubber-check habit and several outstanding warrants. She was given a choice. Disappear, or do time. Sam really didn't have a choice."

"My God." She drew away from her father.

"He never told you about that, did he?" Gavin asked in a pained voice.

"He never said a word."

"I'm sorry as hell, honey. I didn't know what to do. I was afraid you'd go running off with him."

"And I did run off. Only not with him." She pulled her knees up to her chest.

"I wish I could undo what I did. But I acted out of desperation because I loved you, and I was so damned scared."

Her throat stung. "Why—" she said, and had to pause. "Why didn't you just say so? Why didn't you tell me you loved me? You never said it."

"I thought you knew." He was silent for a long time, staring down at his hands. "You're a parent yourself now. The love happens whether you talk about it or not. You've made choices for Cody—some good, and some bad. But you always acted out of love for him."

The stark truth struck hard. He was right. She didn't approve of Cody hanging out with Claudia Teller. Every once in a while, Michelle would "forget" to pass on a message that Claudia had called. Or manage to schedule Cody for a dental appointment when she knew he and Claudia had plans. Michelle was uncomfortably certain she would resort to devious means if she thought she could keep them apart.

"Sometimes a parent does the wrong thing for the right reasons," Gavin pointed out. "I'm so damned sorry, Michelle. I should have trusted your judgment."

"Are you saying I should trust Cody's?"

"Maybe. Yeah, I am. Look, I failed with you. But you have a chance to succeed with Cody."

"Right now it's Cody's judgment that he doesn't want Sam in his life."

"I suspect he'll come around. He's a kid, thinking about himself first and foremost. He doesn't want to move in the middle of high school—what kid would? But he's also your son. He wants you to be happy, Michelle. Do what's right for you. He'll come around."

"I can't do it, Daddy. I can't force the two of them together and pretend it will be fine."

"You don't know how it will be. Maybe it won't be fine, maybe not all the time. But what is? What the hell is in this life?"

Restless, she got up and opened the doors to the front porch, feeling the harsh chill of the morning air on her face and hearing the sounds of the ranch coming to life—diesel vehicles firing up, the foreman's whistle, the hydraulic hiss of a dump truck. Horses blowing and stamping, the tinny sound of the farm and ranch report on someone's radio. She needed to clear her head, had to think about what it would really be like to marry Sam—a man who had just taken off without a word of explanation.

It scared her when she considered how hurt she was by that. How vulnerable she was when it came to Sam. "I'd better go wake Cody for school," she said.

Returning to the guesthouse, she knocked lightly on Cody's door. No response. "Cody?" she said, and pushed the door open.

Reality registered slowly. The bed that hadn't been

slept in. Closet door carelessly open to empty space. The big duffel bag gone.

Terror broke over her in a dizzying wave. Gone.

Her son was gone.

It was every mother's nightmare. She tore out of the room, screaming for her father, her mind filled with visions of Cody broken, bruised, abused by someone who had picked him up hitchhiking.

Gavin met her halfway across the yard, holding out the cordless phone. "It's okay," he said.

His words barely penetrated her icy, heart-freezing terror.

Her father closed her hand firmly around the phone. "It's okay. He's in Seattle. Here, let Natalie tell you."

Standing in the blanketed yard, her hand shaking, she put the phone to her ear. Natalie was calm, uncharacteristically subdued, as she explained that Cody had taken the all-night bus from Missoula. Dear God. Her son had run away from home last night. No, he'd run away *to* home. He had run away from *her*.

"Let me talk to him," Michelle said. Tears threatened to melt the ice of terror, but she held them in, afraid that if she started to cry, she'd never stop.

"He's on his way to school. He wanted to get there early to re-enroll."

"You let him go to school without calling me?" She wanted to jump through the phone line and throttle Natalie.

"I told him he should call you. He said he would. Later." Natalie hesitated. "Michelle, he didn't explain why he showed up here alone, but I can guess. He's safe. Let him cool off, okay? If you don't give him time to realize on his own how much he loves you and misses you, he might never figure it out."

She was still trembling when she hung up. Her first impulse was to phone Garfield High School, demand that they find him, bring him to the phone. Then she looked across the white mystery of the fields of Blue Rock, and a small, surprising voice inside said No and then louder: *No.* She handed the phone to her father.

"You want me to fly you to Seattle?" he asked.

"No." The word formed of its own accord. "Natalie just said something to me that makes perfect sense. He's got to fix this on his own, Daddy. It's time he made his own decisions and figured out how to deal with the consequences."

Gavin looked at her for a long time. "When you were young, you went away, too. And like a fool I just let you go. I was too stubborn. Are you being stubborn or is this the right thing to do?"

She spread her arms. "Who knows what the right thing is? I just know that what I've been doing lately isn't working. Maybe I was too much of a perfectionist, too demanding. That's probably what made him turn into a rebel in the first place."

Now, with a lurch of her heart, she suddenly understood. It was only natural to distance himself from her expectations. And it was her job to let him find his own way.

"I was smothering him with love, getting him out of scrapes when I should have let him fall and pick himself up again." The decision hurt, but it felt right. She realized that what she really had to do was make the painful choice of letting Cody go. He might discover the answers on his own, or he might not. It was no longer up to her.

At six-thirty at night, Cody stood on the rain-slick sidewalk in front of the town-house complex in Seattle. It was weird, but he missed the dark of Montana, the inky purity of the night in the mountains. Here in Seattle it was never all the way dark, not with the yellow shore lights, the busy ferry docks, and the ribbons of reflected neon snaking along the wet streets. The high bluff framed a view of Elliott Bay, a glittering necklace of lights along the shore.

Today had definitely been one of the strangest days of his life. He had gone to school, handing a re-enrollment slip to the clerk in the office. After the initial paperwork it had been like a regular day. Same classes, same kids.

Same Claudia.

He'd found her at the usual place, a wooded area everyone called the smoke spot. Unobserved, he had stood at the fringe of the woods and looked at her, expecting a theme song to start up or something. He'd watched her throw back her head and blow out a cloud of cigarette smoke, and he'd felt . . . nothing. Not the rush of excitement that used to keep him awake at night, not the heady pride that made him walk tall through the school halls. No theme song, just the boring hiss and spatter of the incessant Seattle rain through the alder and cedar trees.

When she'd seen him, she had squealed and flung herself at him, but her questions had all been about Gavin, and what it was like to have a celebrity grandfather, and why hadn't he ever *told* her that his grandfather had played Lucas McQuaid, and had he saved any of his prescription painkillers . . .

He had tried hanging out with his old crowd after school, but nothing felt right. There was nothing different about them, but it *was* different. The energy had gone flat, like a Coke left out too long. Their jokes sounded stale, their laughter rang hollow. He couldn't share their reminiscences of the Phish concert last weekend. It was as if he had been away for years rather than weeks.

He planned to call Claudia tonight and break up with her. Then, if he could get up the nerve, he'd call Molly Lightning. It was shitty, the way he'd left without explaining anything to her. She probably thought he'd been shipped off to reform school. It wouldn't be the toughest call he had to make, though. He had to figure out what to do about his mom and, tougher still, Tammi Lee. It was his stupid fault she'd lost her job. His stupid fault for chickening out and not telling the truth about what had happened. His stupid fault she'd gone out drinking.

Through the window of the gated entrance, he spotted a movement. A shadow. His heart thumped. Behind him, a wino shuffled along the sidewalk, muttering to himself. Noticing Cody, he said, "Hey, gotta smoke?"

"Nope," Cody said. "I gave it up."

Slowly, his backpack feeling like a load of bricks, he trudged up the walk toward his house. For a few more minutes, he stood listening to the low hum of the hot-tub pump and feeling the moist chill of the Seattle evening on his hair. Then he took a deep breath, punched the security code into the keypad, and let himself in.

The place smelled vaguely of patchouli oil and Natalie's experimental Middle Eastern cooking. She had a performance tonight, and so she'd left dinner in the fridge and a note in fat pink magic marker—*Call your mother.*

"I know, I know," Cody murmured under his breath. He set down his backpack with a thunk and went to put on some music. It was too quiet in the house. He found himself wandering around, feeling more alone than he'd ever felt before. Without really planning to, he found himself in the study, a neat-as-a-pin room with a glass-topped desk, a big angled drafting table, and two computers, their black faces gathering dust. He went to the closet and folded the louvered door aside, and then he realized what he was looking for.

His mom's paintings.

They were stored in the very back of the closet in a large, flat portfolio with three clasps. Working carefully, he took out the canvases and sketches and leaned them against the walls. There weren't very many of them, and he'd only seen them a few times.

He supposed he'd always known the pictures were good—great, even—filled with color and life and movement. They seemed to say something important. Like the painting that hung in Sam's house. But up until today he had always regarded these pictures as something created by a stranger, someone he never knew.

For the first time, he managed to connect the paintings to his mom. He pictured her in the studio at Blue Rock, lost in her work, not harried and tense like she was at the agency. Pacing in agitation, he thought about how she had looked yesterday when he'd told her he and Sam would never get along. In his heart, Cody didn't believe he was wrong. Sam *didn't* want him.

But maybe Cody had twisted the truth . . . a bit. It was pretty obvious Sam was pissed at him, but he'd never actually said he didn't want a son. It was a fine distinction. But if Sam was pissed about Molly, he'd go ballistic when he learned who the real culprit was in the quilt-shop incident.

Cody felt a rank lump of guilt in his throat. He didn't blame Sam for not wanting him.

The reason Sam had left Crystal City didn't have a thing to do with Cody or his mom. That phone call Sam had received . . . In his mind's eye, Cody could still see rage and fear on his face. And something worse—the hurt.

Sam had to take off in order to save his mother, and Cody had done the only thing he could think of. He'd fled.

Now he knew how the filly had felt, driven up to the woods in terror of the snowmobiles. He'd run away, but maybe he'd wound up in a place of greater danger. Hell, he didn't know. He should just stay away from Montana, where he didn't fit in. He'd never fit in.

Feeling restless and unsettled, he grabbed a yogurt from the fridge and scarfed it down, then drank half a quart of orange juice. Then he picked up the phone and jabbed in Claudia's number. Might as well get the easy call out of the way before he decided what to do about the rest.

In the middle of the third and fourth ring, the sound of the buzzer from the security office nearly made him jump out of his skin. Frowning, he hung up the phone. He wasn't expecting anyone.

He was amazed when the guard announced the name of his visitor. *Gavin Slade.* Switching on the lights over the entranceway, he opened the door.

"Hey," he said tentatively.

"Hey yourself." With a jangle of flying-ace buckles and straps, an unsmiling Gavin Slade strode into the house.

Cody followed him inside. "Um, how did you get here?"

"Flew the Mustang to Boeing Airfield. I wasn't planning on taking her out for a long haul so soon, but here I am." The bluewater eyes inspected Cody. "I expect you know why I came in such a hurry."

Cody eyed him warily. The angry energy of defiance coursed through him. "If you came out to lecture me because I blew it with my mom, you wasted a trip. My mind's made up. I don't fit in there."

Gavin scanned the room and Cody realized he was

seeing where his daughter lived for the first time. "Actually," he said, "it's more than that. I guess I came because, a long time ago, *I* blew it with your mom. She needed me, and I wasn't there for her, and she took off." His eyes looked deep and sad. "For seventeen years," he added. "I'm here because this is what I should have done for my daughter all those years ago. I should have come after her."

"This is different. Sam can't stand me, and the feeling's mutual."

Peeling off his leather jacket to reveal several more layers of clothing, Gavin studied a big studio photograph of Cody and his mom, done about five years before. He walked right up to the framed picture and pressed his palm to it. "How old were you in this picture?"

"Maybe ten or eleven." Cody remembered the red Izod shirt, and the feel of his mom's open hand on his shoulder, and the way the photographer had tried to flirt with her.

"I wish I'd known you then," Gavin said. "I feel lucky to have met you at all, Cody. Look at all the time we lost, with us being so stubborn." He turned to face Cody. "I don't know what went on between you and Sam, but the one who's getting hurt is your mom."

Cody's throat felt dry as sandpaper. Gavin was right. She had been happy and flushed and calm up until last night. Up until Cody's big lie.

"It took a kidney failure to get us back together," Gavin said. "What's it going to take this time? A heart attack?"

"You don't understand," Cody said. "You don't understand how bad I am." He felt too miserable to be embarrassed when his voice broke.

"Then make me understand, Cody."

The genuine caring in Gavin's quiet voice reached out to Cody. "You're not going to like it," he said. And then his voice steadied, and he told the truth. He told his grandfather what he had done.

Gavin gave a low whistle. "That's pretty damned bad."

"See? Sam'll never forgive me, and who can blame him?"

Gavin was quiet for a long time. Cody's stomach knotted. He hated what he'd done. Hated what a jerk he'd been. Finally, Gavin spoke. "I think I get the picture. You know, Michelle doesn't have the sort of troubles your grandmother does, but that doesn't meant she doesn't need you."

"What does she need with a screwup like me?" Cody demanded.

"You're only a screwup if you don't know how to straighten out the mess you've made," Gavin pointed out. "Nothing'll ever feel right again until you do. You know that, don't you, son?"

"You're right," said Cody, filling up with elation and terror.

Sam stood in the shower, letting the too-hot water pound down on his head. There was nothing, he thought, *nothing* worse than dropping your mother off at rehab. He felt as if a bomb had gone off in the middle of his life, and pieces lay scattered about, unrecognizable.

He'd had to pry her away from the dim, smoky cocoon of the honky-tonk; he'd listened to the familiar protests and promises; he'd hardened his will to her desperate pledges. Then he'd spent most of the day getting her checked in at the facility in Missoula.

"We did it again, di'n' we?" she had said, staring woozily out the truck window. "Stepped over the line.

Tried to fit in with respectable folks, where we don't belong. We're still on the wrong side of the tracks, Sammy. We always will be."

During the drive home, the rage had struck Sam hard, as it always did. What the fuck had LaNelle Jacobs been thinking, blaming the robbery on Tammi Lee? All the slights and slurs of years past had suddenly come back on a wave of resentment. Five years of peace and quiet in Crystal City had lulled him into thinking the past didn't matter.

Sam turned off the shower. Slinging a towel around his waist, he picked up the phone and stabbed his fingers impatiently at the numbers.

"Blue Rock," said a familiar and unwelcome voice. Jake Dollarhide.

"Sam McPhee here. I'm looking for Michelle."

"I'll see if I can get her on the intercom." Sam heard an unpleasant sneer in Dollarhide's slow drawl, and suddenly the years peeled back to expose the gaping wounds of the past. He remembered all the times he had tried to call her long ago, all the times Gavin and his staff had put him off.

"On second thought," Sam said brusquely, "never mind." Without further explanation he hung up and got dressed.

Screaming gusts of wind kicked up a ground blizzard, and everyone with a lick of sense stayed indoors. Not Sam. Not tonight. He was exhausted to the last inch of his shadow, but he had to see Michelle.

He wasn't sure what he'd say to her. He'd never had anyone to talk to in the middle of a crisis; he was used to going it alone. Still, he owed her an explanation. After all, he'd stood her up.

Have dinner with me tonight. She had sounded so excited. Fresh and alive, the Michelle he had known as a young man. But a lot had happened since her breathless invitation. He had lost his cool with Cody, and the incident made him wonder just what sort of father he would be. His mother's fragile sobriety had been shattered, reminding him that loving someone carried hazards that could crush even the stoutest of hearts.

It did not escape him that the other time he had disappeared from Michelle's life had been on his mother's behalf. The reason had not changed. Michelle was strong. She knew how to keep herself safe and secure. No matter how much Sam loved her, he also loved his mother, who could not survive without him. Michelle's very strength was her Achilles' heel. She had trained herself not to need, want, desire. And perhaps the habit was so ingrained that now she no longer remembered how to want something.

But when he saw her through the window of the studio, standing and staring at her canvas, he knew there were mysteries inside her he could not guess at. They would reveal themselves to him gradually—but only if he knew the right way to unlock them.

When he knocked at the door and stepped inside, she folded her hands in front of her. "Sam."

"I had an emergency," he said. "This was my first chance to call."

She stood quietly in the warm glow of the studio lights. He told himself to explain the rest, yet the words wouldn't form. When it came to his mother, he was private and intensely protective. And even a little ashamed, as if his mother's disease were due to some weakness in him. The silence opened a gulf between him and Michelle.

Last time they were together, he had proposed to her. Now he couldn't even make small talk.

The ground blizzard pounded at the windows and doors. Michelle shivered, and he saw that the fire in the woodstove had dwindled to embers. To occupy himself, Sam wrenched open the iron doors and added a quartered log.

"Cody told me what happened when you found him and Molly in the barn," Michelle said.

He crushed up a wad of old newspaper and stuck it under the log. "He told you his version. Molly's the daughter of a good friend. A nice girl."

"According to Cody, they weren't doing anything that risky. Sam, they're sixteen. It's what teenagers do. We can't stop them. We can just hope they don't do anything rash."

He grabbed a bellows and pumped at the banked embers. "The trouble is, sometimes hope isn't enough to stop them, and the consequences are pretty far-reaching." The air wheezing from the bellows sparked the yellow edge of a flame under the new, raw log.

"You made that clear to Cody. You made it clear he was an accident, an unwanted child. When he came home, he asked me if I'd ever considered having an abortion or giving him up for adoption. That's the first time he's asked me that, Sam. Ever."

Sam shut the stove door and stood to face her. A cold chill hardened in his gut. Doubts buzzed through his mind. He *had* lost it, overreacted. How was it that he'd been so sure of himself only two days ago?

Now he didn't know a damned thing, except that loving someone carried a commitment that could crush you. All his life, he had borne the responsibility for his mother.

The price of that had been that he'd had no parental guidance of his own.

"Well, what should I have said, finding him like that?" he asked.

"There's no oracle that lays it all out for you. You just have to pray you get it right most of the time. When it comes to sex, Cody knows the decision is his to make, and all I can do is hope that whatever he decides, it will keep him on course with who he is and what he wants to become."

"You didn't answer my question, Michelle."

She held out her hands to the stove, warming them. "I suppose I would have told him to wait, to be careful. I would have reminded him that he has all the time in the world." She fixed her gaze on Sam. "I would have told him I know it's damned hard to wait when you're sixteen."

"That's naive as hell. The kid is a bundle of raging hormones—"

"He knows when to stop, Sam. I have to trust that. If I can't, what sort of a mother am I?"

Sam envied Michelle her conviction. He realized now that he doubted his own ability to be a good father. God knew, he wanted to be, but he was afraid he'd screw up.

"I'm sorry I made that remark to Cody," he said. "Maybe I just don't have enough patience and understanding to handle him—I guess I proved that by blowing up at him." He gestured toward the door. "I should stop in and talk to him."

She was quiet for a long time. Shadows sculpted her face, and he couldn't read her thoughts.

"Michelle?"

"You'd better go, Sam. This isn't a good time for a discussion with Cody."

His heart lurched. "He's taking it that hard?"

More silence strained between them. Michelle bit her lip, hesitant to speak, and pushed her hair out of her eyes with a weary motion. "This just isn't a good time," she repeated. "I don't know what to think, except that you and I don't work until you and Cody figure out a way to get along." She opened the door to the howling night. "I won't let myself be torn to pieces by the two of you." Her good-bye was as brief and painful as the cauterizing of a wound.

He drove home, the chill inside him expanding. Damn it. Last time he'd seen Michelle, he'd asked her to marry him. Two days later, she was practically throwing him out. Sam squinted at the dry, blowing snow. He was tempted to turn back, but the doubts—and the remembered words of his mother—held him back.

"Don't go chasing after her again." Only yesterday, his mother had admonished him in a tequila-harsh voice. "Don't go getting your heart stomped into the ground."

He told himself not to jump to conclusions. They'd work out their problems. But no matter what he told himself, he still remembered that Michelle hadn't tried to find him years ago.

Saturday

Chapter 51

The next morning, Michelle was still wearing the sterling-silver earrings she had put on for her big night with Sam. The night that never happened. It seemed like ages ago. Miles ago. A lifetime ago. With Sam, she had known a love so deep that it left her gasping and haunted her still. Watching him leave last night had crushed her, and it was far worse now than it had been years ago, because now she understood exactly what she had lost.

She took off the earrings and made a fist around them. Something had broken down between her and Cody and Sam, and she didn't know how to make it right. She didn't know if it could be made right. Maybe she should have told him Cody had disappeared. The fact that she hadn't was revealing in and of itself. Regular couples would discuss the issue right off, up front, and confront it together.

Instead, she had resisted telling Sam that after his quarrel with Cody, their son had taken an all-night bus to Seattle.

That was important, overwhelming. She should have told him. Yet she hadn't. Why?

Because it would make her look like a failure. A mother who lacked control of her own son. She was tired of feeling like that. She was embarrassed. She imagined people saying, "Her son took off on her." People's opinions shouldn't matter, but to Michelle they always had.

She hadn't seen her father since breakfast the day before. He'd gone to the air park. She had spent the day painting and worrying and waiting for Cody to call.

He hadn't.

It was all she could do to keep from jumping in the Rover and racing across three states to him. But she forced herself to stick by her decision. The old Michelle would have done that, and the old Cody would have expected it. But things were going to be different now. Different and new. Until Thursday night, she had thought Sam would be a part of it, but now she wasn't so sure. The child they had made together should be a part of their love. Instead, he had become a symbol of their doubts and differences.

It was just as well that she had come to see those differences now rather than sinking even deeper in love with Sam. The thing to remember was the hurt. The sense that, when all was said and done, the past few weeks had been an interlude. By nature, an interlude had to end.

Sam McPhee was all her heart wanted. But she was so scared. Was she to spend her life with this ache of yearning in her chest, the walking wounded of failed love?

She had made a studious effort not to try to second-guess Sam. Who knew what he was thinking, blowing up at Cody and then disappearing like that? Maybe everything got a little too real for him. Maybe he started thinking about what it would be like actually to be married, to be the father of a difficult teen. Maybe it was not what he wanted after all.

And so she couldn't look to him for comfort. Her wounds had to stay private. The pain was too raw, too sharp to show anyone yet.

The past weeks must have happened to someone else, she thought. Her giddy happiness with Sam felt surreal, a fairy tale made of myth and spun sugar. No one's life could actually turn out like that, she realized. But her hopeful, foolish heart reminded her that at the center of every fairy tale lay a truth that gave the story its power.

Lord. Even now. Even after last night, she was still dumb enough to hope. It was a shock to realize that even though she loved Sam with everything that was in her, it wasn't enough. Her throat filled up, and her eyes swam, and she blinked frantically. She decided to go riding, work on her painting, try to feel normal for a while.

And maybe, please God, maybe, wait for the phone to ring.

The crisp edge of winter kept its hold on the ranch even though a dazzling sun kept trying to warm things up. On her way to the barn, Michelle passed the calving shed, hearing sounds of bovine distress and a few well-chosen swear words. In the lot adjacent to the stockyard, protesting steers were being loaded for shipping to some rodeo or other. A dark-skinned young man, carrying a bucket of oats for the horses, tipped his hat in greeting. She remembered how enchanting she had found all of this when she had come to her father, eager and shy, to live as his daughter for the first time. They couldn't have known then the turns their lives would take, and she had never dreamed she'd be back here again, loving this place even more, if that was possible.

On a day like this, Blue Rock was the idyllic place in the imagination of everyone who had ever dreamed of the West. The rim of mountains, the fields of snow with bunchgrass showing through, the clusters of buildings and ranch vehicles spoke both poetry and permanence.

She heard a grinding of tires and saw a car turn in from the main road. Sunlight glared off the windshield of her father's Cadillac as it parked in front of the old building she used as a studio. Shading her eyes, she watched two people get out of the car. Her heart seemed to drop to her knees.

Cody and her father didn't see her as they went around back to the trunk. They were both wearing leather flight jackets and weary grins. She couldn't believe it. Couldn't believe her father had gone after Cody, and that Cody had come back to Blue Rock. Yet it made perfect sense. Gavin had done for Cody what he should have done for Michelle—brought him back to the place he belonged, whether he knew it yet or not.

Her throat stung as she watched her father and her son facing each other—Gavin tall and white-haired and distinguished, Cody slender and intense. They spoke for a moment, then Gavin clasped Cody's shoulder in a way that was so awkwardly male that she couldn't help smiling through her tears.

For so long, she had thought Gavin had been no father at all to her. But last night, she had sat down with the blank book the transplant team had given her months ago, when she had first agreed to the transplant. The pages had stayed blank, as empty as she had been before coming to Montana. Then last night, she had lain in bed and written in the book, and by the time she finished, she understood

that Gavin had been her father in the only way he knew
how. She had written of the precious time she and Gavin
had spent together seventeen years ago. An early-morning
ride on horseback. Lazy afternoons on the porch, watching the mountain wind ripple through the fields of
avalanche lilies. Evenings by the fire, sketching while he
read his mail. That was what he had given her. And it was,
she suddenly knew, enough. Enough. *Thank you, Daddy.*

She blotted her cheeks while Cody lifted the lid of
the trunk. He took out something she hadn't seen in a very
long time—her portfolio case.

The tears threatened again, and Michelle pressed a
hand to her mouth. Cody went into the studio, and she
was dying to know what he was up to, but she had something to do first. She went and got the journal and took it
to her father.

Gavin's expression indicated that he recognized the
book.

"Read it," she said, kissing him on the cheek. "I think
you'll like it."

"I love you, honey," he said, taking the gift. "Now go
see your boy. He's got a lot to say for himself."

"Thanks, Daddy. Thanks for bringing him home." She
kissed him again, then hurried to the studio to find Cody.
"Hey, stranger," she said from the doorway.

His shoulders stiffened, and the reaction stung her.
Lately it was automatic, the way he braced himself for the
worst. He turned to face her. "Mom," he said. "Mom, I'm
really sorry I took off."

She tried to say something, but no words came out.
She stepped into the main room of the studio, and her
heart soared.

Cody had taken out the paintings and lined them up
against a wall. The light flowed over bold splashes of

color, and she thought about how long it had been since she had looked, really looked at her own work. The paintings were honest and painfully beautiful, filled with truth and emotion. She could see the evolution of frustration, grief, joy. When she regarded the paintings now, they seemed to have been done by someone else. Someone more emotional. More tender. With more of her soul to give. It seemed a miracle to Michelle that these images had come from her. There was one significant painting missing, she realized. It was the snow scene—the one that hung over the mantel in Sam's house.

Sam.

Pushing away the ache of regret, she opened her arms. Cody hugged her, and she marveled at how tall he was, tall and wiry and stronger than she remembered.

"Hey, Mom—"

"Cody—"

They both spoke at once. She gave a little laugh and stepped back. "I'm so glad you came back," she said.

He picked at the bandage on his hand. "I never should have left like that, Mom. It was so stupid."

"We'll get over it," she said, and was pleased to feel actual conviction behind the words. "Cody, I owe you an apology."

His face paled. "Mom, no. I'm the one who—"

"I do." She held up a hand to quiet him. She felt a sting of regret for the way things had been between them lately. She'd always thought it was her job to protect him from being hurt, but she'd wound up teaching him to shy away from emotion. "I was awful to you sometimes, Cody, and it was my own frustration making me pick at you and fuss at you. That was wrong, and—"

"Mom, there's some stuff I need to tell you."

Struck by his tone, she went over to the cushioned

window seat. Cody was somber and tense as he sat beside her. In Gavin's bulky flight jacket, he looked strange and poignantly familiar. His hair was combed, there were no headphones in sight, and when he looked up at her, she saw both Gavin and Sam in his face. "I screwed up, Mom," he said. "I screwed up big-time."

"What do you mean?"

He rubbed his hands on his thighs. "Um, I don't blame you if you get mad at me."

"So just say it, Cody. I can't read your mind."

He picked at the fraying gauze bandage on his hand. "I didn't tell you the whole truth about Sam taking off Thursday night." His voice was low but steady. "His, um, mother—Tammi Lee—got in trouble. Sam didn't say, but I think she was drinking. So he had to drop everything and go help her."

Michelle's stomach lurched. Sam hadn't said a word about this. He had kept it from her, just as she had kept Cody's disappearance from him. She had never known much about Sam's life with his troubled mother. How hard it must be for him, for them both, every day. And her son had held his silence. Her son . . .

"Why didn't you tell me?" she asked Cody, more baffled than angry.

"I didn't know what to do. Everything happened so quick—Sam was yelling at me about Molly and he made me feel so bad, and then he had to go help his mother. She got fired from her job, see? And I'm the only one who knows the real reason why." His cheeks flamed, and Michelle was shocked to see tears in his eyes. "Some guys from school took money from the shop, and Tammi Lee got the blame. Instead of speaking up, I just let Sam go running off to help her, and then I started thinking how much he'd hate me when he got back, so I didn't tell anyone . . . it just got away from me."

She detected a hint of his old sullenness. But she wouldn't stand for evasion, not anymore. "Those are excuses, Cody. What's the real reason?"

He didn't speak for a moment, and she felt a little shock of disorientation as she watched him fighting tears. "I got scared, Mom," he said.

"Scared of what? Cody, tell me."

"I got scared, thinking about what it would be like to have Sam for a father." The admission was squeezed out of him along with the tears he had been struggling to hold back.

Scared. Michelle's heart skipped a beat. She knew then what Sam had tried to tell her the last time they were together—that Cody was in danger of becoming like her. Holding back and hiding from love because it was frightening. Overwhelming. All her life she tried to buy emotional safety at the risk of feeling only half alive.

"I saw how happy he makes you," Cody added, "and I guess I was afraid you'd love him more than me."

"Oh, son." She touched his face. "It's totally different. You have my heart, all of it, and that will never change."

"I'm sorry, Mom. I'm sorry. I'm sorry." His arms went around her. He still smelled like a boy, of soap and outdoor air, and he still needed his mother. As much as she needed *him.*

"I'll make everything right with Sam and Tammi Lee," he said. "I swear I will. I just hope they forgive me." Cody straightened up and scrubbed at his face with the back of his hand. Then he put his arm around her, and the universe came back into balance.

She gazed at him, and in his eyes, she saw Gavin's

eyes. Her father and her son. It took both of them to make her understand that life was short; who knew how long anyone had? When she got to wherever she was going, she wanted to have painted her paintings. She wanted to have loved with a passion beyond reason. She wanted to know that Cody was not just her son, but her friend.

She used to look at him and wonder where her little boy had gone. Now she realized she'd found him. She'd found him in this hurting, confused, and ultimately good kid who was becoming a good man. She paused, drew a breath, tried to think of the right thing to say.

"You know what's even more scary?" she asked. "It's that I almost lost you, Cody. But I think we're going to be okay." She realized that she'd almost lost Sam because she hadn't trusted herself with him. What she should have done was fling herself into the relationship the way she had flung herself into painting. Because it wasn't just the painting that came back to her after its long sleep in the frozen tundra, but life. And Sam had awakened her to that.

She thought about the transplant. Fear and love were sometimes the same thing, both necessary, unavoidable. Now she understood that it was okay to bleed if you know how to heal.

"So we'll call Sam, right?" Cody said. "He'll give me another chance, won't he?"

She put her hands on his shoulders. Lord, but it felt good to hold him again. She had never felt closer to her son. At sixteen, Cody was learning what she wished she had known long ago—that you have to love even though it hurts, even though there are no guarantees. You have to spend it all even though you never know what you'll get in return.

"Oh, Cody." She wanted to reassure him that of course

Sam would forgive him. But how did she know that? She'd had sixteen years to love and understand Cody, to learn who he was. Without all that groundwork, Sam's forgiveness would have to be a leap of faith.

Chapter 52

It snowed later that day. An oppressive quiet shrouded the land, and flying snowflakes pocked the colorless sky. Michelle rode beside Cody in the Range Rover with headlights shining in the bleak day. The heartbeat rhythm of the windshield wipers, batting at the snow, punctuated the silence.

This was nuts, she thought. This was asking for heartache. When Cody had phoned Lonepine, he'd spoken to Edward Bliss, and the news was not good. Sam had taken his mother to detox, then brought her back to the house for a day or two while she found her footing. No, Edward wasn't any too sure they wanted company. And yet here she was, driving her son over to Lonepine, just as they had that first day—Lord, was it only three weeks ago?—before Sam and Cody had any idea they were father and son.

Why did she ever think this was a good idea? Barging back into Sam's life, hoping and praying he would let her back in.

Self-doubt and sheer terror pounded in her gut. In the past, the fear would have stopped her from taking this step. She would have chosen emptiness over pain and joy. Now she knew better. For a short and glorious time she had found the essence of all she desired in the arms of Sam McPhee. It was something she wouldn't get another chance at, something most people didn't even experience in a lifetime.

Parking at Lonepine, she stared out the window at the white-quilted landscape that was starving for spring to come again. Tammi Lee stood out on the porch wearing a big jacket with the collar up and smoking a cigarette.

"You want me to come with you?" Michelle asked Cody.

"Nope. I'm on my own."

He got out of the car and walked toward the house. She realized he didn't need her to prop him up as she had so often in the past, even when it would have been better to leave him be.

Tammi Lee tossed out her cigarette and sat very still, waiting for Cody to come to her. She felt drained, wrung out, as if she had just run a marathon. She hated having her grandson see her like this, but this was who she was—someone who had flown high and crashed-landed more times than she could count. She hovered in a low gully, wondering if she'd rise or fall this time.

"Can I talk to you?" Cody asked. His face looked pale and tight, hands jammed hard into his pockets.

"Sure," she said, her breath freezing in the air. She could listen. Yeah, she could do that.

"It's about . . . what happened with the shop and stuff." He stepped up onto the porch. "That night I borrowed your car, something happened."

Tammi Lee's head began to buzz, craving her meds. She focused sharply on the nervous young boy. He was so good-looking. And right now, he looked as wrung out as she felt.

"It's my fault the money in the cash register went missing," he blurted out. "I didn't know—I—it's my fault."

Tammi Lee sat very still. She was so used to getting kicked in the teeth that she braced herself.

"The cash disappeared when I went into the shop after hours," he said. "It's all my fault."

"Did you take the money?" she asked quietly.

His hands dug even deeper into his pockets. "That doesn't matter. I was responsible. And I blew it. I went to see Mrs. Jacobs today, and I explained it all to her, paid her what was missing. She feels real bad, and she's going to ask you to come back to work. That is, if you want to." He scuffed his foot at a frozen lump of snow on the edge of the porch. "I'm real sorry," he added. "I'll do whatever I have to do to make it right. I just—I'd like to have a second chance."

Tammi Lee felt herself rising a little, hovering above the abyss. Her head pounded, but the pain meant nothing. This was it, she realized. She could forgive this boy and go on from here, or she could let anger and resentment drag her down.

When she looked into his eyes, she saw Sam's eyes. Sam, who'd given her more second chances than anyone had a right to expect. Sam, who deserved a chance of his own. There was really no choice to be made. She stood up and opened her arms. A tentative smile started in Cody's eyes as he hugged her. Over his shoulder she saw Michelle

Turner standing by her car, watching them, one hand pressed to her mouth.

"I think we're going to be all right," Tammi Lee whispered, and she started to soar, lifted by hope. "I think we're going to be just fine."

Sam came out of the main barn and started walking toward Michelle. Her knees felt liquid, threatening to buckle. She was aware of the bruising cold, the snow coming over the tops of her boots, her incision aching.

She used to think healing meant stitching up, scarring over, turning a mess to neatness. Now she understood that she had to let things melt down, unravel, and then come back together in the way they were meant to be.

She had to quit looking for a reason that things happened. This was life, it was messy, and now she knew better than to expect a guarantee. Her heart pounded, she had never felt more alive. She had no idea what the expression on her face was, but she didn't care. When she looked up at Sam, she saw everything she wanted her future to be.

And no matter what that was, it was bigger and brighter than her dreams had ever been.

Hope and fear were locked, unspoken, in her throat. She and Sam walked to the edge of the snow-covered driveway and stood beneath the twisted skeleton of a crabapple tree.

"Cody blames himself for everything that happened," she said at last. "He wants to make things right with you and your mother."

He looked over at the house, where Cody and Tammi Lee stood very close, talking. "I guess I'm glad to see that."

"Can he?" she forced herself to ask. "Can he make

things right? Can *we*?" She twisted her gloved fingers into knots.

"I've been asking myself the same thing."

"Last night, we were both still hiding things. You didn't tell me about your mother, and—" she swallowed hard "—I didn't explain to you that Cody had run away." She forced herself to meet his disbelieving gaze. "He took the bus to Seattle. I wanted to tell you, Sam, but I didn't know how. My father brought him back this morning."

"I guess I'll just let Cody do the explaining, then." Sam held her gaze for an endless moment. "We'll give it our best shot, honey. Okay?"

She managed to choke out his name, and the dam inside her broke like the thawing mountain streams. The sobs of relief came from the deepest part of her, a part she couldn't discipline or control. Sam was a wall of warmth, silent and steady as he absorbed the brunt of her tears. She found a sanctuary, not a threat, in loving him.

"I was so afraid." Her hands clutched at his jacket. "I was so afraid you'd decided Cody and I were too much for you."

His arms slid around her. "Ah, Michelle. Everything's not going to be perfect all the time. But we can survive the mistakes. You know that. You *know*."

"Sometimes I think I'm just not good enough at this," she whispered.

He held her away from him, and dear God, he had the most magnificent face, so full of hardness and soul, weathered by life's joys and sorrows. Snowflakes landed and disappeared on his cheeks, his shoulders. "We'll work it out. You and me and our son."

"*Our* son. It sounds just right." There was a catch in her throat, and she swallowed hard. "I love you, Sam." It was time to say it, long past time. It was so easy. It had turned from impossible to effortless. "I always have, and I always will."

He pulled her against him, pressed his lips to her hair. In that moment, the last of her doubts slid away, and Sam said, "I know, honey. I know."

"You do?"

"Oh yeah."

Michelle closed her eyes as joy settled over them, as silently powerful as new-fallen snow. And like the snow over a stubbled field, it covered everything else—all the flaws and ruts and bruises of the past—with its perfection and purity.